RUNNING WITH WILD BLOOD

A MORIAH DRU/RICHARD
LAKE MYSTERY

Running with
Wild Blood

Gerrie Ferris Finger

FIVE STAR
A part of Gale, Cengage Learning

GALE
CENGAGE Learning·

Farmington Hills, Mich • San Francisco • New York • Waterville, Maine
Meriden, Conn • Mason, Ohio • Chicago

LIBRARY OF CONGRESS CATALOGING-IN-PUBLICATION DATA

Finger, Gerrie Ferris.
  Running with wild blood / Gerrie Ferris Finger. — First edition.
    pages ; cm. — (A Moriah Dru/Richard Lake mystery)
    ISBN 978-1-4328-2966-7 (hardcover) — ISBN 1-4328-2966-1 (hardcover) — ISBN 978-1-4328-2974-2 (ebook) — ISBN 1-4328-2974-2 (ebook)
    1. Police—Georgia—Atlanta—Fiction. 2. Women detectives—Fiction. 3. Murder—Investigation—Fiction. 4. Cold cases (Criminal investigation)—Fiction. I. Title.
PS3606.I534R86 2015
813'.6—dc23   2014031311

First Edition. First Printing: January 2015
Find us on Facebook– https://www.facebook.com/FiveStarCengage
Visit our website– http://www.gale.cengage.com/fivestar/
Contact Five Star™ Publishing at FiveStar@cengage.com

Printed in the United States of America
1 2 3 4 5 6 7 19 18 17 16 15

With heaps of love to Angela, Victoria, Joshua and Ethan.
May all your dreams and aspirations be granted.

CHAPTER ONE

Lake said, "Juliet Trapp told her mother she was taking off to Florida with Wild Blood for Bike Week."

I'll always remember when, where and the exact words Lake spoke. It was two days before Christmas, three years ago.

We had been at the Capital Grill in downtown Atlanta celebrating Lake's promotion to Detective Lieutenant in the Major Crimes Homicide Unit of the Atlanta Police Department. Between chewings of salmon and swallowings of cabernet sauvignon, he said that his ex-wife's garden-club friend, Roselyn Trapp, had called the police station three times to report her daughter, Juliet, a runaway. Lake went on to explain, "The time before that, Juliet left town with a traveling circus and was brought home from Illinois by the Marshal Service. She acted contrite, but I think she enjoyed every minute of riding an elephant. Rich girl's idea of fun."

I said, "That's what happens when parents give their kids a fancy car when they turn sixteen."

"Juliet wrecked the car while she was in Illinois. Her father bought another."

"It wouldn't do to have their precious bumming rides in other kids' Mercedes."

Six months after the circus escapade, sixteen-year-old Juliet Trapp's body was found in a patch of weeds a block from the Wild Blood Motorcycle Club's Atlanta hangout. Sometime on the night of December 28, during Christmas break, she'd been raped and strangled with her winter scarf.

Because of her threat to run off with the club and being found near their clubhouse, those members not in Florida for Bike Week and still hanging out in Atlanta came under suspicion. However, male bodily fluids didn't match anyone the cops rounded up and questioned or those who had voluntarily given specimens.

Today, three years and the Juliet Trapp cold case later, we ate at our favorite restaurant, Il Vesuvio's on Marietta Street in downtown Atlanta. Like other high-profile cases, every anniversary the press honed in on the Atlanta Police Department's failure-to-solve.

My mind came back to Lake as he recounted more of Juliet's tragic end.

"Wild Blood members swore up and down they'd never seen, heard of, nor ever been in the presence of Juliet Trapp. Three submitted to the liar's machine."

At that time, the Atlanta chapter of Wild Blood, a club of one-percenters, had maybe thirty-five members. One-percenters are the bad guys in outlaw clubs. Ninety-nine percent of motorcycle riders are ordinary Joes banded together for the love of their bikes. Not all, but many one-percenters—it is alleged— live off the proceeds of processing crystal meth or crank. I carry around a lot of extraneous knowledge, and how the word *crank* came about is an example. After outlaw motorcycle clubs manufacture their product, they transport it beneath the crankshafts of their bikes. Interesting how words evolve, isn't it?

I looked at Lake who had an interesting expression on his face. "Welcome back to the real world," he said, his smile blossoming.

"What's become of Wild Blood?" I asked. "They've fallen out of the headlines. Have they cleaned up their acts?"

He reminded me that last year two members were convicted

and sentenced on federal drug charges. Since their leader had been spirited into the Witness Protection Program for ratting out two buddies to avoid his own conviction, those roaming free changed their attitudes. At least in Atlanta. "Their clubhouse is still behind a high fence in Forest Park," Lake said, "but you never see any bikes there. A couple of members were suspected in the murder of a rival biker and throwing his body in the Chattahoochee, but it was never proved." His lips twisted. "To give the devils their due, they've never been known to murder or purposely injure a citizen. This time of year they mostly hang out in Florida."

January is not an optimal time to ride a motorcycle, even in the sunny South. "That might mean a trip to Miami."

"It might. Word has come down from on high that the Trapp case will be solved—or else. Since I don't want my head rolling, I've got to do whatever it takes."

Lake hadn't been lead detective on the Trapp case, although he'd worked it. The lead retired last year and the Major Case Commander, Haskell, told Lake to lead the case himself instead of assigning it. Lake doesn't like cold cases. It means looking at the evidence through another cop's perception, working off his or her prejudices.

Mia, Il Vesuvio's owner, came with another bottle of Chianti and did the opening-of-the-bottle ceremony. Armed with a sparkling glass encasing the red wine, Lake lost the look of frustration.

I wasn't through quizzing him though. "Where's Roselyn living now?"

"Massachusetts, but she comes back to the Columns Drive house every year for the anniversary of her daughter's murder."

"She drinking again?"

"You have little faith in your sisters." He set his wine stem on the small napkin. "Roselyn's a recluse now."

After Juliet's murder, Roselyn Crane Trapp and her husband Sherman Hanover Trapp divorced. Roselyn, who drank like everyone else in her set, according to Linda, drank heavily enough to lose her wits and went into rehab somewhere in the Northeast where she met and married a doctor. After the divorce, Sherman sold his computer company and dropped out of sight.

Lake said, "About a year ago a question came up about Sherman Trapp's financial records, bank accounts, etc. We'd been monitoring them for . . ."

"Was he a suspect in his daughter's murder?"

"Couldn't have done it. He was in Augusta when she was killed." The muscles in his face shifted as if, but for that fact, he would have been a suspect. "As I was saying before I was rudely interrupted . . ." He flashed his most charming smile. "There was no activity on his accounts, and when Uncle got curious about him not filing tax returns, they came to us. We're not in the business of helping the tax man but we assigned a young cop to track Trapp. She found no record of his existence, and she's damn good." He drew his hands apart. "He literally cashed out and vanished."

"Took the money and ran. Why?"

"The answer to that is probably the answer to our case."

As the owner of Child Trace, a specialty private investigation agency, I had no involvement in that case, having been up to my eyeballs in foster runaways that winter, but I recall seeing photographs of Sherman Trapp in the newspapers. Lake described him as a hard-ass Hun, and he looked it.

"Maybe he'll respond to the media's reports on the new evidence?" I said.

"He should have by now."

The Trapp case had hit the anniversary headlines with a witness bearing new evidence. While I studied the particulars of

Lake's angular jaws, he told of his interview with the Trapp neighbor who'd come forward to say he'd seen Juliet the night before her murder at the White Dot Reboot in Atlanta.

The White Dot. The first incarnation of that dive, rather than the second, brought on memories. Distracted, my mind shot back to the old White Dot that was within staggering distance of the cop house on Ponce de Leon. It was a late-night place for local rockers, up-all-night drunks and, of course, cops. Lot happened there, like the time the APD cleared the place when an undercover lost his gun. He'd got a little too dance-crazed with sleazy high-steppers, when his gun slipped from its ankle holster and skidded under a booth occupied by a man and a woman lip-locked in intoxicated ardor.

"Where have all the great Atlanta shitholes gone?" Lake asked, adding to my recall.

"Goes to prove Tom Wolfe was dead wrong in calling Atlanta a 'city of go-go materialism and vapid boosterism.' "

"He spent too much time at Aunt Fannie's Cabin apparently."

I asked, "Why did this neighbor of the Trapps come forward now? The news story didn't make it clear why three years later the witness suddenly remembered seeing her at the White Dot Reboot the night before her murder."

Lake's mouth worked with annoyance. "I conducted the interview with Geoffrey Howard a day after the murder, like we did with all the neighbors and friends of the Trapps. At that time Howard said he and friends were at the White Dot Reboot drinking. We took a close look at him and his pals. They were there all right, drunk and rowdy as you would expect."

"These normally good boys?"

Lake grunted and shook his head. "They were graduates of a moneyed prep school and going to Georgia Tech. Howard's pals were not happy to be interviewed in a murder investigation."

Mia set pasta fagioli before us, and, as I prepared to savor the first spoonful, I considered that these money prep school chums of Howard's were probably even unhappier now that their friend amended his statement of three years ago to say that Juliet was with a biker that night. He described the biker to the reporter as an older guy, thirties—I guess he was old compared to college men—who wore leathers, had a bandana tied around his forehead, facial hair and carried a motorcycle helmet.

"Stereotypical," Lake said, letting the soup's flavors cool on his tongue. "Except bikers don't carry their helmets around. That's why they make cable locks for bikes." He tasted again, nodded appreciation, then said, "The coincidence of her saying she was taking off with a motorcycle club, and Howard seeing her with a man dressed as a biker the night before she gets murdered, brings the focus back to bikers."

"I remember they were pissed at being investigated up one side and down, literally to their privates."

"Bikers pass through and hang out in Atlanta for a while, then move on. Since Wild Blood's troubles here, North Carolina has become their east coast HQ, which happens to be the halfway point between New York and Miami on the Narco Highway."

We finished the soup and Mia opened another bottle of wine. My veal parm came and thirty seconds later, Mia brought out Lake's loaded pizza. Lake likes to savor his food so we didn't talk much, at least not about the resurgent cold case. He had his fork working overtime, mouth to plate, until the pie cooled enough to be handled.

Having eaten late and filled up on the pasta and bean soup, my veal dish grew cold while I thought about the return of Roselyn Trapp from the great Northeast.

"Your dinner's cold," Lake said.

"Yes, you may have my veal." Before I got out the last syllable, my plate rested on his.

Ten minutes later, Lake wiped his mouth and finished his red wine. He looked at me, sly sparks in his dark eyes. "If anyone can find out what happened to Juliet Trapp, it's you."

My mouth gaped, then I grinned and shook my head. "You're just saying that because . . ."

"It's true."

". . . you're shuffling a dozen active new cases and you hate cold ones."

"That, too."

"And I deposited the last check from the nutty artists job."

His eyes took on the look of a penitent because he knew that one hurt. It had not ended satisfactorily. Most resolve without happy endings. There was one I still itched to pursue, and that was who killed a man I tried to save in the wine country case. And not that I didn't have current work. Portia Devon, juvenile judge and childhood friend, had hired my agency to find a runaway girl.

Portia's case had loser written all over the file. In a way it reminded me of Juliet Trapp. In another way it didn't. Juliet had been born into a wealthy family and grew into a curious and wayward teenager. The girl Portia hired me to find was wantonly wayward and deemed a delinquent. It all depended on where you were born and how much money your parents had. Juliet's mother had the luxury of drinking in secret in her north Atlanta mansion. My delinquent's mother did drugs in her prison cell. Her aunt worked two jobs. Portia said the girl was into "street" activities. Was that much different than running off to join a circus or riding with an outlaw motorcycle gang?

I told Lake, "I have a case for Portia."

"For Pearly Sue, a piece a cake."

I couldn't deny that Pearly Sue, my assistant, was one bulldog when it came to working a case.

Lake's face showed a rictus of hope. "Roselyn married a doctor while she was up north. Currently they are separated. Will
you go see Roselyn tomorrow?"

Did I want to tackle this case? Tired and dispirited as I was
of humans torturing one another, the answer was a resounding
yes! I'd felt sorry for Roselyn Trapp, a simpering Southern belle
who didn't know what to do with a head-strong daughter and a
mostly absent first husband.

I had left the police department by the time Juliet Trapp was
killed, so I didn't see the butchery done to her, but I'd seen
other victims' bodies and it made me want to cry for her and
spit on the sick slime that didn't have enough humanity to save
his own soul. But more, I wanted to know who did this awful
thing to a girl who, by all accounts, wanted to experience life
without knowing why, or how to do it without getting herself
killed. I wanted to catch the murderer and see him punished,
picture him rotting in a cell, dodging shivs from his more
dangerous companions. There's always someone more dangerous. Jeffrey Dahmer, the cannibal pedophile, met his end taking
a prison shower. I felt good about that for days.

"I see by the flicker of your star-sapphire eyes that you're
already on this case," Lake said, holding up the wine glass as if
in congratulations.

"Maybe," I allowed. "With a little help from my cop friend."

"I can't go with you tomorrow to see Roselyn."

"Roselyn?"

"She insisted I call her Roselyn."

I wondered if she would want me to do the same. Richard
Lake fascinated women like he was a jewel in Tiffany's window.

CHAPTER TWO

The runaway case Portia gave me didn't last long. I found her. Dead under a pile of filthy blankets in a meth and whore house two blocks from where she lived with her aunt.

Portia met me at the morgue. The girl's aunt and a cousin were there.

The aunt said, "Poor chile. Never given a chance."

"A chance?" Portia said, her dark eyes drilling the woman. "Nobody gave her the time of day. You were named her guardian because you said you could control her."

Portia's bark had cut into the woman. "I did all I could."

The cousin looked menacing, so I intervened, "The ME will want to know the name of the funeral home . . ."

The unfortunate girl's aunt walked away followed by the cousin. I put a restraining hand on Portia's arm. "You couldn't make her feel worse if you wanted to."

Portia stormed ahead, toward the elevator. Outside, she said, "I'll wrap things up this afternoon. Send me your final expenses."

"None," I said. "I'd hardly started."

Portia looked at me as if I was one of those who hadn't given the girl the time of day.

"Okay, I lied. I worked the case until midnight."

I told her that after dinner, Lake, always generous with his free time, and I hit the pavement to find those who knew the girl. I learned where she hung out. We found the boarded-up shotgun-style house by the railroad tracks. I heard the scurry of feet out the back door as Lake opened the front door. Lake flashed beams throughout the house, but all we found was the detritus of drugs, alcohol and sex. No live or dead bodies. Until the next morning when I returned.

"Case closed," Portia said. "Go home and sleep."

"Can't," I said. "Got a case from Lake."

Shortish Portia looked up at tallish me. Her eyes filled with curiosity, and her hawk nose twitched once or twice.

I said, "He wants me to look into the Juliet Trapp murder."

"Biker did it," Portia said. "Sure as I'm standing here."

"Keeping an open mind," I said.

"Even though they pimp their women and cook up lethal drugs?"

"Even though," I said.

She appeared to give some thought to keeping an open mind, something she sometimes did. "What can you do that Lake can't?"

"Fresh eyes."

"You're straying outside the bounds of your agency."

"Porsh, I'll be available if you need me to trace a kid, you know that."

And that's when I realized that something bothered Portia, other than my straying outside the bounds of my specialty. I asked, "What do you know about Juliet Trapp?"

She thought a moment. "I can tell you there was a problem, but I'm going to have to . . ."

"Are we talking about sealed records?"

"Expunged, and not of Juliet."

"Who?"

"A family member. Now don't ask me anything more."

She could count on me doing so. "Does Lake know?"

"It doesn't relate directly to the murder, but could be a reason for Juliet's personality disorder."

"Porsh," I said, a hand on a hip. "Is this another uncle-diddles-niece case?"

"It was a long time ago, and the family member is dead."

"I'm going to talk to Roselyn Trapp What-Ever-Her-Last-Name-Is-Now in an hour, so she should know."

"I'm sure she does know, but whether she wants to discuss the matter is another story. She's unpredictable, even sober."

"How do you know her?"

"Mama went to Town and Country School with her father."

Like Linda Lake, Old Atlanta Society—kinked internal moorings.

Having risen at five thirty a.m. to see Lake off, I had time to go through the Trapp files that I helped Lake lug up the stairs to his third-floor loft. There were five boxes of evidence—officers' handwritten reports, tapes of conversations, computer printouts of forensics, ME observes, etc. I began at the beginning and stopped after the second box, my eyes bleary by then.

I dressed and began my unofficial commission.

From downtown, where Lake's loft is situated south of the old rail depot, I got on I-285, got off at Riverside Drive and turned from Johnson Ferry Road onto Columns Drive to begin the trek along the Chattahoochee River. The name of the river means "painted rock" in the Cherokee language. The Cherokee lived in hut villages for thousands of years until they were forced onto the Trail of Tears by Andy Jackson in the 1830s.

I remember rafting the Chattahoochee with my school group and we learned all kinds of neat things about the river that runs through Atlanta—the city's lifeblood, you could say. Columns Drive paralleled the Chattahoochee for several miles and is where old and new million-dollar-plus homes sit on and between rock ridges, and where, before the Cherokee, prehistoric people took shelter. My destination was just past the Atlanta Country Club. I can boast of having played golf there a few times.

There was no number on the mailbox or a sign, but I knew the house. I'd spoken to Roselyn Trapp Pritchett on the telephone and she described in detail the gates and the garden in front of her home. After I announced myself into a speaker, the gates slid back and I drove my vintage Bentley through them, over winding red pavers until I came to the garage set off to the right of the great house. Traditional in style, the two-story long house was built of stone and wood, with brick chimneys in the front and on each side. It looked to be a house with many fireplaces. The wood was painted in the lightest tan you could still call tan and the upper floor sported dormer-style windows.

I stepped from the pavers onto a flagstone path to the door. Evergreen topiary in phantasmagorical shapes lined the path. I stopped to admire a topiary lion sunning on the lawn.

A wavering voice called, "How do you like our lion?"

She stepped from beneath the recessed entryway, and I thought how much she'd changed in the three years since her daughter was murdered. Everyone does, of course. She used to be on the zaftig side. Today her royal blue dress accentuated her thinness. "Good morning, Mrs. Pritchett. I like it very much."

"Our garden is our solace," she said and turned to go beneath the shallow porch overhang.

I followed. "Gardens are that," I said, following her.

The floors were highly polished hardwood, and off to my left was a winding staircase slapped up against a white wall. The lathe-turned balusters looked like brass candlesticks and the banister was of the same polished wood as the floors.

"Come this way," Mrs. Pritchett said. "Our daily girl made coffee and tea."

"No trouble, please," I said, delighted at tea or coffee. They would make excellent props for this difficult conversation.

"None," she said and led me into the kitchen at the back of the house. Nothing remarkable about the kitchen. Island in the center of a long room, expensive appliances, marble and granite countertops, travertine floors. What else would I expect? Except it was colorless, dull. The "daily help" was a pale woman of about forty who prepared a tray. Biscuits and butter. More props, and hopefully delicious ones at that.

The woman's name was Lois. She followed Mrs. Pritchett from the kitchen onto a lengthy lanai and set the tray on a low marble-and-glass table in front of a wicker sofa with baby blue and cantaloupe orange pillows. A lime green love seat and sun-yellow chairs were grouped to the sides and across from the sofa and the table. Roselyn Pritchett sat on the love seat, and I sat in a chair. Lois served coffee for me, tea for Mrs. Pritchett, and placed biscuits and strawberries on Spode plates. Silver salvers held cream, butter, cinnamon and sugar. Lovely setting, delicate china, inviting food, I still wished I was not here at this time for this reason.

Pulling teeth, I thought, and, buttering a biscuit, I tried to ignore Mrs. Pritchett's slow, rather mournful moves like endlessly stirring sugar into her tea and tearing apart a biscuit by quarter-inches.

"We do love a biscuit, mid-morning," she said, sprinkling cinnamon on the bread.

"I love a biscuit any time," I said.

Maybe I spoke too fast, or too loudly, or didn't use the editorial "we" that made her cringe.

Hunched in her blue dress, she was like a blue dragonfly with transparent wings twitching on a green leaf. She said, "My appetite isn't what it used to be."

I nodded, showing I understood. We were almost finished

eating so I thought I might as well get to it. "Lieutenant Lake asked me to speak to you on his behalf."

She looked at the last bite of her biscuit sitting on the blue patterned plate. "You were once with the police, Linda said."

"I left to start my agency, Child Trace."

"Our daughter isn't . . ."

"I understand she's not missing, but in my capacity, I often find out why they're gone. In that sense, I'd like to find out what happened to Juliet."

She'd shrunk further into herself when I spoke her daughter's name. "Well, we know what . . ."

When she didn't go on, I said, "Lieutenant Lake is in charge of the case, I want you to know that, and he will never rest until whoever did this is caught."

"It's been three years," she said quietly. "We're glad he reopened the case . . ." Her voice trailed off.

Unsolved murder cases are never closed, but the investigation had fallen into a time stall, waiting for new leads to serendipitously spring up.

If Roselyn were a kitten, she couldn't have mewed more. "We married again, after it happened. But we never forgot. Dr. Pritchett and we are separated, just for now. Just until we . . ." She looked like she was about to spiral downward, but suddenly caught herself. "It's a lovely sunny day. Would you like to walk along the river?"

Thank God for something to do. I was about to jump out of my skin at her disassociation from herself. I think it was Mark Twain who said, "Only kings, presidents, editors, and people with tapeworms have the right to use the editorial 'we.' " I would add schizophrenics because a shrink once told me that it was a common symptom in that devastating disease. Not that schizophrenics purposely disassociate, but because of their mental disability they are not able to integrate their thoughts, perceptions and imaginations. Which made me wonder about Roselyn. Was she purposely disassociative?

I had on a suit coat, and she fetched a shawl warm enough for the coolish January day. I followed her from the lanai through a vine-covered arbor. "The grapes are pretty in summertime," Roselyn said. We passed a fountain that probably burbled in the summer and came to a fence. A path snaked to the river bank, and we strode wordlessly side-by-side until she spoke as if to herself. "We didn't get flooded out when the rains came like last year."

"You're lucky. So many homes did."

She looked at me, a smile smearing her face. "The river is not so fierce here."

"Nor deep," I said.

This section of the river, not far from the boat ramp at Johnson Ferry Road, is popular with rafters. The three-mile stretch to Paces Mill is what Atlantans call The Hooch. As young kids, Portia and I, along with myriad friends, spent countless summer days bobbing along The Hooch, sometimes jumping in to wade to a deeper spot to dog paddle. Later, as teenagers, we brought coolers of beer and smoked cigarettes and jumped off the diving rock further down the river. Every other summer someone drowned, although no one we knew. I considered myself lucky when I contemplated my recklessness. Portia wasn't much of a daredevil, fearing her bag of bones would drop and never surface.

I glanced at Roselyn. She looked as if she'd read my last thought and said with a show of enthusiasm, "We had an alligator come on the bank once."

"An alligator!" I couldn't believe I'd spoken with an exclamation point like a child.

"Big as life he was, too. Everyone was in such a flurry. Park rangers came and got it, of course."

I recalled, but not aloud, that as a rookie with the APD, I was with investigators when I first met Betsy, the Chesapeake Retriever and her handler, Eleta. Betsy had sniffed out a body jammed in rock and bramble on the bank about fifteen yards downstream from this house. It was in the wine country case that I was recently reunited with the talented pair. It's a treat to see a search-and-rescue dog work with a handler that knows her dog.

Roselyn meandered to a cleared place a couple of yards from the bank where a bench had been placed. She brushed the seat with her shawl, and we sat.

"We're happy you came," she said. "We don't know that we could talk to the lieutenant, although he was always a gentleman and patient."

Lake is always patient, with old ladies especially, but Roselyn wasn't much past forty-five. She just looked old and frail.

"Where is Mr. Trapp now?" I asked.

She looked at me like I'd asked where they took the alligator. "Why, we've no idea. We didn't stay in touch."

"Is he still in Atlanta?"

She suddenly got interested in her fingernails. "He may be."

She claimed not to know if he remarried, and she knew nothing about his finances except that, before he departed, he gave her enough to live out her life. Her strange elusiveness told me she knew more about his whereabouts than she was prepared to admit. She was particularly reticent about his relationship with his teenage daughter. She said, "We don't know that he had one . . ."

I was ready to get this over with. "Tell me about Juliet's plan to take off for Florida with a motorcycle gang."

My question was way too crass, and her breath caught in her throat. "Well, she was always saying she was going off with someone." She watched her thumbs twiddle. "She had the wanderlust, as our daddy used to say. He had it, too. It was in the Crane blood, but passed us, thank the Lord."

"Where is your daddy?"

"In Oakland Cemetery. Mama, too. Our Juliet's passing was too much of a strain. On all of us."

To say nothing of murder. "Was she close to her grand-daddy?"

"Lord, yes."

"Anyone else in the family?"

"Her cousin, Marcus. He used to come here . . . Oh my, it brings up old . . ."

She had a habit of trailing off. "Memories?" I asked. She shook herself and I asked, "Where is Marcus?"

"He's buried next to his granddaddy. Over from Juliet."

"How old was he when he passed?"

"Marcus was thirteen."

"Accident?"

She closed her eyes and didn't speak for so long I thought she'd gone to sleep, except that her lower lip quivered.

I said, "I'm sorry if I've brought up sad remembrances."

Her eyes popped open. "Yes, well, we won't speak of Marcus." If Marcus's last name was Crane, it would be easy for Webdog, my computer investigator, to get the story, even if Marcus changed his name and moved to a different planet. The deceased Marcus could be the family member Portia alluded to. Armed with a little more information, Portia would tell me about Marcus and Juliet. She knew I could keep the secret of the scrolls.

"Did your daughter hang out with motorcycle riders?" I asked. "Any come to the house?"

I hadn't meant the question to be a family insult, but Roselyn's eyes got wide and she said that our daughter most certainly did not. They were, she asserted, dirty men and we would never allow them near our daughter.

Sounded just the type Juliet might want to hang with.

I asked, "Was Geoff Howard a friend of Juliet's?"

She sniffed. "He wished. His idea of music is noise."

"But he liked Juliet?"

"When they were children, but afterward they grew apart. He was a couple of years older."

"Was there a problem?"

A tic made one eye flutter like bees buzzed it. "He thinks he saw our Juliet before . . ."

I asked, "Could you tell me what happened the day and evening before Juliet went missing?"

Having read the initial reports this morning, I knew the answer she'd given police when the investigation began. Roselyn reiterated much of what was in the reports. The day of the night of her disappearance Juliet came home from a tennis lesson, said she was tired and went to bed. She rose, ate a sandwich, went into the garden to read and then to her bedroom to watch television. There was no quarrel at all. "She was sweet that night," Roselyn said. "She made a nice cocktail for us."

"By us, do you mean you and Mr. Trapp?"

"Mr. Trapp was traveling that night."

"Were you alone?" She sighed an answer. The batting tic had to be bothering her. "Just you and Juliet?" She sighed again.

The next morning Juliet wasn't in her bedroom when the daily help, Lois, went in to "do" her room at nine o'clock. Being on holiday break, Juliet slept late. Lois was the first to notice the window open and the gardener's ladder leaning against the house. It was supposed that sometime after Juliet had gone to the garden, she'd laid aside her book and gone to the garage for the slide ladder. Roselyn heard nothing during the night, but the family closed their rooms while sleeping.

When Lois reported Juliet missing from her room, Roselyn

went to the garage and saw that Juliet's car was still parked there. She called Mr. Trapp, and he told her to call the police. He then rushed home from Augusta where he'd been in conference with clients. Augusta is two hours east of Atlanta.

Given her history of running away, and Sherman Trapp's bullying, police reluctantly formed a small search party of professionals, neighbors and dogs to search the river bank, yards and country club grounds. Geoff Howard had been among the searchers, who said at the time he knew nothing of her whereabouts. The same Geoff Howard who three years later said he saw Juliet at the White Dot Reboot with a biker on December 27. An anonymous man discovered Juliet's body in south Atlanta, miles from her home. The medical examiner put Juliet's death at between nine p.m. and midnight on December 28.

I asked Roselyn if she knew that Florida's massive winter Bike Week was taking place the following week, and she said that *we* certainly did not.

I started to rise from the bench. "Thank you, Mrs. Pritchett, for your . . ."

She reached out and touched my arm with a shaky hand. "Oh please dear, call us Roselyn. If we didn't have to have the names of our two husbands, we wouldn't."

"You can take your maiden name," I suggested, settling back onto the bench.

Rubbing the tic, she said, "Crane is our maiden name, so nice and simple, but we've made our bed."

"Roselyn, you called police twice to report Juliet missing after she told you where she was going. Did she say *when* she intended to ride with a motorcycle gang to Florida?"

She seemed like a spirit drifting in the space around us. "She promised she would leave a note, but she didn't."

Since she didn't go on the ride, that made sense, but I didn't

25

say so. I asked, "Did she always leave a note—before taking off?"

"No, but with motorcycles, she said she never knew where she would be." Roselyn apparently realized she needed to say more. "You see, Juliet would tell us so we wouldn't worry, but not when exactly. We forbade her going, but she'd slip away. We always called the police immediately, and they always found her where she said she'd be."

"By we, do you mean she told Mr. Trapp, too?"

"No, she didn't tell him. That was up to . . . After she'd gone."

"Her father might have stopped her."

She shrugged as if this might or might not have been true. Strangely strange.

Juliet Trapp's name had been entered into the National Crime Information Center Missing Persons list twice. Lake had told me that Roselyn said "we" didn't go ourselves to fetch Juliet because Juliet would be angry at being treated like a child.

Much better to be carted off by the cops or the Feds.

Except for these excursions, Juliet was a fine young woman. She didn't have a drug or alcohol habit and was a regular church-goer—a singer in the choir and a ringer of hand bells. During the time Roselyn told me this, the nervous tic stopped. She appeared as grounded as she could be. "Our daughter wanted to experience the world." A tear slipped down her white cheek. "Her advisor at school told us not to stifle her enthusiasm for life. He said she had a special gift."

"I'd like to speak to the advisor. What's his name?"

"Mr. Stuart, if he's still at Winters Farm Academy."

I asked if there was any reason that he wouldn't be, and she said that he'd had a rather unfortunate automobile accident.

"Roselyn," I began, not happy to be saying this, and she may have picked up unhappy vibes from me because she turned her shoulders away. "Most girls run away because they're unhappy.

The unhappiness stems from relationships within the home." She turned her head and frowned at me. "For instance, daddy can occasionally come home drunk and yell at mama, but if the girl sees love between them, she'll see it as just the way it is. But if there's constant mental or physical misery, she'll often take off to escape the misery."

She bowed her head. "It wasn't that way us. Sherman would never yell or get physical. He never paid enough attention to us to want to."

"What about Juliet?"

"He never laid a hand on her from the time she was born. He never even raised his voice. He was not an affectionate man but he was not abusive. We told Lieutenant Lake that several times."

"Another reason girls leave is they've lost someone they love. Perhaps Marcus's death . . ."

She looked at her hands and clutched them together to still the tremors. "She never spoke of Marcus after . . . that."

"What did Marcus do?"

She looked upward as if the answer might be written across the stark blue sky. Then she looked at me, a blur of pain in her pale eyes. "He hung himself in his closet." She put her face in her shawl and sobbed. Ten minutes later, we walked back in silence.

Before I left I had one request, and she granted it.

Juliet's room was exactly as she'd left it except the window was now closed. Roselyn invited me to inspect anything I thought held a clue to Juliet's murder, but she left with vague words about dressing for something. Or nothing. A trait of the dissociate recluse.

Juliet was a neat freak of the first order. I went through her closets and drawers. Nothing there that shouldn't be. The police had taken anything of interest and my search led nowhere.

CHAPTER THREE

Geoff Howard was picking his guitar in the three-car garage of his parents' modern glass house, also on the river. His mother had, with flat-footed irritation, led me to him. "He lives in that garage. His father is threatening to turn him out if he doesn't get a real job."

I thought about the new information Howard had given the police and the reason for his recollection. I'd read Lake's report, but I was anxious to hear it from him.

The few strums I heard weren't too terrible. Atlanta has plenty of clubs where he could get a start. I thought again about how Portia and I snuck off in her mama's car—before she was a legal driver—when we were barely Juliet's age to hear Dead Elvis and Neon Christ. Not exactly joining the circus, but not being busted by the Marshal Service either.

Geoff Howard looked up when I walked through the laundry room door into his computer and musical world that was housed in a three-car garage with no cars in it. No wonder dad was mad.

"Won't you people ever leave me alone," he grouched.

His mother walked around me. "I don't care how old you are, Geoffrey, you will not be rude to visitors in this house."

He hunched a shoulder in a "whatever" way and did several competent pasodoble crescendos. His mother marched out, closing the door, and Geoff set his guitar on its stand. "Well?" he said, his head canted.

"Who are the *you people* that won't leave you alone?" I asked, stepping toward him.

"You know." I shook my head. "You people are the cops, investigators like you."

"How do you know I'm an investigator?"

He grinned and stood. "I may be a madcap inventor, but I look at the papers and see television from time to time."

"There was news about me in the media recently?" My involvement in the artist case never made the Atlanta papers.

"No, but you caught the creeps that kidnapped those two girls."

"I came to see you because of the Juliet Trapp case."

"No kidding."

"Whoever killed her wasn't kidding."

His mouth twisted into a manifestation of touché. "Look, Miss . . . Your name escapes me . . ."

"Dru. Skip the miss, just Dru."

"Call me Geoff. I'm thirsty. Sparring with a heroine makes me thirsty." He was on the move toward a refrigerator in the corner by a gardener's wash stand. "What can I get you to drink?"

"Coke is fine," I said when he opened the frig door, and I spied the labels on soft drinks.

He ripped open a Heineken for himself. "Never too early for a brew."

He sat at one of his computers, and I sat in the seat next to a guitar on its stand. I noticed that the guitar was the Stradivarius of guitars and wondered who'd paid for it.

"My dad," he said and grinned. He was classically hand-some. He had longish dark hair and fair skin and obviously was not an outdoors man. His eyes were cobalt, about the color of mine, and his mouth was wide and loose—the kind of loose that looks sexy, the kind of mouth Lake possessed. Geoff was either blessed with gorgeous teeth or had expensive dental work. He continued, "I'm an engineer by education, graduate of the great institution down the road, Georgia Tech. A hundred-and-fifty-thousand dollars later, I can't find a job."

"An engineer that can't find a job?"

"Not all engineers are created equal. I'm a civil engineer. Cities are paring back and are not hiring civies. So I'm engineering in the new world of civility. The Internet."

And so, while drinking his beer, he told me that he wasn't interested in performing, but about his Internet start-up dream, the dreams of World Wide Web billions. If I got it straight, Geoff was developing a social computer network for guitarists. So what if it seemed narrowly focused, they laughed at the idea of an around-the-clock weather channel. When the subject became too technical and my mind lost focus, I brought him back to the reason I was sitting across from him.

"Who is not leaving you alone? The Atlanta police?"

"I guess we have to discuss it. One, Lieutenant Lake all but accused me and my friends of killing that girl . . ."

"Wait," I said, holding up a hand. "I know Lieutenant Lake. I read his reports. He doesn't accuse you. He checked out your bona fides at the time of the murder, and now that you've given a different statement."

"Can you put *attitude* in a report?"

"I get your point. Why didn't you tell the story at the time of the murder?"

He blew out slowly. "If you read the report you can tell me."

I waited.

"I was so drunk I was in an alcoholic blackout phase. I don't know how I got home that night except that my friends told me they drove me. They all backed me up. I don't binge-drink anymore, but I used to in college. Stupid, but I did."

"What caused the revelation?"

"Sounds crazy." He shook his head. "I slipped on ice and hit my head on a low stone wall in Piedmont Park. Sliced it open. Here." He stood, turned away and separated hair on the back of his head. "See the gash."

I did. The pink stood out on his white skull. "And you got your memory back."

He sat. "Parts. Doctors called it TMR or something like that. I'll give you the name of my doctor and permission to discuss the theory he put forward as to why I recovered some of my memory of that night. During a complete alcoholic blackout, memories are not set in the brain. My doctor said that night at the White Dot Reboot I laid down hazy memories before the blackout. Right after Juliet was killed, I didn't immediately recall that I'd seen her. By the way, that was the night of my last blackout. I will never drink that much again." He crushed the empty aluminum can for emphasis. "It scared me away from hard liquor."

As if only hard liquor caused blackouts. But I didn't say it.

He continued, "I recalled a lot of things that I'd forgotten, not just in that blackout. It was like the trauma awakened a part of my brain that was dozing. Anyway, I didn't independently remember seeing Juliet until the other day when I saw her photograph on television and heard what her dippy mother said about Bike Week. It just leaped into my head, seeing her and the guy. It was weird, too. It wasn't a biker bar. Lots of weirdoes and cops and media and students, but no bikers." He spread his hands apart. "That's it."

I nodded to indicate I understood. I'd heard other instances of blackout memory recovery, and I asked him if he'd been sleeping well at the time of the blackout. Fatigue has a lot to do with the severity of a blackout. He said that he'd been up all night the night before. It had to do with the incoming freshman pledge class.

"Had you ever seen the guy, this biker, before?"

"Never."

"Why did you tell your recollection to a reporter instead of the police?"

"He came around. He asked. I knew the cops would be around after that hit the news. And now you're here, too. I wish I had been sober. I would have gone up to Juliet and told her to ditch the guy, but I wasn't."

"Any problems with the Trapp family?"

"Between ours and theirs?" I nodded. "They keep to themselves except to go to the club occasionally. My folks are social, very social."

"What about Trapp family squabbles?"

"You met them?"

"Roselyn Trapp."

"Dotty, but nice. He's a cipher."

"That's not real definitive."

"I never had anything to do with him. He was quiet, kind of stern."

"Mean?"

"No, just not real nice. He took off after . . ." He shrugged. "Just split."

"What did you do the next day, the twenty-eighth, the day Juliet was murdered?"

"Took pills for my hangover. Hung around the frat house, shot pool, played cards, ate dinner, went to bed."

"You ride a bike?"

"Mountain bike." He gestured to a bicycle hanging on the wall.

He knew what I meant. "Motorcycle."

"No, I told the cops."

"When was the last time you talked to Juliet?"

"Maybe a month before . . ."

"Did you know about her escapades?"

"I heard about the circus. I thought it was pretty cool."

"You thought she was cool?"

"She was sixteen. I was in college."

That didn't mean he didn't develop a thing for her. Maybe he went to talk to Juliet about hanging out with a biker and things got out of hand.

"Did the police ask you for a DNA sample?"

His mind quickly made the leap. So did his legs and propelled him up off the chair. "You can leave now."

"I just asked."

"You're asking me to give one, aren't you?"

"I just asked . . ."

"The answer is no, but I will if I get suspected of anything."

I looked up at him. "Sit down. Investigations are seldom polite. Describe what you recall about this biker and Juliet."

He sat, stared a bit, then gave in. "I told the cop, Lake, the recall is not sharp; it's like a film shot in a fog. She was walking by, and I wouldn't have noticed, except for the guy. A biker in a punk bar? Weird. One of my friends said something like 'Hey, Harley boy, Hank don't sing here.' The guy looked us over. I could tell he was mad. I looked closer at the girl. It was Juliet all made up. She was laughing. The whole thing was funny to her. I wanted to say something to her, but I couldn't. Man, I was wasted."

Right then I knew he'd seen Juliet. I'd already gotten a good feel for her personality. She'd witnessed her neighbor, drunk on his butt, and he'd seen her with a biker. I'd guess she knew Geoff had a thing for her.

I asked, "Did the biker wear a jacket with a patch on the back?"

"Yeah, there was something on the back."

"Wild Blood?"

"It was at an angle, but yeah, I think so."

"We wrote the guy off as a sensation-seeker at first," Lake told me via cell phone. "His friends say he's an introvert who every once in a while breaks out and does something out of character for attention."

"He's an inventor."

"He's a paranoid."

"Did you check out what his doctor says, and his friends?"

"We're on it."

"I believe he saw Juliet and her killer that night."

"Nothing's impossible."

"You're the one who said it was interesting her saying she was taking off with bikers and then being seen with a biker with a patch on his leather the night before her murder."

"You can buy patches online."

"On the other hand, you've got to wonder who else she told, and why would her killer dump her body near the clubhouse if he was a club member?"

"Well, what I'm wondering is, where for dinner?"

"You choose. I'm off to Winters Farm Academy. Juliet's advisor."

"Sad case."

"Don't profile him. Let me judge without prejudice."

"Well without prejudice, I'm off."

He hung up.

Winters Farm Academy, my IT investigator told me, had once been a large tract of land off North Roswell Road owned by a man named—what else—Winters, one Thomas H. H. Winters to be exact. His ancestors had set up a one-room school for neighboring farm children. By the time THH had passed on, the school had a hundred pupils and had become known for its classical music and arts program. Winters Farm was also known for its English riding stables. It appears he endeavored to instruct farm kids in the finer things of life. Not founded as a school for the money-challenged, I'm guessing that THH didn't like it that country boys were called rednecks and girls were pregnant at thirteen.

Wilton Stuart, Juliet's advisor, Webdog said, had graduated from Duke University and went on to get his master's from the University of Alabama and his doctorate from the University of Florida. The brass nameplate on his door told me that his full name was Wilton Johns Stuart. I knocked and he opened the polished wooden door. Wilton Johns Stuart was every bit as polished as his door.

"Miss Dru, am I correct?"

"You are."

"I'm Wilton, come on in."

His office was as immaculate as his clothing. From the neck down, he was GQ perfect. His head, however, was a mess. His hair was parted and sculpted with care, but his features . . . I'd seen the results of burns before—the skin grafts, the rigid scarring. He wore thick-framed black glasses and his smile was a slit in his face.

"Please sit," he said, gliding his hand toward a leather barrel chair. He sat in its twin and made sure the press of his trousers was straight. "Your assistant said you wanted to talk about Juliet Trapp."

"That's correct. I've been asked to look into her life, particularly anything that may have led to her murder."

He tilted his head. "I believed the police had gone into her background very thoroughly."

"Sometimes perspective is gained by distance."

"Three years' worth?" said the skeptic in him. "Well, I know nothing more than I told them."

"How well did you know the Trapp family?"

"Not well. They weren't ringing up all the time interfering with Juliet's education, second-guessing my advice, if that's what you mean?"

"Did you find that odd?"

"Refreshing, rather."

"Who did you interact with most?"

"Oh, Roselyn Trapp, whenever interaction was necessary, and that was when Juliet toddled off on one of her adventures."

"Like the circus?"

"Indeed." He smiled, remembering. "Juliet would be nineteen now. She was thirteen when she came to Winters Farm, thereabouts. She had a different advisor at first. In her second term, I became her advisor when Mr. Chapin retired. Freshmen were put with Mr. Chapin because he was good with nervous adolescents. After that, they were reassigned to others of us."

My notebook was poised on my knee; my recorder sat on the edge of the table next to my arm. "What is Mr. Chapin's first name and is he still in the area?"

"Samuel. Samuel Chapin. He retired to Florida and recently died."

"What of?"

"Old age, I assume. He'd been in poor health his last years here. I can tell you that he failed with Miss Trapp. He . . ."

I interrupted to ask, "Do you call your students mister or miss?"

"Yes, as we are mister or miss to them. Reciprocal respect, we call it."

I liked that. "Sorry I interrupted. How did Mr. Chapin fail?"

"As good as he was with incoming students, he wasn't the type of advisor Miss Trapp needed. He tried to mold her into a fine student, but she was not going to be molded by man or woman—and I would add God, whatever God's gender."

"I get that about her. How did you approach advising her?"

He reached up to touch a high cheekbone, and it stung my fingers to see him touch the crinkled redness. He said, "I advised her to be herself. Now before you think I'd encourage her to join a troupe of acrobats and animal trainers, I'll say that I would not. But I didn't scoff. I rather liked her spirit and determination. When she returned from wherever the spirit took her, we discussed the trip—the who and what and why of it. She intrigued me."

"I can see that. Are you married?"

If his face could get redder it would have. I'd never seen a better example of high dudgeon.

I raised my palm against his indignation and told him that I was not suggesting, or accusing, or inferring an illicit attraction or connection to his advisee. He calmed a bit and said he supposed it was the way of the world to suspect a liaison between student and teacher, what with teachers taking advantage of pubescent students and being on the news practically daily. He said that he wasn't married; he had been, but his wife lost her life in the same accident that almost took his own. I apologized and said I was sorry for his loss.

I could tell he was ready to kick me out, so I said hurriedly, "Was Juliet a good student?"

"She teetered on the edge because her mind was elsewhere a lot of times, but when she had tests she studied with incredible concentration and was able to make up for her daily coursework, which was hardly stellar. She was a C-plus, B-minus." He touched his shirt collar. "That was too bad because she possessed a superior intellect. She was a sophomore when she was killed. I told her that she needed to take the last two years of secondary school seriously if she wanted to get into a first-class university. She looked at me once and said, 'I don't think I'll be going to university, Mr. Stuart. It's for the *hoi polloi*. I want more out of life.' "

"That more being?"

"Last we talked, which was just before the holiday break, she wanted to be a writer." He paused and looked grave, as if thinking that Juliet would never realize her dream. He took a deep breath, then said, "She wanted to travel all over the world and write about her adventures." His eyes glistened at the memory of a favored young woman who had done things that he probably wished he had done or could still do. I wasn't going to ask if he'd married young. It was hard to gauge his age since his face had been partly destroyed, but I thought him about forty. I would find out more about him from Webdog.

He said, "Forgive my reminiscing. It's not often you encounter a spirit like Juliet Trapp." He rose and so did I. "I'll be happy to help in any way that I can, but I must attend a meeting now."

He wasn't fast shuffling me because of anything I'd said. The secretary to the advisors had told me he could only give me fifteen minutes.

I asked him, "Did you speak with Juliet over the holidays?"

He thought a moment. "Not speak. I saw her twice when she came to ride horseback with a friend." He directed my attention to his bank of windows. "My office looks out on the riding ring."

So it did.

The girl on the hunter-jumper looked like she'd been riding all of her life, and probably had been. This part of north Georgia is called "horse country" for a reason. Stables abound. Horse-lovers from Atlanta and the suburbs board their horses for large sums of money. Next to owning and operating a boat, it's a toss-up which costs more. I've heard the caveat that boat ownership means acquiring a hole in the water into which you throw your money. The best I'd heard of horse ownership was that a woman needs two animals: the horse of her dreams and a jackass to pay for it.

Watching her was a red whippet of a man approaching middle age. He wore sunglasses and a smile as bright as the winter sun they guarded against.

The sunny smile behind the shades belonged to Master Hoyt Fagan. It said so on his name tag. Too tall for a jockey, yet he had the physique. I stuck out my hand and introduced myself. "Master Fagan, I'm Moriah Dru with Child Trace."

The smile disappeared. "Child Trace?"

"I'm here about Juliet Trapp. She was a student of yours, I understand."

"Let's back up," he said. "First, call me Hoyt. It makes me feel like an adult in this swirl of adolescent hormones and humor. What's Child Trace and what does it have to do with that darling girl who was brutally murdered?"

He'd said a mouthful. I explained that at one time I was an officer with the Atlanta Police Department and now owned a specialty PI agency, and that Detective Lieutenant Richard Lake asked me to apply a fresh brain to the case.

He brushed back his red pompadour. The sides of his hair were cut quite short. "About time they got on her case again. Damn, that was a terrible thing to happen to Juliet. Still can't get with it. Anyone asked me, I'd say that little gal would live to be a hundred. Never saw a better example of *joi de vivre* in a human."

"I'm a believer."

He looked at the girl posting to the rhythm of the horse she rode. "Juliet should have been brought up in Big Sky Country where a girl is the equal of men."

"I notice you call her Juliet. I talked with Mr. Stuart who

said the girls are called by their surnames like teachers are."

"I call my riders by their first names. They call me Mr. Fagan. That's the way I like it."

I doubted that's the way Mr. Stuart liked it. I said, "I was born in Atlanta. I don't know Big Sky Country."

He looked at me and grinned. "Not to slight women in the South and what they did to hold their society together after the Civil War, but you better believe that women who traveled West in the Conestoga wagons were tough as the men, otherwise they wouldn't have survived. They battled heat, cold, cholera, lack of food and water, the desert, high plains, to say nothing of an occasional Indian raid, which is portrayed out of proportion in movies. Indians wisely left wagon trains alone unless their food and water source was muddied or destroyed by them. Western women today are admirable descendants of their female ancestors. That's how I see Juliet."

"I see her as an intelligent, curious Southern girl aching to break out of a lackluster home life."

"You got that nailed tight," he said. He called to the girl on the horse. "Joyce, ball of foot higher than heel. Vertical line— ear, shoulder, hip, heel." The girl straightened and adjusted her seat by throwing her shoulders back.

When he looked at me I detected a faint sneer. "To further comment on your astute observation, see how much easier it is to give *Joyce* instruction rather than *Miss Higginbotham?*"

I thought of a comeback, but said, "How did Juliet sit a horse?"

"Terrible." He laughed. "But she was intrepid. Jump anything. Never lost her seat. Great balance, but otherwise poor technique. She'd grab the mane and over the rails she'd go."

"I assume she wasn't on the riding team."

"You assume right. Didn't have the patience to do the drills." He canted his head at Joyce. "See her bob like her head's a metronome, like the weight on a pendulum? Joyce is the opposite of Juliet, always predictable. Practice, practice, practice. She'll never be an inspired rider, though."

"But she will win ribbons."

"Oh yeah." He picked a gold pendant watch from its fob pocket and consulted it. "Look, I got to get going. If I can help you with anything . . ."

"Did you see Juliet during the Christmas break?"

"I was in Florida for the hols."

He hadn't exactly answered. "Wilton, Mr. Stuart, said she came here with a friend. Who was that?"

"I couldn't say for sure, but she often rode with her friend Bunny."

"Bunny?"

"Brandle goes by Bunny. Don't call her Brandle, she'll ignore you. She never returned to school after Juliet was murdered. She just disappeared."

"Disappeared? As in . . ."

"No one knows for sure, but one rumor was that she went to live with her uncle in Switzerland. He's with the embassy there."

"What about her parents?"

"They're actors. Off-Broadway. Grads of Winters Farm Academy." This time his sneer was more than faint. "A credit to us all," he said.

Nothing like an Irish sneer. I should know. My family came from that nation during one of the famines. "Did her parents travel back and forth to their home here?"

"Far's I know they don't have a home here. Bunny lived with her aunt. I met the aunt a couple of times when she came to watch Bunny ride. She had remarkable balance and guts."

"The aunt?"

He grinned. "I wouldn't know about that. Her name is Louise and she has a home design business." Hoyt turned and gave

41

a backward wave. "See you around if you want to ask anything else."

As I got to the gates of Winters Farm Academy, a distinctive roar reached my ears. I looked in the rearview mirror. The gates opened and, at the state road, the motorcycle on my tail braked abruptly as if the rider hadn't seen me stop until the last second. I like motorcycles, and the one idling behind me was a black beauty, a Harley, one of the Dynas like Lake's. Without seeing the logo, I knew it was a Harley by its sound at idle—that irregular hacking rumble. The rider wore a full helmet and black leathers. He seemed as intent on watching me as I him. I think he meant to intimidate me. I turned left to go south and the biker turned right to go north. He must have reached a hundred in three seconds flat.

CHAPTER FOUR

Dennis "Webdog" Caldwell graduated from Georgia State University magna cum laude and currently attended graduate school at the Georgia Institute of Technology, known as Georgia Tech. Poor boy—literally—he'd worked for me since his sophomore year at Georgia State, hacking and cracking information that helped solve many cases. I'd spoken for him in his quest for a full scholarship to Tech, but it wasn't necessary. His intellect and grades were the driving force behind his free ride to a master's degree in some arcane computer specialty.

I told him what I'd learned about Wilton Johns Stuart and asked for a deeper probe. The wife, the accident, anything and everything. Not that I suspected Stuart of wrongdoing, but I like to know all I can about the people connected to a case.

Then I gave him another name, Samuel Chapin, and said that he had retired from Winters Farm Academy and resided in Florida.

"Samuel Chapin, retired to Florida—with a million other elderlies. That's broad, boss."

"He recently died."

"That narrows it. May take half an hour."

We pay private computer investigative agencies good money to run down routine information, all of which is fed into Webdog's supercomputer—fifth generation.

I said, "Chapin retired after Juliet's first year at the school."

"You looking for a connection between Chapin in Florida

43

and her wanting to ride to Florida with a motorcycle club?"

"Noodling my brain, that's all."

"Now for my news," Web said.

I liked the excitement in his voice. "Shoot."

"Sherman Hanover Trapp is in a coma and has been for more than a week."

More than a week. The same amount of time that Geoff Howard's revised witness account hit the headlines.

Web continued, "Botched suicide. Identified by fingerprints. Was using the name Hanover. Just Hanover."

"You're kidding."

"That's the scoop from Dirk's."

We considered Dirk's Detectives our best source of public information, and sometimes they would go outside their mandate and do some real digging.

Web said, "Hanover missed his temple and got his cheek."

That happened often when a self-shooter jerked his hand when pulling the trigger.

"That shouldn't put him in a coma."

"Complications from drugs. His body was on meth overload."

"You still working on Geoff Howard's bona fides?"

"He is developing a website. I employed some of my special skills to check it out."

"And?"

"His invention is not too different than other online networking sites. I wouldn't call it revolutionary. He uses the standard building blocks. PHP is the scripting language most used for developing web pages and is embedded in HTML. PHP's was borrowed from Java, C and Perl, and runs on a web server like Apache that is configured to take PHP code as input and create web page content as output. It is deployed on most operating systems and platforms. MySQL would be employed to store multiple databases. They all borrow from each other's codes, even use cheat codes including the granddaddy of them all, the old Konami."

"Stop! Is this something I really need to know?"

"Uh, not unless you want to build your own social network."

"Just don't get yourself thrown in jail and out of Tech."

"He'll and they'll never know."

"Get photos of everyone you check out."

"Natch."

Lake was pissed that he hadn't been informed by the Chattanooga PD that the father of his murder victim had tried to kill himself, didn't succeed and was in a coma.

While Lake fumed, he cracked peanuts and tossed the hulls on the floor of the original Longhorn Steak House on Peachtree Street. Chewing nuts, he recited facts he'd gotten from the Chattanooga chief of police.

The man calling himself Hanover lived with a woman named Jean Ann Scott somewhere in the mountainous boonies. She came home and found him on the bed bleeding from the head. She called the cops and when they couldn't find any identification, they ran his prints. Trapp had been in the military.

Trapp was helicoptered to Chattanooga General where he lay in a special care unit for coma patients. They expected him to recover because he could breathe on his own. He'd apparently also been poisoning himself with drugs.

The police chief told Lake that they didn't know Sherman Hanover Trapp was the father of Juliet Trapp. The chief then wondered why Lake or someone in the APD wasn't keeping tabs on Mr. Trapp. Lake shot back with the fact that Mr. Trapp apparently didn't want to be found, having shed two of his names, but that all three of his names were in databases as the father of a murdered Atlanta girl.

"Is the Scott woman still at the house?" I asked Lake, thinking of the drive to Chattanooga.

"She split. CPD is going to call me back with an update."

Lake's sirloin was served with potato wedges and mixed vegetables. With his steak knife, he waved to the veggie section of his plate. "You want my carrots and broccoli?"

I'd passed on the potatoes that went with the filet mignon so the extra veggies suited. We ate in silence, and when Lake had finished his steak he perused the dessert portion of the menu. "What to share a mile-high pie?"

"Nope."

"Good, neither do I." He ordered the ice cream dessert and two cups of coffee.

I told the waiter no coffee; I'd had three glasses of wine. Enough to put me into a good sleep. I said to Lake, "I don't know whether to go to Chattanooga first or Naples."

"Ah, Naples, then Venice, then Rome."

"There is no Rome, Florida."

"Nonsense, there's a Rome in every state. It's only right." The coffee came and Lake doused it with sugar and cream. "Go to Chattanooga. Find the Scott woman," he said. The waiter set the towering pile of calories in front of Lake. "Hanover, as she knew him, might have confided in her."

"That's what I'm thinking. When you next talk to the Chattanooga chief, let them know I'm coming into their territory and that I'm licensed for concealed carry as a PI."

"You have to personally check with the Tennessee State Highway Patrol about carrying."

"You cleared the way for me already. Thanks for that. Surprising that the chief agreed, since you talked ugly to him."

"You're entirely welcome. Check in with him when you get there."

"Thanks. Maybe I won't carry."

Chewing and piling more ice cream on his fork, he said,

"Keep it in your glove box."

"I always do."

Bunny Raddison's name was in the police file as a school friend of Juliet's. Roselyn had told Lake that Juliet wasn't fast friends with any one girl because girls her age bored her. Lake had interviewed a couple of the girls in Juliet's class and they said the same thing. They liked being around Juliet, said she was a hoot, a girl with a quick wit and sharp tongue, but not someone who became a best friend. I was learning a great deal about the sixteen-year-old girl who possessed intelligence, charm, wit and pizzazz, not to leave out a lust for exploits. She was stand-out different than girls of her moneyed and social standing.

I would guess that the majority of mothers of the girls at Winters Farm Academy were in the Junior League. The Junior League (an organization to which my mother is a member, even though she's unaware of it now) is still tied to its blue-blood, old-money roots. It began in 1901 when debutante Mary Harriman, daughter of railroad baron E. H. Harriman, founded the organization with nine deb friends, one of which was Eleanor Roosevelt. They embraced the settlement house theory of bringing culture to the poor and immigrant communities. Volunteer middle-class workers would live side by side with slum dwellers to bring enlightenment to the poverty-stricken, thus motivating them to get off their lazy butts and help wipe out poverty. Pie in the sky, my father would say. Today, with chapters in towns that harbored snobs, the League's work is volunteerism and charity. Mother's chapter was into redistribution of wealth by selling year-old clothes. Rich women would go through their closets twice a year and get rid of those old Saks outfits and price them so that middle-class women who wanted a Saks label could purchase one for half the price. If there was a trickle down to the poor, I never saw it. They used the money to hold other events like beautifying a particularly rotten area of the city. Those saplings and shrubs sure meant a lot to hungry folks.

I was being snotty myself, but most Junior Leaguers feel a cut above. Mothers pass those superior feelings on to their daughters. Those daughters, in turn, band together against the non–Junior League crowd. They go to expensive schools where everyone is of one mind. But every once in a while a girl rebels. At Winters Farm Academy that girl was Juliet Trapp. I admired her. She was me when I was in school—twirling to a different drummer with a mother who never was there for either of us.

I told Lake about Bunny Raddison and we agreed to put Webdog on her trail.

"If I can find her," Web said, "we can Skype."

CHAPTER FIVE

During the War of Yankee Aggression, as we Southerners call the Civil War, Chattanooga was a railroad town like Atlanta. Still is. The Yankees liked to pitch their battles around these hubs, and you can tell by the number of battlefield parks and Civil War attractions in the city that it suffered mightily in that war.

I remember as a kid Daddy driving us from Atlanta, a hundred-mile one-way trip, to visit his uncle who had terminal lung cancer. What a bleak trip that was. The Chattanooga riverfront was a slum and the entire downtown had a dilapidated sorry ambience, despite the incredible beauty of the land around it. Lying between ridge and valley in the Appalachians, the city is surrounded by mountains. Cliffs border the city's streets and brace the rivers and lakes. Anyone who's driven toward Nickajack Lake has seen signs advising, "See Rock City," which is on top of Lookout Mountain. As many times as I've been in Chattanooga, I've never been tempted to see Rock City.

Today, as I drove across the John Ross Bridge (named for a Cherokee chief) and turned onto Riverfront Parkway, then segued onto Amnicola Highway into downtown, my heart sang. The city had pulled itself together with the help of determined citizens. Now it sparkled like its lakes—the Chickamauga and the Nickajack—both birthed by the Tennessee River.

At the police station, I was expected. Officer Lauran Brown stepped smartly toward me with a couple of sheets of paper for me to sign. Under the Auspices of Child Trace, Inc. of Atlanta, Georgia, and the Chattanooga Police Department, I was to locate and interview one Jean Ann Scott, a citizen of Chattanooga, in connection with the shooting of Sherman Hanover Trapp, formerly of Atlanta, Georgia, currently deceased and known as Hanover in the city of Chattanooga, state of Tennessee. I signed and asked where I could find the office of the Tennessee Highway Patrol. It was, Brown said, District Two, which served Hamilton and other counties and was located on Cummings Highway.

But not so fast, Miss Dru. He'd been informed by THP directive that unless I had credible evidence that said Jean Ann Scott posed a danger in the carrying out of my duties, I would not receive permission to carry a weapon, including gun, knife, or other lethal weapon, to and including a Taser, on my person unless and until such danger proved imminent. Made sense to me, *if* she wasn't the one who pulled the trigger resulting in Trapp's head shot.

And, no, Officer Brown said, the CPD had no idea where Jean Ann Scott lived. She'd dropped out of sight. The hospital hadn't seen her since Trapp was moved to the coma care center. He said that the house she and Trapp had rented had been let to another family. The leasing company informed me that Jean Ann Scott had been the renter of record and that she'd paid in cash and was never late with the rent.

Thanks to Webdog's good work in locating Jean Ann Scott's current address, I walked to a home at the Cottage Court Apartments, a low-income complex that Jean Ann Scott shared with a woman named Anna Paxton. No relation to her as far as Web could discern. I turned on my pocket recorder and knocked. It was for informational purposes only and could never be used for legal evidence.

Jean Ann Scott had a vapid prettiness that would turn ragged in middle age, especially if she didn't take care of herself. Her features were even and her hair still thick despite being tortured with home dye. It was a shade of brass with an inch of black roots. Her eyelids were blue and her mouth red. She looked to be thirty. Skinny and apprehensive, her left eye twitched and her left shoulder had a hitch. They spasmed in harmony.

"This about Hanover?" she asked.

"Yes, ma'am," I said, showing my identification.

I stood on the concrete slab under the overhang of the brick complex waiting to get in out of the cold. It's cold in the mountains in January. Jean Ann had on clean jeans, a red shirt and a hooded sweatshirt. She said, "He's in a coma."

"How long were you with Hanover, who is known in Atlanta as Sherman Hanover Trapp."

"Year-and-a-half until he shot hisself."

"How did you meet him?"

"Through a friend," she said, her forehead furrowing. "Why are you asking me these questions? Are you from the city?"

"Atlanta. This isn't about you."

She didn't relax much. "Okay."

"What was Hanover's last name?"

"He said to call him Hanover."

"Do you know why he shot himself?"

"Got the crazies is all I know."

I stamped my feet to give her a clue.

She didn't take it. "I got to go to my job," she said.

"You have a car?"

She sneered. "If I got a car, I wouldn't be here."

"Did Hanover have a car?"

"A motorcycle."

"Where is it?"

"Somebody stole it."

"Before or after he shot himself?"

"Day before. I got to go."

"I'll drive you."

"You want to talk some more?"

I told her that I did, she nodded and we walked to my car. She said she worked the three-to-eight shift at The Tire Store six blocks over.

I turned where she told me to and asked, "Did Hanover talk about his daughter?"

"I don't know nothing about a daughter until a policeman told me Hanover had another name and all about her getting killed. That's when I decided to split. I can't do nothing for a coma."

The smell of cigarette residue emanating from her skin, clothing and hair damned near overwhelmed my nose. "Are you certain he never talked about his daughter being murdered in Atlanta?"

"I just said . . ."

"Did he talk about his ex-wife?"

"Once maybe. She was nuttier than a fruitcake. He had some money, Hanover did."

"He was a very wealthy man. Did he have a lot of cash?"

"How would I know? He never shared any with me. He was tighter than a tick on a hog."

"Did he buy the drugs you shared?"

She looked at me. "It was our arrangement. I got clean when he shot hisself."

I'd seen plenty of hardcore druggies. She wasn't one, but maybe she got a late start. Was she a poor girl from the hills? I wondered who her folks were and if they were still living and what made Jean Ann take up with a man named only Hanover and how she wound up in this low-income place that she shared for expenses and no car to get to work.

She directed me to pull up in front of The Tire Store and

52

grabbed the door handle.

"Wait," I said.

"Can't. Can't be late."

"Did Hanover belong to a motorcycle club?"

She stared at her hand holding the door handle. "It's been real hard for me since he shot hisself. He'd go off for a week sometimes, come home stinkin' of oil and gas."

"Did you ride with him?"

"I'da like to, but he never let me."

"Did you meet any of his riding buddies?"

She shook her head. "They were all a secret far's I was concerned."

"Where was his bike when it was stolen?"

"Chained in the back yard. Next morning he about had a fit. A biker friend came and Hanover told me to take off." She opened the door and looked over her shoulder. "When I got back, Hanover was packing his shit in his duffel. I liked him okay. He said he was near done here and he was getting a ride the next day. Never said where to. I said what am I supposed to do with this place? He gave me three months' rent in twenties, just like he got them from the bank with the paper still around them. That all I got for all I did for him. The next day he shot hisself."

I asked, "Do you have any of the money he gave you?"

"Naw. I had to pay to move in with Anna."

"Where did he keep his cash?"

She fled the car, slammed the door and ran into The Tire Store.

I decided to stick around and pick Jean Ann up after her shift, but first I'd check if the hospital could give me any useful information . . . maybe even a look at the elusive Mr. Trapp.

Except that Trapp was no longer in residence. His brother

had taken control of his body once he died. I demanded to speak to the director, an elderly doctor with a fuzzy memory.

"Mr. Trapp died four days ago," Dr. Alfred Denton said, running his hand over his longish white hair. "I think it was. Here, let me get the medical file up."

It took him fifteen minutes to get Trapp's medical file to the computer screen. He kept forgetting passwords. Meantime, I asked for the name of Trapp's brother. He couldn't recall, but said it would be in the records. "Oh yes, for the record it's in the records." His idea of humor.

"Ah, here it is," he said. "It was exactly fifty-two hours that he passed on."

"I thought he could breathe on his own."

"Yes, well, he could actually, I think. Here, yes, he'd been removed from the breathalyzer . . ."

Were we talking blood alcohol levels here?

He looked at the screen. "Uh, the catheter, and uh, let's see, feeding apparatus stayed in. So, he was periodically removed from the respirator, but since he was in a coma . . ." He pointed at the computer screen as if I could see it, but I couldn't because he had told me with prissy emphasis that I couldn't read the patient's medical records. His reading them for me was okay, it appeared. "Here, here, right here it says he had lost kidney function. Of course his food intake consisted of a mixture of thiamin, glucose, electrolytes, and naloxene to reverse the narcotic overdose he suffered."

"The typical coma cocktail," I said.

He frowned and blinked. "Well, it's not always the same."

"How was his wound healing?"

"Wound?"

"The gunshot wound?"

"Oh that. Nicely I suspect."

Did this doctor ever look at Sherman Trapp? "Did his brother sign a release form?"

"Oh yes, yes indeed. Several, as I recall." He wheeled his chair away from the desk and opened a file drawer. After many minutes, he looked up perplexed. "They don't appear to be here."

"Did you witness him signing the forms?"

"Ah, I believe, that is, yes, I was away last week."

"Did Mr. Trapp have visitors?"

"The police came that first day. I think . . ." He fidgeted. "I guess they were satisfied all was in order."

"They'd lost interest in him, hadn't they?"

"I believe that is correct. His brother started coming to visit him. Let's see, I believe, yes, let's see, visitors have to sign in." He looked in a file and seemed perplexed. He waved a hand. "Oh yes, that would be kept in the ledger at the desk."

"When he died, did you call the police?"

"Why no, that wasn't necessary. Coma-related deaths are considered natural. We never do."

"I'm no doctor, but I know he didn't die from coma."

"Let's see." He consulted the computer screen. "Yes. Pseudomonas pneumonia. An opportunistic pathogen." He made as if to wax his moustache with this thumb and forefinger.

Or an opportunistic murder.

At the desk, he showed me the signature of the brother. It was a scrawl connecting the initials R. T. The signer hadn't bothered to print his name on the allotted line.

I got the name of the funeral director and left him grooming his facial hair.

The body of Sherman Hanover Trapp, a.k.a. Hanover, had been cremated and his bagged ashes placed in a container that the brother supplied. "What is the brother's name?" I asked.

The funeral director looked up the paperwork and said, "Robert Thomas Trapp. He came for the cremains just this morning."

The lugubrious director said Robert Thomas Trapp didn't say what he intended to do with his brother's ashes. He described the brother as a stocky man in a suit that didn't fit well, a man with a clean-shaven face that looked as if he had just shaved a beard. His lower jaw and mouth were white and pimply.

"How would you describe Trapp's corpse?"

"He'd had a traumatic injury to his left cheek. He had been in coma so his skin was flaccid. That's really all I can tell you."

"Did you embalm him?"

"No, that is not required for cremation. We have refrigeration, and a public viewing was not offered. Only the brother viewed the body."

Maybe it was seeing my mental grasping for words that made him continue. "There are certain procedures that all crematories must follow. The paperwork was complete and the fee paid. We provide an ID number, much like a metal dog tag, that stays with the body through the process and is attached to the deceased's bag of ashes. We present the ashes to the next-of-kin or other authorized persons in a cardboard box. Mr. Trapp brought a canvas tote that had a coffin on the front with the words 'Think outside the box' in gothic letters. He said he was having the urn inscribed for burial in the family's vault, which, he said, is located in Atlanta, Georgia."

Think outside the box—what class. The funeral director nodded as if he'd read my thought.

Web confirmed my belief that Sherman Hanover Trapp did not have a brother. His sister, Elise Lane, lived in Birmingham with her husband, Roger. He gave me the phone number and I called her with the bad news. "Actually," she said, "I haven't seen

Sherm in years. He became estranged from the family in college. I'm so sorry he's gone, and I don't know what to do. I'll have to call Roger."

I told her that because a man posing as Sherman Trapp's brother took possession of the cremains, I didn't think there was anything for her to do but pray for Sherman's soul if she was so inclined. She sounded relieved, and I asked her why she and her brother had become estranged.

"I'm five years older than he is. He was always a strange kid," she said. "You never knew what he was thinking. He could and would go for days without conversation. His answers would be one syllable until he snapped out of it. Our dad was a man of few words and introverted, but he was a nice man, kind. Our mother was a chatterbox compared to those two."

In that respect, Elise had taken after her mother. "Are you saying that your brother wasn't nice?"

"He wasn't nice or not nice. He was very into himself. Then he married a woman who was as strange as he. I only met her once when our mother died. I don't know how Sherm hooked up with her, but her being an heiress was a plus in her favor. He always went for the money. If he loved anything it was cash. I was shocked when Juliet was killed. Neither of them called to let us know. We found out about it on the news."

I told her what I knew about his life with Jean Ann Scott and asked if she could believe that Sherman shot himself.

"As I said I haven't talked to him in years; well, not since Juliet was buried. We came to the funeral. It was a very strange feeling. Of course it was, her being murdered and all. We hardly spoke at the services. I talked to that nice policeman, Lieutenant Lake. Thank the Lord he was there. He made us feel halfway comfortable around Sherm and his wife."

She hadn't answered my question. "But would Sherman shoot himself?"

"Never in a million years. He loathed guns. Our daddy was a hunter. Sherm wouldn't touch the things. He wasn't a violent man, just weird. By the way, I'm the only one called him Sherm. He insisted on Sherman from everyone else. He knew I'd tease him for being a prig if he protested."

I said, "At the time he is said to have shot himself, he had overdosed on crystal meth."

I heard her intake of breath through the cell. "Are we talking about my brother?"

"He called himself Hanover and got around on a motorcycle," I said. "We know that after his daughter's death he sold his computer business in Atlanta and moved to Chattanooga. He lived a near-hermit's life. So said Jean Ann Scott, the woman he shared his house with."

"What happened to his money?" Elise asked.

Wonder if she was thinking inheritance? "He had money, Jean Ann said, but wouldn't share it with her until the day before he was shot when he gave her three months' rent."

"That's Sherm. Three months' worth for putting up with his moods."

I said, "He apparently spent money to buy their drugs."

"If I didn't know better, I'd think you were talking about another man. Two things wrong here. Sherm absolutely hated drugs, illegal and legal. It's a good thing he had good health. He really believed his body was a temple. He preened all the time. My goodness, how I remember seeing him before a mirror all the time. No, he definitely would not put a chemical in his mouth. One time he had a painful ear infection. He wouldn't have anything to do with the meds; just quietly gutted it out until the ear healed. My brother would not touch drugs, and he sure as shootin' wouldn't pay good money for anyone else's."

★ ★ ★ ★ ★

I waited for Jean Ann to come out of The Tire Store at eight o'clock. Ten after eight, a man came out and locked the door. Hard to tell his age, muscular rather than fat, he wore a short tan raincoat over a cheap brown suit. His eyes were close together, spliced by a straight nose. His hair was longish and dirty-blond. Apparently you didn't need Brooks Brothers on your back or a classic side-part haircut to work in a tire store.

I got out of the car and approached him.

"I've no money," he quickly said, spreading his arms.

I grinned. "Sorry if I scared you." I held up my hands. "No weapon."

He relaxed. "Can't be too careful in this neighborhood."

"I'm Moriah Dru. Must be some neighborhood if a woman can frighten you."

"Kids here frighten me." He looked me over. "I'm Dave. You don't belong here. You want something?"

"I'm waiting for Jean Ann."

His gaze held an unspoken question, then he broke eye contact. "You'll be waiting a long time then." I made a noise like *what?* He said, "I recognize your car now. You dropped her off." I nodded. "She came in the front door and went out the back. I thought she was hanging up her coat. Nope. She did a bunk." He seemed resigned as if such things happened regularly.

"Did she get into a car or on a motorcycle?"

"I didn't hear a bike. She always walked. Like she walked away from the job I gave her."

"Did her companion, a man named Hanover, come into the store?"

He thought about the question for a tic too long and shook his head. "I felt I could trust her so I'd skip out at six for a bite to eat, and she'd mind the store until I got back to lock up."

He'd skipped answering. I said, "Hanover got around on a

motorcycle. He was interested in, you know, the life. Jean Ann ever talk about that?"

"Hmmm," he murmured, as though ruminating on the question. "I guess it's time for me to ask why you're asking. You're law, aren't you?"

"Used to be. Private now, in Atlanta, here in your town to follow up on a murder case."

"Murder, huh? We got enough murder in this town." His crooked teeth showed when he tried a grin. "Don't bring no more."

"Big city, big-city problems."

"Hanover do a murder in Atlanta?"

"No."

"So he rides a bike. What's that got to do with your murder case?"

"Maybe nothing, but he had a biker friend I'd like to locate."

He bristled. "I ride. Not all riders are criminals." He walked away and got into a beat-up Honda parked at the side of the building.

Tetchy.

Jean Ann Scott's roommate opened the door three inches and said that Jean Ann was not at home and she didn't keep up with her comings and goings. That evening I returned to Jean Ann's apartment and her roommate told me to go away and not come back. I said, as the door slammed in my face, for her to call the police and report Jean Ann missing.

It was eight thirty when I reported to Lake. I told him I needed to have a chat with the cops about motorcycle clubs and hopefully find someone up here willing to talk about Trapp, if my hunch was right, and he tried to get information from club members. "I'll find a motel and follow the leads tomorrow," I said.

"Think about Sherman Trapp," Lake said. "There ain't a Chinaman's chance in a Mexican kitchen he infiltrated a biker gang."

"From what Jean Ann said . . ."

"You will not go it alone, Dru."

I didn't reply.

"Did you hear what I said?"

"I heard."

"No contact with one-percenters until you have an army with you, or me. I'll wrap up here in half an hour then hit the road."

"Lake, I'm perfectly capable of . . ."

"Thanks for the tips, but the Trapp case is still mine."

My face flamed, my tongue flared. "You jerk, you can't cut me out . . ."

"Dru. I'll overlook your anger. I'm not cutting you out. We'll always be partners, but like any partner, male or female, I will not put you in harm's way."

I blew out long and slow. "Sorry."

"Get us rooms and find a good restaurant. We'll talk this out when I get there."

The downtown hotel had an attractive restaurant; however, the food was cold, overcooked and bland. Lake didn't seem to notice as he loaded fried catfish and fries and hush puppies from his fork into his face.

After ordering a wedge of cherry pie, Lake started to launch into a lecture on modern autopsy practices. I held up my hand. I'd brought the subject up, regarding the odd handling of Trapp's death, but I didn't relish watching Lake eat cherry pie and talk autopsy. So he finished the dessert and then relaunched.

"Fifty years ago, an autopsy was routine," he said. "As a part of health care, they were performed on most patients who died in a hospital. Your coma care center is a hospital that requires its staff to be licensed physicians, nurses, technicians, etc. But for the last ten years, postmortem examinations are performed on about five percent of corpses."

"That's surprising."

"Not surprising are the reasons," he said, "which are grave concerns for the medical and insurance establishments. Health insurers do not cover postmortem examinations. They save their zillions for the living."

"I didn't know that you had to file a claim with an insurer for an autopsy. Isn't it something the hospital, or doctor or the state would require and therefore pay for?"

"When faced with a suspicious death, our department requests the crime lab do an autopsy and the taxpayer pays. But in the case of hospitals and doctors, sometimes there's a contract with a municipality, but the real kicker is they have no incentive to investigate a suspicious death at their facility. They fear it might reveal malpractice. I've seen stats where probably one in four hospital deaths have a misdiagnosis associated with them. Do you believe Trapp's death is suspicious?"

"I believe everything I've seen and heard up here is suspicious."

"Trapp was in a drug-trauma coma."

"He didn't die from that. Officially, he died from *Pseudomonas* pneumonia."

"My godmother died from hospital pneumonia many years ago. She'd had her gallbladder removed and was on a ventilator."

"Like Trapp."

He stared as if abstracted. "It's diagnosed by a blood test."

My mind melded with his. "What happens to leftover blood samples?"

"After testing, the remaining blood, or plasma or whatever, is disposed of in a biohazard container. But the doc should have the test results in his computer."

"Bet he doesn't; bet he didn't do a blood test. Bet he was guessing that Trapp had hospital pneumonia."

"You talked to the man, I didn't."

"That means I have to call him and ask."

"Either way it doesn't prove anything."

We'd learned that lesson time and time again. "I know, but . . ."

I looked at his empty pie plate that was smeared with the impossibly red gel of cheap cherry pie.

CHAPTER SIX

When we work a case together that involves cooperation with other jurisdictions, we book two rooms, preferably adjoining. Unless imprudent to do so, we sleep together in one and Lake climbs out of bed before dawn to return to his room. This anticipates what occurred that evening after dinner.

I'd stripped, bathed and was donning comfortable lounging pajamas when the hotel house phone rang. Had to be a wrong number. But it wasn't. The concierge said, "Someone to see you, Miss Dru. The Chief of Police, Forest Smarr. May I put him on the telephone?"

Foreboding rode through me. "Please do."

"Good evening, Miss Dru," he said, his voice low and resonating.

"How can I help you, Chief Smarr?"

"I'd like to speak with you. The bar is quiet now."

"Lieutenant Lake arrived this evening. Can we include him?"

"By all means."

"His room number is five-forty-two. Have the clerk contact him."

His pause was slight, but there. "Sure, I'll do the official summoning."

I wondered what his investigators found out about us. Because he would have checked us out.

★ ★ ★ ★ ★

We sat in a corner of the long low-lit room. Lake ordered a beer, I ordered wine and Chief Smarr—Forest, as he'd directed us to call him—ordered ice tea. I wasn't going to call a chief of police by his given name, not until I knew him better.

"I got a call from the doctor at the coma care center," Smarr said. "Dr. Alfred Denton thought I might like to know that you, Miss Dru, interviewed him about his patient. I think you confused the doctor."

"He's easily confused," I said.

"I know the man. He appears that way, but he's a dedicated professional."

"What was his problem?" Lake asked.

"He wanted to know if he'd done anything improper by signing the death certificate of Sherman Hanover Trapp, a.k.a. Hanover, and releasing his body to the mortuary."

"Did he?" Lake asked.

"I don't know." He stared at me a few moments too long. "It was my understanding that Miss Dru came here to interview Jean Ann Scott."

I stared back just as long. "That is true, and I did."

I told Chief Smarr that I hadn't finished the interview and decided to come back to her workplace and drive her home, giving me more time to ask a few more questions.

He said, "In the meantime you went to talk to Dr. Denton."

I told him that I went to see Trapp, and to my great surprise, he had already been cremated. His body was released to a man who was not his brother, *although* he said he was *but* offered no proof other than a signature on the call ledger.

Lake gave me the look, like I'd been too emphatic, and said, "You can understand Miss Dru's consternation, but we know coma patients are susceptible to many ways of dying."

I spoke up and said that Dr. Denton shared information freely with me, even told me that the police had come once to see that the patient had settled in, but hadn't bothered to visit again.

Lake's expression warned me not to get into a good guy–bad girl slanging.

Chief Smarr settled back in his chair. "We had no reason to further check on Trapp. Failed suicides are for the docs and shrinks. The matter was over."

"Even when you found out he was connected to a murder in Atlanta?"

"Didn't know that until Lieutenant Lake here informed us. Meantime I've had research done on the murder of his daughter. Brutal as they come. My take is the pain got to be too much, he shot himself and then died of complications of coma. Nothing suspicious there."

"Then a bogus brother showed up."

He was pretty good at keeping his face impassive. "You know, Miss Dru, and you, too, Lieutenant Lake—that case comes under your purview. I have my hands full in this city. I got citizens who change their names to avoid whatever they want to avoid, even us. I got bogus people out the wazoo right here in river city. Are you going round-about to say that a crime or crimes were committed here in connection with these people?"

Lake touched my foot with his, then said, "It appears that Trapp came here to find out something. Here's a rich man, a pillar of his Episcopal church and the country club, a dapper dresser, who's living in a shack on a dirt lane with a woman he hardly knew with only a motorcycle for transportation. No identification with him. Trapp's sister paints a picture of a brother that would never touch drugs or a gun . . ."

Chief Smarr held up a hand. "All that goes out the window when a loved one gets murdered like his girl did. Haven't you seen that in your career?"

"I'll grant he could have lost his mind," Lake said. "But I

want to know more. The evidence is too sketchy."

"You want to continue investigating in my jurisdiction?"

"I would like your help, too."

"I guess we can cooperate with our southern big-town neighbor. Used to be Chattanooga was bigger than Atlanta."

"Maybe still would be if another man named Sherman hadn't decided to torch Atlanta and Atlanta got mad," Lake said.

Smarr laughed. "Couple of Shermans causing trouble for my city doesn't escape me. But I like my city's size. Would you keep me in the picture as you go about investigating my citizens?"

Lake and I both assented with a good-natured laugh.

Chief Smarr turned to me, "You get anything more out of Jean Ann Scott when you went back to fetch her at the tire place?"

"She'd disappeared." He pushed back a little, and I told him about the turn of events when I drove back to continue the interview at The Tire Store.

He asked, "Did you check her home?"

"Twice. The second time the roommate told me to go away and not come back."

"I'll handle the roommate, see if she knows where she'd go. What did Jean Ann Scott say in this interview?"

I took my recorder from my sweater pocket. "Give a listen."

I snapped on the small recorder and listened to myself introduce the recording.

"This is Moriah Dru, Child Trace, Inc., talking with Jean Ann Scott of Chattanooga about her relationship with Sherman Hanover Trapp, known to her as Hanover."

Jean Ann: "This about Hanover?"

"Yes, ma'am."

Jean Ann: "He's in a coma."

"How long were you with Hanover, who is known in Atlanta as Sherman Hanover Trapp?"

Jean Ann: "Year-and-a-half until he shot hisself."

"How did you meet him?"

Jean Ann: "On the street. Why are you asking me these questions? Are you from the city?"

"Atlanta. This isn't about you."

Jean Ann: "Okay."

"What was Hanover's last name?"

Jean Ann: "He said to call him Hanover."

"Do you know why he shot himself?"

Jean Ann: "Got the crazies is all I know. I got to go to my job."

"You have a car?"

Jean Ann: "If I got a car, I wouldn't be here."

"Did Hanover have a car?"

Jean Ann: "A motorcycle."

"Where is it?"

Jean Ann: "Somebody stole it."

"Before or after he shot himself?"

Jean Ann: "Day before. I got to go."

Chief Smarr listened to the rest of the recording and said, "You have a copy?"

I handed him the recording. "Made just for you."

Forest Smarr left us with a questioning expression riding his jaw bone. "See you in the morning, nine sharp?"

After a quickie night cap, our love-making matched that tempo—what I call need-sleep, peck-on-the-cheek sex.

The next morning, though, we made up for the rapidity, showered and drove in Lake's off-duty car to the police department.

A sharp young officer led us into the conference room. There, my mouth fell open. Not at the two trays piled with assorted donuts—though later I could laugh about them—but at the ten men and one woman who had their heads turned to, and their eyes focused on, us.

"Good morning!" Chief Forest Smarr called out. I was glad we were three minutes early. Wouldn't do to keep these self-important people waiting. "Take a seat," the chief invited.

Our places were to be smack in the center of the long rectangular table. I was across from a suit that looked like FBI or Secret Service.

"I'll do the introductions," Chief Smarr said. "Starting to my left."

He rattled off names I would not remember. In turn these names belonged to Alcohol, Tobacco and Firearms; the Tennessee Bureau of Investigation; North Carolina Drug Enforcement; the Chattanooga Police Department's Drug Assist Force; the Hamilton County Sheriff's Office; the FBI guy across from me (he winked when Chief Smarr said his name); the Tenth District Drug Task Force; and lastly, the Assistant U.S. Attorney, whom I'd met before. His name was George Ryan. Once these introductions were made, the door opened and in came our very own Commander Haskell, APD's Major Crimes Commander, followed by the director of the Georgia Bureau of Investigation. Lake's arm was touching mine and I felt it stiffen. He's not fond of the GBI director.

The gang was all here.

Chief Smarr said, "We are gathered in the interest of clearing the streets of Tennessee, Georgia and North Carolina of vermin from the Wild Blood Motorcycle Club. This motorcycle club has been officially declared a public nuisance in all three states. They are headquartered in Raleigh and have a clubhouse here in Chattanooga and Atlanta." Handouts were passed. I looked at one titled Federal Authorities Seek Indictments of the Following Members of the Wild Blood Motorcycle Club.

It listed their addresses, birth names and their a.k.a.'s, which read like something from the comics. Dingbat and Snoozer were from Raleigh, Drano and Wasp hailed from Tennessee and Gonzo and Roach were residents of Georgia.

These vermin were arrested and charged with narcotics, firearms, child pornography and various public nuisance actions like wheelies at crowded events. If convicted of the more serious crimes, each would face up to twenty years in prison and as much as a $25,000 fine.

Smart-mouth Lake said, "Where are they going to get that kind of jack if they can't sell porn and crack?"

The overly serious U.S. Attorney rose and said that the ATF had spent the past two years investigating the Wild Blood Motorcycle Club that had formed more than twenty years ago and in the interim became a criminal enterprise. "Our partnership involves many law enforcement projects," he said. "The Federal Safe Streets Task Force, the Northwest Georgia Criminal Enterprise Task Force, the Raleigh Safe Streets Task Force, the Appalachia High-Intensity Drug Trafficking Area, and the Tennessee Anti-Gang Initiative. The ATF enforces the law that one-percenters think they're above."

The ATF man thanked the men and women from each agency, project and initiative that resulted in the arrest and charging of six men who were a menace to society. In turn, every agency's spokesman (and the one woman) made a similar speech, during which Lake reached for two donuts. The coffee pot was passed around several times. Given my three cups at the motel buffet and two here, my back teeth were floating.

After the verbal back-patting was over, Smarr turned to us. "I have given these agencies a copy of the recording you gave to me last evening. We will be working diligently to find Jean Ann Scott and will pursue an investigation into the death of Sherman Hanover Trapp of Atlanta, with the goal of eventually locating the killer of Juliet Trapp. If any of the Wild Blood Motorcycle

Club are involved, we will find who they are." He sounded more confident than I felt. He went on, "Let me say this. Not one of the men on this indictment list has been charged with murder, although several have been charged but not convicted of assault, pimping and statutory rape. You can imagine that witnesses have moved away or recanted rather than face these cockroaches."

Vermin. Bugs. I began to itch.

Chief Smarr addressed Commander Haskell. "We will get up to speed on your murder case and help move heaven and earth to find the killer. If you will remain behind, the rest of this assembly will separate and get to work." He looked at the men, and one woman, who'd folded their briefcases and looked ready to bolt. "Congratulations on the fine work you've accomplished. We've more to do, so let's go to it."

I rose, as did Lake. We exchanged glances. Lake was super pissed. I was not happy either. We were being X-ed out.

Commander Haskell said to Smarr, "Give me a few minutes with my people here."

Haskell stepped into the hall and stood in front of Lake and me. Lake waited for his commander to say what we expected to hear. "I talked to the ATF guy last night. He's real gung-ho to convict those bastards and I don't blame him. If the Feds can hang a murder rap on the bikers, it's a capital case."

"Sherman Trapp's death may or may not be suspicious," Lake said, teeth nearly snapping. "But Juliet Trapp is my capital case."

Haskell gave a short, curt nod. "I'd say Sherman Trapp's death is suspicious, but that's still a Chattanooga case. Juliet Trapp stays with you. Don't feel left out. Those men in there needed to congratulate themselves on investigations that led to charges. Feds are Feds, ATF or FBI doesn't matter. The federal attorney is a Class A a-hole, but he's good and he'll nail every inch of those bikers' hides to the indictments. Chief Smarr's with me, I'm with you. Continue your work on the case. I know you don't need me to caution you, but I will. Don't poach on federal territory."

"Are they claiming biker crimes as their sole territory?"

"On the federal charges. However, remember that if they have two murders, it could constitute a conspiracy and will broaden the scope of the bikers' criminal enterprise."

"You're saying they could wrap the Trapp cases in RICO and take them away," Lake said.

"They will tread lightly, having been bitten. Remember when the Feds went after that Hells Angels' honcho for all the mayhem that gang was causing? The Feds failed to meet the RICO requirement that the club had a *policy* to deal guns and drugs. Policy is the operative word with RICO."

"If these six Wild Blood bikers acted on their own, there's no RICO, as I understand RICO."

"That's true, but the U.S. Attorney aims to link the three individual chapters and call them conspirators."

"We haven't had problems with Wild Blood recently," Lake said. "Those Georgia boys under indictment with the Feds now belong to the Chattanooga branch."

"There's still a clubhouse in Atlanta that gets some use. And we haven't tested every Wild Blood for semen yet—just those who were in Atlanta at the time of Juliet's murder and volunteered."

"How many bikers in these three branches are we talking about?"

"Over a hundred."

"Six out of a hundred? Sounds like a PR campaign against Wild Blood to me."

"Don't be saying that in public," Haskell warned.

"I won't be saying anything in public until I have something to say," Lake said.

Haskell waved and went inside.

I looked at Lake. "Only you ate donuts during the speechifying."

"You would notice," Lake groused. "And count."

"Just lookin' after your waist."

I followed Lake outside and to the parking lot. He nudged my arm. "You see him?"

Nodding, I said, "I do."

The FBI guy, Grady Locke—if I remember his name right—leaned against a shiny black Crown Victoria, arms and feet crossed, staring straight at me. His black shoes had a mirror shine. His brown hair was cut agency short. He was medium height and slender, and his dark suit, white shirt and red tie were likewise agency perfect.

Lake peeled off, saying, "I'll walk and get the car."

"And leave me with the Fed?"

"He winked at you. He likes you. Capitalize on it."

With that he was gone. That's my lover, quick to pimp me for the cause.

Locke sauntered toward me, his eyes taking inventory of my hips, chest, face—a superior grin showing fine white teeth. He stopped and said, "Happy to meet you at last. I'm a fan of your work, Miss Dru. You have made a name for yourself and your agency, Child Trace."

He'd gotten through my defenses, the jerk. "Thanks, Special Agent Locke. I heard in there that you do good work, too."

His palm went to his chest like he was going to say the Pledge of Allegiance. "We try."

"Don't we all."

I asked, and he said he worked out of the Memphis Bureau. "I can help you," he said.

"How so?"

"Work with me and I'll get you what you need."

"What do I need?"

"Someone on the inside of the club. A CI can be very helpful."

A CI was a confidential informant. "When they're helpful."

"Mine are." I guess he couldn't help his sniff of self-importance. "I was interested in the Trapp case from the get-go. My specialty is violent street gangs, which includes OMGs—outlaw motorcycle gangs. I was immediately struck by the victim saying she was going off with Wild Blood."

"A recent development—a new eyewitness—indicates a biker, not a club."

"The last person to see her alive, right?"

"The eyewitness or the biker?"

He bounced back on his heels. "I like prickly."

"Look, I'm starting from the beginning, and that begins with Mr. Trapp's behavior after his daughter's death. I'm making no assumption regarding the Wild Blood club. If our witness's drunken recall can be credited, we know of a single biker."

He cast a doubtful glance. "Wild Blood was the predominant OMG in Atlanta at the time. The biker could have been one of them."

"Those in town were exonerated. It was her mother who used the club's name, and her mother is very vague."

Why was I upholding an outlaw motorcycle gang like Wild Blood? Yes, I was prickly standing here being patronized. My prickliness had to do with Grady Locke, not the club or the case.

"The dead girl's father's coming here suggests a connection to Wild Blood," Locke said. "Several of the Atlanta club members came here after being harassed by the APD."

I could argue with that, but I didn't want to discuss my case with him at all.

Locke said, "OMGs are on the rise and compete with thirty-three thousand other ethnic and prison gangs, and we are but a small force against them. They're well organized and will do whatever it takes to make money, including murder, robbery, fraud, extortion, and prostitution." Sounded like something out of his handbook. He kept going. "OMGs are different than other street gangs. Terror is engrained in what they call 'The Life.' Like the scumbags we talked about in the meeting, they enjoy hurting anyone who gets in their way." I held up a hand to say something, but he hurried on, "I know, they stress in their public relations attempts that they don't bother citizens who don't bother them, but citizens have been caught in the cross-fire of their constant wars for territory. It's my mandate to take down these gangs through new initiatives and partnerships." While my mouth was stuck on idle, his flashed a smile of beaming brightness. "What do you say? Shall we form a partnership?"

Where the hell was Lake?

I said, "Does your new initiative include the old initiative of using bureau undercovers and confidential informants?"

"You are a clever girl. Yes, new meets old when exigencies . . ."

"Cops and bikers become partners."

He shifted his slender hips. "You used to be a cop."

"Never an undercover." *Although I have disguised myself before in a very dangerous operation that almost got Lake and me killed.*

"Beautiful as you are," he said, his throat closing around the words, making his voice husky and longing, "no one would believe it."

Where the hell was Lake?

"When can I talk to your CI? We could use a new lead or two."

"We?"

"Lieutenant Lake and I."

He of the throaty voice said, "I thought maybe you meant you and me."

"Murder is state business."

He snapped back to his concern. "Mine, too, if I can prove it's connected to a violation of federal criminal statutes."

I ran fingers through my wind-mussed hair. Time for some straight talk. "I'm looking into the murder of a young girl who had itchy feet, but so far I've found nothing that says she was involved in gangs or illegal activities. I want to talk to a biker who might give me something, a lead to the man who raped and murdered her."

Jangling change in his pocket, he again tried charm. "I admire your obsessive compulsion and that you grind away at a case until every layer is exposed. You don't give in, and you love being right."

I simply stared at him.

He looked past my shoulder. "Ah, I see your ride arrives." A breeze ruffled his short brown hair. "I share the same attributes, and that's why I believe we can work together." He trained his eyes on Lake's car, then shifted them back to me. "I look forward to working with an investigator who is smart as she is lovely." He turned to go. "I'll be in touch."

I got in the car.

Lake stared at my profile for a few seconds. "Was I in the nick of time?"

"He promised to call," I said, trailing my voice with yearning.

We had an early lunch at Southern Fried Diner, then Lake left Chattanooga. I wanted to see if Jean Ann had returned home or to The Tire Store and told Lake I'd be back in Atlanta by dinner, or hoped to.

Jean Ann's roommate told me through the crack in the door, which was on a chain, that she didn't think Jean Ann would be coming back, and that the police were on their way to talk to her, thanks to me. She admitted Jean Ann acted "weird" and "jumpy" and left most of her stuff. She would not let me in to go through her room without a warrant, which I could not get, so it would be a job for Chief Smarr.

Dave was not at The Tire Shop. A fatish girl named Tina was manning the counter and phones. She said Dave had hired her at a bar last night and that today he had gone to his club. The bruise on her jaw kept jumping up and down.

"What club?" I asked.

"Who wants to know?"

All of a sudden she'd gotten hinky. That's when I noticed fangs where the bruise was. My God. She had a cobra tattoo climbing up her neck, the head of the fanged one just breaching her jaw. This led me to believe Tina was a motorcycle groupie and got a job interview with Dave at a biker bar. Probably the same with Jean Ann; like her, Tina and Dave were pieces in the Trapp puzzle.

"No need to get hostile," I said to Tina, who looked as mean as the snake crawling onto her chin. "I know he's in a motorcycle club, just not which one."

She snorted. "Only one in this town."

"Thanks," I said. On the way out I noticed Dave's framed picture on the wall. The lettering beneath it told me that David Melvin Barstow was the manager.

Since I'd learned where Wild Blood had its headquarters, I drove to Webber Road. The clubhouse sat on the corner of a main thoroughfare and a street that could have been an alley. A six-foot spiked iron fence surrounded the long white building. Judging by the bay doors, it had once been a garage with a storefront on one side. The plate glass windows were boarded.

The club's patch was painted on the white boards. The patch depicted a gold skeleton riding a speeding black motorcycle with red wings streaming from the biker. The door to the store was painted gold and black. Four Harleys rested inside the compound. It wasn't long before I heard the *po-ta-to-po-ta-to* of an engine, then the rider revving the bike to a mean pitch. The iron bars parted by automatic opener and the rider flashed through on a Road King, a handsome bike, one that Lake coveted before he bought his Electra Glide. The Road King turned and flowed in front of me. I thought it wise to move on and let up on the brake. Before I knew it, the Harley zoomed past on the right side of my car and cut in front of me before I'd gotten my foot on the gas pedal. He stopped abruptly. I noticed the club patch on his back and the rockers above and below. Wild Blood. Chattanooga.

That reminded me of the first time I observed the Hells Angels patch up close. I happened to be in California visiting a friend whose brother was in the infamous motorcycle club. The brother's wife woke up one morning to find her kid missing. The case delayed my vacation for two days, but I found the girl. Her real dad had taken her to Oregon, away from the outlaw bikers. The irony was he lived in a compound of right-wing lug nuts. The real dad went to jail for two years. The little blonde girl was reunited with her tattooed mother after the authorities deemed the home was fit.

Cutting the remembrance, I studied the biker who had pulled in front of me. He wore a second cut—a neat little patch with a 1% sign inside a blue diamond rhombus. The biker stared through the half-helmet's visor for a brief moment, got off, cut the V-twin engine, kicked the side-stand down and walked toward my window. On one side of his chest was written in Old English script: By Blood Possessed.

I pressed a button and the window glass slid down. He

removed his helmet.

"Hi, Dave," I said.

"You wanted me."

"Tina called?"

"Yeah. Like a good girl. And along you came."

"She didn't tell me you rode with Wild Blood." *Nor did you.*

"She told you too much."

"I guessed. Tina looks like a biker chick. The snake and all."

"You know biker chicks?"

"I located a Hells Angels' kid that went missing."

"Then the Angels owe you. Go talk to them."

"Not their problem."

"What can I do for you?"

"Information."

He laughed. He genuinely got a kick out of my seriously stated desire for information. "In case you don't know, we're a secret club."

"I don't want passwords or handshakes or initiation rites. I want information on a murder in Atlanta."

"I know about it."

"Did you know the man calling himself Hanover?"

"You asked me that before." I nodded. He stared, then twisted his lip. "He came around asking about joining the club. As we say, you have to ask how, you're not cut out to be one of us."

I said, "Members of Wild Blood that were in Atlanta at the time of Juliet Trapp's murder were cleared. The Angels and Outlaws were all in Florida."

"Gearing up for Bike Week."

I told him that I didn't see his name in the police reports of the members' interviews so I assumed he wasn't in Atlanta at the time. He shook his head and crossed his arms. He said that he had a job here. I asked if his friends talked about being interviewed. He answered with a shrug. I grinned, "I guess it's pointless to ask if there was any loose talk about raping and murdering a teenager in Atlanta?"

His eyes shifted and when they came back to stare at me they were gray marbles.

"Is there anyone in the club I can talk to?" I asked.

His mouth turned up, but wasn't exactly a smile. "You can talk to most of the members. Some aren't too friendly, but good-looking women are always welcome companions in the bars. Don't be rude. I wouldn't ask about rape and murder, I was you."

"I get you. Where are the bars?"

"Round about."

"You won't tell me?"

"Don't want you hurt."

"I hear you're fixing to lose some members."

He looked perplexed.

"The indictments," I said.

"They got good lawyers. They'll be back in four-and-a-half years."

"Not many Harleys in the lot," I said, waving backhand toward the fenced enclosure. "Couldn't they get bail?"

"They'll bail. Like I said, they got good lawyers. They got jobs, like me." He put on his helmet. "I got to get back. Tina's new."

Dave swung away. I liked him, I think.

I drove three blocks and heard the rip of a police siren behind me. I looked in my mirror. A black Crown Vic. I pulled over and rolled down my window. Not just any Fed, the FBI Fed. He smarmed toward the side of the car and gazed at me. "You live dangerously, Miss Dru."

"You mean Tire Store Dave?"

"I mean Dave 'Michelin' Barstow. Don't let his boyish charm fool you."

"I hadn't noticed boyish charm, but thank you for caring."

"Say, let's clear the street; there's a coffee place on the river by the museum."

Following him, I drove through the shabby neighborhood and got to Riverfront Parkway. The coffee house was beautiful and inviting, as it should be, being close to the Hunter Museum of American Art. I adore art museums and thought about ducking in after coffee, but it was getting on in the afternoon, and I wanted to be home before dark.

Already over-coffeed, I had tea. Locke settled in with strong coffee and caloric cheese bread. I had a sample of the tomato basil flat bread. Yum.

"How do you know Michelin?" he asked.

I didn't reply, undecided what I would tell him.

He ate half his bread. He was an elegant man, an elegant diner. He didn't wolf down food, or gulp when he drank coffee. He wiped his mouth and raised an eyebrow. "How do you know Michelin?" he asked again.

Briefly I outlined the Trapp, Jean Ann Scott, Dave Barstow connection. "Remember the tape this morning?"

"Sure do. It's on its way to be analyzed."

"Like I'd faked it?"

"No, for voice vibrato. When liars lie, the voice tends to shake, sometimes imperceptibly."

"Jean Ann could have been lying."

"Were you?"

"I don't think I fibbed once, which is unusual for me."

He grinned. He may not have wolfed his food, but he did his grin.

I said, "Why did you follow me?"

"To see where you were going and to keep you from doing

81

something, uh, irrational."

"Like talking to a Wild Blood." He nodded. "FYI, I didn't go there to talk, but to check out the clubhouse. Out comes Dave."

"You interview anyone else here?"

"Medical examiner who didn't autopsy Trapp, and the funeral director who let his ashes go with a bogus brother."

"PI work's a bitch."

"Not like you suave Feddies."

"We can get down and dirty."

"Not Special Agent Grady Locke, not in a million light years."

"You can call me Grady. I'd like that."

Then he went on to mischievously disabuse me. When he said he'd become an FBI spy fifteen years ago, I looked at him like I didn't believe him. He vowed it was true, that he'd been an undercover in Raleigh. Just out of college with a law degree, he fit right into the scene. From narcotics, he went into street gangs, which included motorcycle clubs. "They've always fascinated me," he said. "In another life I might have been a member. The extolled club camaraderie has its appeal."

I didn't think club camaraderie was Agent Locke's forte. I said, "In another life I might have been a hooker, but let me ask this: you've rounded up six members from three clubs with a total membership of around a hundred to prove the whole organization is corrupt. Why are they not individual bad boys from three separate clubs who've committed crimes? How can you cobble them together and prove organizational corruption?"

"We can do that because they are officially the United Federation of Wild Blood, a corporation they set up so they can sue anyone who poaches on their patch or colors. And they trade illegal substances across state lines between each chapter."

"You mean they sell drugs and guns to each other?"

"Yes, and to other clubs, some of the bigger ones. We currently have an ongoing operation to discover how much commerce these Southern boys have with clubs to the north, even into Canada."

"Therefore, the need for CIs and undercovers."

"Honestly, the undercover business is tricky for an agent. We prefer someone we can turn."

"Like a biker who sells out for a reduced sentence."

He finished his bread and wiped his mouth. "Got it."

I told him that my agency traced a daughter for one of the Hells Angels' women. Along the way, I learned some biker lingo and lore and that they didn't give a rat's ass if they were misunderstood; that they believe they are persecuted for their lifestyle, but mostly that they're being used by law enforcement to get bigger budgets and glory for themselves.

He laughed. "That's their tune. Read any story where a one-percenter gives a quote, and you'll find that's what they all say." He gave me a look of admiration. "When you get on their good side, you're a saint, as you've done. But they don't tell you the truth. Not one-percenters. Reveal anything about the club and you don't get kicked out. They take you out in a box, sometimes in pieces."

"When I was police in Atlanta, we had our share of club rivalries."

"That was what?—seven, eight years ago?" I nodded. "Three years ago, U.S. Customs and Border agents in Atlanta arrested a motorcycle gang member wanted on a murder charge. He'd been in Venezuela and was returning to get his day in court, according to his attorney. He was a member of the Banditos. He and other members attacked members of the Flaming Knights because their red and gold motorcycle club colors too closely matched the colors of the Banditos. That, Miss Dru, is typical activity. I grant you the popularity and perception of the clubs has been up and down—mostly due to the era in which the young ones join, specifically the wars in which they fought. One-percenters of the mid-eighties were tamed when a myriad of them went to prison on narcotics, gun and assault charges. And after Hollywood got its fill of angry biker movies, the clubs spent the next twenty years keeping a low profile and cleaning up their image by doing community service. The wild ones who came out of Vietnam got long in the tooth and established Bike Weeks in places like Myrtle Beach and Florida so the bad boys could show off for the tourist crowd. During those halcyon years, the clubs kept to themselves but grew into national associations as the populace's perception changed. The big ones like HA are worldwide. Unfortunately, along came the Gulf Wars and Afghanistan to give us a fresh crop of experienced killers. That's where the Wild Blood mostly come from. They traded their Humvees and tanks for tats and Harleys."

"Have any of your CIs been outed and killed?"

"The former leader in Atlanta is still in Wit Protection as far as I know. Our operation shattered that chapter, which is our goal. It didn't hurt that they made headlines in the Juliet Trapp case. Another example: the ATF pulled off a classic case in oh-eight when they infiltrated The Mongols. Four agents earned their patches while reporting on the club's activities. The sting resulted in dozens of arrests, even the club president. Hundreds of search and arrest warrants were carried out. The club was enjoined not to wear their insignia in public."

"I heard that's been overturned." I'd finished my tea and pushed the cup away. "Thanks for the tea and the info. By the way, who's the head of this Wild Blood federation?"

"Each chapter has its own leader. Chattanooga's is Nelson Warner, road name Rassler. He's called that because of the term 'full nelson' in wrestling. He is a wrestler, too. Tough boy, and smart. Ex-paratrooper."

"He isn't being indicted."

"Like I said, smart. The thing about Rassler is he's in it for the ride, and he likes a close brotherhood like the military."

Did I see a little admiration in this Fed for a member of an outlaw motorcycle gang? "I've got to get back to Atlanta before I lose the light."

A couple of times I caught him looking at my left-hand ring finger. He glanced at it again and said, "Just when I was going to ask you to have dinner with me."

"Appreciate it, but . . ."

"You still want me to find you someone who knows something?"

I gave him a hard stare. "If you know anything about the Trapp murder case from your snitches you'd better say so and now, and tell us why you haven't already."

"Whoa. No. I volunteered to try and help you. The Trapp case never came up with our operation."

"Okay," I said, feeling better getting that out. Did I believe him? He was a Fed, after all. All seeing, all following.

"I'll see what I can do. Just for you, for your case."

"Is that a bribe?"

He laughed and ran his finger along a line in the wood of the tabletop. "That's not my style." I believed him. He was a man who used charisma as an offense.

He said, "FYI, Wild Blood members are going to West Palm for a funeral. These things are big with the brotherhood, especially if one of their own gets whacked by a rival gang member." He paused and looked introspective. "Bikers from all over are gathering in Miami and Fort Lauderdale for the Alligator Alley Motorcycle Ride. But our WBs have a stop in West Palm to bury a brother from the Raleigh club. A week ago a bar fight started when one Riley 'Big Red' O'Rourke spoke to the girlfriend of a local White Stallion. This club makes no pretense of being anything other than white supremacists. They operate

85

in the land of Latinos and blacks, both minorities being the same in their book. Inferiors. Anyway, White Stallion, Joseph 'Candy Ass' Johnson, whose name is a farce since he's a big brute, sliced O'Rourke's throat. Docs tried to save him but he died three days ago from an infection. Candy Ass is in jail on a second-degree murder charge, but that's not enough for our Tennessee, Carolina and Georgia boys. Retribution will be had at or after the funeral."

"You suggesting I get in the middle of a rumble?"

"Hell no. But my operative will be there. He won't speak directly to you, but he might be persuaded to talk by ditch."

That was cop talk for a one-time cell phone.

This cloak-and-dagger stuff reminded me of when I was hunting for two little girls. I met a vice snitch in a Catholic Church. While I sat in a pew in front of him, he whispered what he knew in my ear. I could only hope Grady's snitch could get me as much info as that vice snitch did.

"Have you talked to your CI about me?"

"I gave him a heads-up. It's up to him, but he did tell me that when he became a prospect in the club, he heard members talk about giving donations for the rape and murder of a girl in Atlanta. He said maybe time has loosened lips." Grady shook his head. "Don't get too hopeful."

By donations he'd meant bodily fluids and DNA. I asked, "When is Wild Blood headed for West Palm?"

"Once they're out on bail, those going will stage a meet and all ride together. It won't be part of their bail agreement, but since they'll eventually plead to the federal charges, jumping bail is minor. West Palm Beach ought to be interesting when they hit town."

"Are you going to be there?"

He lifted his head and searched my face as if he was going to ask me if I was wearing royal blue contacts. "I can be there.

Maybe we can have that dinner."

Maybe not.

I'm sure it was Grady who tailed me back to Atlanta. The driver of the older Volvo didn't try to hide, sometimes pulling in right behind me. In the fading wintry light, I couldn't tell if the person driving was a man or woman. Could have been Grady since he was slender and not overly tall. He said he'd keep in touch. Did he mean bumper to bumper?

Lake must have been in a situation where he couldn't answer his personal cell, and I didn't feel I needed to call his duty phone.

CHAPTER SEVEN

I didn't have to tell Roselyn the bad news about Sherman. Her sister-in-law, Elise Lane, had called to offer condolences and suggest a memorial service for Sherman.

Roselyn said to me, "If we had his ashes we could have a proper service."

I said, "You can have a service without the ashes."

Roselyn shook her head. She looked over the river. We sat on the bench where we'd sat before, and she told me the alligator story again, disassociated as ever. "Where are his ashes?"

"In the possession of the man who told the authorities in Chattanooga that he was Trapp's brother."

"Sherman didn't have a brother."

She'd already said this six times and I amended my statement to include the word imposter. "His imposter brother."

"What would he want with Sherman's ashes?"

Another question already answered. "I don't know. He may have had something to do with Sherman's death."

"Of course he killed our Sherman. Sherman would not shoot himself."

"He was shot in his left cheek and you said that Sherman was left-handed."

"He played golf right-handed."

"We believe Sherman moved to Chattanooga to hunt down his daughter's killers."

"We knew he would."

In my first interview I'd asked her in several ways where Sherman could be and she answered: we don't know, in as many ways.

She said, "We knew Sherman to be very vengeful. No slight gone unpunished. That was our Sherman."

"Why did he think he could find his daughter's killer in Chattanooga?"

She looked very tired, unfocused. "We don't know."

"He got around on a motorcycle. Did he always own one?"

She seemed to come to life. "A what?"

"A motorcycle."

Amazed, she answered, "Why would he drive a motorcycle?"

Lake and I had hypothesized, and I suspected she did, too, if she didn't outright know.

I left thinking about *our* Sherman. Was he cold and uncaring as she'd first told me, and was his vengeance as cold as the man seemed to be, or had his daughter's murder turned him into a hot-blooded avenger? Did he shed his hatred for guns and drugs to become a druggie biker who would disappear for a week, then come back stinking of oil and gas?

Webdog had a surprise for me. "Brandle Bunny Raddison is missing."

Something pressed against my rib cage and made it almost impossible to breathe. "From where?"

The riding master had it wrong. Bunny never went to Switzerland where her uncle, Joseph Raddison, was with the embassy. With the change of administrations in Washington, he was assigned to the Prague embassy. Bunny's actor parents said they had no idea where she was and seemed remarkably unconcerned, according to their agent in New York. Webdog also contacted her aunt in London. Louise Raddison said that Bunny moved out after Juliet's murder to go to New York and join her parents on stage. It didn't work out. She didn't have a guess where Bunny had gone after that. Web concluded, "Lost in the theatrical void, I presume."

"If she's alive," I said. "I don't have to ask you . . ."

"On it. If she's in the theatrical world she probably changed her name. Dirk's and my other contacts haven't gotten a line on a Brandle or Bunny Raddison. Her mother was Babe Brandle before she married Trevor Raddison."

"Babe and Trevor sound like loving parents."

"They are currently playing in 'Cat on a Hot Tin Roof' in Denver."

"Hook me up with Babe, will you?"

"Their agent will talk to you."

"I want Babe, or Trevor."

"I'll try, my insistent boss."

"Who else have you taken apart?"

"Chapin, Samuel, died last August. The death certificate reads failure to thrive. He suffered from mild Alzheimer's. The nursing facility's personnel will not divulge any information."

"What's Pearly Sue doing?"

"Great minds think alike. She's packing for Naples."

"Anything on the riding master?"

"Hoyt Fagan is an accomplished show rider and instructor. Forty years old, never married, wealthy background, born in Wellington, Florida, to old money. Plays polo and is known as a ladies man. He rides a Hog and drives a Porsche. Speed freak." A Hog was a Harley-Davidson motorcycle.

All roads seem to be leading to Florida.

Back at Winters Farm Academy, I turned the engine off in the visitors' lot just as Fagan came out of the Federalist administration building and walked down the steps. He wore a hacking jacket over tan breeches. His shirt was called a ratcatcher. It had a stand-up mandarin-style collar with an untied stock tie. On the phone he'd said he was going to a hunt club outing. I've often wondered how an equestrian show shirt got called a rat-catcher. I'd looked it up once and learned that the men who hunted and trapped vicious rats in London bound their necks with cloth chokers to keep the jumping rats from attacking their throats. I love knowing needless bits of trivia.

I got out of the car thinking that to some ladies Hoyt Fagan would be handsome enough, but I'm not partial to red-headed men.

Hurrying toward me, he said, "As I said on the telephone, I told you all I know about Juliet Trapp."

"You told me that Bunny Raddison went to Switzerland, but she didn't."

"That's what I heard. I didn't buy her plane ticket or see her off." His words flashed through the air like lightning.

"You knew that her uncle was with the American embassy in Bern."

"Bunny told me that. She was fond of her uncle, more so than her neglectful parents. What a pair of egoists."

"Actors have to have egos."

His snicker was bitter. "They came to Atlanta to perform in a Tennessee Williams play. Bunny heard about it on TV. Her hometown parents returning to triumph in a play everyone dreams of starring in, and she heard about it on TV. She came to school upset that morning."

"When was this?"

"Late November, about a month before Juliet was killed. She skipped school a few days, then Juliet died—was killed—and I never saw Bunny after that. She never came to the funeral and everyone was surprised."

"Why did you think she was going to Switzerland?"

He hitched a shoulder, more relaxed as if he'd prepared an

answer. "I heard it around. I can't recall anyone telling me, although I said something to Wilton and he'd heard the same rumor, if it was a rumor. Maybe she went and came back."

"Her uncle said she didn't."

"This school is full of imaginative students. Someone makes a suggestion and an hour later it's gospel. Now really, Miss Dru, I must run. Can't be late or I'll lose my position."

As I walked up the steps of the administration building I saw his silver Porsche glide from around the building and pass the circular drive.

I'd been told by phone that Wilton Johns Stuart was absent and would return tomorrow. My appointed time with Dr. Eugene Fetterman was near. Dr. Fetterman was senior principal of the school. Each study had its own principal and he, it would seem, was head of all the junior principals.

A woman in her late thirties was at a copy machine when I walked into the spacious and stylish office. She didn't hear me, but I didn't feel like interrupting so I watched her efficient movements until she finished the job. When she turned, she looked surprised and a bit nervous. "You must be Miss Dru."

"Yes," I said, "here for Dr. Fetterman."

"I'll just run and tell him."

Eugene Fetterman looked like a runner. Somewhere in his forties, he had thinning brown hair, and his narrow face made his eyes look overly large. He reminded me of a priest we once had. Portia and I called him Father Fly for his bug eyes. A few years after he'd come to our parish, he left the priesthood to live with his partner.

"Welcome. Let's have a cup of coffee or tea," Fetterman said, and I walked around the long desk, through a stile, and followed him into his office. His movements were quick but supple. He invited me to take a seat across from a square table that served as a conference or work table. He didn't invite me to use his first name.

The woman at the copy machine came in. He looked up at her. "Mrs. Taylor, this is Moriah Dru of Child Trace. Would you kindly fetch the tea and coffee things prepared in the cafeteria? Then we can begin our discussion."

Mrs. Taylor gave me a shy smile and scurried out of the room.

Dr. Fetterman said, "She's a teacher's aide. Her youngest daughter will graduate this year, and we'll lose her. Not all teacher's aides are created equal."

"You said that you had someone who would talk to me about Bunny Raddison."

"That would be Mrs. Taylor."

"What can you tell me about Miss Raddison?"

"Probably not much more than you already know. I suspect she's in New York. I was sorry to lose her. She had raw talent that needed training. As you know, her parents are actors, graduates of this school, and she has that same sense of drama in her life and work." He sounded like Bunny had lived a long life and had an extensive work history.

Mrs. Taylor returned and we chose our drink, mine being water and the other two settled for tea. Scotch shortbread lay on white plates. My stomach took delight, but I wasn't going to be the first to snap one up.

Fetterman folded his hands on the tabletop. "Mrs. Taylor is the mother of Lawrie Taylor, a schoolmate of Juliet Trapp and Bunny Raddison. The three were friends before the accident."

My eyebrows went up. An accident. Juliet's murder?

Mrs. Taylor spoke in soft, deep-south tones, "I see you haven't heard, judging by the look on your face, Miss Dru. My daughter had a terrible riding accident. She is now a quadriplegic."

I thought about Hoyt Fagan and the girl I'd seen posting on the horse and felt tears threaten to bubble for a girl I never knew and a mother who sat here stone-faced with an iron-willed determination not to break down. "I'm sorry to hear that," I said.

"Thank you," Mrs. Taylor said, looking at Fetterman.

He said, "It was a terrible thing and the fault of all three girls: Misses Trapp, Taylor and Raddison. They were staging a steeplechase race, which is absolutely forbidden on this campus."

Mrs. Taylor said, "My daughter Lawrie is, was, a beautiful rider. She steeplechased in Cumming, Georgia, and at Callaway Gardens, and was in training in Wellington, Florida, but here the girls don't race horses, either on the flats or over jumps."

I said that I wasn't aware that steeplechasing meant racing, which was untrue.

I could tell Fetterman itched to educate me on the subject.

"Steeplechasing began in Ireland," he began. "A race went over a hunt course from one church's steeple to end at another. Thus the term. This was cross-country racing on the hunt field, rather than today's track steeplechasing."

"Excuse me," I said. "If it's not allowed, how was there a course for them to race?"

Mrs. Taylor and Fetterman exchanged glances. Mrs. Taylor got the nod from Fetterman. "They set it up at night. It was crude and that was the trouble. The next morning they put on boots and britches and . . ."

For the rest of her life Mrs. Taylor would not be able to finish that thought by speaking it aloud.

"Miss Taylor and Miss Raddison were excellent riders, but Miss Trapp was not," Fetterman said.

Mrs. Taylor squirmed in her chair.

Fetterman went on, "Yet it was she who baited the other two girls into the race."

All of a sudden my heart rate upticked. "Where was Hoyt Fagan in this?"

"He knew absolutely nothing about it," Fetterman said with enough certainty to forestall more questions. "It was Juliet Trapp's idea. She led the planning."

Mrs. Taylor sat forward, hands folded across her stomach.

Fetterman glanced at Mrs. Taylor's distress and asked if she was all right. She nodded and he continued, "Miss Trapp admitted she coerced the other two girls into the dangerous race." He looked at me and I knew I was going to be schooled some more.

"Hurdle steeplechase fences can be plastic, pine or synthetic hedge. The fences are fifty-two inches tall at the maximum and are moveable. They are designed to collapse should a hoof accidentally strike the fence. The horse is trained to jump at regular stride, which is optimum since it can keep up its speed after the jump. But sometimes that's not possible as the horse approaches the fence. Horses are also schooled on how to jump out of stride, which decreases the horse's speed and can affect his jump."

Mrs. Taylor rocked back a little. "The fences were wrong, the height was too high and not collapsible. And their horses were not trained to jump out of stride." She pulled the words from the back of her throat like they were taffy.

One of these two would eventually explain what actually happened. I cringed, not wanting to hear, but needing to.

Fetterman said, "The jumps weren't wide enough for steeplechasing. When all three girls went over simultaneously, Miss Taylor's horse got squeezed in between the other two and was knocked by Miss Trapp's horse. Miss Taylor's horse went to its knees, throwing Miss Taylor onto her neck. Neither of the other girls was injured, although Miss Trapp fell from her horse and scraped her leg. Her horse did not fall."

Slowly Mrs. Taylor began to shatter. Her chest sunk and her eyes leaked tears. All the air had left the room, it seemed. I couldn't breathe. Mrs. Taylor said, "Excuse me" several times and I looked for her to run from the room, but she stayed in her chair, clutching the arms.

I don't know how long we sat in that terrible tableau, but I told myself to gather my wits and break into that abysmal silence. "Terrible story. When did this happen?"

"In late May, the day before school was out for the summer," Fetterman said, then paused. "Approximately eight months before Miss Trapp was murdered."

I'll say this about the senior principal, he didn't shy away from frank talk. I told him that there was nothing in the law enforcement reports that related to Juliet's murder about this tragedy, even though the police had interviewed several teachers at the school including himself.

Fetterman said, "As surprising as it would seem to you, when every little incident that happens in a school is trotted out on network and cable news, this never made it. There was a small report in the community newspaper, no names, just that a student had a riding accident."

Holding tight to the chair arms, Mrs. Taylor rasped out, "That suited us. We didn't want Lawrie's accident sensationalized. Even after Juliet's death, we kept our silence. Whoever murdered her would be punished by God. Just as she would be."

My mind reeled, but understood that Mrs. Taylor still harbored anger for Juliet Trapp. She hadn't wanted her murder to ameliorate the lingering hatred she had for the girl. Southern belles can and do harbor such feelings for the rest of their lives, sometimes with justification. More reasonable and unaffected heads would say that Juliet caused the accident, but that she didn't deserve to die for it. By God's or anyone else's hand.

Fetterman said, "Miss Raddison, who has a flair for drama, never spoke of it again. Miss Trapp apologized, did not return to school for the last day of term, and then sought to join a circus. Her father persuaded authorities to bring her back.

Disappearing was a ritual with Miss Trapp. She was a sensation-seeker." He steepled his fingers.

Mrs. Taylor picked up in the same sour tone as if Fetterman had not interrupted. "The attorneys settled the case. I don't know that given her personality, how deserved punishment would affect Juliet."

Harsh words. "Did Juliet visit with Lawrie?"

"Mr. Taylor thought it unwise when she tried."

Fetterman appeared not to hear Mrs. Taylor and said, "Perhaps it was collective guilt or wanting to evade notoriety that kept the student body quiet. We're rather special here."

They both fell silent, and I directed a smirk at Fetterman.

He looked critically at me. "I don't know that the steeplechase accident had a bearing on Juliet's murder, but we, Mrs. Taylor and I, thought you should know. You can do with the information as you wish."

Getting back to the purpose of my visit, I asked, "Do either of you have a clue where Bunny Raddison is now?"

Both sat unyielding. I'd asked two people who didn't care.

I got to my car when I heard a motorcycle engine *pop-pop* into a power burst. It came from the side of the administration building, circled the flag island and bolted for the road. Before I got into my car I looked toward the admin building. Fetterman stood at the window watching me, or maybe it was the biker that got his attention. Quickly, though, he stepped away.

Lake shook his head like he wished he could reverse time. "My predecessor about tore his hair out because there were things about the case he couldn't get a grasp on. You can see from my reports at the time that I believed people were holding back for whatever reasons."

"But," I said, "the primary focus was on the motorcycle club and that her body was found in an inner-city neighborhood twenty-five miles away. According to your predecessor's files, nothing happened at the school that would cause anyone to think Juliet's murder might revolve around an incident there."

"That was the case then, but this secret now coming to light gives a couple of people motive. Mrs. Taylor and her husband, to be sure."

"Mrs. Taylor tried to contain her anger at, and hatred of, Juliet. Enough surfaced to make me wonder if they were enraged to the point of hiring a thug to murder her."

I told Lake what Webdog had reported—that Hugh Taylor was the president of a company that buys automotive parts from overseas. He practically lives in China and was there when Juliet was murdered.

"Rich men hire others to do their dirty work. Why is Taylor's wife a teacher's aide?"

"Parents are encouraged to get involved. There's another daughter at the school."

"Why did they choose this time to tell us about the accident?"

"Only one reason I can think of. We're trying to find Bunny Raddison. They believed Bunny had either gone to New York or Switzerland. Now that we've been asking questions, they apparently think it prudent to tell us their side. It's interesting that I went there to get a clue on where Bunny could be, and all they talked about was Juliet."

"Guilty conscience?" Lake asked. "Wonder why the school kept Juliet since she disappeared regularly."

"Money. Dirk's Detectives told Web that Sherman Trapp was a major benefactor of the school."

"Trapp's dead now. Samuel Chapin died recently. Geoff Howard opened up a can of worms when he told that reporter about the biker in the bar with someone who looked like Juliet."

"I believe it was Juliet."

"And I believe what you believe."

"We need to find Bunny Raddison. Before the killer finds her first."

CHAPTER EIGHT

Web had nothing new on Bunny Raddison; neither did Dirk's Detectives. I told Web about the steeplechase tragedy, that Lawrie Taylor wound up paralyzed, that Juliet was murdered shortly thereafter and that Bunny Raddison left the school abruptly, first going to New York and then disappearing.

"Work off family names for an alias," I suggested. "Uncle Joseph, Aunt Louise, Father Trevor, Mother Babe. Focus on New York and Atlanta. I have a feeling she's in Atlanta, probably show biz. Get me in contact with her parents."

"I've hassled the agent," Web said. "They work and party all night and sleep all day. There's *just* no time to talk about their daughter, besides the agent told me Babe and Bunny did not get along when Bunny went to New York. I asked if it was mother/daughter jealousy, but he wouldn't commit. He did say Bunny turned into quite a stunner. Bunny's what now? Nineteen? Mama's probably forty plus."

I'd looked up the biographies of the Raddisons and saw several photographs of Trevor and Babe throughout their twenty-year careers. Both were beautiful, and the last photo showed Babe to have retained her beauty, possibly through surgery. The couple didn't always act in plays together, but wherever one had a gig, the other was there. Biographers called the couple a true love match since their days at Winters Farm Academy.

★ ★ ★ ★ ★

Grady Locke had left a message with Webdog and I returned his call since he'd told Web it was urgent.

"Wild Blood is on the move," he said.

"Leaving when?"

"The Chattanooga clubhouse is jammed with bikers. Sometime tomorrow, I expect."

"Your snitch hasn't told you?"

"My guy isn't necessarily in the Chattanooga chapter, but he will be riding with the club in West Palm Beach. If the opportunity arises, he'll contact you. It's possible that he won't be able to without arousing suspicion. Just so you understand."

"I'll go to West Palm then and wait. I'll let you know where I'll be staying, and you can give him the info, etc."

"Since I'll be with you, he'll know. How about I pick you up at eight in the morning?"

The idea of riding with Grady from Atlanta to West Palm, some nine hours, didn't have me jumping for joy. "I never go anywhere without my car. We can meet up there."

"Not a good plan. I'll be by in the morning."

Geoff Howard had made the case for the lone-biker-as-killer theory, and I couldn't ignore Sherman Trapp's actions, what he must have believed. "All right, but you'll have to convince me why my car isn't acceptable."

"I'll see you in the a.m."

"I live at . . ."

"I know where you live. Shall I come to the cottage in Peachtree Hills or the loft by the railroad tracks?"

Lake's loft. The nerve of him, checking me out. "I'll leave a message at this number," I said and hung up.

I cooked dinner at Lake's loft. Something simple since Lake's culinary tools were limited. A chicken simmered in the crock pot with onions and carrots. After loading his ricer, Lake contributed pre-prandial libations of Blue Sapphire martinis. He had two bottles of an un-oaked fruit-forward Chardonnay chilling. I'm not fond of the big buttery Chards. With a lot of oak aging, the fermenting grapes take on a butter smell, feel and taste due to a chemical called diacetyl.

At the rustic table we'd sanded and refinished in the fall, I explained Grady's plan for morning.

"Ain't going to happen," Lake said, carefully settling his wine glass on the placemat so as not to ring the table's satin finish. He lifted a fork full of chicken and rice to his mouth. I grinned. He chewed slowly and forcefully as if on a hunk of Grady's flesh. Swallowing, he said, "Bastard."

Lake is not usually jealous. I'm the jealous one in this duo. "Grady knows it's no good hitting on me," I said, then drank and swirled Chardonnay in my mouth.

"He'd be happy to get into your silk undies, but he's a Fed, too. They have agenda." He stood, and with deliberation, uncorked the second Chard.

"I have no option. I want to contact his CI, and it's his party."

"No. It's going to be our party." Lake was deadly serious. "It's still a city of Atlanta murder case, not a federal case. That his so-called snitch might be able to help us doesn't make it his case."

"I have to have Grady to get to the . . ."

Sitting, he hooked one of my pinkie fingers with his. "But you don't need to be Grady's pawn."

Pawn was not a word I liked. "You think he's setting me up for something."

"Bait." Lake filled my wine glass and his. "Worst case is to rush in and save you from getting killed by the psycho who killed Juliet."

Even for me that was a stretch. "I've got something to say

about putting myself in a psycho's way."

"You do, but Grady doesn't have a clue about you."

"So what's the answer?" As if I hadn't set it up.

"I'm going."

"You, me and Grady?"

I was genuinely excited. My sneaky persuasion had succeeded.

"Grady can do what he wants, when and where. Tomorrow we're cruising to West Palm together."

I hate it when he gets ahead of me. "You already talked to Commander Haskell about going, didn't you?"

"I like the way you bat your eyelashes."

Grady wasn't happy about the plan, but what could he do? We had a legitimate reason for going to West Palm Beach, that being to question persons of interest, and Lake's superior got the come-ahead with the Palm Beach County authorities.

My cell phone played one of my favorite Mozart concertos. Although hearing it at three in the morning wasn't as uplifting as at midday. The display did not identify my caller, and when I answered a male voice said, "Trevor Raddison here for Miss Moriah Dru."

"Speaking." The word didn't come out clear through my clogged throat.

It took a second or two for my head to put it together. Trevor Raddison in Denver. After the play. The party in the background, in full swing.

His voice was commentator perfect. "What can I do for you, Miss Dru?"

"It's about your daughter, Brandle."

"Ah yes. Well, she hasn't shown up here, and she knows the name of our agent if she wants to keep in touch. That really is all I can tell you."

There were a million questions I wanted to ask, but I sensed his hurry to get back to the post-play festivities.

He said, "I have the mayor here to go over our next year's schedule." He'd pronounced it shedsule.

"I won't keep you," I said to the creep. "I need to find Bunny."

"Why? Today girls of her age are all about freedom from rules and guidance. They strike out on their own. There's really not much you can do about it."

"Was she unhappy in New York? Is that why she left the stage?"

"She was never on stage. She is not an actor, but a singer that needs more training. Even so, Babe and I don't star in *operettas*. I'm afraid Bunny was rather disappointed in us."

"Where are her favorite cities—places where she's spoken about, where she might go?"

"Well, New York, of course."

The only town in the world for stage people. "It's important that I find her." He didn't respond. "She may be in danger."

"Danger? Bunny?"

"I think she might have information on who killed her friend Juliet Trapp."

"I can say with absolute certainty that she doesn't. Her mother asked and Bunny told Babe that she had no idea why Juliet was murdered. So horribly too." I could feel his stage shudder through the ether. "If that's all . . ."

"If Brandle Raddison is alive and well, she is not using her given names, Mr. Raddison, nor her nickname. My investigators are experts in locating people. We've tried various combinations of yours and other family members' names to no avail. Did she ever have an imaginary friend with a special name?"

"Ah, I see where you're going." I could imagine him lifting his chin, scratching a cheek with an elegant forefinger. "She named herself Bunny because she didn't like Brandle. That pissed Babe off, of course." He chuckled dramatically. "When she was six, she named a new puppy Rabbit, which she thought was hilarious. Oh, and she loved it when I called her Bunny Bean." He paused. "Does that help you?"

I doubt she was calling herself Bunny Bean. "I'd like for you to call me if you think of anything else."

"I will certainly do that, and your man has our agent's number. Should you need more information, he can certainly relay it."

"Thanks for your time," I said, mentally adding *asshole*. "Go back to your party."

He rang off.

Lake rolled toward me. "I can tell by your voice how that went."

After I said a few choice words for Trevor, I rolled with my back to Lake.

He put his chin on my shoulder. "I want you to relax, Dru."

I shifted that shoulder. "I know. We've got a long road tomorrow."

"Don't let the bastards affect your emotional responses. You're the objective investigator. Don't allow the case to take *you* over."

"You asked me to."

"I didn't ask you to jump on a fast freight. You need to step back and let the theories rest. They'll be there in the morning."

When I turned to face him, he wrapped his arms around me. One of the qualities that had initially drawn me to him, besides his incredible good looks and nature, was a shared zeal to end the horrors we found on the job, to the victims and to ourselves. When you spend your days surrounded by brutality, it can't help but become a part of you. You fight to ward it off, but it invades your consciousness. The incredible acts of sadism that had been forced onto Juliet Trapp could only be mitigated in the apprehension of a person that was so depraved he couldn't see a beautiful human being, but an object to destroy. There was too damn much of this kind of thing in the world. And now, my beloved, who shared my fervor, was telling me to step away.

Wasn't going to happen. When Lake kissed me, I felt myself responding but just as quickly my mind raced back to the unconcern expressed by Bunny's selfish egoistic parent. Lake pulled away, knowing the passion building inside me had dissipated. Some moments later, I was deep into sleep until the seven a.m. train stormed past.

CHAPTER NINE

A Harley-Davidson is a wonderful machine. About a year ago, Lake invested in an Ultra Classic Electra Glide, and although I'd ridden short distances as a passenger, I had no qualms about heading off to south Florida sitting in the sofa seat with much-appreciated back and arm rests. Around Atlanta, when Lake sheds his squad car, he rides his Dyna Glide. I've spent many hours on that bike, racing up and down north Georgia mountain roads and tearing up and down Atlantic coast beaches—where they let us ride—clutching Lake's middle, my butt rubbing raw in the saddle seat. I loved every minute.

I had on my maroon leathers and sexy Maui Jim sunglasses that Lake bought me for Christmas and stood on the sidewalk watching Lake roll the Harley from the storefront that used to be an art gallery. Since no garages attach themselves to the cotton warehouse, he leases a first-floor store front solely for his motorcycles and other assorted toys. Next to his guns, his proudest possessions are his motorcycles (one a vintage Harley), street and mountain bicycles, rock-climbing tackle, jet skis, golf clubs, a small boat and assorted fishing paraphernalia.

Slanting winter sunrays hit the Electra's ember red paint like sparklers on Independence Day. Stowing the last of my gear inside the hard saddlebags and snapping them shut, I donned my open-face bell helmet with visor. I don't do full face shields—too claustrophobic.

I was ready to ride.

Atlanta's interstates can be deadly for bikers, but once free of the city's skyline, we shot down I-75 in fifth gear. Seventy-five at ten in the morning on a weekday is heaven on two wheels. Lake popped it into sixth gear and set cruise control. The miles sped by. In an hour we'd cleared Macon and rolled on toward Valdosta where we would eat and refuel. The Ultra Classic can go an easy hundred-and-eighty miles on a full tank.

The Ultra Classic Electra Glide is Harley's flagship motorcycle with fairing to keep the winter wind drafting around riders and passengers. Lake's sacred Dyna Glide didn't have a ride as smooth as melting butter, and I didn't miss suffering hot legs because the exhaust header crosses too near the frame, but it depends what a biker wants. The Dyna is fast and sporty. The Electra Glide is a touring bike, complete with stereo and a communication system.

Our purpose in riding the bike to Florida wasn't to infiltrate biker ranks or even hide our identities. Lake looked every bit the square-jawed cop that he was. I didn't particularly look like most PIs, but I didn't look like a biker gal, either. The plan was to approach the club members politely because being impolite could get you in trouble. One-percenters are usually polite, even possess a courtly attitude when things are even-keeled, but a disrespectful word could get you maimed from one of your own club members. That would make most people polite.

Our attitude was: we aren't here to investigate your club's beef with the Feds, we're here seeking information on the murder of a sixteen-year-old girl in Atlanta, Georgia. We don't care what illegal activities you're into. We don't believe a member of your club murdered the girl, but we believe you might have some knowledge because bikers are aware of what's going on in their communities, more so than most citizens. Bikers hear rumors. Bikers are wary of other outlaws either in other motorcycle clubs or in street gangs. Bikers respect the law when the law respects them. Bikers are a special breed, an all-American breed that love their women and children. The accolades I'd brought away from my experience with the Hell's Angels ran out.

A writer, Donald Charles Davis, wrote a book about an ATF sting involving the Mongols and Hells Angels. He called motorcycle outlaws "ghosts from America's frontier." Like the religiosi who came to America to escape persecution from onerous laws and mores in Europe, and the Manifest Destinyites who left the East Coast for the same reason, bikers seek freedom to live as they wish, as men were born to live according to their particular insular attitudes.

Attitudes. Everyone has one.

As if Lake had sensed my musing, he spoke into my headset. "Enjoy being cage free," he commanded. A cage is biker-talk for an automobile. "Fire up some music if you want."

Lake had installed a GPS/MP3/Bluetooth cell phone and radar into the bike's audio system.

We arrived in Valdosta, and I dismounted at the colonel's fried chicken place. My butt was only marginally numb, but it can get that way in a cage ride, too. My job was to order while Lake filled up.

As I portioned out white meat chicken, mashed potatoes, gravy and slaw, I heard the Harley and saw people staring out the window. The man and the silver Super Glide Harley looked like something out of a movie—beautiful machine and handsome man walking with grace. He took off his helmet.

Grady. That ass. He'd followed us.

Coming inside, his laser eyes focused on me.

A bike enthusiast shouted, "Cool wheels."

Grady gave him a half-smile and a wave. Then he stood next to me.

"Fancy meeting you here," I said, not bothering to lower my voice.

He grinned like we were old pals and whispered, "Let's not talk wise. We got witnesses." He glanced around. People were overtly watching. I shrugged so what? He said, "You about ran me out of gas."

I said quietly, "Why did you follow us?"

He sat saying, "I just happened to pick the same route as you."

I sat across from him. "Don't kid me."

He sure loved to grin. "Okay, I saw you were leaving. That's quite a machine Lake owns. The Atlanta PD must be paying cops good these days."

I ignored that. "The FBI's transportation crews work fast."

"It's my personal bike. I rushed home and fortunately it was gassed and ready to ride. I couldn't keep up with you otherwise. Hundred miles an hour." He breathed in ecstatically. "Wonderful."

I heard another Harley and people ooh-ing as Lake walked in. The bike enthusiast gave him a thumbs-up, which Lake returned.

Seeing Grady sitting at the table with me, Lake halted, a dark look spread across his face, and then he stepped forward. "Grady," he said, "I wondered if that wasn't you tailing us."

Lake knew and didn't tell me. First demerit of the day.

Grady rose. "I'll leave you to your meal. I have to gas up, or I'll be pushing the damn thing."

"How far are the WBs ahead of us?"

"An hour. Which way you going?"

"I-10 to 95."

"That's the way they'll go," Grady said. "I'll go the Turnpike."

"See you in West Palm."

"Don't let your tune-up be our tune-up."

"We're not there for a beat down."

"Be nice then."

When Grady was out of earshot, Lake said, "I see you're steamed. Sorry, but I didn't want you craning around to alert him." Which pissed me off even more. He bit into his chicken, chewed, swallowed and then said, "Just kidding. I wasn't sure it was him, but the rider stayed behind me even when I slowed."

"I don't like being tailed."

"He's keeping an eye on us, which makes sense to a Fed. They don't want anyone but themselves solving biker crimes, lest it dries up speaker fees and book deals."

Technology is a wondrous thing. Swooshing down the interstate at high speeds wearing only a half helmet that they call a brain bucket for obvious reasons, I could take a phone call from my technology specialist.

Webdog told me he'd learned (through spurious computer machinations that I didn't need to know about) that Wilton Johns Stuart had no children, that he and his wife were having a vicious argument when her fatal, and his injurious, accident happened. The insurance company conducted an extensive investigation and interviewed witnesses who said there was shouting and fist-shaking going on and that the driver, Wilton Johns Stuart, wasn't watching the road when the Lexus slammed into the concrete barrier, flipped and burst into flames. Two men pulled Stuart out, but his wife was trapped alive and died. Wilton's recovery was long and painful. Also the insurance company found out that Maria Stuart was planning on divorcing Wilton because he was unfaithful. Further probing by the insurance company revealed that his infidelities ran to nude pole dancers. According to a neighbor friend of Maria Stuart's, Wilton spent recklessly at the clubs, depleting the couple's savings. Maria wanted out. The neighbor also said that Maria had recently been seeing a man and made no secret about it.

"He's still at it," Web said.

With wind flowing by at ninety miles an hour, I marveled at the clarity of the cell signal. And at the rapid radar beeps. That alarm had Lake slowing and gliding at the speed limit past a state trooper staked out on the median holding a radar gun.

I'd momentarily lost the thread of Web's conversation and said, "He's still at what?"

"The strip clubs. He spends a lot of time and jack at Twenty-Four Caret. There's three clubs in metro Atlanta. He lives closest to the Roswell Road club."

"You hacked his credit card companies?"

"His personal computer. Excel. He keeps his personal expenses on the program. His password is his addy."

His address? Even I know better than that.

Web said, "He's loaded. Deep pockets. Does Twenty-Four Caret ring a chime?"

Twenty-Four Caret. Bunny. Of course it could be coincidence, but I never liked coincidences, until they proved to be coincidences.

"Web, you're in for a fun assignment."

"Why am I rolling my eyes?"

"You're going undercover. So here's what you do. Dress like a sex-starved student . . ."

"Which I am."

"I'll pretend I didn't hear that. Check out these places. You have a photograph of Bunny Raddison. Show it around, maybe you'll even spot her."

Web said, "Here's the thing, these rabbity clubs are all owned by a single person or entity, Peters Brothers, Aaron and John Peters."

I asked, "What children's classic does that name bring to mind?"

Silence on the cell. Then I heard Web catch his breath. "That's the sound of stupid. The answer is: Atlanta's Joel Chandler Harris. Br'er Rabbit. Brother Rabbit. Should I vet Aaron and John Peters and their business?"

"Hold off. Let's let Lake and the APD look into their operation. When I get back I'll have another talk with Wilton Johns Stuart."

Web said, "Stuart's spreadsheets show he owns motorcycles and a Lexus . . ."

"What kind of motorcycles?"

"Couple of Harleys. He's owned them as long as he's been keeping his spreadsheets."

"Go on."

"He's got a houseboat docked at Tinny Allen's Marina at Lake Lanier. He spends weekends on it and buys his groceries at the Piggly Wiggly in Buford. He buys cat food, ergo he has at least one cat; he's filed two complaints against his Roswell neighbors for noise violation for dogs barking in the night. He buys his clothes at Neiman-Marcus, but I see no record of him buying feminine articles, jewelry, etc., therefore he doesn't date, and . . ."

"Web, file it and when I need it, I'll ask."

"You got it."

"Round up photographs of the principals connected to the case and email them to me," I said.

"You got it."

Before I rang off I thought of something else. "Also, in your spare time, look into the creds of Grady Locke, FBI out of their Memphis Tennessee bureau."

"The sound you hear is me rubbing my hands. Government. Could present a challenge."

"I didn't hear that."

★ ★ ★ ★ ★

We caught up with Wild Blood in St. Augustine at a rest stop on I-95. Pulling into a parking slot, we got their attention. Their Harleys were lined up as if on the showroom floor—choppers, bobbers, short chops, cruisers, a couple of Dynas. Bikers lounged and smoked and gabbed and fiddled with their bikes and helmets and generally seemed to ignore us. Three came from the low tan building that housed the restrooms.

Sixteen bikes lined up meant sixteen men in their contingent. They ranged in age from elderly to twenties. Most were heavily bearded except for two. One was Tire Store Dave, a/k/a Michelin. They wore vests, some over tee-shirts, others were bare-chested. Ah, January in St. Augustine. Lots of tattoos going on, too, forehead to neck to arms.

Half hour before we stopped here, we gassed up at a massive truck stop in Jacksonville, known for taking care of bikers. That's how Lake learned that Wild Blood always stopped at the St. Augustine Rest Area to pay respects to a member who, several years ago, lost a knife fight at the third urinal on the left. The knife wielder, a member of the Doomsday Prophets, was last seen at a Jacksonville bar two nights later, and, story goes, was then cut up and fed to the fishes. At any rate, he's been missing since last seen there. There's murderous bad blood between the WBs and the DPs.

Watching them go into the men's restroom in twos and threes, then come out with somber faces was interesting.

I removed my helmet, shook my hair free, all the while watching Michelin. Michelin's flat hand came up to shade his shades against the bright southern sun. Having recognized me, his mouth turned down. Halting once or twice, as if to rethink the advisability of recognizing me, he managed to make it halfway to where we stood.

"Hi Dave."

He nodded to me and said to Lake, who made a show of balancing his bike on the kickstand. "Nice ride."

"Thanks." Lake looked up. "You have a good trip on that RK?"

"No problem—so far." He looked at Lake like there might be a problem about to break out.

"No problem here," Lake said. "Stopping to take a whiz."

"You following us?"

"Nah. But I bet we're going where you're going."

"Why's that?"

The posture of the two men had the brotherhood alert and chest puffing.

"Alligator Alley Ride, this weekend."

There's always a biker event in south Florida, even in January.

Dave said, "We're going to a funeral first."

"Bummer. Sorry," Lake said, securing his helmet on the gas cap, taking off his leather jacket and letting his shield and gun show.

Dave stared at the gun. "I did the Alligator ride last year. Didn't see any cops."

Lake shrugged. "Cops are people, too." He folded his jacket, as I did mine. He stored them in the hard shell. "Look about that whiz, I got to go."

He walked away and Dave studied me. He looked behind him at the brotherhood eyeing Lake as he walked by. Lake threw up a hand and gave a genial wave and a closed-lip smile. They didn't smile but they didn't jump him.

I said to Dave, "Seems I see you in places I don't expect to see you."

The bikers suddenly seemed restless, ready to move out, apparently not interested in Dave's discussion with a woman.

Dave said, "That's 'cause you're following me."

"I still want information on that Atlanta murder, and the death of Trapp, since he was the girl's father."

"We been through this."

"I've got another line on the girl's murder, so I'm not hot to trot after information from your club. Who died, anyway?"

"A Raleigh brother originally from West Palm. We're going to bury him and who killed him."

"Did the cops catch him yet?"

"He's in jail. Won't be for long 'cause they'll carry him out in a bag."

One of the bearded brothers had sauntered over and, ignoring me, said, "What's up, Michelin?"

"Her and I met before in Chattanooga."

I had bearded's full attention. He stared, his yellow hazel eyes hard as marbles. "Where?"

"At The Tire Store. She knew Jean Ann."

Knew? Past tense? That didn't sound good for Jean Ann.

He broke eye contract, looked at Dave and said, "Crank up."

Lake came out of the tan building and trotted around the bikes as they exploded to life.

"They'll be waiting for us," Lake said.

And they were.

There's a hierarchy in group riding and exacting etiquette. The leader and the tail or sweep rider are the most experienced. The riders might look like they ride double file, side-by-side, but they don't, unless they want to intimate. They ride double file, staggered, the leader riding in the left-third of the lane. The second rider stays a few seconds behind in the right-third. The rest follow in the same pattern. On curves and roadways where a bike needs more room, riders fall in single-file formation, widening the gap to four or more seconds behind the rider in front. That's the formation the Wild Blood brotherhood used as they rode in the slow lane at about sixty miles an hour.

Lake drew up to the leader, never getting his front tire in front of the road captain's bike and made a circle with his right arm, thus asking permission to join in. The leader raised his arm and brought it forward, meaning follow me/us. Lake slowed to let the brotherhood get ahead. The last man in line, the sweep, slowed to let Lake into the formation on the left, thus keeping his position as sweep. The leader took us single file into the passing lane and we stayed there doing a legal seventy-five.

Nearing the Cocoa Beach exit, the leader signaled a stop by throwing his left arm over his head meaning pull off at the next exit.

The biker bar was called Indian River Hideaway. A dozen Harleys and other makes were resting on stands.

The leader took off his helmet and approached us. He was a tall man, fifties, neat salt-and-pepper beard, looking a lot like Kenny Rogers. He raised his shades briefly and let them fall back on the bridge of his nose. "Lose the badge or move that garbage wagon."

Lake said, "I got a lot to carry in this garbage wagon, but I'll move on. I'm not here for trouble."

I'd taken off my helmet and started to put it back on.

The Road Captain said, "You a bike cop?"

Lake shook his head. "Homicide."

"You may be here to ride Alligator Alley this weekend, but it's a couple days until the ride." He insinuated we were here for other purposes, too.

Lake tossed his head toward me. "She's working. I'm not a Florida cop. I wear my shield because I don't want anyone thinking I'm pulling a fast one. I'm Detective Lieutenant Richard Lake with the Atlanta Police Department. This here's Moriah Dru; she finds lost kids."

"Who's lost?" he said, turning his biker shades on me.

117

"A girl named Bunny Raddison, only she doesn't call herself Bunny Raddison anymore."

"What she calling herself?"

"I don't know. Her friend, Juliet Trapp, was murdered in Atlanta three years ago."

He bobbed his head. "You talked to Michelin. He told me. Nobody in our club did it, so if you're hoping to sweet-talk someone, forget it."

"Can I ask your name?" I said.

His mouth twisted into a grin. "I'll tell you 'cause I think you're square with me. Nelson Warner. I answer to Rassler when I'm on my bike."

Lake said, "The Atlanta murder case is mine. I talked to a few of your members back then. I'm satisfied they didn't do it."

The look he gave Lake was a mix of calculation and doubt. "I got to get inside." He turned to go but looked back at me. "Where you hanging in south Florida?"

"A hotel by the airport," I said.

"Look out for us at the Double Yellow Line at Lake Worth Beach. Round midnight. We can talk about Alligator Alley."

With those parting words, he walked away, then turned back again. "Not tonight. We got business."

Could he be Grady's snitch?

Lake said before he fired up the Ultra Classic. "Looks like we'll be going back to Atlanta by way of Alligator Alley."

I didn't know about that.

The bike roared and we sped away. Rassler never looked back.

Lake kept up a steady eighty miles an hour down I-95 to Jensen Beach and across the causeway to his favorite beach-side restaurant. The Laughing Dolphin, he says, fixes the best fish tacos in Florida—in all the Southeast, for that matter.

118

He was right.

I ate during my conversation with Webdog. Food is so sacred to Lake he doesn't like talking while eating. Me, I can eat, talk and listen at the same time.

"Someone else is looking for Bunny Raddison," Web said. "Her name is showing up in search engines. A partial resumé calls her a singer of torch songs. No clubs named. She's not a dancer at the Peters Brothers' clubs. Isn't now or hasn't been. Dirk's found a search where a person identified as a lawyer was seeking information on a Brandle Raddison, also known as Bunny Raddison. The person states Bunny's sick mother desires urgently to get in touch with her daughter. I called Babe's agent. He said it had to be a hoax, that someone was trying to get to Babe Raddison. It's all about them, of course."

Gassed up with food and fuel, we got underway just as the storm hit. Lightning leapt from the sea and spread across the purple atmosphere in shafts of dazzling radiance. The wind threatened to knock the bike sideways, but Lake sped up to keep the forward momentum against the slamming force. A deafening crash of thunder rolled over us like the hell was ready to rise.

Then, just as quickly as it erupted, the squall tore away, toward the mainland.

We checked into adjoining rooms at the hotel, and I went to soak in the tub while Lake went to the Palm Beach Police Department to have a friendly chat about our stay. Georgia has limited license recognition agreements with Florida, among other states. As a licensed investigator I am able to enter into Florida to perform work for a thirty-day period since the murder case originated in Georgia.

When Lake returned, he didn't look happy.

"What's up, pup?" I asked, buttoning a silk blouse. I intended to find a quiet, elegant bar and order a double Blue Sapphire martini.

Before he spoke, Lake ripped off the red tee shirt with the Harley logo and tossed it on the chair. "Who should greet me on arriving at the PBPD, but your Fed pal. He wanted to know where you were."

"Did you say, 'In bed waiting for me'?"

He unzipped his blue jeans. "And now I'm here, and in great physical need for nurture."

"In time, detective."

He pushed the denim off his hips. "I didn't talk to the chief, but the captain I spoke with is on edge."

"Feds put everyone on edge."

"They're bracing for a biker war."

"Uh oh, our Wild Blood buddies?"

He kicked the jeans free of a foot, and they soared across the room. "The hostilities will be between Rassler and his bail jumpers versus a ragtag local OMG group of maniacs who are equally dangerous because they don't know any better. They will be aided by some Doomsday Prophets."

The group of maniacs were the White Stallions and the Doomsday Prophets were eager to avenge their Jacksonville member who became seafood. Naked now, Lake turned for the bathroom and a shower.

I called to his back. "Are you sorry we're in this?"

"Nope. I miss street rumbles." He went toward the bathroom snapping his fingers like a dancer in "West Side Story." The man has rhythm.

I went through the door into my room to finish drying my hair.

Lake looked divine in blue slacks, a white Polo turtleneck and tan sport jacket. My butt hurt despite being swathed in exquisite silk. My body moved in a forward motion in its effort to alleviate monkey butt.

I suggested we head out to City Place, where elegant bars awaited our attendance. The cab ride was short: Belvedere to Congress to Okeechobee. The cabbie recommended The Palms Bar and Grill and dropped us off on Hibiscus.

The place was a little chi-chi for Lake's taste, but at least it wasn't like the Italian place we'd passed where the snowbirds were hooting it up on the sidewalks. I'm not partial to outdoor restaurants in touristy places, especially at night. People drink, voices raise, and before you know it, it sounds like a full-scale riot committed by middle-agers acting like teens.

The drinks were superb and Lake asked for a menu.

"I'm still taco-full," I said.

"Smells good in here." His hand went to his tummy. "A rare piece of beef will hit the spot."

While he studied the menu, I felt nerves dancing across my shoulders. Someone was watching. I looked toward the entrance. Somebody ducked. "We're being watched," I said.

"I figured."

"The Fed?"

"Don't think so. Grady stayed to talk to the chief when I left. I spotted a tail riding back to the hotel. Blue Buick, five years old."

"Not a good tail since I just saw him duck. Does Grady know where we're staying?"

"Yeah, I told the captain." He shut the menu. "He asked."

I didn't see the tail while I watched Lake devour prime rib. I shared his salad and ate all of his undercooked veggies.

When dessert came, so did Grady.

"Bother," I said.

"Then you won't mind if I tell him to fuck off."

"Do it."

Grady came to the table, pulled out a chair and sat.

"Have a seat," Lake said.

"You folks don't look too happy to see me."

"Not at this particular time," Lake said.

I looked at Lake. "I thought you were going to tell him to fuck off."

"Didn't I?"

Grady laughed. *A Fed with a sense of humor.*

"Was that your man tailing me?" Lake asked.

"You made him?"

I laughed. "Peeping around door frames? At first I thought it was you, but then the tail wouldn't even make a good sneak thief."

Grady looked like I'd just called him a sneak thief. Which I had.

Lake swallowed a bite of coconut cake and asked, "What did the chief have to say?"

"I'm welcome. You're not."

"You don't say."

"Apparently he's done some checking on you."

"You ratted us out."

"Not me." He laid his palm on his chest, a move I'd seen before. "I'll tell you the deal. We're partnering with the local task forces on a narco sting, and it includes the motorcycle gangs. Home-growers like the White Stallions and incomings like the Doomsday Prophets and the Miami Hotshots. He doesn't want anything to screw it up. He's in a race with Orlando to see who puts more biker scum in federal prison."

"Don't look at me," Lake said. "I don't plan on screwing up anybody's operation, narco or otherwise, and that includes whatever you got running."

"You two could get in the middle with the bikers."

I gave Grady a wide smile, even let my eyes shine excitedly.

"We're going to see our riding buddy, Rassler, at their biker bar, and then we're going to the funeral of his friend." You'd have thought I was twelve and said we were going to Disney World.

"You met Rassler?" Grady asked, and Lake nodded. Grady looked thoughtful. "He's a decent guy, for a Wild Blood. You know a lot of these guys got screwed up in the wars and came back with mental problems. Then there are losers who never went to war but are born that way. You take Rassler, though, and a few others, they're regular guys who love motorcycles and have a live-and-let-live attitude. Now you take the war-bonkers, when they came home their nearest and dearest didn't understand them so they found a group of like-minded, same-experienced men and bonded. The thing people don't understand about one-percenters who sell drugs or guns or women is that it's an individual thing. The clubs don't sanction illegal activities, and that's why ninety-nine percent of the time we can't get them on RICO. Some members sell illegal stuff, some don't. Those who don't don't condemn those who do. It's an 'every one has a right to make a living' attitude, and if that living includes something illegal, so be it. It's his own right and his own ass if he gets caught."

Lake said, "If that's the way it is, you might as well quit before you join forces in the sting."

I said, "Doesn't make it legal, moral or ethical."

He looked from Lake to me. "You have the right attitude, Miss Dru. That's why the Chattanooga bail-jumpers are going to jail as soon as they get back. They'll plead and go to prison for at least five years." He rose. "I'll be keeping an eye on you, or my crack shadow will, just to make sure you don't stumble into our action. Otherwise, I'll see you around."

Neither Lake nor I bid him farewell.

Lake stuffed the last piece of cake into his mouth and was chewing with the look of a peeved bulldog.

I said, "If he only knew what experts we are at losing tails, he wouldn't bother."

The bulldog left and the Cheshire cat appeared.

CHAPTER TEN

Our plan was to take a few hours off and go to the beach. We ate a late breakfast at a wonderful place called He Sells Sea Shells right on the beach, just yards from the Atlantic Ocean. Their crab benedicts were nothing short of terrific.

No sooner had we spread a blanket borrowed from the hotel and got lotioned up with sunscreen than Pearly Sue called.

"I'm coming there," she said.

"To Palm Beach?"

Palm Beach is the exclusive town on the east side of the Intercoastal Waterway. The Intercoastal separates West Palm Beach from Palm Beach.

Pearly Sue said, "Not exactly. Not the city, the county of Palm Beach. City of Wellington."

Wellington. Hoyt Fagan. "Is there a connection between Samuel Chapin of Naples and Hoyt Fagan in Wellington?"

Lake, who had reclined on his elbows, presumably to people-watch, sat up.

Pearly Sue said, "I hope you don't mind me following up on a hunch, and I would have called for a go-ahead, but Web said you were tied up with biker gangs and . . ."

"Clubs, Pearly Sue. They don't like being called gangs."

"Oh I know. I dated a boy from Waycross who would as soon slit your throat if you called his club a gang."

"I hope that's a hyperbole."

"I'll look that up. I learn so many fancy words working for you."

Don't for a moment think Pearly Sue's not sharp. She's the sharpest knife in the block, except for Web. The vast difference between them is that Web's an introverted savant and Pearly Sue's a gregarious smarty-pants who loves to talk and enter beauty pageants. She ain't Miss Georgia Peanut for nothing. Any target in her sights, though, best be wary of her charm.

"So what is taking you to Wellington?"

Lake and I exchanged glances.

"The week before Samuel Chapin died," she said, "Bunny Raddison had gone to see him."

Lake's keen hearing, despite a stiff wind and bad cell static, had heard what she said. He got up. I stood, too.

"How's that connected to Wellington?"

Lake was shaking out the blanket while Pearly Sue explained, "Listen to this. It's connected to the school and Fagan's a big bug with horses in Wellington, all of Florida really. Mr. Chapin's private-duty nurse was worried about Mr. Chapin after Bunny left because he was very upset. He told her that Bunny had learned something about the school and mentioned Mr. Fagan's name. Mr. Chapin did not tell the nurse what Bunny told him, but that it was something he needed to think about— before he acted."

That Pearly Sue can sure spin it out.

She went on, "When I talked to Web he told me that Winters Farm Academy riders that excel go to Wellington to train and enter events. Mr. Chapin used to have two girls visit him when they were in Florida to ride. They came with their parents or Fagan. The nurse looked up the names for me. Lawrie Taylor and Brandle Raddison. Lawrie Taylor stopped coming to see him, but Brandle came by herself and told Mr. Chapin that Lawrie had been in an accident. Then she had to tell him that

Juliet had been killed. The nurse said that had really upset him. Then suddenly Brandle didn't come anymore, either."

"What's your destination in Wellington?"

"Web told me that Fagan keeps his horses at Hackensack Stables. He's a trainer and got an interest in the stable. I thought I'd go there . . ."

"After you've finished there, we'll meet up with you for lunch at the mall. There's a restaurant there called Beaches Café, something like that. Are they expecting you at the stable?"

"Yes, I called to talk to Fagan, although I knew he wasn't there, but in Atlanta. A woman name of Robin said Fagan wasn't expected for another week to get ready for the winter hunter festival."

"Did you identify yourself?"

"Yes, I said I wanted to talk about Bunny Raddison. She remembered her and said she wasn't Hackensack material. Very snooty, Robin was. But nice, too. She agreed to see me because she took a personal interest in all her girls, some of them were Winters Farm girls, and she wanted to help me find Bunny."

"Did she seem eager to help you find Bunny?"

"Seemed to me too eager."

The Beaches at Wellington was a chain that had started in Lake Worth in the seventies and slowly spread across south Florida. The menu was limited, but that didn't bother Lake. A roast beef with Swiss cheese and onions would do him just fine. Add slaw and American fries, which looked exactly like French fries, and he was a happy man. I had a turkey sandwich, fruit and slaw. Pearly Sue had a vegetable salad. She dribbled vinegar and oil from little jars. *Got to keep the figure for the pageants.*

"Anyway," Pearly Sue said after the waitress got us condimented and departed. "Robin said that Bunny had come to see Fagan. Bunny also told Robin that she was in show business and had changed her name to Margery Williams. Do you know who that is?"

I stopped my slaw-ladened fork's journey to my mouth. "No idea."

Lake shook his head.

"Well, I said to Web that it looks like he was wrong and that Bunny wasn't using some kind of play on her Bunny name when she went into hiding, but, that Web, so smart. He looks up the name on his computer and voila! Margery Williams wrote *The Velveteen Rabbit.*"

I laughed. At Bunny—and at Pearly Sue's delivery of the coup. "What was Bunny doing at the stable?"

"She wanted to see Hoyt Fagan, but Robin told her Hoyt was in Europe showing horses. Robin said she'd leave a note with his answering service that Miss Margery Williams wanted to talk to him, but here's the thing, Bunny said never mind, she'd get back with him. She hurried away and didn't leave a number. Robin said she seemed beside herself."

"When was this?"

"Right before she went to Naples to talk to Mr. Chapin. It must have really been important what Bunny told him, because the nurse said he wanted to think it over before he acted. And it must have upset Bunny, too, because Mr. Chapin said Bunny was very nervous. When I brought up Juliet's name, the nurse said that Mr. Chapin never really liked Juliet because she was truant and wild as a buck. The nurse said Mr. Chapin was sorry for the way it ended for Juliet, but blamed her own self for what happened to her."

I recalled Wilton Johns saying that Chapin couldn't mold Juliet like he could other students, and Lake looked like he was trying to decipher Pearly Sue's jumping narrative.

I said, "Did Robin say if she told Fagan about Margery Williams's visit?"

"She said she wrote a note and put it in his box. He never made mention of it, and she forgot about it." Pearly Sue gave a slide-eyed smirk. "Hoyt Fagan had a lot of women coming to see him, Robin said. Like he was a big star."

Lake had finished his meal and wiped his mouth. He said, "Okay, let's see what this means. Let's suppose that Bunny sees or hears something that causes her to go to Fagan's stables to consult or confront him about this something. He's out of the country, so she goes to her old advisor and tells him what she's seen or heard. It's enough to upset a mentally challenged old man and he starves himself. Did he starve himself because the news made him lose his appetite? Or was he already on his way down . . . ?"

Pearly Sue interrupted, "The nurse said he was always in good spirits and had a good appetite."

"Because," Lake said, following his thought, "a week later he'd failed to thrive. That must mean . . ."

Pearly Sue looked horror-struck. "Somebody helped him fail to thrive."

Her stare reminded me of that W. Somerset Maugham short story classic, "The Appointment in Samarra" where a merchant's servant sees Death in a Baghdad marketplace and flees to hide in Samarra. The merchant goes to the marketplace and asks Death why she threatened his servant. Death says, "I was surprised to see him because I have an appointment with him tonight in Samarra."

I told Pearly Sue to find out if Chapin had any visitors after Bunny left and who they were.

"He didn't have any," Pearly Sue said. "I asked. His nurse was sad that such a nice old man died a lonely death."

Lake said, "If I may, I'd like to get on with my supposing."

I didn't say a word. Pearly Sue sat upright, folded hands in lap, all ears. I also noticed Pearly Sue's salad bowl. So much talking, so little eating.

Lake said, "Ladies, what I was getting at is that Bunny Raddison most likely lives in these parts if she found out something about the school and sought out Hoyt Fagan. Otherwise, she would have sought him out in Atlanta."

"True," I said.

"Let's also look at what she would be doing here, what she was good at."

Pearly Sue said, "She rode horses here, but not very good and not for long, Robin said."

"Singing," I said.

"That, too," Pearly Sue chimed in. "Mr. Chapin's nurse said she sang for him when he asked her to. The nurse said she had a voice to make the angels weep."

"Therefore," Lake said, "she's working in a club or doing stage work down here."

"If she's still down here," Pearly Sue said.

I asked, "Would she be using the name Margery Williams?"

Lake said, "I'll take a wild guess. Not glamorous enough."

I looked at Pearly Sue. "Have you got anything going in your personal life for the next several days?"

Her big eyes lit up. "You want me to find her."

"That's the idea," I said.

"I'm good to go. Web's already got my cats."

Cats? "At the office?" I asked.

"When he's there, which is all the time, but they use the kitty litter."

But will Web remember to change it?

Lake stood. "I'm ready to go."

We spent the afternoon working out of our hotel rooms, contacting every supper club, dance hall, dive and show in town.

We ruled out the Cuban clubs, of which there are many and

ones I've always loved. Castro was a hard ass, as was Batista before him, but they couldn't squelch the Cubans love of song and dance. Every time I went to get a drink or use the bathroom, I rumba-ed there.

"What does American fusion mean?" Lake asked. He was surfing on a hotel-furnished laptop.

Lake, the food specialist, didn't know?

I said, "Fusion restaurants combine culinary delights from all regions."

"The American fusion establishment says their show and dining experience is second to none," Lake said. I rose and looked over his shoulder. "They have the regular entertainers' photos here. None are Bunny. So, we'll move along without knowing what exactly the chef fuses with what cuisine."

And so it went. Major lounges that featured live entertainment had websites. To those that didn't highlight their entertainers, I put in a phone call. No one had a Bunny or Brandle Raddison singing there. None had a Margery Williams.

"Not Bunny's style," Lake said. "Look at this. It appears burlesque is making a comeback, or so this joint is advertising. Look at these babes." I did. There was a lot to those babes.

"Want a little burlesque action tonight?" Lake asked. "There's a place over on Clematis Street that's got what they call a Cupcake Burlesque show."

"Sorry, my horny darling, but I don't think that's Bunny's genre. Skip to cabarets."

"You're no fun. Okay, so . . ." In time, he said, "All's I'm getting is where I can buy Cabernet Sauvignon and the price."

"C-a-b-a-r-e-t."

"Gotcha. Here we go. Care for a trip to South Beach in zizzling Miami?"

"Could happen."

"At Cabaret Artistique it says here: our singers, dancers,

mimes, magicians and comics display a distinct mix of cunning virtue and old-fashioned mischief, characteristic of the nineteen-forties."

On a hunch and hope, we found ourselves in a chauffeured limo heading for South Beach in Miami and the Cabaret Artistique.

CHAPTER ELEVEN

Lake had been told by the reservation lady at Cabaret Artistique that the dinner presentation—which was simply a piano bar singer—was booked and had an extensive waiting list. However, the champagne show that began at nine thirty and, though booked too, usually had cancellations. She also said the waiting list wasn't long so we ordered a table for two in the event one became available. I almost backed out when I heard the price. A hundred-twenty dollars for a table and a bottle of champagne. I would have asked what kind of champagne, but Lake didn't. He reeled off his credit card number like it was a library card.

We had time to find the right clothes and asked the concierge at the hotel where we might rent party clothes for a cabaret night in Miami. For a hundred bucks, he took our sizes and promised something extra special.

I thought my dress was extra special, although I'd never have bought it. Because I'm tall, it was shorter than the designer designed it to be. It was a one-piece chemise, having a black satin skirt and black lace bodice. A wide red satin sash was sewn at the drop-waist. Good thing I'm slender. The five-inch heels had to go. I'd tower over Lake. I settled for two-inch red pumps and a red beaded bag. A small black feather hat, known as a fascinator, was part of the package. In the end I decided I liked it and perched it on my head.

Lake whistled when I came through the connecting door. He

looked handsome in a black suit with narrow gray stripes, a pinkish dress shirt and a black tie—a little gangsterish, but he'd look smart in farmer's overalls. I whistled back.

The outfits rented for seventy-five bucks each and that included dry-cleaning. Lake told the concierge we were delighted not to have to cart the clothes to the cleaners, thanked him and peeled two twenties off his roll as a tip. No problem when you're flush.

The limo had a well-stocked bar and was going to cost another hundred to get us to the show, then an additional hundred to get us back to the hotel. Plus the mandatory tip. No problem when you're flush.

Settled comfortably with a gin and tonic, I clinked glasses with Lake. Our first trip to South Beach together. Our first night at a cabaret.

The chauffeur asked if we wanted total privacy and we said not. We weren't going to be *up* to anything in the back seat and he was especially chatty. He told us that South Beach was the area between First and Twenty-First Streets going north and south. The millionaires' playground is bordered by the ocean on the east and Biscayne Bay on the west. We were on a causeway when he said, "Downtown Miami is totally separate from Miami Beach."

We cruised in comfortable silence onto the north end of Ocean Drive, heading south under a royal blue sky. A lovely area like this can make one forget the crap places in the world.

Lining the boulevard were flat-roof white and pastel structures not more than four stories high. Wide sidewalks had cutouts for royal palm trees that brushed the building facades tenderly like lovers on a starry night.

The structures gradually grew more stories, and a few blocks from Casablanca, where I'd eaten outdoors several years ago, we came to the Cabaret Artistique.

The neon-lit art deco building that housed the cabaret took me back to a time before I was born, to a time I knew solely from movies and art museums and history books.

Lake forked over the limo's charge, arranged for the chauffeur to return at eleven thirty and gave the valet attendant fifteen dollars. When you're flush, you're flush.

Seeing the long line on the windy boulevard wasn't encouraging, but we moved along so that I didn't feel rooted to one spot in heeled shoes that began to pinch my feet. We arrived at the host's dais and Lake said, "The Champagne Show. Richard Lake."

"Ah yes, it looks like we can accommodate you, if you'll agree to share the table with a distinguished gentleman."

Bummer.

Lake said of course, we'd be delighted. *If he's delighted, I'm delighted.*

We were shown to a small round table about three feet across where three plush armless chairs snugged together. The reserved sign read: Mr. Montague. However, there was no sign of the man himself. I took in our position regards the stage and counted eight rows from it. I recalled the escalating ticket prices and that the most expensive tables included those ten rows from the stage. We were sitting in the most expensive section.

Sinking into the cushioned chair, I was immediately carried back to old movies I'd seen with my mother. Her favorites were set in the decadent glory of the nineteen-thirties. I looked at Lake who observed me with amused discernment; no doubt to gauge my reaction to the opulent interior and its phantasmagorical lighting.

I said, "If Cole Porter were here, everything would be perfect."

He raised his chin and sniffed. "You do have a thing for Cole Porter. Perhaps 'Night and Day' will be on the program."

"Bet it will," I said. "Otherwise the producers have overlooked the signature tune of the era."

A surprisingly wonderfully expensive champagne arrived and was elegantly opened. Before it was served, Lake said to the sommelier, "Perhaps it would be best to wait for Mr. Montague."

The man smiled. "I wouldn't. He comes and goes. He's the producer of the show."

Jackpot!

Lake smirked. Did he arrange this? His stare told me not to question.

I kept watch for Montague, the producer, and Lake said, "You're going to fling that feathery thing off your head if you don't stop swiveling it."

Halfway through the bottle of champagne, the chandeliers slowly dimmed.

The audience went silent in the darkness. The swishing of timpani was joined by the rising rumble of bass drums. The groundswell of drums ended with cymbals crashing. Then silence. Sweet violins and snare drums began a hypnotic undulation, then oboes and flutes joined in the sway. The call of French horns brought the stage lights slowly to life. Finally, the bravura of trumpets and trombones brought the whole thing to a crescendo.

A spotlight slowly zeroed in on a figure standing at the head of four steps on the stage. The Master of Ceremonies, dressed in white formal attire, surfaced. He looked like a refugee from Merle Norman—the pancake, the eyeliner and shadow, the bright red lips. An obvious mime, he beamed an insinuative smile so bawdy there was no mistaking we were in for a wanton evening. He turned for the dark door behind his back. Looking over his shoulder, he stared long and then grinned a provocative warning. Abandon temperance all ye who enter my seductive establishment.

I was so rapt I didn't hear Mr. Montague slip into his chair.

"How do you like our emcee's welcome?" he asked quietly and placed another bottle of champagne on the table.

"Swell," Lake said.

I smiled at Montague. He weighed about three hundred, was bald as a cue ball, had three chins, baby skin and a merry smile. He wore a tuxedo.

"Actually it's pretty standard," he said in a low voice. "Guests expect it after the movie."

I inferred he referred to the movie *Cabaret.*

"It is highly effective," I whispered.

He raised his flute of bubbly. "Welcome Richard Lake and your beautiful companion. She could grace my stage." He turned his continuous smile to me. "Do you dance?"

"Only in the shower," I joked.

A waiter brought an iced bowl of shrimp and condiments to the table. The spotlight dimmed until the room was almost black. A thrill of restive anticipation wavered in the air along with the quiet timpani. The show was going to start. I touched Montague's arm. "Thank you so much for your hospitality."

"It is you who are hospitable. You see, I keep this table for those who come late and are willing to share. Most are not willing; some get quite vile. That is why I treat you with all the fine champagne you can drink." He started to rise. "I wish you . . ."

"Mr. Montague, wait," I whispered, sensing that wasn't really his name and he might not even be the show's producer. He sat back in the chair and I pressed on, "We are here to enjoy the show, but also to find information about a singer."

His perpetual smile faded into perplexity. "In my show?"

"Maybe. She's not in trouble. She could be in danger."

His smile returned, this time as one of intrigue. He reached into his jacket pocket as the stage lights rose on a stageful of feathered dancers. A cymbal crashed.

He said, "Present this after the show. Miss Audrey will speak to you."

I took the backstage passes and pressed his hand. "Thanks."

"Good luck in your search. Now sit back and enjoy the show."

We did enjoy the show. The energy of the singers and dancers was astounding. My only complaint was with the female star. She had a pleasant voice for choir, but not strong enough for a nightclub act. Her best number was "My Heart Belongs to Daddy," although I squirmed at the suggestion of incest. She was dressed like an eight-year-old. I see too much of the real thing to be entertained.

The black men were the best dancers—so clichéd but true. The impeccable choreography took the audience through historical periods of song and dance—from Japanese geishas to American flappers. A handsome dancer pulled a fortyish woman from the audience up onto the stage. The audience got a kick out of her embarrassment when he pulled her butt against his crotch and did a little grind. If she wasn't a plant, then I'm happy we sat eight rows back.

Lake enjoys circus acts and farcical humor more than I do, especially tasteless scatological jokes. Clowns, jugglers and a trapeze act, which made me nervous, livened the audience. The elaborate sets were spectacular, the colors glorious. There was partial nudity, but the bodies were so gorgeous and graceful I imagined I'd entered an artist enclave where they painted nudes. I didn't feel the burlesque was pornographic, but there were many simulated sex acts.

One of my favorite acts was a tribute to Gypsy Rose Lee of fan dance fame.

The show ended with a fabulous cancan.

Twenty minutes after the finale, we found ourselves backstage in search of Miss Audrey. I lost hope of ever finding her in the chaos of costumed human flesh. Every woman looked like a dazzling show girl. Some were bare-breasted while others had a few beads covering their pertinent parts. There were at least two arguments going on. One bare-breasted dancer seethed at a man wearing blue jeans, a green dress shirt and a polka-dot bow tie. He was evidently a choreographer or a crew member and taking an ear-pounding. "I will not be upstaged again," she yelled, almost in my ear as we scooted past the two. "Get over it," he yelled back.

Lake had taken my hand so we wouldn't get separated in the swirling melee and headed for a corner where there appeared to be an office. The office turned out to be the men's dressing rooms. He urged me right to where a tall, thin, dark-eyed man held a clipboard. A line of costumed performers looked nervous as they made their way to stand in front of him. He scribbled notes, and—I could tell by the stroke of his hand—check marks. What the checks were for was a mystery, but I noticed that the costumes they wore were in wonderful condition. That's not usual with troupes. There's the wear-and-tear factor, along with misfittings.

The beanstalk of a man was the only official that appeared to be in charge except the man wearing a bow tie with jeans. We waited until the last performer was checked off, then Lake went up to him.

"Yeah," the tall man said, not bothering to look at us.

"We're looking for Miss Audrey."

"You found her." He-she went on without paying attention to us, "I don't audition after the show. There's a sign-up on the bulletin board." His voice was high-pitched, but definitely male.

"Excuse us," I said with determination.

His kohl-lined eyes took in my chest, then Miss Audrey snickered. "No need to check you out for implants."

"I beg your pardon," I said, not really affronted. Or not yet.

"I'm a cop," Lake said, showing his wallet identification.

"That act's over," Miss Audrey said. "Auditions in spring. Try then."

He started to walk away. "I am a cop," Lake said, separating each word and giving it definition.

Miss Audrey looked at him, really seeing him for the first time. "You'd be good. The manly, square-jawed look."

I wouldn't want Lake auditioning for Miss Audrey, although one wrong word or move and Miss Audrey wouldn't be painting her face for a while.

"Mr. Montague sent us," Lake said. "Won't take a minute of your time."

"At least you're not here to serve a subpoena. You'd have crammed it in my face first thing."

"I don't serve subpoenas. I'm looking for a missing girl."

He started to say something wise, but apparently thought better of it. "Shoot, but hurry it up. I got more bad news to give."

"Are you firing performers?" I asked.

It's off-putting when a man in black lipstick grins. "It's the highlight of my evening." He slipped the clipboard into the pit of his arm. "Contracts are for six months. After that, singers and dancers are re-evaluated."

"What about seniority?"

"There's no such thing. The girls and boys know if they don't stay sharp, they're out. I had a few tired puppies in the show tonight. Can't have that. Mr. Montague is a nice ol' boy at the table. Backstage, he's a tyrant. It pays to keep rotating and adding new blood."

"I want to show you a photograph," Lake said, opening his jacket to take out his cell. He brought a photo to the screen and held it out. "We're looking for this young woman, nineteen thereabout, a singer . . ."

"Can you be more specific?"

"Give me a chance," Lake snapped, offering Miss Audrey the cell phone that contained Bunny's photograph, one that was three years old. "Her name is Brandle Raddison. She goes by Bunny, but I doubt that's how you would know her—if she's been one of your performers. She is a natural blonde as you can see, but she may be anything, and with makeup . . ." He twisted his upper lip. "Hell, I wouldn't know my own mother wearing stage makeup."

Miss Audrey bestowed her black grin on Lake. "Don't know a Brandle or Bunny. We had a Brandy, but she was over the hill a couple of years ago. She works at an all-night gin dive."

I said, "How about the name Margery Williams?"

"Is she on the lam or something?"

"Long story. She's not a fugitive, but she may be in danger."

He raised his eyebrows. "Intriguing."

Miss Audrey reminded me of a transvestite I'd known from Savannah. I've always had a thing for characters. "The young woman we're looking for is said to have a voice to make angels weep."

Rolling his head and eyes toward the ceiling, he said, "They all think they do."

"You could use a new feature singer," I said.

"You noticed. Good voice, no pizzazz." He removed the board from under his arm. I've never seen a clipboard quite so packed with papers. "My notes," he said, flipping through the pages while he spoke. "I wish I had a number for this singer we had a month ago, but she left no forwarding address. These people are gypsies. They go on to other troupes and can be anywhere on the globe."

"Why'd you let her go?"

"She went AWOL in the middle of a show. That doesn't go here."

"I can tell," Lake said.

Miss Audrey gave me a smeary black grin. "This singer actually did have a voice to make angels applaud."

"What was her name?"

He handed me a photograph. "Margery Williams."

As setups go, he'd done well. He hadn't registered a tick at the mention of Margery Williams.

He turned to leave. "You can keep her photo. Good luck in your quest."

The white face paint on his neck confirmed what I concluded. He'd been in the show. The mime.

The Master of Ceremonies.

rags hustling nearly naked broads under bras dangling from the ceiling supports. I leaned into Lake, "Biker broads are mighty fulsome."

"Crank for melons."

"You gotta love the barter system."

Since it was stuffy and hot, no one wore leathers, and the few shirt patches I saw didn't belong to our Wild Blood friends. Lake pulled me through the crowd to the bar where we stood five deep. Beer and hard liquor drinks passed over my head and money made the return trip. Better have the correct bills; you weren't getting change. And don't expect to get what you ordered. We got two American beers that Lake called panther piss.

Four or five women of varying ages were on the small bandstand, some bumping, others grinding in approximate rhythm to the music. I looked closely at each nearly naked form and face as we passed. I didn't expect Bunny would be among the brassy blondes and the one atrocious redhead who looked drunk, stoned or both. Plumpish, there wasn't a good-looking body among them, but hell, it was one in the morning, and I was sober, the champagne having long seeped from my pores.

Pushing past the video games and pool tables, I noted another bouncer stationed in the corner. We stepped onto the patio where patrons were keeping two tiki bar mixologists busy. It was a few decibels quieter but that's because the girls were hard at work giving their prospects arm rubs and heavy-lidded stares.

I stood next to Lake at the rail. A few wooden steps would take us onto the sand, over dunes to the beach. "Our guys aren't here," Lake said.

"Funeral tomorrow, turned in early."

"Likely," Lake laughed. "Looks like we can get that walk on the beach now."

Suddenly a familiar voice boomed out, "Law dog! Hey ya!"

Silence fell with a thud. Lake winced.

Rassler made his way to the rail and raised his fist, knuckles out. Lake met it with his own.

Rassler looked at me. "Good lookin' babes don't get the bump." He put his finger to his lips and then against my forehead. I felt anointed and since I'm not partial to strangers pawing or laying an unexpected kiss on me, I smiled and my breathing returned to normal, sort of.

"Things going good?" Lake asked.

"So far. You missed the live entertainment." He took out a pack of a popular cigarette brand. "Packed up half an hour ago."

"Everybody getting ready for the big ride?" Lake asked.

"Funeral first," Rassler said. "You're invited."

"Who else?"

He lit his cigarette. "Anyone wants to come. You can't keep people out of a graveyard, but there'll be plenty of you there." Through a stir of smoke, his eyes roamed each of our faces. "You still looking for your girl?"

"Still looking," Lake said.

"I want you to meet someone. Don't know if he'll help. Get my meaning?"

"Sure," Lake said.

I wasn't so sure what he meant. Were we to meet Grady's snitch?

We followed Rassler inside, past the video games and pool players, around the bar, down a hall and into a large room as noisy as the main barroom.

Into this tumult of deep male voices launched through handlebar mustaches, I heard a loud pop and a wounded roar. I turned in the direction of the action. Pink liquid was shooting into the air and a burly man was holding his eye, stomping like a mad bull.

"Joe Blade," Rassler said.

"What?" Lake said.

"The man I just told you about. Damn." He laughed. "Looks like he's run up against a champagne cork."

We followed behind Rassler.

Champagne? A biker drinking champagne?

When the man who ran up against a champagne cork stopped stomping, a blonde ran forward and sopped his face with a napkin. He pushed her away. "Goddamn, fuckin' bitch!"

"Sorry, baby," she repeated several times, buzzing around him like a confused honey bee.

He was a stumpy guy with black hair and black beard; his dark skin looked fashioned from rawhide. A scar slid down his left cheek. She was a platinum blonde with dark leather skin and the body of a porn star.

"Now's not the best time for introductions," Lake said.

Joe Blade noticed us and before he growled, he saw Rassler. "What the fuck's so funny?" he said, wiping his eye and elbowing the blonde away.

"Gotta watch those killer corks, Switch," Rassler said.

"Fucking thing about took my eye." He pulled the napkin away from his eye. It was fluttering, trying to open, but the redness was beneath the eye. It had caught his high cheekbone, which saved him.

The blonde said, "Sorry, babe. It got too shook up."

"Who the fuck shook it up?"

"My purse. Sorry, babe."

Blade motioned to Rassler to follow him. "What's this about?"

We followed Rassler for about three steps. Blade stopped, Rassler stopped, we stopped. Rassler said to Blade, "I told you about the cops that want information."

Blade looked from Lake to me. He said, "You a cop?"

"Used to be. Private now."

"You looking for a missing girl?"

"We got a possible lead tonight," Lake said. "She was the friend of a girl who was murdered in Atlanta three years ago. We're seeking information . . ."

"Yeah, I heard." He took a wet napkin wrapped in ice from the bimbo and dabbed his cheekbone and eye. "I remember that case and the stink it made for the club. We ain't no angels, but we don't murder and rape school girls, either. Let's go outside. I need fresh air."

Off the private room, a back door led to a wooden patio overlooking the Atlantic Ocean. Blade and the blonde moved away—to where she stroked his back and he lit a cigarette and messaged his cheek.

Rassler said, "We got mostly non-affiliated riders here tonight, so the club rented this room in case trouble comes."

"Are you expecting trouble?"

"We got lookouts at The Sanction where White Stallions hang. They probably know Switch's here. He and Big Red served in Iraq with the Army. They'll try a first strike. We put out a white flag until the funeral's over." He looked at Joe Blade. "Then he'll light the bomb that burns their fucking clubhouse to the ground."

He reached into his pocket for a cell phone. "Texts, calls—we'll know when they're on the move. Matter of time."

Blade had smoked his cigarette taking deep drags. He patted the blonde on her cheek and walked over. "Here's all I know." He flipped the butt into the sand.

The beach, the world's biggest ashtray.

He stared at me, dared me to comment. I stared back.

He went on, "Back then, this was after the kid was killed, I rode into Atlanta. Met this babe, stayed a while." He paused and shrugged. "Don't matter now. I kept running into this poser hanging in bars asking fool questions, getting on my nerves. He

148

wants patches, a one-percenter patch. I told him patches ain't copyrighted so go get him one. I hoped the douche would, so next time he comes in, we'd knock the shit out of him and rip the cut off his ass."

"A lone wolf," Lake said.

"He's a RUB, you know what that is?"

"Rich urban biker," Lake said.

"Not worth a shit."

"He have a Harley?"

"Got himself a shiny Custom V-Rod."

Rassler chimed in, "Nothing like your dresser, Law Man. What you carry in that thing, anyway? Your ol' lady's closet?"

"Just about," Lake said and grinned. His smile touched the bikers and they laughed. "When did you last see this RUB?"

"Can't tell exactly. I wasn't payin' attention. I split with my Atlanta ol' lady and headed for Florida. The Atlanta club split because of the girl getting herself killed and them getting the fault."

"Describe the poser."

"White. Douche bag." He looked at me. "S'cuse me, sugar, some people are like that."

"He give a name?" Lake asked.

"Don't remember." He rubbed his cheekbone. "We called him Fetch because he'd go get us food. Dumb fuck. Do anything for a ride."

"If I showed you photographs, could you pick him out?"

"Maybe. But don't flash no pictures at me tonight."

"Besides being a poser, what was his demeanor?" I asked.

He smiled, maybe at the word *demeanor*. "I wouldn't take him for a one-percenter. Being one ain't all about killing." He gestured at Rassler. "He don't carry a weapon or ain't broke the law in over ten years, but he don't fault anyone has to. We're a band of brothers. We do what we have to, knowing we won't be judged. Not many in the club didn't kill in Nam or Iraq or Ghannie. That ties us together." He steepled his fingers and pushed them tight. "We know how and when, and ol' Fetch itched to know what it was like to kill."

With that he turned to his blonde babe. "Come, Joycie, let's get us some of that champagne." He looked at me. "It's Joycie's birthday."

"Thanks, Blade," Lake said. He looked over at Joycie. "Happy birthday, girl."

Blade hit Lake's upper right shoulder with his fist. "Call me Switch."

It was going on three o'clock in the morning. Rassler had left for the main bar, I stopped at the ladies and joined Lake to head out.

Halfway through the crowd at the bar, where the ranks waiting for brews had thinned, Rassler lunged forward, then stopped suddenly. At the door, Joe "Switch" Blade was talking to a large man with a Swastika tattoo on his neck. Switch was making ameliorating gestures, holding his hand up, palms out. Michelin was behind Switch. Two other Wild Bloods materialized beside Rassler.

It was then that I started thinking of Joe Blade as Switch.

So fast I hardly saw it, Swastika brought the side of his hand down to chop Switch's neck. Switch dodged and charged Swastika. Michelin hit Swastika from the side. All three went down.

Hell had fired up and the crowd loved it.

The Jolly Black Bouncer brushed by me; and two other giants behind him waded into the fist-fighting, kicking, floor-brawling combatants. Thirty seconds hadn't passed. I looked at Lake. He seemed fascinated. I didn't know how I felt. Rassler grabbed my arm. "Out back," he said. "Now. You're cops. Hurry."

That was when we finally had our walk on the beach, that lovely south Florida evening under a low-hanging winter moon, the stars as sharp as ice crystals, the black waves singing over the sand.

At the hotel, I fetched my computer, went into the Media Suite and looked for a computer with a printer. I printed out photocopies of the photographs Web had sent me, got back to the room to find Lake sound asleep.

CHAPTER THIRTEEN

I'm easily amused. Lake circled the rental car around Palms Garden Cemetery. A spiked, wrought iron fence kept the dead in, otherwise, who knew? They might run out and vote. I didn't say that to Lake for fear of an unappreciative groan.

At the white stone gates, at intervals, the uniformed cop held up a hand to allow other boulevard traffic to flow past the line of bikes and cars waiting to enter the city of the dead.

The crowded graveyard was aptly named for its variety of palms. They too were crowded—from the short but showy Sago Palms to the Royal Palms that waved against a bright blue sky as we passed beneath them. Windmills, Sabals, Queens, Fans, Majesties, all created an atmosphere that said this would be a wondrous resting place, if one wanted a resting place. Not me. I don't like the thought of being in a box.

My mind returned to the line of Harleys, Nortons and BMWs grumbling ahead and behind us. The throbbing of explosive pipes was enough to wake the dead. The shuddering sandy soil surely had their bones rattling and rolling. That I could see, not one biker wore a helmet. In Florida one wasn't required. In outlaw jargon, they were called organ donors.

We'd been given a police decal for the back and front windshields of our rental car. PB's chief was happy to allow Lake to act as a cop, because, like all police departments, he was short on uniforms and detectives. Lake's badge hung prominently around his neck. Our Wild Bloods had already accepted us as furniture.

Lake had on black linen slacks and a cotton guayabera shirt. The pleated, pocketed shirt hid the subcompact Beretta in its pancake holster that nestled in the small of his back. A second gun, a Beretta Storm, rode in a holster on his belt.

I, too, was dressed in black—pants, blouse and jacket. The jacket covered my pockets. In my left was a cell phone and Bunny's photo from Miss Audrey and various photographs I wanted to show Joe Blade to see if he could identify his Rich Urban Biker. In my right pocket, my Glock 17 was secured in its pocket holster. The PB police chief had granted me temporary carry permits since we shared information from our visit to the Double Yellow Line biker bar. My BUG, my back-up gun, a Glock 26, rested in an ankle holster beneath my wide-leg trousers.

All that to say, anyone looking at us would believe we were armed since we sported official IDs on thick neck ribbons. Mine said Child Trace, Inc. but looked, at a passing glance, like a cop ID. It was large with Private Investigator printed at the top. It displayed my photo, a certified true crest, my license number and an authorizing signature. I did not and could not carry a badge lest a citizen mistake me for a real cop.

We segued away from the biker line, to the right where cars were parked, mostly belonging to cops and the media. I hadn't taken two steps from the rental when Grady sidled up. "You got a bulge in one pocket," he said.

I didn't look him up and down as he'd done me, but I knew there wouldn't be a bulge in his immaculate jacket to show he carried an underarm weapon, nor was there a slight hike in his shoulder that underarm carry gives someone who's not practiced at carrying that way.

Lake looked at him. "It's in the air, Grady. Not all gangbangers are here to pay respects. You got a count on expected attendance?"

"A thousand maybe."

"For an unknown piss-ant biker?"

"He's a Wild Blood member; that's all they need to know. They came to square off against each other, given the chance; or gawk at the expected brawl. You catch the one last night?"

"Got out of there."

It was on the news. The cops got there late and there were no arrests, but it served to put the city on notice that biker tension rode into paradise.

"Rassler help you with your case?" Grady asked.

We brushed past Needle Palms crackling dryly and around Pindos and came to a fenced plot with a stone that told us the Matthews family occupied several graves. We skirted past the fence lined with bougainvillea.

"Rassler knows nothing," Lake said.

"He wouldn't tell you if he knew something."

Lake laughed. We walked side by side, over the lane curb onto the grass that led between two rows of headstones guarded by King Palms. Grady filled us in on the man being buried. He said that as giants like Big Red went, he was known as a gentle man with a love of women, which had gotten him killed. He was a member of the Raleigh club because his Army buddy from Raleigh had joined. In the last few years, Big Red spent most of his time in Florida except when the club rode together to meets across the Carolinas. Big Red worked construction when he worked.

Behind me, the roar of bikes seemed louder, and I turned. So did Lake and Grady. A biker signaled something then did a wheelie and ripped ahead of the line. I caught the famous or infamous cut and rockers of the Hell's Angels.

Grady said, "You get some rivalry with those guys, but they coexist with Wild Blood. HAs are an old club. The founders of

WB were every bit as hard core, but didn't want the reputation. Some, but not everyone, put their killing, doping, and whoring to peace-time use."

I didn't tell him, nor did Lake, that Rassler had invited the Hell's Angels to the funeral.

Grady turned to look at the line of bikers streaming in. "Speaking of which, Raleigh's here," he said, motioning with his head.

As they thundered by, I studied the Wild Blood patch with the rockers. The one above identified the club and the one below spelled out RALEIGH. To the side was the letters MC. Some wore a 1% rhombus on the left shoulder.

Grady said, "You see the leader on the red bike?"

"The stumpy guy with the black beard?" Lake asked.

"Joe Blade. They call him Switch."

"Ouch," I said.

Grady said, "Fearless on a bike, fearless with his hands. From what I hear, the Switch handle is just that. Never known to use a knife. Big Red's Army buddy."

Lake and I glanced at each other.

Lake had been told by the chief that Palms Garden was an old cemetery where many of the city's fathers and elites lay beneath the stones. The O'Rourke family had a plot in the cemetery and their only son, Riley "Big Red," was to be planted in it today. I didn't see a soul that looked to be a family member, much less the mother and father of a giant called Big Red.

We weaved and shouldered our way through throngs of bikers, some startled at seeing three people not wearing cut, sleeveless denim, or leather, or visible tattoos—until they caught the badges. They growled and spit, then went back to their conversations. Lots of fucks and fuckers being said, Lake noted. They were paired with all the adverbs and adjectives known in the English language.

The last of the attendees were in place at O'Rourke's grave. On the gold-draped stand stood an obviously hand-painted casket with the motorcycle club's colors and a patch on the foot. I spotted Rassler and the Chattanooga brothers milling around the head of the coffin. The Raleigh boys were at the sides and the Birmingham chapter at the foot.

I wondered if there was some kind of strategy in the stations of those nearest the bier. I looked behind me. Pressing forward was so much human flesh in leather, cattle pens must have been emptied to supply the hides.

The crowd quieted. The service was to begin.

My knee bumped an O'Rourke headstone. I was standing on a double grave that had an extra-wide monument. On it were two clasping marble hands. Above them were the words "Our mother. Our father." Big Red was named after his father, now buried alongside his mother. They'd died on the same day three years ago. I'd read that Big Red was forty-two years old. There was a story there that I would read about in tomorrow's newspaper and hear on local television. I spotted obvious reporters behind a line of tape and television cameras encroaching whenever a cop wasn't watching.

My skin started to hum. The voltage in the atmosphere was amped to the max despite the fanning palms doing their damndest to make this day a celebration of the dead.

"Don't anyone light a match," Lake said.

I'm tall but I still had to stretch to see around the men standing in front of me. The preacher wore long robes and a stole as he walked up to the platform that held the casket. He wasn't Catholic, but I had no idea what faith he represented.

Grady said, "The O'Rourkes are Protestant, Presbyterian."

That answered that.

Holding a microphone, the preacher began the service with a prayer, and those bikers in front of me removed whatever head gear they wore except those with do-rags. Bad hankie hair maybe.

The silence quivered with tension and I was glad for the "Amen."

Immediately, Rush's "Ghost Rider" flared from speakers hidden in palms. I thought it an apt song. When Neil Peart, the drummer and lyricist for Rush, lost his daughter and wife, he went on a motorcycle journey across America, and then wrote the song.

When the track ended, the preacher did the "we are gathered together" thing. The preacher paused, stepped back and Steppenwolf's "Born to Be Wild" erupted from the speakers. The crowd let out a collective yelp.

Those immediately behind me moved suddenly, and I turned. Two men dressed in leather from neck to toe moved in behind us. They spoke quietly to Grady. I couldn't make out what was said. Despite being on the other side of me, Lake appeared to understand. It's some phenomenal hearing that he possesses. Lake frowned. The men in leather disappeared, one going one way, the other another.

"What was that about?" I asked Grady.

He gave a very brief, but obvious smile that said, *wouldn't you like to know, little girl?* Before I kicked him, he said that the White Stallions and the Hounds of Hell from Miami were here without their colors. Also amongst the uninvited were "shitheads from the Latino and black neighborhoods." The ATF had identified them, Grady said, then added, "They weren't wearing cut, but I bet before the service is over they'll be fly."

I think that meant wearing patches.

While we discussed this, the preacher read a passage from the Bible. It rang out in enunciated tones through the speakers, as if the preacher wanted everyone to hear and believe.

"I declare to you, brothers, that flesh and blood cannot inherit the kingdom of God, nor does the perishable inherit the imperishable. Listen, I tell you a mystery: We will not all sleep, but we will all be changed in the twinkling of an eye, at the last trumpet. For the trumpet will sound, the dead will be raised imperishable, and we will be changed. For the perishable must clothe itself with the imperishable, and the mortal with immortality. When the perishable has been clothed with the imperishable, and the mortal with immortality, then the saying that is written will come true: 'Death has been swallowed up in victory.' Where, O death, is your victory? Where, O death, is your sting? The sting of death is sin, and the power of sin is the law. But thanks be to God! He gives us the victory through our Lord Jesus Christ."

Halfway through that passage from Corinthians I had my doubts about it being right for a biker funeral, but when the preacher said "Amen" a collective, testosterone-laden "whoop" blew through the air.

Into the whoop came the Eagles, "Life in the Fast Lane."

I swear every biker sang. They must have been nipping from flasks. I haven't heard that much dissonance since I went to a David Allen Coe concert and we all sang "You Never Even Called Me by My Name." At midnight. While drunk.

Once the song ended and voices settled, the preacher read from another Bible passage: "To everything there is a season, A time for every purpose under heaven: A time to be born, And a time to die . . . A time to kill, And a time to heal . . . A time to weep, And a time to laugh, A time to mourn, And a time to dance . . . A time to lose; A time to keep . . . A time to keep silence, And a time to speak; A time to love, And a time to hate; A time of war, And a time of peace."

As expected, the blaster fired up another motorcycle song, this time Bruce Springsteen's "Born to Run."

I'm thinking funeral as an excuse for a heavy metal concert.

Certainly the crowd was much less restive than they had been before the music.

Next up, The Doors, "Riders on the Storm." I've always loved that song, the thunder and rain effects. It was inspired, they say, by "Ghost Riders in the Sky," a cowboy song.

I reasoned that biker music must be standard at funerals. It certainly had a calming effect on the crowd, but I stayed alert, wary.

The music died and the preacher said, "I am the resurrection and the life. He who believes in me will live, even though he dies; and whoever lives and believes in me will never die. Amen." He held up a cross. "Go with God and our Lord Jesus Christ brother Riley O'Rourke."

After a quiet interval, the casket was lowered into the ground by some automatic button. Shovels began to fly; their blades had the club's patch painted on it. The Raleigh club was literally burying their dead. I got a good look at Rassler who worked his shovel demonically, his face red with sweat. The silent crowd was rapt with awe. It was then I sensed something in the air, a quiet determination. At the same time, something moved rapidly to my left. A man rushed forward, passing not six feet from me, weaving through the biker fraternity intent on seeing their brother buried. They'd let down their guard.

I looked to my right. Lake was several steps away and still unaware of the man's forward motion. I reached into my pocket for the 17 and followed the man wearing a muscle shirt with a rearing horse on the back. He moved fast, and had his fist around a small gun at his side. I saw it plainly because I was behind him, closer now, as he moved through the bikers. The ones that had seen the rearing horse man with the gun rushed a step or two behind me. I heard my name. "Dru!" It was Lake. He was parallel to me, five steps over. "Dru!"

The would-be shooter and I were leaving a commotion in

our wake. The grave shovelers halted. Rassler turned. Switch—on the other side of the coffin—paused. The shooter raised his gun hand. I aimed low in case I was jostled into an errant shot. Two shots rang through the air, cold and sharp.

Mine got him in the buttocks.

His bullet went into the palms.

He faltered a step forward, then went to his knees. I felt the stampede, then the pause of movement. At least fifteen bikers jumped the prone, injured man and began stomping him. Grady spoke rapidly into a police radio. Lake stared at me. Rassler portaged around the carnage. Parting the crowd, he came up at the same time Grady arrived with his FBI contingent, the ATF and the police. The cops waded into the men bent on murdering the gunman.

Lake stood next to me. He didn't say anything, but his eyes were narrow with anger.

Rassler said, "You saved my life." Switch came up and raised his fist in salute.

I couldn't respond for the hollowness in my chest. It was like someone or something had pulled a plug and drained away my core. I feared what lay ahead, what Lake's expression was telling me. I simply could not speak for fear my body, its organs, would shut down.

The faraway voice was Rassler's. "You okay, girl?" He gave me a side hug.

I think I nodded and watched six burly cops pry bikers off the body of the would-be assassin. I didn't look down, though I knew he was dead.

"Come with us," Grady said gently, taking my gun and my elbow.

As we left the O'Rourke family plot, I heard a murmur, and then a rousing number sprang from the speakers: "Bat out of Hell" by Meatloaf.

Lake walked behind us, jaws locked, eyes like hard brown granite.

Better if they played AC/DC's "Highway to Hell" for me.

Chapter Fourteen

The man I shot was a nineteen-year-old illegal named Juan Torres. A lot of things happened after that, but none had Lake talking to me. I tried a *to hell with him* attitude, but didn't quite get into it. In the end Grady told the Palm Beach County and city authorities that, as part of an interstate case the Atlanta Police Department and I were involved in, I was now in federal protective custody.

Protective custody? "I was here legally," I shouted at Grady. "You knew every step I took."

"It's the only way to get you out of here," he said. "I've cleared it with the U.S. Attorney in Miami. The police will investigate the murder of the illegal by his OMG rivals. We'll be on the next plane."

Without looking at me, Lake said, "She'll be on the next plane. I've got a bike to ride."

Grady seemed doubtful and said to Lake, "You aren't responsible for the kid's death, but I wouldn't want to be riding the highways alone."

"You do what you do, I do what I do," Lake said.

I said, "I'm riding with Lake."

"Not a good idea," Grady said.

"Am I charged with something? Am I under arrest for shooting an illegal alien who was trying to kill people burying their dead?"

"No, but I could think up something."

"I'm riding with Lake."

Grady shook his head and looked at Lake.

Lake said, "Don't worry about me. I got Annie riding shotgun."

It should have been funny, but no one laughed. Shadows shifted on each of their faces.

There would be a reckoning for sure.

I asked Grady if I could have a word with the police chief.

He was reluctant, but said, "Don't admit to anything."

How idiotic. "Nothing to admit to."

I sat in the chair staring at the stern-faced chief. He said, "The heads of those clubs are powerful men. Clubs fall apart when they lose their leaders. But your actions saved their sorry lives. Joe Blade is a trained killer. The country and state, the highways and cities, would be better off with him dead."

There were several cogent things I could have said, but didn't. "I don't judge."

"You react."

I didn't admit to reacting. "Grady said Joe Blade never killed anyone."

He looked like he wanted to spit. "That we know of. People he doesn't like go missing."

"Speaking of missing, Joe Blade may have provided a valuable clue to our case in Atlanta."

He waved away the valuable clue. "Did you want to say something in your defense regarding the action at the cemetery?"

"What I want to say is that I wish I wasn't in the custody of the federal authorities. I'm not afraid of state, county or city justice."

His eyes cut through my shaky bravado. "I know your reputation. Saving kids will hold you in good stead with any jury you'd face. But it wouldn't come to that. The DA was scratching his head when that son-of-a . . . the FBI put the clamps on you."

I told him that I understood he, and other jurisdictions, had an operation with the Feds involving drugs and guns against several clubs. "Why would a shooting at a biker funeral change that?"

"I don't know that it would, but you have valuable information you can't discuss with me because Grady and my superiors told me not to question you."

"We both seek valuable information. I gave you a statement that was witnessed by at least a dozen people, including police and the Feds. The valuable information I came here seeking is information on a girl's murder in Atlanta."

He looked less peeved, but only a bit. "This is not a question as in an official interrogation, but did you find that valuable information?"

"I'm not admitting to anything, but I hope so."

"From Joe Blade?"

"I'm not supposed to admit to anything."

His grin was more of a smirk. "You think you can waltz into biker territory and start quizzing these guys about a murder?"

Hadn't I? "Bikers are people, too."

He shook his head and stood. "All right, Pollyanna, go now with your Fed."

At the PBPD's motor vehicle depot, Lake stood next to his red Harley, his arms folded across his chest. The beautiful bike, the lovely man . . .

I had to get a handle on my emotions. Lake gave the stand a good kick and fired up the bike. I got into the rental. He followed me to the car agency and waited outside while I returned the car.

I unstrapped my helmet from the rack and strapped it on and

mounted the back seat behind Lake and we were off to the motel to fetch our things.

Lake had wavered between sympathy for me in front of his peers and aggravation when no one was looking, but he hadn't spoken nor caught my eye, and I knew why.

At the hotel, I removed my BUG snug in its holster and threw it on the bed, turned and faced his back. "So let's have it."

He laid the duffel on the bed and unzipped it. "Nothing to have," he said, not looking at me.

"Do I ride back with Grady or you?"

That did it.

He laid his shoes in the bag. "If that's what you want, go right ahead, Annie Oakley."

I'd gone from Pollyanna to Annie Oakley in under an hour. "If you'd been in the same place I was, you'd have done the same thing."

Into the duffel went his leather shaving kit. "Where in your police training did it say it was all right to shoot people in the back?"

"There was no other option. He raised his gun. I was too far away to bring him down. If I yelled out I put people around him in danger. He was going for Rassler or Switch."

"It wasn't your place . . ."

"I should have let him shoot them?"

He turned for the dresser drawer, grabbed his socks and shorts and threw them into the duffel. "They're scum bikers. They live to die."

"I don't live to let one human purposely kill another."

"You've killed purposely."

Once, to save his life, yes I had.

I said, "I didn't shoot to kill the illegal, and you know it. This is going nowhere."

"Dru, it wasn't our fight. Recall the off-duty ATF agent a few years back. The one who went into a convenience store in the middle of a robbery? He shot the robber, but the cops came and saw him with no uniform and a gun. They killed him. You put your life in jeopardy over two outlaws."

"I don't know that Rassler is an outlaw."

"He is. You just happen to be taken with him."

"Taken! What a jerk thing to say."

"Okay, I'm a jerk. You like the guy. I sure as shit don't trust him."

"He helped us."

"Not us. You. And that's a maybe."

"I believe Switch's description of the poser. He's helped *us.*"

"I'll look into it."

"Whoop-de-doo."

"Now, Rassler owes you, and so does that other dirt bag, Switch. You sure know how to make friends."

"And maybe because of their help I'll be able to solve *your* murder."

"Cease your investigation of Juliet Trapp."

"Too late. I'm committed. You know I never give up."

"Bull Dog Dru."

"Where are you going with this?"

"You let Grady take your gun."

"Standard operating procedure in a shooting. I'll get it back. I'll have to testify when they try the killers."

"I'm packed. You riding with me?"

"You're the one that brung me."

"I'll be downstairs."

While I packed I reflected on the reason for Lake's anger. The Feds had gotten the upper hand by my action. Grady got me under his control, and therefore Lake, and it made him fighting mad.

In the hotel parking lot, Lake stood by his bike holding what looked like a tiny piccolo. I recognized it as a GPS tracking device.

"Courtesy of your pet Fed," Lake said, mounting and cranking the pop-pop-in-a-tin-can, pulsating machine. I barely got seated before he burned off.

He swung from the ramp onto I-95 heading north and tossed the device into the weeds. Those things are expensive, so Grady was going to be pissed.

My suspicion that we wouldn't be riding Alligator Alley home had been borne out and it was because of me.

When we reached the off-ramps to Port St. Lucie I felt Lake suddenly stiffen. I asked what was wrong. He shook his head. Thirty seconds later, I knew. The collective snarl of motorcycles had reached my ears seconds later than his. I looked back but couldn't determine if they were friend or foe, or neither. Lake kept a steady speed at eighty. Soon they were immediately behind us. The road captain was hand-signaling and his voice was full of static through the General Mobile Radio Service, known by its initials GMRS. Lake slowed and gave an okay. Rassler came around us, and held out his right hand with a two-fingered peace sign. He rolled in front of Lake and another WB came around, giving the same hand greeting. Lake responded with his left hand. Rassler and his comrade zigzagged into staggered formation. The one hanging back signaled something to Lake. Lake slowed. Two more riders passed us and fell into formation; then two more, until we were in the middle of the pack.

"Just great," Lake said through the helmet intercom. "Blade's pack is behind us. We got us a motorcycle escort."

"They were supposed to ride Alligator Alley today."

"They'll make us pay for diverting them."

I didn't think so. This was war to them, and war was fun.

"Did you fear something happening to us?"

"No, but they did. Sit back and enjoy your new friends."

"Always need new friends."

At one of Melbourne's exits, we lost Switch's contingent.
Damn, I never got a chance to show him photographs.

We forged on to Daytona. Rassler gave a few hand signals
that meant something to Lake and spoke into the radio without
much accompanying static. "Base to Lake."

"Go ahead."

They talked about a plan that I didn't fully understand, but I
heard Michelin's name and Rassler say, "Park at the family
friendly. Clear."

"Will do. Clear."

Lake switched back to Bluetooth so I could hear him but
Rassler could not. "Getting off," he said.

It was clear to me they spoke in code because GMRS
transmission can be heard by anyone nearby.

Once on International Speedway Boulevard, where the motels
were jammed between fast food joints, Michelin moved behind
us. Rassler traveled on, got in the left lane and stopped at a red
light. Turning, he led his minions into a motel parking lot. This
two-story inn advertised itself as extended stay. I don't know if
those checking in would extend their stay with eight burly, tattooed men debarking from their Harleys in the parking lot.

Across the street from the extended stay, Lake pulled into a
motel advertising super cheap rates for families. Michelin was
right behind us. Guess he was our lone guard now.

We dismounted. I removed my helmet, and Lake went to the
duffel and took out binoculars. "Trouble behind us. We were
followed."

"Wild Blood didn't have trouble finding us," I said.

"You told Rassler where we were staying?"

"Not exactly."

"You said by the airport," Lake said, training the binoculars on the interstate overpass. I looked at our crowded surroundings and hoped trouble didn't find us here. Rubbing my sore butt, I kept watch on the overpass until I heard motorcycles on the move. Wild Blood members across the boulevard rode two-by-two to refuel at the nearby gas station. As soon as they finished gassing, it was Michelin's turn. We gassed last.

Rassler rode up as Lake replaced the nozzle. Rassler hit his left chest just below the shoulder with his right fist. Lake returned the greeting. "Y'all doing all right?"

"Doing good," Lake said. "Didn't take long."

"White Stallion fuckers went to Double Yellow Line, but the law dogs were waiting for them. Fuckers are after cop blood, too." *Meaning Lake and me.* "A few Doomsdays and Bad Asses are keeping company, looking for a fight. We'll keep communication to a minimum since we're on public radio."

"I can pair you," Lake said and Rassler nodded. "Switch coming, too?"

Keeping his eyes trained on the overpass, Rassler said, "They're riding up 1-A and will cut back to 95. They'll be in front of the Stallions. We'll be behind them."

"If they engage . . ."

Rassler held up a hand. "There they are." I turned to the interstate to see a staggered line of riders passing overhead.

I took out photographs and urged them on Rassler. "Have Switch look at these. See if his rich urban biker is one of them."

After our pursuers cleared the overpass, Rassler put the photos in a saddlebag. He said, "The Stallions and their ilk are unpredictable, like that idiot got himself killed at the funeral." He smiled at me. "They want cred, but they're mostly mean posers. Watch yourselves."

When he rode away, Lake glanced at me and got on the Harley. I mounted the back saddle. When the bikers left the extended stay and got in formation, Lake pulled out of the family friendly with Michelin behind us, riding sweep, and, with signals understood by all but me, we hit the ramp to the interstate.

Since Lake had little to say to me—thanks Rassler for the funeral reminder—I tuned in my music player and listened to traveling music. First: "Low Spark of High Heeled Boys."

Every once in a while I'd hear Lake speak to Rassler, but didn't know what was said. We got to I-10 and headed west to I-75 and stopped in Lake City—a hundred fifty miles of easy riding but still hard on the backside. We met up with Switch's five-biker contingent at a rest stop near the pet walk area. The only walker was a middle-aged woman holding the leash of a small non-pedigree dog that was lifting his leg against a palm tree.

Switch spoke to Lake and Rassler, "The ass-wipes laid back and waited for you to pass back on I-10. We took the back roads and got here from the north."

"Nice cat-and-mouse," Lake said.

Rassler said, "It's going to come to an end. They won't ride into Georgia without their brain buckets."

"We got them outnumbered," Switch said.

"Hey, gents," Lake said. "We got to think about the authorities here. I'm a cop, not a vigilante."

Rassler looked at me. "She's not a cop."

Lake responded, "She's got a PI license to defend."

"You want to lay up in a motel, that's fine by me," Rassler said.

"Me, too," Switch said. "We need to settle this and quick. I don't want the fuckers in my own yard."

Looking grim, Rassler said, "There's gonna be blood, might as well be a fair fight in the . . ."

The sound blasted into my consciousness, the growls

overpowering the eighteen-wheeler noise of the interstate. Adrenaline burst through my nervous system. My heart beat against my chest wall. Lake's face tightened into a mask of command.

They came at us, rounding the exit, two by two.

The bystanders recognized a biker war when they heard and saw it, and ran for the building. Lake ripped the Velcro on the duffel and brought out two Beretta .45s and two extra magazines and handed a set to me. I had my BUG on my ankle, but the .45 stood me in better stead in a gunfight. The extra Beretta .45 was Lake's BUG. The magazine held ten bullets. We had forty and I prayed we didn't need more. As happens when a fight is imminent, my training kicks in, my head clears, my heart restrains itself.

I stared at the enemy blasting closer.

The lead biker slowed, and one by one the bikes lined up side-by-side across the road in the pet walk area. Poor lady with the white mutt was rooted to the earth while the mutt barked its lungs out. The bikers paid no mind. I wanted to run to her and get her out of the way, but I would only put her and the pooch in immediate danger. I hunkered behind the bike with Lake, waiting for their move. The pooch lady, having recovered her wits, picked up the dog and scurried behind the palm tree.

The White Stallions revved their motors, but didn't roll forward. I spied black flags fluttering behind the riders and assumed the white blotch on the flag was the likeness of Juan Torres, their fallen comrade; one that I'd caused to fall, and one that four Wild Bloods stomped to death. All were now in jail. One of those was Switch's brother. Unlike me and my part in the killing, they hadn't gotten FBI preferential treatment. *Why the hell was I thinking this when the shooting was seconds away?*

They drew their guns, about a dozen of them, firing bullets that popped and barked off concrete and asphalt. Lake held his fire, and so did I. So did the Wild Blood members. Lesson one: in a gunfight never waste ammunition. Unless one of them brought out a bazooka, they weren't close. For fifteen seconds guns literally blazed.

Then Rassler and Switch mounted their bikes. So did the others. Rassler pulled out, then Switch. They led their pack toward the Stallions. There was a pause before the face-off started, neither club close enough to do damage to human or bike.

I slumped below the back saddle. Were these bastards really intent on killing each other? Or just intimidating one another? It was craziness, these angry men, shooting up a parking lot. It was my fault that these men played at war—men that wore stupid patches, spouted mindless killer creeds, had misogynistic philosophies, ridiculous nicknames and demonic club names. Bah, testosterone-laden adolescent males playing shoot-'em-up games. I'd killed men before and been shot at. This wasn't war; this was showing off.

This was—oh, I don't know—eerily surreal. A waste of ammunition; combat without hostilities. Then I got it. No one wanted to die on this sunny day, in this public place. No one had the heart to kill.

The firing paused again. That's when I heard sirens.

Lake said, "Up, let's get going."

We mounted and Lake ignited the pistons.

Wild Blood, being closest to the exit, led the retreat, without Lake and me.

The Stallions flew past, then Lake, like a bat out of hell, took off with a wheelie and a rush. There was no formation, just a couple dozen bikers getting out of dodge before the sheriff's posse caught up.

Lake stayed well behind the Stallions until they quickly regrouped and shot off the next exit—to head south, I hoped.

We caught up with Wild Blood and I blew out a relieved breath. I didn't hear sirens yet, but they would be on us soon.

Rassler gave the word on the radio: "Scatter. Two-by-two off exits. One right, one left. Hail."

I couldn't see him, but I pictured his right fist to upper chest.

Nobody down; no disabled bikes. I began to laugh and then I heard Lake laugh, actually giggle, through Bluetooth. He said, "That was fun."

He actually said that? My Lake? A testosterone-laden adolescent male?

At the next few exits, a couple of our band of reluctant warriors swung off to go in opposite directions. The sheriff and the highway patrol were going to have a helluva time pinning anything on any biker, particularly if those who took pot shots had the good sense to toss their weapons in the nearest river or pond. Lake had a potential problem if caught. He was a cop, although neither he nor I had fired a shot. No bullets, no matching rifling.

"You have a dilemma, my love," I said.

"Don't I know it," he said, a lilt in his voice. Gone was the surliness. "It's you."

"And I'm not talking."

We went home over north Florida's back roads into southwest Georgia and finally ventured onto I-85 near Fort Benning where Lake gassed up.

Afterward, sitting in a burger joint eating, I called Web.

"The FBI is looking for you two," he said.

"I guess so."

"One Grady Locke wants your heads. You got something that belongs to him?"

"Not anymore."

"I still don't know where you are."

"He asks, you've heard from me. Better yet, call him back and tell him that he'll find what he's looking for on the Okeechobee Street ramp onto 95 heading north. Clear."

"Clear."

Lake folded the paper over the last bite of his second half-pound burger and rose. "Let's ride."

I didn't want the rest of my burger anyway.

Thirty seconds after we got rolling, my cell played Mozart. I answered, "Yes, Grady. What's new with you?"

"You shouldn't have."

"That's my thought, too. You shouldn't have."

"If I don't find that tracker . . ."

"Tell it to the Attorney General."

"Is it too much to hope it wasn't you in the rest stop shooting?"

"Never fired a shot. Our escorts were out to rattle their sabers. A regular Mexican stand-off. Is that okay to say to a Fed?"

"This is serious, Miss Dru."

"Just Dru is fine. Like before. Like when you invited me to dinner."

I think Grady was grinding his teeth. He asked, "When will you be in Atlanta?"

"Some time this evening."

"We need to talk right away. You know where the bureau office is?"

"Not tonight. Gonna soak my sore butt."

"You need to check in with me. I'm your handler."

"Aren't you special."

Lake was pointing at his own chest.

I said, "Let's meet at the International. Lake will be with me."

"Watch yourselves. They're all still out there, including those you consider your friends." He added, "Oh, by the way, you've still got an escort. Switch and Rassler don't want to see anything happen to their old lady."

"I'm not their old lady."

"You should have heard their radio chatter. See you this evening."

I ended the connection and spoke to Lake. "It seems the Feds are intercepting Rassler's and Switch's phone calls."

"They shouldn't have been talking on public radio."

I took a deep breath. "I don't want to be anyone's old lady."

"That's a high compliment, my girl."

"Not when bikers prostitute their old ladies."

"Only if the ol' lady wants to work for the cause. Our values aren't the same, but they do have them. One is that if someone saves his life, he will sacrifice to the death to save that person from harm. In this case, that's you."

"Then I'd better do my best to keep them on the straight and narrow."

"No ratting on the Feds. You'll lose your license and go to jail."

Lake had gotten over his mad, evidently. He was positively chatty. I said, "I didn't ask for this. I just acted to stop a killing."

"Conversely, their rivals have a target on your back for killing a scum brother."

"I wounded him. Wild Bloods killed him, or rather he committed suicide. What did he think was going to happen once he started firing?"

"He was a kid, a probe, looking for the fast track to full cut and colors."

"Is this the time to comment on Hog Heaven?"

"Enjoy the ride," Lake said.

I'd almost unwound by listening to the mellow voice of Norah Jones when Lake interrupted on the headset. "Our company's closer now, meeting at West Point. Rassler on lead, Switch in the middle, Michelin as sweep."

"You communicated with Rassler on public mobile radio?"

"I paired Bluetooth to his Android."

"I can't let you out of my sight."

"If there's going to be a war, I want people around me who are determined to save your ass."

"You hunks of testosterone had your chances at the rest stop. I'm relaxing with Norah Jones."

"You have a road name." He swooped the bike between Switch and Michelin.

"I can't wait to hear it."

"Wonder Woman."

"I like it."

"You'll always be Hippolyta to me."

I once persuaded Lake to see Shakespeare's *Midsummer Night's Dream*. Since then, when the situation calls for it, he calls me Hippolyta, Queen of the Amazon warriors. As Hippolyta says in the bard's comedy, *"This is the silliest stuff I ever heard."*

CHAPTER FIFTEEN

We walked into the International Lounge on West Peachtree Street. The International is a good place to meet because no one cares what you're wearing, be it an outfit out of "Scheherazade" or looking like you warmed your hands over a barrel under a bridge. Lake and I in our leathers and jeans wouldn't turn a head. Grady sat at a round booth in the corner smoking a cigar. A straight-up martini glass was at hand. This was one of the few places in Atlanta where smoking was allowed due to a special license given to martini and cigar bars. In the back was a cool room filled with cigars from the corners of the globe.

Grady wore his Fed duds, and no one seemed to wonder why a biker and his chick were meeting with law enforcement. Winter in Atlanta brings out the costume in everyone. And this lounge was every bit as international as its name. In the booth catawampus from us sat a man wearing a flat old-fashioned golfer hat and a kilt. The woman he was with was Indian—assumedly since she wore a sari and had a dot on her forehead.

I looked down at Grady. "Did you get it?"

He couldn't have looked madder. "Miami did. That was a juvenile thing to do."

"What judge would okay a tap for someone in protective custody?"

"You weren't in physical custody. I let you ride with a policeman, but I wanted to keep tabs on you."

"Like I was going where?"

He rolled the cigar in his mouth. "Wherever your quirky mind takes you."

Lake scooted into the booth opposite Grady and I sat next to Lake. The Indian woman across the way seemed to be paying attention to me. I grinned. She beamed back.

"Are those two our new tails?" I asked.

Grady slaked the cigar tip against the deep ash tray in front of him. "You'd joke at your own funeral."

Lake said, "I'm tired, Grady. I'll write up an account of the shootout, but it was a stupid show and a waste of bullets."

"A hundred and ten rounds and still counting," Grady said, sticking the cigar back in his mouth.

"And that was just the semi-auto handguns," Lake said. "There were some revolvers and I heard an illegal automatic. A Trejo pistol, if I'm not mistaken, using twenty-two calibers. It fires in bursts rather than one continuous stream." Lake was a firearms expert and he once told me that a Trejo pistol is illegal in the U.S. It's made in Mexico and quite valuable to collectors.

"You're not mistaken," Grady said. "And you're saying with all this shooting going on, you didn't fire?"

He inhaled from the cigar. I hate cigar smoke.

"Nothing to fire at," Lake said. "They were never close enough to hurt or get hurt. Each side would have needed long-barrel assault rifles. Find the guy with the Trejo. I'm sure he wouldn't ditch it."

"From the witnesses, the GBI and state patrol figured where each side was during the shooting. More than five-hundred yards is a long way to wage urban war."

"I left town with Dru. We were on our own until we got company. We didn't start it."

Grady removed the cigar from his face and looked at me. "I need a statement for the U.S. Attorney in Miami. The family of Juan Torres wants to know about the shooting that led to their son's death."

"Their *illegal* son's death."

"They're here on a green card. He snuck in. There might be circumstances."

"I don't care if he was an alien from Mars, I shot him to stop him from killing someone. You were a witness."

"If the U.S. Attorney doesn't have a problem, and I can't see that she would, you're still part of the state's case."

"I've called my lawyer, Grady. That's about all I'm going to say."

"What's your next move with the Trapp murder case?"

Lake said, "My next move on any case is a shower and a bed."

"I hear you," Grady said, sipping his martini. "Keep me informed."

"I never did get with your confidential informant," I said.

"He's still around."

Lake said, "Grady, if you know what this snitch of yours has to tell us, better say it now."

"I have no idea. You understand how CIs work. They look for specifics, but collect a lot of extraneous info." He looked hard at Lake. "I heard one thing, though. There's something rotten at the school the Trapp girl attended. You've got people working that angle, don't you?"

I wondered how long Grady had a tap on Webdog. He wouldn't dare tap Lake.

Grady pretty much shut up after that, so we left him sipping and smoking.

After a shower in Lake's half bath—the kind of shower where you sit in the bathtub and use a spray hose attached to the faucet—I was asleep by the time Lake finished the leftover cake in his frig. When the seven a.m. train from Birmingham woke me, I found Lake had gone, leaving a note. "Missed you last night. You pick the restaurant tonight."

I sat next to Webdog. It was good to get in the office and sit next to my geeky computer genius. He poised his hands over the computer keyboard and rattled the keys. He turned the monitor so that I saw the sheet on Marcus Crane, Juliet's cousin, who, according to Roselyn, had hung himself when he was thirteen. Web said, "There you have it." *It* was a computer copy of the medical examiner's report, not an easy thing to obtain.

"You hacked into the medical examiner's computer?"

"Piece of cake. It should be open records."

"Except for autopsy photos, written reports usually are for law enforcement," I said. "But this was a kid. Why wasn't his report sealed?"

Webdog hunched his shoulders. "Screw-up."

It listed the cause of death as fracture of the hyoid bone, the result of strangulation. Death by misadventure.

Web said, "There's more. According to the Fulton County Sheriff's Incident Report, he also tried to kill Juliet. He left a note, but then the whole thing was turned over to the juvenile courts, and we know who that means."

Web and I exchanged glances. He had created software for Portia's records that he said even he couldn't hack. But I wondered . . .

My immediate call to Portia raised her ire. "Where'd you get that? Webdog didn't hack my files, did he?"

"No, Porsh. He got it from the Fulton County Sheriff's office. They still have the incident report where he tried to kill Juliet before he killed himself."

"Those incompetents should have given me that report to seal. Assholes. Here's what you don't know. Marcus began show-

ing signs of schizophrenia the year before his death. Trapp
forbade him in the house because he was too aggressive toward
Juliet. Marcus started calling the police, accusing Trapp of
molesting Juliet. He wrote a note, tried to drown Juliet and
then—thinking that he had succeeded—hung himself. There
you have it. It's got nothing to do with Juliet's murder."

"I wonder."

"I don't. Now, unless it's relevant, I don't want to hear about
it again."

"I am feeling chastised but I don't know why." I waited.
"Porsh?"

Nothing like an earful of dead air.

Pearly Sue and Web had split the nightclub/cabaret calls and
were both getting the same results. From New Orleans to
Richmond, Virginia, neither club promoters nor show producers
had heard of or interviewed anyone named Margery Williams or
Bunny or Brandle Raddison. No refugee from the acclaimed
Cabaret Artistique had presented a resumé. And no, they didn't
have a young singer with a golden voice, or yes, all their singers
had golden voices.

Lake called and told me that the APD found that Aaron and
John Peters, owners of the Twenty-Four Caret nightclubs, were
not sleazeballs as many nightclub owners are, but respected
businessmen as far as their public persona went. They had
inherited the strip club business from their father who started
out in New Orleans and expanded as cities allowed nude dance
clubs to open. Neither brother had official residences in Atlanta.
"Aaron lives in Natchez. He's forty-five with a wife and three
kids, two at Tulane and one in private school. John is fifty,
divorced and lives in New Orleans. He is the hands-on guy, but
they have a management company that runs the clubs in the
cities where they exist."

Web reported on his three-night forays to the Twenty-Four Caret clubs. "They're all designed along the same line. One long room with a main stage running down the center so men can line up on each side of a stage. There were several poles and dancers on this stage. The back wall has two tiny round stages, big enough to hold one pole and dancer. The places have no windows and are loud. I'm not fond of pink and purple neon and the strobes are bright enough to knock out the eyes. A guy named Zack runs the three locations. He gave me the run, and I talked to a lot of girls."

Nah, better not mention lap dances. "Tough duty, right?"

"Yeah." Web seemed to yearn a little. "There was this one with a Hello Kitty tattoo."

"And?"

"Don't ask me about her brain."

"Any of those nubile lovelies working their way through college?"

"Odd that you should ask. Several claimed they were, though I doubt they had their GEDs."

"No Bunny?"

"Not even a tattoo."

"Wilton?"

"He's a regular at the Decatur club, Zack told me. I saw him. Came by himself. The bouncer said they let him stash his Harley inside the chain link fence by the dumpster."

"They chain link the dumpster?"

"Divers. One died in there."

"What kind of Harley does he own?"

"One of the Dynas."

"Moving on, what else can you tell me?"

"You have a good ride?"

"Wonderful. Still feel a bit saddle sore, though."

"Grady Locke works out of the Memphis Division, is

considered an arrogant ass, but a good agent. Commendations. Divorced, one boy, eleven, cystic fibrosis, lives with Grady's widowed sister, who has two children of her own. Grady owns the house she and the kids live in. Currently dating a prosecutor in Memphis."

"He also owns a Harley-Davidson. Lots of them in this case."

"Lots of people own bikes today. Hog's stock's up like crazy. Fifty percent market share in the U.S."

"You invested?"

"Yeah, when Lieutenant Lake went to buy his second one."

I made an appointment to see Eugene Fetterman. He wasn't delighted, but I insisted on a visit in the afternoon after the last class ended.

The rest of the day was spent visiting Harley-Davidson motorcycle dealerships and used lots to track down a shiny V-Rod. I started in the north Atlanta suburbs, the first on Alpharetta Highway.

I should have had Lake with me. The salesman thought he saw a sucker. I asked for the manager or owner of the dealership. He said they were in a meeting, but he had a sweet little bike for me.

"I'm inquiring about the V-Rod," I said.

His look was incredulous. "Little muscle in your life?"

"How could I go about finding the V-Rod sales records from four or so years back?"

He bobbed his head. "That would be the manager or owner."

"When will they be out of their meeting?"

He looked at his watch. "They'll go directly to lunch. I'd say two o'clock. Can I ask a question?"

"You want to know why I need V-Rod sales records?"

"That's what I'm thinking."

I showed him my identification. "I'm looking for a missing

girl. Child Trace is my agency and I find missing persons."

"She run away on a V-Rod?"

"With a little help from a male friend. How popular is that motorcycle? My friend has an Ultra Classic."

"Lovely machine. Different animal. Your V-Rod ain't a dresser. It ain't called muscle for nothing. I've been riding fifteen years, and I can tell you, I wouldn't buy one. Terrible mileage, can't put your feet where they should be, and besides, it's a beast on the twisties. High maintenance, too."

"I'm looking for a buyer who didn't know much about motorcycles or the life. Kind of a loner who hung around club members asking questions. What they call a rich urban biker."

"Plenty of them around. When did all this happen?"

"Three, four years ago."

"Hmmm. We don't sell a lot of V-Rods, especially to inexperienced riders. We steer them to a more manageable bike. Now if he was experienced, I'd talk up the Wide Glide. Now that's a sweet ride. You don't want to have to massage your butt after an hour's ride, to say nothing of the hot pipes. Jeez."

"Whatever the bike, an inexperienced rider has to learn."

"Best way is bike school."

I knew about the schools. I asked, "People actually go to school to learn to ride a motorcycle?"

He chuckled. "I bet half don't admit it; hell, probably more than half. Bikers see themselves as macho."

Did Lake see himself as macho? Probably, although he was smart enough not to let it show. And was this guy talking about himself, too?

I said, "You know bikers. Do you think someone wanting to join a club would go to a riding school?"

He cackled this time. "If he's under eighteen in this state, he has to get a certificate of attendance at a school to get a Class M license. Over that, well I know some get something like a

Sportster or a beat-up Fat Boy and take it on the back roads. You're going to lay it down while you're learning."

"That's what I'm thinking. If you didn't want to go to school, where's a place around here where you would learn to ride?"

"It's all built up now. Didn't used to be when I was learning. Now, I'd go to the school. Ain't no indignity in that. We're affiliated with a school over Marietta way."

An intrusion of male voices came into the showroom with a whoosh of the door. A glance told me they were management. My salesman broke away and went to talk to the men.

After a few nods, they came to where I stood next to a neat new Sportster.

"What's this I hear," the larger of the two men asked.

I greeted the guarded men and offered my credentials.

"Child Trace, Inc. You're a private investigator?"

"I am."

"You think somebody bought a V-Rod here and kidnapped a child?"

I looked at the salesman and shook my head. "I'm looking for a missing child. It's possible a motorcycle rider might have been . . ."

"We don't show our records without a subpoena." He frowned at the salesman. "Don't know what he told you, but that's how it is."

"I understand." Lord knows how many times this dealership and the manufacturer had been sued. "Your excellent salesman gave me some insight on the V-Rod." I patted the saddle of the Sportster. "This here's more my style." I put away my credentials and said, "Thanks."

He seemed somewhat mollified. "Get the paperwork together and we'll see what we can do."

He knew, of course, I didn't have a chance of convincing a judge to open his sales records on an obvious fishing expedition. Not even with Portia, who was miffed at Webdog and me right now.

On the way to the next dealership, I called Lake. "You take a motorcycle riding course when you started riding?" I asked.

"What?"

"Did you go to motorcycle school?"

He grunted. "Probably should have. Laid my scooter down often enough, but I don't recall knowing there was a school. I was thirteen when I started riding."

"Forgot, you're an old fart."

"APD motorcycle cops go to school. There's all kinds of classes. None of our guys are beginners, but they take experienced rider courses, motorcycle maintenance, trauma. It's good to get a tune-up every once in a while. How'd it go at the dealership?"

"Need a subpoena to let the fingers do the walking."

"Suspicion, word of a biker isn't enough. You didn't name names, did you?"

"You mean like, 'Did a man name of Hoyt Fagan buy a V-Rod from you?' "

"Stupid question, please disregard."

"I suspect I'll find the same stone wall at other dealerships."

"Yep."

And I did. At two others before I gave up.

Biker school intrigued me so I headed for Marietta.

A sign at the gate read:

"Dwight Baines Motorcycle Riding and Racing School. We now offer a Bystander Assistance Program to reduce injuries and fatalities to motorcyclists. Our program is based on the First Responder GA HERO Curriculum. We focus on Trauma rather than First Aid. This program is a must for road captains, tail gunners and group road trips. Logo Patch and CEs for

Professionals."

I was sold on the school already.

I found the owner in a converted horse barn where every kind of motorcycle rested on kick and wheel stands in the main aisle. Dwight Baines shook my hand with force. He was in his early fifties, and had thick white hair and a thin goatee, the kind that reminds me of a billy goat. The school rules were posted on a wall that used to be a hosing-down stall. All students, the sign said, were required to wear over-the-ankles boots with rubber soles, long pants, long sleeves, eye protection and a Georgia Department of Transportation–approved helmet and full-fingered gloves. "Classes convene rain or shine. No refunds for classes missed; no admittance if late for class. A re-scheduling fee will be charged."

Beginner classes began at $350. Another sign read: "Ask about our special racing packages that begin at $650."

I showed Baines my creds and explained my quest. He led me into a small office that was once a tack room with enough room for a desk and two chairs, a credit card machine and a couple of rolling files. I took a seat as did he.

"First off, call me Dwight. I got a good eye for students who will be talented riders and a good eye for those who don't need to go anywhere near a motorcycle. You ride?"

I explained Lake's bikes. "I'm happy to be a passenger."

"You'd be an excellent rider."

I laughed. "You trying to recruit me?"

"I want everyone who even thinks of getting on a motorcycle to train, here or someplace else. Even passengers need training. Passengers can cause confusion to a rider and a wreck if they don't understand the machine."

I told him I was looking for a particular type of rider that may or may not have attended his school and why I was interested in him.

"How far back?"

"Hard to say. I learned that he owned a late-model V-Rod three years ago."

"Tough bike for a starter."

"I don't know that he started on that bike, but I talked to a one-percenter who said this poser with a shiny V-Rod hung around biker bars asking stupid questions. He called him a RUB, you know what that is?"

"He didn't know his name?"

I shook my head.

"Rich urban biker. Pain in the ass. All show. I'd rather run up against a teenager riding a crotch rocket than a RUB. Do I know this one-percenter?"

"Are you one?" I should have guessed sooner that he was widely known and knew a great many riders in the community. As Michelin Dave said, *Bikers have jobs, too, you know.*

He laughed. "I used to ride with a club, but don't any longer." He hadn't answered my question exactly. As the owner of a riding school, maybe he wouldn't want it known that he rode with an outlaw outfit. He went on, "Settled down with a wife and two kids, one in college, one in the Army. It's like the Marines. You never leave the Corps or the club."

"I think the RUB wound up in Chattanooga."

"Wild Blood. Got some problems up there with the Feds."

I told him it was a long story how I came to talk with several of the club members, and that they were willing to tell me what they knew about the Juliet Trapp case since they were suspected in her murder.

"It all comes back," he said, frowning. "I knew a couple of the Atlanta boys she accused."

"That's not exactly true. She didn't accuse a particular person. She told her mother she was riding to Bike Week with Wild Blood."

He shook his head. "At sixteen? Not collectively. Maybe a single member likes young girls. Club doesn't need that kind of trouble. They got the bad apples out and now they get left alone." He leaned back. "Sometimes I want to get away, have a few beers and ogle the dollies with the members, so I take myself to a bar." His grin was crooked, showing cigarette-stained teeth. "As time has passed, it's been less and less. You know, old-times' sake can get maudlin or ridiculous."

I smiled. I liked this guy.

He went on, "There was a lot of talk and anger at the time. You get a club pissed at being accused when they're innocent, well . . . If they done it, they'll admit to it, at least to themselves and each other. They won't admit their bad deeds to the law."

"Or me."

"Someone in the club told you what you needed to know; now you got to put it in place."

"Do you think they actually know who this guy is?"

"Whoever it was told you, they didn't pay attention to the poser because he was a joke. But something about him was off kilter. You have to find out what for yourself."

And that's why I'm here. "The poser stopped coming around suddenly."

He nodded.

I asked, "So, have you a clue?"

"The V-Rod don't ring a bell. I'd remember some poser on that muscle machine. But lot of Harley makes attract posers."

"Maybe he was here on a different machine."

"That'd be my bet. Let me give it some thought. I told you I get a fix on the potential of my students. I've been at this teaching for fifteen years and I can't remember all the way back. I'll have to think on it, even ask around if that's okay with you."

"I was going to ask about other riding schools."

"You got an age for this poser?"

189

"I'm guessing. Not real young, fortyish. Someone who could attract a young girl."

His expression became thoughtful. "You know, talking on this, something's creeping around in my head about what happened to that girl."

Seeing my anticipation, he pressed his lips and shook his head.

CHAPTER SIXTEEN

Dr. Fetterman's greeting was meant to sound as if he didn't know what information he could possibly add to what he'd already told me. I'd told him on the phone that it was a sensitive matter and he seemed perplexed. Now he seemed not to care, as if he'd bulldozed my concerns under the administration building.

I told him about Bunny Raddison showing up in August at Samuel Chapin's nursing home in Naples, Florida, with information about the school that upset Mr. Chapin. A week later Mr. Chapin was dead.

"What information?" Fetterman asked. No lament for the deceased here.

"It concerns Mr. Fagan."

"Hoyt?" He almost gagged on the name. Then he spoke more calmly. "He practically lives in south Florida when school isn't in session, even sometimes when it is. It has to do with horses. I know while there he frequently visited Mr. Chapin—who was elderly and ill, I might point out."

"Mr. Fagan often visited Mr. Chapin before Lawrie Taylor's accident and Juliet Trapp's murder. The girls accompanied him sometimes."

"How is this relevant to today?"

I hate the word *relevant*. "Bunny learned something and went to Mr. Chapin to confide in him."

"That sounds like Bunny being dramatic."

"She also went to see Mr. Fagan at the Wellington stable, where she identified herself as Margery Williams." I hesitated to see if Fetterman connected the name of *The Velveteen Rabbit* author to Bunny, but he showed no signs that he did. "Mr. Fagan was not at the stable."

"Have you addressed whatever concerns you have with Mr. Fagan?"

I said that I had not, that I thought it prudent to talk to the senior principal first in case the matter was or would became delicate.

"I understand what you're saying, but Mr. Fagan lives in his own world and seldom shares much of it with us here. He's an excellent riding master and we're proud of our equestrian program, but beyond that, I know nothing about him."

"Here's what can become *relevant*," I said, putting a bit of emphasis on that overused word. Fetterman's eyebrows curved upward. "We're not the only people looking for Bunny Raddison. She's using an assumed name. Why?"

"I haven't the foggiest. Ask her overrated parents."

Gee, I thought they were the pride of Winters Farm Academy. "The police suspect, and I can say this with certainty, that Bunny Raddison was working in south Florida when she learned something about Winters Farm Academy and sought out Hoyt Fagan. Did Bunny subsequently get in touch with Fagan? We don't know, but we know she went to her old advisor in Naples and upset him with what she'd learned. The police believe, and I include myself in this supposition, that what Bunny saw or heard or read was about this school, rather than Hoyt Fagan. I don't believe she would confront someone she feared."

"I wouldn't bet much on that."

"Why do you say that?"

His eyes appraised me, then he said, "You don't know Bunny." How could I refute that? I asked, "Do you have any idea where Bunny Raddison is today?"

He looked affronted, as if I'd accused him of heretofore lying. "Of course not. I would have alerted the authorities."

I don't think he meant he would have called me. "The police will talk to Hoyt Fagan. Do you have any reason to believe he knows something about this school that could damage its reputation?"

"Damage? Of course not. The steeplechase accident happened well before Juliet Trapp's death. It was something unsanctioned that kids do. Mrs. Taylor and I thought it prudent to tell you about it."

"There could be a revenge aspect to her murder."

"Revenge? Someone killed Juliet Trapp because of a riding accident?"

"It's odd to me that it didn't occur to anyone after she was murdered?"

"No one thought there was a connection. Juliet Trapp was a wild kid who ran off with whatever and whomever took her fancy. Her parents were negligent. They should have taken her car away."

"When I talked to Mr. Stuart, he seemed to admire the wild aspect of her personality."

He rubbed his forehead. "We all have different personalities; even as educators. We don't think alike. Mr. Stuart has his opinions."

"Did he encourage her to take these flights of fancy?"

"Of course not. Mr. Stuart, if you'll forgive me bringing up a tragedy in his life, is somewhat constrained by his own accident. He would admire someone who was free to be adventurous. One would like to think one's appearance has no impact on how people see and perceive us. The truth is the flawless have an easier time than the flawed. And Mr. Stuart, by virtue of a horrific accident, is horribly flawed."

"I'm intrigued by certain aspects of his personality."

"What's that?" he asked sharply.

"He rides a motorcycle."

He looked at the ceiling then back at me. "What are you implying?"

"He was almost killed in a car crash. Yet he's taken on more risk."

"Maybe risk to him means something different than it does to you. Perhaps he feels he's had more than his share of bad luck."

"Or maybe he doesn't care about life any longer."

"I'm not a psychiatrist, Miss Dru."

"Nor am I. I guess it's more logical given his circumstance—and what you've said about the flawed—that he frequents strip joints."

"Miss Dru . . ."

"I don't care about his sexual tastes . . ."

"I would hope not."

". . . but his actions could disgrace or damage the school."

"Poor Wilton. Your perception of him has sunken to this."

I'd either truly disgusted him or he was a pretty good actor.

He said, "Is there anyone else you would like to excoriate here?"

"There's always the chance that Bunny's sudden discovery has to do with Mr. Fagan himself, as you pointed out, and not the school. Mr. Fagan is known to love the ladies."

"If you are suggesting . . ."

"Just wondering is all, like I wonder if Mr. Fagan had or has taken up with any of the female staff at WFA."

"That's ridiculous."

"Or maybe with the wife of one of the staff, past or present?"

"Where are you going with this preposterous guessing game?"

"Dr. Fetterman, don't you understand this school and its instructors, and masters, and principals are undergoing scrutiny?"

"Because of what some hare-brained drama queen thinks she saw or heard?"

"The questions come back to why Bunny Raddison is running all over the U.S. in hiding. Her voice is magnificent and she is a lovely girl. Why isn't she promoting herself and advancing her career?"

"You think she's in danger?" He rose. "If she is, it's not from anyone at this institution. Talk to her nutty parents. If she's hiding from anyone, it would be them. She's competition for the mother." He came around the desk. "You have raised some provocative questions. Juliet's murder isn't about the school; it's about her running off with strangers, possibly those in a motorcycle gang, and . . ."

"Doesn't have to be a gang, Dr. Fetterman."

"There's new evidence of that. Read the newspapers."

Apparently he was referring to Geoff Howard. I said, "It's looking more like a solo rider. A club like Wild Blood wouldn't have a pedophile in its ranks. It's more likely that a school would."

He winced. "Don't you people even try to connect anything of the kind to Wilton Stuart or Hoyt Fagan, who both ride motorcycles. As friends and colleagues, they often ride together."

"One thing I don't think is that either is a pedophile. And they may have had more in common than motorcycle riding."

He flared his shoulders as if I was going to speak of naked women and pole dancing.

"I've got an appointment now," he said, rushing to the door and turning the knob. He looked back at me. "Don't concern yourself with this school's reputation, and Bunny Raddison will show herself with a tale taller than any you've ever heard."

With that I could agree. If she was able.

It was five thirty when I got back to the office.

First item, Wilton Johns Stuart had left a message for me.

Second item, Pearly Sue came in and announced that Webdog had taken excellent care of her cats and that she was taking them home. A sniff around the room told me that Webdog had taken care, at least to change the cat litter. My nose is very sensitive to odors, especially rank ones like that which used cat boxes give off.

Third item, while I spoke with Dr. Fetterman, Webdog was digging into his background. Pretty solid academically. English Literature, with a specialty in Shakespeare; a master's degree in Greek History and a doctorate in Higher Education and Administrational Leadership. He was thirty-eight, married with no children. His wife was an ordained minister in the Episcopal church. Dr. Fetterman was also in charge of the Sunday school curriculum.

"There's got to be a skeleton," Pearly Sue said. "I'm good at sniffing skeletons out of pious closets."

"Go for it," I said.

I punched Lake's number. He answered, "Hi doll, where we going for dinner?"

"I'll cook pasta."

"Your house it is."

"Did you find Fagan?"

"He's fox hunting."

"I wouldn't have thought . . ."

"Or rather coyotes. They don't run down cute little red foxes any longer; the hounds are after Wiley Coyote."

"Where?"

"Wisackee Farms twenty miles south of Americus. He left

word on his voice mail."

"Nice of him to keep us informed."

"All persons of interest should—solely for our convenience."

"Want me to go?"

"You'll probably pass each other on Interstate 75. The hunt is over tomorrow."

"I think we should use the cat-and-mouse approach when he gets back."

"Your approach has upset a mouse."

I let this sink in. "Fetterman already reported me?"

"Yep, he invited me to his suite of offices to clarify some misconceptions you laid before him."

"Tattletale."

"He uninvited you to ever, ever set foot in his realm again."

I summed up what Web had found on Eugene Fetterman, and Lake asked, "Do I have to kiss his ring and genuflect?"

"While on your knees, take a chunk of the anatomy at the end of his back."

"Just for you, my sweet. Now, to the important event of the day. What wine should I purchase?"

"Come empty-handed. I know just the cabernet."

My return call to Wilton Johns Stuart went to the answering machine. I gave up trying when I reached the parking lot of the wine store.

Lake can boil water and pasta. There was a period of time between his separation and divorce from Linda Lake that he lived alone, or mostly alone. I'm guessing there were women in his life who may or may not have hung their clothes in his closets before me, but we don't discuss that. Anyway, during that period he ate spaghetti—with marinara sauce, meatballs from the grocery's freezer, Alfresco, with clams and garlic, pesto and sometimes plain butter. Ragu and friends kept him alive. If there was a leafy green in his life I don't know about it. Yet, like me, he is a health and exercise fanatic. Tonight I was preparing my favorite sauce, which is a Bolognese. A round table for four sits in a corner off my small kitchen. We toasted and Lake got busy with the fork and twirls. He's very adept.

We finished two bottles of a medium-priced cabernet sauvignon without talking about the case. For the first time in weeks, I didn't even think about it. Lake pushed back after blueberry shortcake from the freezer. "Umm, that was wonderful. Reminds me of my bachelor days."

"So who, back in your halcyon days, made Bolognese sauce for your spaghetti?" I asked.

"I have to say bologna's not bad in marinara sauce. I didn't think of that back when I was cheffing for myself."

I grinned. "What I cheffed up was not a marinara sauce; it was a real ragu. A ragu is a meat sauce with tomato, it is not a tomato sauce with meat. You can use different meats like Italian sausage or pork. I used pancetta, veal and chuck. Heavy cream adds a touch of richness." I looked at his plate and the empty bowl of Bolognese. "I think we've had this discussion before."

He reached over and put a finger on my chin. "I know the sauce comes from Bologna, Italy, and you make the classic rendition using goat's cream."

"Fooled you. I didn't have goat's, so I used cow's."

"I wondered why the taste was off."

I touched his shin beneath the table, twisted my mouth and stared without batting a lash.

"Susanna's coming Saturday," Lake said. "Hopefully we'll be speaking by then."

His liquid brown eyes had a habit of splitting my heart down its seams. "Maybe."

He stood and pulled me up. "I love you, Moriah Dru. I truly do." He pushed hair off my forehead and kissed me there. Then my nose, and a cheek. Standing in my bright kitchen, the man I love hugging his body to mine, my sweater began to expend and contract with my breathing. He kissed my mouth, his body as tight as a bow string.

"Lovemaking before dishwashing?" I said, pulling my face six inches from his.

"Your call," he said, his voice already husky. "Which is more important?"

At four thirty in the morning when I woke, Lake was gone. Since Lake brews barely drinkable coffee, I was happy that he didn't have time to go through the coffee-making routine. Staring at the dishes on the table and the pots in the sink—it's at times like these I wished I'd chosen the alternative. But then, swamped by a wave of memory, my heart ker-thumped while I scraped plates and pots and thrust them into the dishwasher.

Back in the my bedroom, I dressed in flannel lounging pajamas and looked forward to two cups of very strong hot coffee. Out of habit, I flipped on a local news channel and walked into the short hall that led to the living room. My cottage was what they call a double-shotgun house. You walked in the front door from a wooden porch, entered the living room, went through an arched double doorway into a dining room. On from there, a single door led into the kitchen. There was an outside locking door at the back of the kitchen by the refrigerator that led onto a summer kitchen or mud room, or both. On the west side of the house, two bedrooms were aligned, separated by a bathroom big enough for a pregnant gnat.

At the end of the hall, before I turned for the kitchen, I glanced left into the living room and saw street lights from the half-open blinds. I paused in the dining room. I'd left the kitchen light on and I didn't hear noise, but a vague awareness caused my stomach muscles to coil and knot. I trod slowly through the dining room into the kitchen. I didn't expect there to be anyone and there wasn't. But there was an alien smell . . . I inhaled deeply. The scent was oily, faintly smoky, reminding me of frankincense . . .

Before I took another step, Ski Mask popped from the hidden side of the refrigerator, a knife extending from a gloved hand.

Taki, my instructor, was in my ear. *There is no dishonor in retreat to give yourself time to collect your thoughts, gain footing, attain and adjust a defensive stance.*

I was in a confined space; his rush was aggressive. Dressed in a long-sleeved shirt and pants, no jacket, he was my height but had me by twenty pounds. He held the knife in his right hand. His head, swathed in the ski mask, angled as if his aggression faltered. That I hadn't turned to flee seemed to confuse him. I broke retreat and moved to my left at the same moment he lunged. The knife passed close by. I gripped his right arm. We were almost shoulder to shoulder as I held his attack hand at my side, the knife still firmly in his glove. Before I could get him in an arm lock, I had to dodge his throat thrust and nearly went down when he pushed a foot against the back of my knee. He was also skilled in Korean techniques.

Together, we careened against the small island, sending a bowl of fruit clanging to the floor. Now the knife blade was waist high, the blade lying flat. I had him pinned so that he couldn't get the edge turned to cut me. We wrestled half standing—tugging, pulling, breathing hard. Then he twisted so that his free hand could circle my neck. His half-turn allowed me to sling my left leg back as far as I could. Slouching at the knees, I turned my body away from him. He tightened his grip. I turned my side to his chest and swung my arm up and over his choking arm while I twisted and turned, using my foot to pivot away. I slammed my bent elbow into his neck.

He yelled and reared backward. The knife clattered to the floor. "Bitch!"

Making himself a battering ram, he came at me.

I backed away, far enough for a roundhouse kick, one of the easiest against a head-on attacker. No need for a spinning hook or back kick. I lifted my leg, snapped my knee and kicked his head with the sole of my foot. Barefoot, it hurt like hell.

Momentarily stunned, he staggered. And I had misjudged my equilibrium. While my body was off balance he rushed me. I'd need to regain posture and stability, pivot and do a spinning back kick, but I was too close to the wall and the stove. I reached to grab his mask. I wanted to see my attacker. He grabbed my arm and hit my head with his fist, and before I got in a position to clip a knee, he pushed me against the island and ran. He stumbled over a small step ladder he'd overturned, giving me time to reach for his shirt collar. He whirled, his wide eyes filling the ski mask—and unmistakably filled with murderous intent and pain. I straightened my fingers, held them close together, thumb in, and struck his upraised arm with the pinkie edge of my hand. I'd hit a nerve in my hand and felt the zing up to my elbow. It was momentarily too numb for the fight. There was a millisecond when our eyes locked. I'd recovered enough to back off two steps, focus and correct my stance for another roundhouse, this time to the gut. But he whirled and ran for the back door.

His footsteps thundered down the back steps and over the deck. He'd come through my neighbor's yard, pushing through a jungle of magnolias and overgrown azaleas, and would return the same way, over to the next street. Standing on the deck, breathing out slowly to drain the adrenaline, I watched as thin streams of milk flowed into the night sky.

Nothing like a few Korean kicks and chops before coffee.

★ ★ ★ ★ ★

"That settles it," Lake said after he told me crime-scene techs were on the way to take control of the knife and go over the scene, which was my house. "You're not out of my sight until I find that bastard."

"*We* find that bastard."

"I should have anticipated this."

"That my attacker keeps his movements fluid at a dojang? I've got to get back to Taki. I'm rusty."

"He could be a paid killer."

"He wasn't cold enough."

"Huh?"

"He smelled."

"He fart or something?"

"He might as well have. Testosterone and adrenaline tend to accentuate body soap or perfume. That's not cold-blooded."

"Perfume?"

"You know, after-shave or cologne, something you eschew—not the testosterone or adrenaline, of course. The man reeked like a funeral at a Catholic church."

"Dru. Be serious. This isn't his last go at you."

"I am serious, and I suspect the same. I wonder what I know that I don't know?"

"He thinks you are a danger to him."

"I hope to be, once I know what he thinks I know."

"Would you get dressed and come to the shop."

"No, I'm going to pay a visit to Wilton Johns Stuart."

"That could be the lion's den."

"I don't think an educator attacked me right after you left. And you know what that means?"

"Your attacker was watching."

"I hate being spied upon."

"Take care of yourself and keep in touch. We can meet for lunch."

"I'm glad your appetite wasn't ruined."

Chapter Seventeen

Stopping for donuts first, I went by my office before heading north to Winters Farm Academy. I recognized what was causing my nerves to jump like they'd neared an open flame. Post-adrenaline survival letdown. Add to that, second-guessing what I should have done. I should have gotten him in an inside close lateral instead of an outside, a better move in the quarters that was my kitchen. As a technique it was sound, but, worse, I wasn't fast enough to get him in an arm lock. I wanted to see the bastard's face, and for that fraction of a second, I lost focus. I was serious when I told Lake it was back to the dojang and Taki for a tune-up. I don't fancy myself much more than competent at martial arts, and don't have an advanced-degree belt. I know the moves I'll need for attacks upon me or someone in danger—the chops, kicks, locks, thrusts—and I know that to be effective they must surprise and/or happen fast. To keep tuned, I needed Taki.

While mulling the missed opportunity to unmask my attacker, I kept watch behind me. I didn't see an obvious tail, but Peachtree Street in the morning is a wacky maze of lane-changing speeders and ancient creepers. My attacker probably knew where my office was. As a private detective I've had my share of tailing. I like to know everything about a subject and his or her habits so I don't have to park at a lot or curb while someone sits in an office for four hours before lunch break.

I thought I'd be in first, but Webdog was at his computer and

Pearly Sue beat me by enough time to make a pot of coffee in a kitchenette that she'd decorated like something out of the tea room in a miniature dollhouse. Cute, cute, and even cuter.

I stuck my head in and said good morning.

"Miss Dru!" Pearly responded like she hadn't seen me in a year.

"You're bright and early," I said. "Put a double load in that maker, will you?"

"I always do for you," she said, adding another heaping scoop. I sat at the ice cream table, surrounded by white wrought iron chairs with fancy blue gingham pillows.

Pearly sat across from me. "I went to church last night."

I held back a snarky remark. Pearly Sue is so wonderfully Southern in all she does, but beneath the exterior is a penetrating, somewhat nasty mind. She'll waste words but at the end of the chatter she delivers the verbal coup.

"Do you want to know where?" she asked.

"You're Baptist, aren't you?"

"Yes I am, and I'm here to tell you that most of us dance and sing and take strong drink, but that's not where I went. I went to Grace of God Episcopal."

"Ah, I'm on your wave link now. What is Dr. Fetterman's wife's name?"

"She is The Very Reverend Sharon Fetterman. In our church at home our pastor is called Pastor Stokes or Preacher Stokes. These fancy churches have different kinds of reverends. A Reverend is an everyday ordained clergyman. A Very Reverend has a higher office but is not a bishop or abbot or abbess. I bet people in First Baptist have no idea what an abbess is, except it could be an abscess." She giggled, looked at my waiting expression, then pressed on. "Then you've got the Right Reverends. They are bishops and other high muckedy-mucks. Most Reverend is an archbishop."

"Did you speak to The Very Reverend Sharon Fetterman?"

"I did. The service was short and only thirteen people were there. Thirteen, I sure don't like to be in a place where there's only thirteen people. When you can't divide a number, it's not a good number."

What about dividing it by one, I wondered, but skipped the mention because it could take a while. "How did you approach The Very Reverend?"

"Well, Webdog told me that the Trapps were Episcopalians at the Grace of God so I told her that I was an investigator with Child Trace and we were looking into the death of Juliet Trapp. She was so sad to hear that, not that I was investigating, but that Juliet Trapp had been murdered and her killer was still on the loose."

"What did she say about Juliet?"

"A troubled girl who was looking to find her identity. Brandle Raddison also went to the church. Her parents used to, but that was before they became famous actors. The Very Reverend said that she only met them once. She's only been at the church for five years since she married Gene. That's what she calls Dr. Fetterman."

Which I thought was only right, since that was his name.

She went on, "They met in Louisville where she's from and he lived for a while. He was a summer school teacher in her town, and they met at an ice cream social that summer before he went back to school to get his doctorate. They kept in touch and then got married. Isn't that a lovely story?" I nodded, thinking it rather usual. I got up to pour two cups of coffee and she continued, "She said that poor Mrs. Trapp came to church, but didn't participate in the array of social programs the church provides for parishioners. She talked a little about *the confused* and how the church had volunteer therapists that could help those who'd *lost their way*. Get what I'm saying?"

"The Very Reverend thought Mrs. Trapp drank too much."

Pearly Sue bobbed her head. "She said how awful that Mr. Trapp had killed hisself up in Chattanooga and that she prayed for his soul. She said that she and Gene were in Chattanooga at that time for an Episcopal Women in Clergy conference. Did you know that traditionalists still don't like women preachers?" I nodded. "Then Dr. Fetterman came in and The Very Reverend introduced me. He turned three shades of green and said that he'd said all he was going to say to private detectives about the Trapp case and gave his wife a hard stare. In church even. And *her* a woman of God. Then he left and she stood up and said it was nice talking to me and that she hoped we found the killer and Bunny. She really liked Bunny."

Dr. Fetterman as Robert Thomas Trapp? Not according to the funeral director's description of the imposter.

My cell rang. Lake. "Where are you?" he asked.

Pearly Sue waved her fingers at me and left with her coffee.

I said, "The office, about to bandage my ear."

"Pearly Sue."

I gave him a Pearly Sue précis and he said, "I had an officer check his background. He's thirty-eight and been married five years. Lot of time to develop bad habits."

"It wasn't he who attacked me, and so far, there's no motorcycle in his background."

"He doesn't have one licensed in this state. He owns a Jeep Cherokee and a Dodge car. He's not a native Georgian. He was born in Akron, Ohio. No record. No fingerprints in his name. As you know, private school staff do not have to be fingerprinted."

"That's due to change."

"He'd be grandfathered, unless he gets into trouble."

"Speaking of fingerprints, have you examined the knife my attacker dropped on the kitchen floor?"

"Techs on the scene found only smears. It is an expensive hunting knife, handy for gutting deer." He didn't need to tell me that. I'd shuddered over it while I waited for the forensic crew. "It's off to the lab for DNA. Normally we wouldn't send it, but since it was used in an attempt to murder one of APD's favorite ex-policewomen, it'll get some tender loving. We'll get a report sometime in June."

I passed the topiary lion, giving it a thumbs-up. His barber had done a fine job on his leafy green mane.

After several minutes—as I was about to give up and go around back, maybe down to the river and wait until Roselyn came to sit—the door opened. Lois gave me a small, sad smile. "Not too good today, Miss Dru."

"I just have a quick question."

"Miss Roselyn is sleeping."

"Can I ask you something?"

"Well, we sign a form at our agency that we don't tell on our clients."

"I don't want gossip on how many pills Mrs. Pritchett takes a day. I'm looking into the relationship of two people who are dead. You practically live in this house. I want your perspective."

"That's why you came?"

"I will ask you the same question I would ask Mrs. Pritchett if I could."

"Come in then."

I said, "Let's sit under the arbor over there."

"I must be quick. Miss Roselyn might awake at any time."

"We will be."

She sat on the white slats like she was ready to propel herself off the bench at the notion of madam's awakening.

I said, "After Mr. Trapp sold his business, at some period of time he moved to Chattanooga. Our investigation shows that he likely went up there to learn who killed Juliet. There's a motorcycle club called Wild Blood. They have an Atlanta affiliate. Juliet said that she was riding to Florida with Wild Blood. Why did he think it was the Chattanooga club and not the Atlanta club?"

She looked like I'd said a mouthful in Swahili and was translating each word in her head. "The police talked to the Atlanta gang," she said.

"True and came up with no suspects. Not a hint. Why would he pick Chattanooga? Because it was the closest Wild Blood chapter to Atlanta?"

"You know, there was talk about that town. I remember . . ." Her mental internals were whirring.

"Yes," I urged.

She bit her lip, still unsure. "Well, you know they used to write these notes . . ."

"Who's they, and what notes?"

"Miss Juliet and Mr. Trapp. They said more with notes than with their own voice boxes. He'd write her a note before going to work and she'd write back. Poor Miss Roselyn . . ." Lois's mouth turned down. "She felt cut out."

Maybe that's why she never told me about the notes.

Lois sat blinking as if wondering if she'd betrayed her mistress. She couldn't have looked more guilty than if she'd inadvertently told me about an illegitimate child. I couldn't promise to keep her confidence, but I mealy-mouthed by saying, "Mrs. Pritchett said as much to me. How was their relationship, father and daughter?"

She apparently decided this question was all right. "Unusual in a way, but they got along good, usually when Miss Roselyn wasn't around. She has her expectations. Her ways, you know?"

"We all do, Miss Lois. Perfectly normal."

"Yes."

Dare I ask? "Where are these notes?" I held my breath against hope.

"He used to save them in a safe drawer in his office. It locks."

I let pent-up air leave my lungs. Hoarders have their place, especially in investigations. "You said there was talk about Chattanooga?"

"One morning, it wasn't long before—well, before she passed—that Mr. Trapp asked Miss Roselyn when was Miss Juliet's field trip to Chattanooga. Miss Roselyn didn't have a notion what he was talking about. He said like, 'Never mind, I'll call the school. Her note didn't say when.' "

"I need to see these notes," I said.

"They're not here anymore." Talk about feeling let down. Then she said, "I believe they're in Miss Roselyn's safe deposit box at the bank. I drove her there the day they buried Miss Juliet. She keeps things there she never looks at again."

Wilton Johns Stuart stared at me when I came into his office. His ruined face was more disconcerting than the first time I'd been here, which happened to be the only time I'd seen or spoken to him in person. I'd tried to schedule a sit-down with him for a few follow-up questions that came to mind, but he was always busy. Too busy even to talk on the phone. Which always makes one wonder.

With his face framed by hostility, my cordial greeting fell on deaf and deformed ears.

"Sit down, Miss Dru."

I sat like a chastised student.

"You are attempting to defame me."

"Not true," I said.

"My private life is my business; not yours or the senior principal's."

"Is that why you don't teach in public schools?"

He nearly spit. "Whys and wherefores of what I do is also my business."

"You must understand, even if you don't want to, that when we at Child Trace investigate a crime or suspicious disappearance, we investigate everyone, and that includes everyone, going back to diaper days. Sometimes to get information we have to ask hurtful questions—to those we're talking to and those we're speaking of." I gave him my best contrite look. "Sorry I ended my sentence with a preposition, but that's how it came out."

He lowered his eyes to stare at slender scarred hands that were folded neatly on his desk. I watched anger melt into sadness. "You can't possibly understand," he said. He looked up. "I was a nice-looking man, not handsome, but I had my share of girlfriends since grade school. I married the wrong woman. She didn't like this school. She didn't like kids. Maria was a beautiful woman, and she constantly told me that I could make something of myself if I quit this low-paying job and became a stockbroker. I inherited money, Miss Dru, but not enough for her. Because I inherited, I pursued teaching, which had become the most satisfying thing I'd ever done. I am not cut out for business. I love to learn and to share what I've learned with others. Young people thirst for knowledge, even the slackers, if you present it right." He unfolded his hands and sat back. "After the accident, I returned to the classroom, but my appearance put students and parents off. As a freak, I was no longer effective as a teacher, so I became an advisor to those who hadn't an aversion to such grotesquery." He paused a second, maybe for me to placate his shattered psyche.

Then he continued. "We should have divorced after the honeymoon was over. I tried to make a go of it, but after several years we found ourselves in separate sleeping quarters. After that, I had a few flings. She didn't want me, but she didn't want me enjoying anyone else." He sighed and pressed his lips. "I

211

wish I had died in that crash. I wish I was man enough to end it here and now, but I can't stand the thought of the grave."

"Yet you ride a motorcycle, and I've seen your maneuvers."

"Maybe someday a careless driver will hit me, and it will be over."

"Do you know where Bunny Raddison is?"

He hesitated, a sure sign he knew and was going to lie. He said, "I used to. She went to New York after Juliet's death. She left a note for me. She loved writing notes. She and Juliet were always writing notes and texting, like if things didn't come from the mouth, it didn't count as conversation, and they couldn't be held accountable. It was Juliet who, in essence, told me that."

The same way it was with her father.

"What did Bunny's note say?"

"I was debating whether to show it to you after your initial visit here. I didn't lie about being busy when you called those times. I could have made time for you, but I was and am still debating whether to show you a personal note to me. It has certain implications. Then, of course, came your trashing of me to Dr. Fetterman, of all sanctimonious people."

"While you continue to debate with yourself about handing me the note, which I strongly suggest that you do . . ." I stopped when he smiled. It was a nice closed-mouth spreading of the lips, the smile of a once good-looking man who'd participated in his own repulsion. "Would you elaborate on Dr. Fetterman's sanctimoniousness?"

"You don't quit, do you Miss Dru? Everyone's grist." I waited. "The Jewish have a word for it. Chutzpah. Are you Jewish, Miss Dru?"

"Not that I know of, and my family's devoted to ancestry. Plain ol' Irish Catholic forwardness."

He turned sideways in his chair, then looked over his

shoulder. "I should offer you something to drink. My own throat is dry."

"I'm good. I won't take up much more of your time."

"I will have all the time in the world now. I will resign after I give you the note."

"You're kidding."

"I have few pleasures left. Yes, I frequent strip clubs. You get to know the regulars, become a regular yourself, and it's like a fraternity of like-minded men." *Like cops and motorcycle clubs.* "After your conversation with Dr. Fetterman, he called me in. He is appalled at the idea of me having a lap dance—a wounded teacher who creeps out half the students—daring to dishonor *his* school. Since my accident, I've helped more strippers than I'll ever help students again. Those young women give me pleasure, and I return the favor. Now, don't think I'm a fool. I know they like my money and what it can buy them—from breast implants to groceries." He waved a hand. "Smack, too, probably. I'm beyond caring."

When I was with the APD, I'd sat across from a dismemberment killer while he dispassionately described his method. I didn't feel as chilled as I did now.

He said, "I am a self-inflicted failure."

I wasn't going near that analysis. "I thought before the accident you were going broke, and that's one of the reasons your wife was leaving you."

"Not so. You can look into my financials and investments. My wife wanted more than the plentiful allowance I gave her, and so she spread rumors that I was gambling and drinking and whoring away *our* money. She was one of those who would always want more."

"You collected insurance on her, didn't you?"

"Yes, if it's any of your business."

He'd said it so mildly I couldn't feel put off. Not that I would be. "You don't have to tell me. I can find out."

"Seven hundred and fifty thousand."

And no one to spend it on but strippers.

He opened his middle drawer and took out the folded piece of pink paper and handed it over. He'd kept it handy, and it showed wear where it had been opened and closed many times. I smiled when I saw bunnies lined up at the top and her name. The note read:

> *I'm out of here.*
> *Now.*
> *I can't stand being around anyone who loved JT as much as I did. I know you especially did.*
> *It was you and your bike that killed her. I am going to New York and become a star. I won't stay in touch because it hurts so much.*
>
> *Bunny.*

It was apparent that Wilton Johns Stuart loved Juliet. But did he kill her?

"Bunny's parents had other ideas," he said, breaking into my thoughts. "About her becoming a star. Mama was to be the only star in that family."

I asked quietly, "Are you to blame for Juliet's death?"

"I did not kill her, but Bunny was right. I bought the bike a year and several surgeries after my accident and gave her that first ride. The rush was as addictive to her as me."

"What kind of bike?"

"A Harley-Davidson V-Rod."

"Tough bike for a beginner."

"I wasn't a beginner. I owned several Harleys before my accident. In one of the lowest moments of my life, I sold them all. After I recovered, I bought the V-Rod."

"You were Juliet's advisor. Wasn't motorcycle riding ill-advised? Wouldn't it appear to be inappropriate between student and advisor?"

"I don't think anyone knew about Juliet's and my jaunts but Bunny. It wasn't inappropriate."

I expected him to say, *we loved each other*. And probably they did.

I asked, "Were you with Juliet the night before she was murdered?"

"You mean was I the biker that Geoff Howard saw?" I nodded to indicate yes. "No, that would be gross stupidity. I'm hardly unrecognizable."

"The young men were drunk."

"It was not me. Let me explain. Juliet and I rode several times after the school term ended. That was last June. Summer school was to begin and Juliet had to attend because of the work she'd missed when she drove to Panama City during spring break and stayed with surfers when everyone else returned. I told her that we needed to stop our rides. I was adamant. She was spiteful for a while. She could be that when she didn't get her way. Most of the kids here are spoiled rotten."

He claimed he didn't know if she'd taken up with another biker, but said it wouldn't have surprised him.

"Have you heard from Bunny?"

"I heard *of* her," he said. "She apparently left New York and disappeared into the wasteland."

"I understand you and Hoyt Fagan are riding buddies."

He grinned too much, looking macabre. He needed to stick with closed-mouth smiles. "We'd take our bikes to the mountains sometimes. He was the only staffer who whole-heartedly welcomed me back after the accident. Therefore, I forgave him for what happened to his pet horse rider."

That was out of left field. "Lawrie Taylor?"

"You know about that?" he asked.

Had he brought that up to smear his buddy Fagan? I said, "I heard that it was the girls' idea, and they'd deceived the school staff."

"The three girls set up the jumps, but Hoyt knew about it. He told me the day before it happened that Bunny and Juliet were determined to beat Lawrie in a steeplechase race. His money was on Lawrie because she was the better rider by far."

"Why didn't you stop it?"

"How was I to know there would be an accident? Kids do things that get them hurt, or even killed, that no one can predict. Juliet told me that Lawrie had been ahead, but then laid back to let her and Bunny catch up. She got caught in the middle and was squeezed going over the jump. Hoyt was devastated and blamed himself."

Which refuted Dr. Fetterman's certainty that Hoyt knew absolutely nothing about the planned steeplechase.

CHAPTER EIGHTEEN

Lake made the trip from south of downtown to meet me at Cabe's Q on Johnson Ferry Road, a forty-minute jaunt for the best pulled pork barbecue and cracklin' corn bread in the South, although some Carolinians would argue. We'd ordered iced teas and settled in with butter bean soup and I caught Lake up.

He listened to the summary of my conversation with Wilton Stuart and seemed curious about his disavowals. "You think he had a thing going with Juliet?"

"I think they had a thing started. He encouraged her *joie de vivre* and was obviously in love with her. I think Juliet most likely felt sorry for him and felt herself on the cusp of an adolescent passion but wasn't quite there."

"If he was as repulsive as you've said, wonder why she wasn't put off?"

"I wasn't repulsed exactly. I rather like him, but I wouldn't kiss his face." Lake feigned an expression like I'd kicked him in the wrong place. "If it happened to you, I'd kiss your face, okay?"

"You're hard, Miss Dru. Very hard."

"I think he stopped the bike rides before he was too far gone."

"He confessed, didn't he?"

"After a fashion."

"But did he kill her?"

"I'm going back and forth."

"Which way is the wind blowing now?"

217

I couldn't say.

Lunch came and we halted all talk and wolfed barbecue, slaw and the aforementioned corn bread. The banana pudding with meringue on top provided the perfect finish.

Lake paid and we walked outside. "If you can't persuade Roselyn to give you the notes, I'll try for a court order."

"On the word of a maid that she might or might not have put notes in a safe deposit box?"

He brushed hair from my face and kissed my cheek. "Don't let anything happen to your face. I couldn't stand it if you were marred."

"Ass."

I waved once again to the laurel lion and pressed the door bell. Wilton Stuart had given me a way around approaching Roselyn about the notes without compromising Lois. Anxious to persuade her to let me look at the notes, I pressed again, thumb a little long on the button.

I heard footsteps and expected Lois to greet me. However, Roselyn drew in the door and stepped back. She looked like a wraith from a bad zombie film. Her hair stood on end, and the gown she wore hung like a shroud. She glanced at me, "We weren't expecting you." She looked down at her gown and spread the skirt portion with her hands. "This ol' thing. We're not proper for company."

Yet she answered the door herself.

From the back of the house, Lois rushed forward, frazzled, and I knew something had happened. She herded Roselyn and I, like two cats at a stand-off, into the antique-filled living room. I sat on a Queen Anne chair and Roselyn sat on the Duncan Phyfe sofa. Lois stood, looking uneasy.

"Dr. Pritchett wants to come see us," Roselyn said. That statement had her eyes bulging with fear, or loathing, or wonder.

Who knew?

I explained to her that Mr. Stuart had told me about notes he'd exchanged with Juliet and that Juliet liked to trade notes with other students. I said, "That made me wonder if Mr. Trapp and Juliet communicated through notes?" Glancing at Lois, I perceived her relief.

Roselyn giggled like a silly seven-year-old and rose. Lois stepped forward. I followed them from the living room into a hall.

Roselyn said to Lois, "Please prepare a tray for us."

When Lois left for the kitchen, I fell in step with Roselyn and said, "I'd like to see Mr. Trapp's notes, if that's all right with you."

"Mr. Trapp's notes?"

"To Juliet."

She clutched her breast and faltered on—through the lanai onto garden flagstones. The air smelled faintly smoky and a greasy feeling began in the pit of my gut. I walked beside her, using the same slow mincing steps as she.

Being deliberately unkind, I asked, "Don't you care who murdered Juliet and Mr. Trapp?"

She shook her head. "Juliet is gone and will never come back to us. We know that Mr. Trapp killed himself."

"I don't think so. He was trying to find Juliet's killer, and I think he did. And he died because he did."

She appeared untouched. "We can hardly believe Sherman would do something like that."

Like what? "Please Miss Roselyn, let me look at the notes. If they aren't helpful, I'll give them back."

She halted near the gazebo by an old-fashioned brick barbecue pit, and laid her hand on a row of bricks. "We've burned them."

I let my eyes follow her gaze. Paper ash fluttered at the bottom of the pit.

Stupid bitch. Open mouthed, I stared at her. "Why?"

I heard a crash and looked toward the noise. Lois had dropped the tray of tea and coffee and biscuits on the flagstones.

Roselyn looked like she could cackle. "It is our duty to protect Mr. Trapp's private correspondence." She turned away. "Now we must rest and get ready for Dr. Pritchett's visit."

I had to wonder about this Dr. Pritchett. Eudora Welty wrote about weird souls like this. No wonder Juliet took off as often as she could.

Lois had regained herself enough to show me out as Roselyn wavered toward the staircase.

When Roselyn was out of earshot, Lois whispered, "Before she did it, I saw the note about Chattanooga. Miss Juliet wanted two hundred dollars to go on a field trip to Chattanooga." She looked over her shoulder at the stair-climbing Roselyn. "Miss Roselyn got very angry reading it. She always hated their note-writing. She called Dr. Pritchett to come and get her. She plans to go back north."

"Back to Chattanooga," I said to Lake.

"Bail was revoked on Rassler's playmates," he said. "They're set to plead."

"I need to locate the biker that came to see Trapp when Trapp told Jean Ann to get lost."

"You think he killed Trapp?"

"Likely," I said. "Someone unknown to Jean Ann."

"Unless Jean Ann is lying."

"Grady sent a copy of the audio tape I made to their crime lab for voice interpretation. He said certain characteristics could show if a person is lying."

"Why don't you call your friendly source and see if they've gotten results?"

"I can't understand why he hasn't called *me*. I thought he cared."

After a few more comments, we rang off.

Web had left a message and I called him. "Your girl has a clue," Web said.

"My girl being . . . ?"

"Pearly Sue thinks she's found Bunny Raddison. Pearly Sue's not here right now or I'd let her tell you."

I thrilled at the very idea. Pearly Sue has a knack for understanding people, their motives, why they'd go where they'd go, what they'd call themselves if they went on the lam, and so forth. "Where is Bunny?"

"Atlanta."

I'd always had the feeling she'd return to Atlanta. Bunny was as Georgian as peaches and as Atlantan as Scarlett O'Hara. "Where in Atlanta?"

"The Golden Ram on West Peachtree."

"Know it."

I watched him arrive in his silver Lexus. He handed the valet a bill and the valet handed him a ticket. The valet was careful not to look at his face.

He carried an overcoat and, crossing the street, hunched himself into it against the cold, windy night. He hadn't wanted to come. He said he had hearing problems since his accident and the noise was too bothersome. I told him I'd made reservations and was counting on him. He curtly accepted.

Walking unhurriedly up the sidewalk, I stepped beneath the canopy of the Golden Ram Cabaret. The red and black lobby was already crowded with people who'd come for the midnight show. The first presentation started at eight o'clock, but our interest was in the opening act of the second show.

There were three doors, ushers at each. I was Door Number

Two. An usher saw me through the center door and indicated the way to the table.

Developers, renovators and entertainment magnates had done wonders with this 1940s brick building. Before it was born-again into a nightspot, it had been a tavern where regulars drowned whatever sorrows they had, or neighborhood business-people dropped in for one or two pops before hitting the interstate for the home 'burb on the north side of town. Then a couple of decades ago, the light went on in the combined heads of the City Council. Why was this wide boulevard wasted on dumps like the tavern? Precious resources were slipping through the coffers so sots could have a place to hang. In other words, ten regulars drinking cheap beer and whiskey wasn't adding to the tax base like a pricey nightclub would—one that served up expensive entertainment with twelve-dollar martinis and hundred-dollar bottles of champagne.

As faux art deco went, the interior wasn't bad. I liked it that the stage was low, not more than three feet off the floor, although I'm sure it could be raised for different types of entertainment.

Tonight was blues night, featuring two famous New Orleans singers that had caused the ticket prices to soar to nearly a hundred a seat.

Wilton sat at the table I'd reserved. Without taking his eyes from me, he fished a Cuban cigar out of his coat pocket, unwrapped it and put it between his lips. There was no smoking here. He was a man that liked to lick and suck on an unlit cigar for the tobacco taste alone.

The newspaper reviewer had described the voice of the warm-up vocalist as *finely tuned with a sensuality and subtlety not heard since the torch singers of yesteryear.* My mother liked Billie Holiday and played her records endlessly when I was growing up. I pushed thoughts of Mama from my mind and concentrated on the girl on the stage. If that was Bunny . . .

Her voice was throaty and yearning and very unlike descriptions that I'd heard of Bunny's angelic voice. Could a soprano become a contralto—a woman named Bunny a vamp? Maybe because she looked exotic, she could.

The thin young woman had jet-black hair, green eyes and the longest legs I'd seen since the showgirls at the Miami cabaret. She strutted the stage in a long silver sequined gown slashed to the crotch. Black underwear—I presumed she wore panties— peeked from the slit.

Wilton bent his ear to me. "It's not her," he said.

When her set ended, the audience rose and gave the singer a well-deserved ovation.

Couples got up to dance to canned foxtrot tunes on the small floor near the stage.

Wilton rose and tossed the unlit cigar onto the table like this whole affair was a colossal waste of his time. He laid more than enough money on the table to pay handsomely for our glasses of over-priced, over-oaked red wine. Those sitting near us gaped at his face.

He bowed. "Goodnight and thank you." His thanks wasn't sincere, and those patrons observing this exchange looked at me like beneath my perfectly normal face I, too, must be a monster. I could have cried for Wilton, but I had another rendezvous.

I threaded my way through the tables and the crowd in the lobby, leaving the club in time to see the valet hold the door for Wilton to enter the driver's side of his car. He drove away and Lake pulled up to the curb.

The wind was swirling as I slide into the passenger seat of the unmarked. It was no challenge following the Lexus to the midtown hotel. Pulling my coat around my body against the wind, I walked next to Lake into the lobby. The bar was situated in the back corner of the atrium.

Wilton's head was bowed to the Golden Ram singer's like they were two spies in a noir intrigue. I noticed the cigar in Wilton's mouth. So did the concierge of this tobacco-free hotel. He cut off our advance so that when Wilton and the singer looked up to see him beeline toward them, they saw Lake and me in his wake. The girl jumped up and fled up a wide hall, presumably to the elevators or stairs. Wilton stood and handed the unlit cigar to the concierge, who departed, holding the cigar like it would blow up in his fingers.

Oh, did I mention the singer's name?

It was Conejito de Frijole. Bunny Bean.

Wilton looked from Lake to me. "You took me for a bad liar, I see."

I said. "I know a few Spanish words—like frijole."

His one good eye looked defeated and aroused in me a combination of shame and understanding. He said, "Since you insisted I go to that detestable place, I had to tell her in case she saw me in the audience."

"Still, the show went on," I said. "Unlike others."

He flung himself back onto the loveseat. "Bunny's toughened."

Lake pulled a chair close to Wilton and leaned into him. "She flees when she sees someone from the old life. Why is that?"

Wilton's upper right lip flicked. "You couldn't possibly understand."

"Ah, but I do," Lake said. "I investigated Juliet's murder three years ago."

"You'll ask, and I will tell the truth. Bunny knew I would never give her away. As far as I was concerned, she would surface when it suited her, and I told her so. She was very disturbed after Juliet's murder."

"Who's the threat to her?" Lake asked.

"I don't know that anyone is." He cocked his head. "Maybe you."

"Thanks for your cooperation," Lake said, sitting back and folding his arms across his chest."

"It seems to me," Wilton said, and made small rolling motions as if he contemplated with a cigar between his fingers, "your investigation is no farther along than it was three years ago."

Lake looked his craftiest, *Like you can't possibly guess at what we know.*

I asked, "Where has Bunny been?"

He took out a cigar and unwrapped it. Another expensive Cuban that will never see fire. Holding it between the first and second fingers of his left hand, he spoke of Bunny's depression after Juliet's murder and escape to her parents in New York. When that didn't work out, she traveled to London with Aunt Louise who owns a home there. Bunny was home-schooled by English tutors until she passed their high school equivalency. She repatriated to south Florida where her father got her an audition with a troupe of entertainers.

Wilton waved the cigar. "The producers loved her, of course. They were devastated when she left suddenly."

I pictured Miss Audrey devastated. Melodrama times ten.

"Why did she leave mid-show?" Lake asked.

"You'll have to ask her," he said and looked across the room.

Bunny skip-hopped over. She'd taken off the wig and removed the stage makeup and changed into blue jeans, tee-shirt and sandals. We stood, and she plopped herself into a chair like a fourteen-year-old would.

A boisterous ginned-up couple had come into the lobby; otherwise, we were alone except for the watchful concierge.

The woman, having caught sight of Wilton, recoiled and elbowed her husband, who stared at Wilton like he couldn't believe his own eyes. He pulled his wife into the hall as if Wilton might jump up and reel after them.

Lake looked like a troubled but compassionate priest.

Bunny said to him, "How would you like to suffer what Wilt does?"

Wilton looked at Lake. "Bunny thinks I should wear a mask like the Phantom of the goddamn Opera."

Bunny said, "I'd love for Wilt to compose an opera for me."

I recalled my literature class and studying that horror book by Gaston Leroux. It is better known by its various movies and stage adaptations, but I immediately saw a parallel between Erik, the deformed phantom, and the woman he loved, Christine, the Angel of Music—with Wilton, the deformed advisor, and Bunny, another angel of music.

As if catching me thinking about the Phantom, Wilton said, "I would never abduct Bunny to my lair, but I will protect her from those who would harm her."

But would Bunny, like Christine, risk her life to expose her jealous admirer for his crimes? And what crimes?

"Ask me what you want," Bunny said.

"Are you all right?" Lake asked quietly.

Lake was going to come at her softly. Across from me sat a wily young woman who would better respond to candor.

"I'm good," she said.

"I was sorry to hear about Mr. Chapin," Lake said, sympathy folding into the tiny crinkles around his eyes. "He was well respected."

"He was my friend."

Lake mealy-mouthed around for another several minutes before I asked, "Bunny, who are you afraid of?"

She breathed in, "I'm not afraid."

"We're here to help you stop running."

She couldn't maintain eye contact and looked at her black-painted fingernails.

I said, "Before he died, Mr. Chapin told his nurse about your visit with him. He was quite concerned."

She swallowed hard. "I'm going back upstairs. I'm tired. My throat's about to kill me."

"Would you like something to drink?" Lake asked, again softly, as if she were Susanna, his daughter.

"I've got something in my room," she said, and made a move to rise.

I said, "Sit down." She stared at me, but sat back. "Let's get a few things clear. Did the steeplechase accident have anything to do with Juliet's murder?"

"Huh?" Her wide blue eyes blinked.

"I'm talking about Lawrie Taylor's injury."

"No!"

Lake said, "We just learned about the accident a few days ago—three years after Juliet's murder. Seems everyone at the school kept it hush-hush. Why?"

She shrugged a shoulder. "Everything's to protect that place." We waited, and she continued sulkily, "Our parents pay a lot of money for us to go there, to keep us away from what life is really about. It's a good school and all, but I'm out now, learning what life is really like. Juliet had a head start on me."

I said, "About the riding accident, Mrs. Taylor still holds a lot of animus toward Juliet even though she's dead."

She gave the shoulder shrug again, so common in young people and so annoying. "Mrs. Taylor pushed Lawrie too hard. Lawrie wanted to win so her mother could brag that she beat Juliet and me."

"Nobody won and Lawrie lost. A lot." A blur of pain filled Bunny's eyes. "You wrote a farewell note to Mr. Stuart saying you loved Juliet."

She jerked up a little. "It wasn't a G-L thing."

"Never considered it. You kept in touch with Mr. Stuart even though you blamed him and his bike for her murder."

She looked at Wilton, who I'd noticed squirmed a bit at Bunny's answers, and particularly at anticipating this one. "He gave Juliet her first ride, but she would have found a biker creep."

"Who was this biker creep?"

"Someone she took up with after Wilt dropped her."

Dropped her? Like a boyfriend drops a girlfriend?

"Do you know his name?" Lake asked.

Shaking her head, she said, "I only saw him once with a helmet on. He was her secret."

"Why?" Lake asked. She shrugged. "Older guy?"

The shoulder shrug again. "I think so." She looked down, letting blonde hair veil her face. "I'm thirsty."

Wilton got up and said, "Give me your room key, I'll get you something."

She took the plastic rectangle from her pocket and handed it to him. "Just water for now." He asked if we wanted anything and we said no. He was happy to go.

"Think about clues she gave about him," Lake said.

She looked like she was giving it some thought, but eventually said, "No clues."

In my opinion, she was lying.

"Why did you go see Hoyt Fagan at Hackensack?" Lake asked.

She flashed her eyes. "Why are you investigating me?"

Lake contemplated her for several seconds. "You and Juliet Trapp were friends. She was murdered. You left school suddenly and didn't go to her funeral. I've investigated people with better behavior than that."

"Okay, okay," she said, with spirit. "I couldn't stand it there without Juliet. It was so horrible what happened. I'm—I'm just now getting my mind right."

"Why did you try to see Hoyt Fagan and then go to see Mr. Chapin?"

She kneaded the back of her neck, giving herself a moment. "I had some things on my mind, and I needed to get a career going before I got too old. I could always rely on Mr. Chapin to give me the right advice. Hoyt, too."

Hoyt, not Mr. Fagan?

I reminded her that Mr. Chapin's nurse said that he was upset, but Bunny remained adamant that what she and Chapin talked about was not connected to the school.

I asked, "Why did you leave the Miami troupe? Miss Audrey wants you back."

She forced a laugh. "I'm the wrong gender."

"Was that the reason you departed abruptly, mid-show?"

"I had cramps. I had told Miss Audrey, but he/she said I had to go on. I couldn't . . ."

Cramps, a girl's fall-back excuse. I told her I heard a different version from Miss Audrey.

"He lies," she said.

I was sure Bunny was lying, too.

Wilton came back with a Coke and three bottles of water. I was thirsty and drank half mine.

Lake asked, "Did Juliet have a boyfriend before she hooked up with the biker creep?"

She snickered. "I wouldn't call him a boy."

"Can I take a wild guess at something?" I asked. She bobbed her head. I gave her a précis of what I thought happened at the Miami cabaret—that during the show she saw someone in the audience she knew and didn't return to the stage. "I also think you saw that same someone when you were performing in West Palm and were upset enough to seek out Mr. Fagan and, not finding him at the stable, went to Naples to see Mr. Chapin."

She drank off some water and shrugged, in effect saying, *It's your story.*

Lake asked, "Why are you hiding?"

She studied the water bottle. "I wasn't hiding. You found me."

Wilton spoke at last. "You are still afraid." She drew her legs up and clutched her knees with her arms. Wilton said, "You need to trust someone. I'll always be here for you." It was in his eyes, his unequivocal adoration of her.

"They never caught on," she lamented, letting her watering eyes roam Lake's face. "I wouldn't be believed." She looked at Wilton. "Not even you would believe me."

"We know a lot more now than we did then," Lake said, his softy side re-emerging.

She breathed in, then sighed the air from between her lips. "I have to think about this some more. I don't want to get anyone in trouble. I really just want to forget and get on with my life."

"You're talking about a student and a teacher, right?" I asked. Her eyes were like a lamb's. "Was Juliet involved with this teacher?"

She gave Wilton a beseeching look as if asking him to confess here and now. "She really loved you, Wilt."

Wilton held up his hands against the obvious implications.

She leaned forward and grinned, not merrily though. "I didn't mean that way, Wilt. You were her mentor, you could never be her lover."

He sat back, grim reality riding the scars on his face.

Bunny shot up. "I'm very tired. I have a lot to think about."

"Can I come tomorrow?" I asked.

She danced from one foot to the other. "Sure." She looked at Lake, then me. "You need to find out for yourselves, though." And with that, she was off with a hop-skip.

Wilton looked too stunned to move. But his lips said, "Not me."

Chapter Nineteen

Daylight snuck between the blinds like the certainty that something bad had happened or was going to happen. It settled—in my bones and in my blood.

"Wake up, sleepy baby," Lake said, bringing coffee. He placed the saucer on the nightstand and sat on the bed. He brushed aside my hair and kissed my forehead. "You look pensive. Turn over; I'll rub your back before I go."

While he messaged my shoulders, I said, "I have the weirdest feeling. It's about Wilton."

"You dreamed of Wilton?"

"And the cast we've been living with, but I woke thinking of him."

I let Lake's powerful but honeyed hands knead the knots from my back. Without knowing why, I said, "He's doomed."

Lake's hands paused. "He loves the girl, sugar." He bunched my muscles together, then let them relax. "That doesn't doom him."

"She'll break his heart, all over again."

"Hearts mend."

I turned on my back and rose to my elbows. "He's with her now, but he's going to lose her."

"You and your caul-enabled foresight."

I sat up. "Being born with a caul means I won't drown."

"And that you have preternatural powers."

Kicking off blankets, I said, "I'm getting my caul-driven

232

preternatural powers out of this bed."

"Watch your back."

"Say that again?"

"Bye."

Bunny had said that we should find out for ourselves.

That we would certainly do. Lake would open that front.

I was confident I knew who Juliet had taken up with, who Bunny had seen in the West Palm Beach nightclub, and then again in the Miami cabaret.

When I thought about my troubling dream, I wasn't so confident that Wilton and Bunny weren't playing a devious game. That occurred to me while I stood knocking on her hotel door, my knuckle raps getting no response, nor my voice when I spoke. "Bunny, it's me, Dru."

At the desk I learned that Bunny had checked out of the hotel at five thirty in the morning. The clever girl had given the slip to one of Dirk's better shadows. He was still in his bubble-windowed van when I knocked on the back door. I could tell by the sharp creases in his suit pants and his bright eyes that he hadn't been sleeping.

It didn't take long to figure out how Bunny had given him the slip. Residents can leave by any number of doors leading to the side streets. They just can't get back in after midnight. They had to go through the lobby until seven in the morning. After studying my credentials, the concierge said that Bunny used the hotel's garage deck down the street. I found the space for number 268 vacant.

I called Lake while I waited for the day concierge to open the door to Bunny's suite. Lake was not surprised she'd skipped; nor was I surprised that there wasn't a clue left in her room. *Wait.* Hadn't Bunny wiped her stage makeup from her face? You don't scrub stage pancake and eye gunk from your skin with soap and water. There are special cleansers and sponges. Those would have been tossed in a trash can.

I'd passed a cleaning cart coming from the elevator. Leaving room 268, I spotted the cart. This early, the cleaning crew was just getting started, but there were a couple of trash liners inside the disposal bag hanging from the cart.

The cart was unattended, but I wanted plastic gloves and a witness or two, so I summoned the crew from a coffee break in a walk-in linen closet. Lying in the bottom of the bag I found the sponges and a piece of paper with a string of numbers. Most likely the numbers belonged to a cell phone. A maid scribbled her name on a piece of hotel stationery indicating that she'd witnessed my removing the trashcan liner. With that, I was off to police headquarters.

Although I don't miss the daily grind of police work, I miss the squad room. I miss these guys—those without gender bias. I'd resigned before I made detective. I was on the fast track and knew it, but so far I've never regretted leaving. I met Lake when I was assigned his partner to patrol Zone 2. Did he welcome me with open arms? No, but Lake wasn't the kind of man that re-arranges his privates in public, farts on purpose, or picks his nose and makes mean-spirited sexist comments. He tries hard not to swear because the habit carried over into his personal life and he has the utmost respect for his daughter, Susanna. He had been going through a divorce when I met him, but his and Linda's divorce was amicable. For Susanna, they decided to be sensible. They're still friends and Linda is constantly asking me when Lake and I are going to marry. I evade whenever I can, but Linda is persistent. Since I don't know if that will ever happen, I can't answer her. *Y'all are sooooo good togetha, and Ricky sooooo loves children* . . . I do, too, which is why I started Child Trace. But there's a difference. I rescue children; I don't raise children. Helping with Susanna on her weekends with Lake is a joy and suits me. I've seen what ambitious working parents do to children. In the end, I don't think I have strong motherly instincts. Those who know my own mother, and believe that those instincts are passed from mother to daughter, might well agree.

In his glass office, Lake spoke with a detective. I sat at an empty desk shooting the bull with two of his detectives. Lake came out of his office at the same time Commander Haskell came out of his. He said to Lake, "I transferred a call to you, Lieutenant."

Lake sat a desk, picked up the receiver and pushed the blinking button.

Haskell leaned against the desk where I sat and folded his arms. "So where you going from here, Dru?"

"I have to find Bunny—again," I said, indicating the piece of paper with a cell number laying in a plastic bag on the desk. "The number probably is a shuffle number."

"The paper the number's written on won't come into evidence, if there's ever a case. Thanks for thinking of the chain, but PIs and hotel maids don't a chain make. Take it to Webdog."

I knew Haskell would say that—with a reprimanding tone to his voice.

"Meantime," he said, watching Lake bang the landline receiver into its cradle, "we're taking the guy apart. If it's a habit, we'll find where it started."

So would Webdog find where it started.

Lake rose from his desk. "Fagan's back in town." He grabbed his coat and fedora—the felt since it was winter. "Let's move."

We caught up with Hoyt Fagan in the tack room. He looked like, to use an old saw, he'd been rode hard and put away wet.

His demeanor was defensive so I assumed he'd talked to Fetterman.

My first question concerned Bunny's visit to Hackensack Stables in Wellington, Florida.

"Sure, I remember Robin telling me that a Margery somebody came by to see me. Hell, I didn't know a Margery. Still don't. This is about Bunny Raddison, isn't it?"

"Yes," Lake said. "She came to see you and then went to see Mr. Chapin in his Naples nursing home."

"Chapin left me a message, but I was in Europe during the summer. By the time I got back to the States, he'd died."

"What was the message?"

"Nothing specific. Just urgent that he talk to me. I can tell you right now, I don't know anything about Bunny, where she is . . . nothing." He paused. "I hope she's all right."

I leaned forward. "Why didn't you stop that disastrous steeplechase race?"

"I . . ." He clamped his lips, and I assumed he did so to give himself time to think before speaking. "I didn't take it seriously. I had no idea—I thought they were horsing around. Excuse the pun. After it happened, I blamed myself."

"Did they tell you what they were going to do?"

"I overheard them in the tack room. I thought they were talking about something taking place off campus. I would never sanction anything like that. We don't. I don't teach steeplechasing. It's a specialty. Anyone interested, there's a school about three miles from us. I somehow . . ." He took a deep breath. "I assumed it was going to happen there."

"Yet you told Mr. Stuart your money was on Lawrie because she was the better rider."

He jerked back. "What if I did? I said it in passing, in general, if the girls ever raced, flat or jumps. I'm surprised at Wilton for repeating an off-hand remark like that."

"It's not fair, is it?" I said.

"Fair?" he yelped. "What happened to Wilton is what isn't fair."

"Nor is what happened to Lawrie."

"Look, am I somehow responsible for Wilton and Lawrie? I'll take Lawrie, if you want me too. I should have been paying more attention, but poor Wilton . . ."

"What about Marie?" I said, giving it puckish emphasis. Then egged on by his guilty shock, I forged on with spurious speculation. "What was their fight really about? What is the real reason Marie was divorcing him?"

His eyes were scathing. "Don't believe all you hear."

"Did Wilton?"

He took a stride toward the door. "I have to leave."

"Not just yet," Lake said, slipping sideways to the door from his position against the wooden wall. Lake hadn't said a word and Fagan knew this was my show.

I said, "Wilton got Juliet addicted to speed and adrenaline. But he wisely cut her off after a while. She took up with another biker, didn't she?"

He flung out his arms. "You think me?"

"There *was* another biker in her life. You read the papers? Geoff Howard saw them together."

He gave me his best one-up sneer. "That exonerates me."

"I don't know about that."

"Geoff sure as hell knows me."

"He take horse-riding lessons from you?"

"No, wouldn't know the ass-end from the nose, but he went to the school. I am known outside the ring."

"You have any idea who her new biker friend was?"

"Not a one, now if you'll excuse me, I have . . ."

"You have nothing until I say you have something," Lake said.

He took two aggressive steps toward Lake. The man wasn't afraid of authority. "Am I under arrest?"

"Should you be?" Lake asked.

"I don't have to take this."

"Fetterman knew about you and Marie," I said.

He whirled. "Nobody knew . . ." He huffed out disgust with himself for jumping to his defense and giving himself away. "I'm not saying another word. You're letting a lot of horse shit fly." He faced Lake. "Bring out the cuffs or get out of my way."

Lake didn't move.

I said, "Did Wilton know about you and Marie?"

"Wilton knew that she and I were friends. That's all. Let the poor woman rest in her grave."

Lake said, "We're not here because of a romantic triangle."

"I'm telling you there was no romantic anything."

"Why would Bunny come to see you at Hackensack when she'd been avoiding everyone, going so far as to assume pseudonyms? Were you two always that friendly?"

Were he a snake, he would have struck me. "I don't date teenage girls. I get enough of their silliness during classes."

"Are there student-teacher affairs at the school?" He blinked. "Male teachers with girls; female teachers with boys?"

He snorted. "You mean are we into the hot student–teacher epidemic? Damned if I know. I ride my horses and make love with mature women."

"Consider this. Bunny's on stage, or in the wings backstage, looking at the audience. She sees someone she knows, someone from the school with a student or a teenager acting in a totally inappropriate manner. Would she come to you?"

"No. She would go to Chapin. I pretty much live and let live. Some of those students, Christ! They've had their first sex experience by the time they're thirteen. Older than that, they think life has passed them by. It's our damn television, video games, Internet, anything-goes culture. Kids are lying around getting fat and screwing each other. Most of the teachers involved with students are sickos looking for the next thrill." He ran a hand through his hair. "Bah, I hate to think about what's happened to our society. No decency anymore."

"If Bunny confided something like that, would you believe her?"

"Why wouldn't I?"

"There are those that call her a drama queen."

"And they aren't wrong. But I swear, she'd tell the truth and shame the devil."

I wondered if Fagan was using a well-known idiom or if he was quoting from the "Henry IV" Shakespeare passage: Hotspur says: . . . *tell truth and shame the devil. If thou have power to raise him, bring him hither, And I'll be sworn I have power to shame him hence. O, while you live, tell truth and shame the devil!*

Who says an interest in the classics is a waste? *I have power to shame him hence.*

"Why wouldn't she go to Dr. Fetterman?" I asked.

A naughty gleam came into Fagan's eyes. "I see what you're getting at. Am I supposed to consider it was Dr. Fetterman that she saw?"

"Any gossip with him?"

"There are those you could ask, who would know better than me. There's a cliché at the school, mostly women, who make it their business to know every nit-picking detail about everyone. I keep myself to myself. I'd rather be in a stable full of horses with the barn on fire than in a room filled with those rumor-mongers."

"What was Mr. Chapin like?"

"Ah ha! You know or guessed it. Nice old guy, but a magnet for gossip and a town crier for spreading it. He'd know if there was anything to Bunny's suspicions."

"Did Juliet take up with a teacher?"

His mouth opened, then he hesitated. "This isn't about Bunny. It's about who killed Juliet, isn't it?"

"Bunny and Juliet were best friends, you know that."

"They were and they weren't. Bunny was a little jealous of Juliet. Both are pretty girls, talented in their own ways, but Juliet lit a room by walking into it. Such verve, a zest for life and love. Bunny could be disagreeable if things didn't go her way. Quite a tongue sometimes."

"Bunny knew that Juliet had a biker boyfriend. Did Juliet confide in you?"

"She talked about some motorcycle guy once when she said horse riding no longer gave her a thrill. Wilton was sorry he got her into riding. Wouldn't be long—I'd bet good money—she'd get her old man to buy her a bike. Sixteen, you think you can handle anything. She'd be flying planes now, if she'd lived." He flung a hand into his thigh. "What a waste."

Lake's phone rang and he opened the door and stepped outside. I asked Fagan to call my office and talk to Dennis "Webdog" Caldwell if he thought of anything pertaining to either Juliet or Bunny.

"Will do, despite your suspicion of me."

"I suspect everyone, except Lake and a judge I've known from childhood, except sometimes I wonder about her." I smiled and left him with a wondering look splashed across that red face.

It was a dreary wintry dusk that settled over the city. Lake and I were discussing where we would dine. I needed a seafood fix, but Lake was bargaining for lean red meat.

I was willing to trade seafood for red meat if he would agree to accompany me to the Fourteenth Street Playhouse where "Menopause, The Musical" was showing.

"You *are* joking," Lake said.

I shook my head. "There'll be other men there. It's enlightening."

"Depressing. Here's the deal. We eat lean red meat tonight, and its seafood whenever you want it for the next month."

My cell phone interrupted the bargaining. The phone call was from Web. After-work hours means nothing to him. I pressed the green arrow on the screen and said hello.

"I found Bunny," he crowed.

"How?"

"Long explanation. You know about fishnet spoof towers?"

He'd explained it to me not long ago. It involved using a spy tool to set up a fake cell tower to intercept cell phone numbers and their locations. "Un-huh. Dirk do it for you?"

"With a little help from my databases." I said I didn't want specific know-how. Web went on, "I heard the ping when she rang his home. She's on the boat. His cell tracking system was even deactivated. A cinch for the spoofs."

"And controversial."

"We're not law enforcement subject to getting court orders and subpoenas."

I breathed out deeply. Web fervently believes information streaming on electronic devices is open to anyone who can retrieve it, even if the seeker has to make it stream.

"Tinny Allen's Marina," Web said. "Peachtree Industrial to Lanier Islands Parkway. Left. Slip R-seventeen."

"When was the phone call?"

"Seven minutes, forty seconds ago."

That's my geek.

"Can I come?" Web asked.

"Not until you get your carry qualifications," I said. Web loves private investigative work, but is not so fond of guns. That was all right with me. My other colleague, Miss Pearly Sue, from south Georgia, had been born with a shotgun in one hand, a rifle in the other and a pistol between her teeth. In her off hours, she can be found at the gun range. Happily, she has not needed to use her arsenal.

Lake got on the phone to Portia and explained the situation. We met her at her Ansley Park mansion where she harrumphed around with a few questions and then signed the search warrant that allowed Detective Lieutenant Richard Lake—specifying his list of qualifications—to board and search the houseboat of Wilton Johns Stuart for the person of Brandle Bunny Raddison. The warrant was very specific and not a no-knock. As an Atlanta police lieutenant, it wasn't his jurisdiction, but it was Portia's. So who's splitting hairs?

Tinny Allen's Marina is one of the largest marina and dry dock shipyards on the lake. Although it was January, Wilton Stuart kept his houseboat, *Advisor,* in the water year round. Pearly Sue's phone interviews elicited the fact that Wilton usually arrived at the dock early Saturday morning. By being a package holder at the marina, he had his own electronic key. He also had weekly garbage pickup, Sunday newspaper delivery, pump-out service, gated parking and a runabout slip beside the houseboat. The runabout was currently in for a bilge pumping. All this cost Wilton a mere ten grand a year. That Pearly Sue could get blood from a stone.

Wilton would take *Advisor* out for an hour or so Saturday afternoons. After returning, he'd call area stores and order provisions. He'd pay a service fee for the goods to be delivered to the ship's stores. Sometimes he went out on a Sunday, but mostly he read. In the morning he'd sit at the umbrella table across from the concrete walkway leading to the slips. During the afternoon he could be seen sitting behind the plate glass salon shield, reading a book or working on his computer. He'd leave late Sunday afternoon. He was friendly and helpful to other boaters, a big tipper—just an all-around regular guy in his spiffy white captain's hat and blue nautical jacket. She also unearthed how Tinny got his nickname and thus his business title. He owned a collection of antique tinplate toys—cars, ships, planes, and motorbikes—which were on display in the ship's stores.

We'd reached the security gate and the young guard studied our IDs like he couldn't read, or didn't understand why an Atlanta police detective and the owner of a business called Child Trace would be wanting entrance into the marina at nine o'clock at night.

"You can call the juvenile court judge," Lake said, waving the paper. "She won't like it but she signed this warrant to search for the girl, or locate material pertaining to her whereabouts. This is the judge's jurisdiction and Miss Dru has been contracted by the juvenile justice system to find Brandle Raddison."

"You think she's here?" the guard asked.

No, dummy, we just thought we'd stop by and roust the snobs.

I leaned toward the driver's window and spoke to the guard. "It was my last contact with her."

"I don't need no trouble on my watch."

"Won't be."

This had to be his first service of process. He'd learn. He stepped back into the guard shack and the security gates parted.

I moved alongside Lake, mimicking his feline moves. It was like stalking a bluebird. Lake is lighter on his feet than me—what with a foot-drag here, a stubbed toe there.

Lake heard something; I felt him stiffen. We backed into the shadow of number sixteen. I hoped no one was in residence in sixteen. No light came from it, while ambient light came from seventeen, our destination.

A man in a long coat and trilby hat pulled low in front came from the starboard side of slip seventeen. Not looking for but anticipating trouble, I wasn't surprised to find a man keeping watch, waiting for us—confirmation that the call to Wilton from the boat was to set us up. There would be at least two of them. Two against two. Bunny and Wilton would be no help. I said a little prayer that they would be no hindrance.

The man in the trilby looked around, up and down the concrete path, and, seemingly satisfied, went back to the starboard side of the boat. Lake motioned me to hurry, and we ran past the bow of the houseboat in slip sixteen, cut to the back of *Advisor* and slipped onto the afterdeck while the thing was still in motion from the action of Trilby. A well-equipped fishing boat bobbed next to the houseboat. The intruders' boat.

"It's a gun under his coat," I whispered. The night was still and cold, and my whisper seemed to echo.

Lake nodded. We drew our weapons, mine a Glock 17—twin to the one Grady took from me at the cemetery—from my backside paddle holster. Lake carried a Beretta Storm in a hip holster. My BUG was snug under my slacks in its ankle holster.

Lake pointed ahead, meaning that I should take the port side, then he motioned right, meaning he'd take starboard. He made a rocking motion with his free hand to indicate we needed to keep the boat's motion equalized.

Easier said than done. It's a boat. We're on water.

The galley was as wide as the boat with large windows opposite each other. I could see Lake through the glass. I could also see Bunny inside, sitting at a table, her head in her folded arms. Wilton sat on a sofa bench, his hair a mess. He held a white bandage to his eye. He was guarded by a short, stocky man with a Sig.

A skinny man with a big head came into the galley from the salon. He bounced like a man on a pogo stick. He also carried a large black Sig. Wilton raised his head and said something. Pogo Stick sprung over and feigned hitting him. I think he said *shut the fuck up*.

The port-side hatch—maybe fifteen feet from me—burst open. I glanced at Lake; he'd backed out of view, toward the stern. Trilby held his shotgun like it was descended from his hand. He grinned and made a come-here hook with his index finger. I shoved my gun into my coat pocket and nodded. He was not going to shoot me out here, not with a shotgun.

He pushed me into the salon, a square, comfortable compartment with a man's taste in furnishings: leather, teak, nautical. He grabbed my arm and pulled me through a passageway into the galley. At first, Wilton's eyes bugged when he saw me, then they filled with tears and apology.

"They said you were pretty," Trilby said, patting my butt. He clearly was in charge. He ran his finger over my cheek as if he were caressing a baby. I wanted to spit on him. He addressed the stocky goon. "Go out, keep watch." He handed Stocky the shotgun and pulled out his own Sig. I moved to my right, away from his sight, and placed my hand in my pocket.

Stocky, holding the shotgun, left through the passageway.

"Sit by the creep," Trilby said, gesturing me toward Wilton's bench seat.

Outrage burst from Wilton's mouth, a bellow to make a bull proud. He rose and shot forward.

"Halt, bud," Pogo Stick said with a thick accent. He raised his gun, now a few feet from Wilton's temple.

Wilton froze. His eyes flashed between me and Trilby. He shifted his weight from foot to foot, the scarred skin on his face as red and tight as a balloon about to pop. Sweat sheened his forehead. He took a step to the side, away from Pogo Stick. Bunny yelled at him to sit. He turned to her.

It happened in slow motion, a moment in enough time for

me to get my finger on the trigger and pull the gun from my coat. Pogo Stick raised the Sig and fired at Wilton, striking him in the head. The roar punched me in the gut. Wilton's ruined skin blossomed into a red rose in the middle of his face. He collapsed back to the bench as if he were a deflating blow-up doll. The horror and shock had time dissolving around me, my gun frozen in my fist.

The tableau was silent and still as we, captors and captives, stared when Wilton's body slid sideways, convulsing on the deck, blood rushing from his head, mouth and nose to form a bright pool that spread like a scarlet pillow for his head.

Trilby looked at Pogo Stick. "The fucking bitch is next. She's the one. Not the blonde. Do it."

The boat rocked. A thud came from the stern. Lake. Or Stocky.

"What's that?" Trilby yelled.

Pogo Stick bounded to rip open the hatch to the stateroom.

Lake came through the doors fast, dove low and rolled toward Pogo Stick, knocking him to his knees, coming up and snapping off a shot at Trilby. I had a clear shot at Pogo Stick's profile.

When the echoes died, I heard Bunny's short, quiet screams.

It took the rest of the night to partially satisfy local law enforcement and the Georgia Bureau of Investigation. Bunny had been carted off to the hospital in hysterics and in no condition to give a statement. My explanation kept to the acts and facts that I'd experienced. It's never good to speculate with people in authority lest opinion be taken as fact. I told the locals and the GBI agents that I had no idea who the men were and who sent them to murder the boat's inhabitants or why, or indeed who that target could be. A total mystery to me.

I sat alone beneath the umbrella on the concrete dock and watched the sun escape the fog's cloak. A light wind chopped the water. Lake was in the salon with the locals and the agents. Finally, he came out and sat opposite me. He said they were calling in the FBI. What he had told them touched on Juliet's murder in Atlanta and Bunny's possible kidnapping by Wilton.

"Wilton didn't kidnap her," I said.

Lake said, "I had to admit APD didn't know that for an absolute fact."

Wilton's and the other dead bodies, including Stocky—who died from Lake's Beretta having come in contact with his skull—were still on the boat when we left at seven thirty, having re-enacted the scene a dozen times, and still under a shroud of doubt. I had a feeling a meeting with Grady was in my near future, too.

The good news was that before authorities stormed the dock, we'd gotten Bunny calmed enough to agree to meet with me at one o'clock in Portia Devon's chambers tomorrow. I advised her to make no statement to the local police until she had an attorney and that the best way to do that was act in no condition to make a statement. Babe Brindle had better watch out, if Bunny ever decided on an acting career.

CHAPTER TWENTY

I love it when I'm right, but it's no challenge when it's a foregone conclusion. I got to my office at nine o'clock after feeding Mr. Brown and saving a bluebird from his claws, changing from night-stalking black slacks and sweater to a pair of navy blue pleated pants, a white turtleneck and a tan cashmere jacket. The sun had perked up and the day promised to be a bright winter day, chilly but not too windy.

Pearly Sue brought me coffee and sat in a comfortable chair opposite my desk. Web sat on the sofa, where he often sleeps, drinking Coke.

"Grady called again," Web said. "He's flying from Memphis."

"Lovely."

"Arrival eleven fifty-five."

"Fabulous. Now, let's go over what you've got for me."

"Late last night, too late to call you, Nelson Warner called to tell you that Joe Blade said the tight-assed guy in the photographs could be the poser. That mean anything to you?"

"Yep. Sherman Trapp."

Pearly Sue was unwilling to let go of what bothered her about what happened at the marina. "They were hired killers."

"Likely. No ID on them. The leader was American or spoke like one. The others seemed foreign, their clothes, their demeanor, Pogo Stick's accent. It's up to the cops to run them down."

Pearly Sue can be a bulldog. "Unless Bunny got herself mixed up with Miami gangsters, I bet they were after you."

I looked at Web, who'd located Bunny on the late Wilton Johns Stuart's boat, thus sending Lake and me into a trap. Webdog's features had an apologetic cast. I held up a hand against his culpability. "You couldn't know what we suspected," I said.

He said, "The Taylors could have hired them. It wouldn't be the first time suburbanites sought vengeance for their quadriplegic daughter. They wouldn't do the deed themselves. But I think they were after Bunny. Wilton could have told them she'd surfaced and he was taking care of her."

I grinned sympathetically. "It's possible. Wilton's not here to tell the tale. Bunny is part of this; I'm just not sure which part. Juliet, too. But her killer raped her."

Web sat tapping a pencil on his knee, wriggling on a line to find a way out of his feelings of guilt. "A hired killer could have raped her, too. Take advantage of the situation."

I smiled at Web, who was a young college student when he came to me, and now in graduate school, he'd become a man. Still, with his open-faced innocence, somehow I couldn't imagine him grasping such extreme sexual deviation.

He said, "It's a violence thing, right?" I nodded. "Lot of men who are womanizers and are married with kids, turn out to be pedophiles. Hoyt Fagan could be Juliet's creepy biker friend."

Pearly Sue's headshake said she disagreed with him.

I asked her, "What did you find out in Louisville?"

Pearly Sue sat straight and ruffled her shoulders, primed to expound. "Well, I told you that the Fettermans met in Louisville where she's from and he lived for a while. He was a summer school teacher in her town and they met at an ice cream social that summer before he went back to school to get his doctorate. They kept in touch and then got married."

I thought about Eugene Fetterman's appearance. He had the build of a runner and I'd thought he'd looked like a priest that

Portia and I used to call Father Fly because of his prominent eyes. He wasn't a man I would be attracted to, but he was nice enough looking, even if he was wont to let his erudition show. English Lit, Shakespeare, Greek History. "Go on," I said to Pearly Sue. For once, she'd paused, maybe because she caught me thinking.

She said, "I talked to two teachers there who'd taught that summer with Gene Fetterman."

"You talked to them at the same time?"

"Oh no. Web ran down the names of the teachers teaching during the summer he was there. There were six. Three had left for other positions or dropped out of teaching. That left Mr. Fetterman, Mr. Bloom and Mrs. Johnson. First, let me say that this school was a school for mostly white children in a blue-collar neighborhood. I found out half the men were unemployed due to a strike. Many of the kids were failing their regular classes, and they had to take remedial classes that summer. Some of the kids were foster children."

My kind of children.

Pearly Sue went on, "I talked to Mrs. Johnson first. She said during the first week, Gene was great with the kids. They'd gather around him. Very popular, he was, especially with the girls that were thirteen and fourteen. There was this one girl, after a couple of weeks seemed under his spell. That's exactly what she said, *under his spell.*" Pause.

Have I adequately described Pearly Sue's large blue eyes when she emphasizes details?

She continued, "He'd take her into the computer room, and there they'd have one-on-one lessons. The girl was making rapid progress and Mrs. Johnson was happy because the girl was on the verge of dropping out of school. Then Mrs. Johnson found out that he was taking her to his Sunday School classes, *and on Wednesday church days, too.*" Pause. "Mrs. Johnson started to notice the touching, how she'd rub his arm and he'd rub her back. Mrs. J started to get uneasy. Then the girl came to school with a new blouse on, one she couldn't afford. Mrs. Johnson took her aside and said, *My, what a pretty blouse* and *Where did you get it? I might get one for my daughter.* The girl was real sly and said it was a secret. *Well!* Mrs. Johnson went right to the office and told the assistant principal, who didn't seem alarmed, but said he'd keep an eye out. One Saturday there was this ice cream social at the church. Gene and the student palled around, and then Gene met this young woman who was just out of high school. He abandoned his pet student for the woman and the student became very upset. She didn't come to class Monday or Tuesday and when Mrs. Johnson heard what happened that Saturday, she advised the school authorities to go to the girl's foster home. Mrs. Johnson went, too. The girl told of touching and sex talk and said that when summer school was over, Gene wanted her to come with him—she actually called him Gene, not Mr. Fetterman—to get his doctoral degree.

"Of course, Fetterman claimed the girl made it all up and that he gave her special attention because, although he could tell she was bright, she was very needy. He laid it off to adolescent hormone imbalance, the girl's messy life and natural jealousy."

Interesting. I asked, "What did Mr. Bloom have to say?"

Pearly Sue laughed. "He called Gene a frickin' faggot and said he kept his eyes on the male students."

"Well, well," I said. "Have you anything to add, Web?"

"After receiving his doctorate, Fetterman taught high school in Wheeling, West Virginia. There was a complaint that got him transferred to a different school. It came from a parent, but the nature of the complaint is sealed. He married, and they moved to Baltimore before coming to Atlanta."

Was Web admitting he couldn't break a seal?

Pearly Sue raised her hand like she was in school. "Want me to go find out about it?"

She would, too. "I think we can look closer to home."

"I've never been to Baltimore."

"Next time we have something doing there, you'll go."

Pearly Sue beamed.

Nothing for it but to answer his phone call. "Yes, Grady."

"Got yourself in deep shit again, huh?"

"Grady, sometimes I'm not in the mood for profanity. I'm tired and this is one of those times. Have you ID'd the killers?"

"From what I've seen, they're the killed."

Wise-ass. "Who were the hit men?"

"You think that?"

"Are you going to tell me you don't?"

"No. Have lunch with me?"

"I can't."

He cleared his throat. "Brandle Raddison is out of the hospital."

"Did she make a statement?"

"No, she's too upset. But she did say she didn't know who those men were. They came in holding a gun on Wilton Stuart and made him make a telephone call."

Someone knew about Web's fishnet software.

Grady said, "Shame about Stuart."

I'd given a lot of thought to Wilton. It wasn't a motorcycle that put him out of his misery, but an assassin's bullet. I replayed the scene in my head. He was a man possessed with his bad appearance, his lost life—to the point of talking about ending his sorry life himself, but he couldn't. What did he say? *Afraid of the grave.* Did he deliberately let himself be provoked in order to be murdered, a suicide by assassin? Maybe he knew, as I knew, that we were all destined to die on that houseboat, and he jumped the gun, so to speak. Or maybe he figured out that Lake was outside and I wasn't alone and that his actions gave me a chance to save myself and Bunny. It's another one of those things I'll never know and will always relive and ponder.

"Miss Dru, are you there?"

"Sorry, Grady. I paused to remember Wilton Stuart."

"Come to my office, you and Lieutenant Lake. We need to clear some things up."

"What things?"

"You'll find out."

"I don't know about the lieutenant, but I might have a few minutes later in the day."

"You sure know how to talk to the FBI."

"I respect the institution. They taught me well at the National Academy." Intentional bragging is something I do occasionally.

"I'll show you my yellow brick if you'll show me yours."

"Bye, Grady."

"Not so fast. An Assistant United States Attorney for the Southern District of Florida is in Atlanta. He knows you're involved in a high-profile case, so he's come to you to review events at the cemetery in West Palm Beach, Florida. See you on Spring Street at two p.m. Good day."

Piss-head.

Even though I didn't recognize the number on the display, I answered my cell phone.

A coarse voice said, "I think I got your V-Rod guy."

Dwight Baines. The motorcycle school guy. I held my breath.

"I looked in the records, I'll eat my helmet if it's not a guy named Mike Sherman. Plops down the bills, big as you please. Kicking myself I didn't catch on when you were here."

Sherman Trapp.

He went on, "Definitely a poser, but he was a good learner.

An earnest guy. I didn't have a problem with him taking that bike on the street. Tell the truth, I wish all bikers took it up when they were at least thirty. By then they got a good head on their shoulders and understand a bike's a serious vehicle and showing off could get you hurt real bad."

"You say this guy was thirty?"

"Closer to mid-forties. I'm just saying thirty's a good threshold."

Whew.

The United States Attorney's Office for the Southern District of Georgia is located in the high-rise Richard B. Russell Building on Spring Street, a facility I've been in countless times. Lately for the Summit on Human Trafficking, a burgeoning problem being tackled by the United States Attorney's Office and the Department of Justice. Hundreds had gathered for the event, ranging from victims, service providers, law enforcement and community leaders. I could see the determination in their eyes to stop smugglers from treating humans like sex slaves, disposable trash. That was months ago, but I've seen no diminution of slaves flooding into the city and 'burbs. Prior to that I was here for a Youth Justice Summit.

I know the U. S. Attorney and most of her assistants, but I was going to be meeting with an Assistant U.S. Attorney from Florida.

The meeting was on the third floor in one of the rooms, stark with institutional ash furniture and used whiteboards. It appeared the last people to use this room were filing for bankruptcy, and this is where they met with their creditors.

Grady sat at a table alone with his briefcase open, apparently reading official tomes. He finally looked up.

I was struck again at his good looks and sex appeal—like Lake. But Lake had an air of grace and good humor, hard to maintain for law enforcement officers who attain high levels and have seen the very worst most decent humans can only imagine. Grady could have been a Ken doll. Plastic and smug.

"Sit down, Miss Dru."

"Think I will, Grady."

"I'm happy to see that your training at Quantico didn't go to waste."

"Why am I here?"

"We are waiting for the Assistant U.S. Attorney for Southern Florida to tell you that."

"You don't know?"

"It's not my place to say. So, as I was saying, I'm happy your training at Quantico came in handy."

"Meaning?"

"It's sad for law enforcement when an excellently trained agent or cop quits the service . . ."

"I stayed my three years, and then some."

"Hear me out." He leaned back in the wooden armchair, an at-ease pose. "I'm happy to see you still serve the people of Georgia. In fact, you've helped other states clean up some of their corruption. For that, I'm happy the Academy trained you. You were one of the youngest ever to attend, did you know that?"

"They told me. I was everyone's kid sister."

"Until you kicked them to the mat. Where did you learn martial arts?"

Strange question, they didn't teach martial arts at the Academy. Lots of fitness exercises, boxing, grappling, but not martial arts. I answered, "Growing up, I lived up the street from a martial arts studio. Portia Devon and I started when we were eight."

"Where did you live?"

"Come on, this isn't about me."

"It is about you. You shot a man to death in one amazing move. You're quite accomplished at self-defense. You and Richard Lake are a very lethal team."

"That's the way we like it. Now how about you answer a question for me?" He cocked his head, a smirk twisting his mouth. "Who were those men?"

"No information so far, but two are likely foreigners. Their clothes make them Eastern European; Bulgarian, Croatian. Killers for hire. Now my turn again. You never disclosed to my satisfaction how you knew Bunny was on that boat. Will you explain, just for me?"

His pretty-please smile was bogus enough to make me turn up my lip. I said, "Did you read the report?" He nodded and when I didn't go on, the smile turned impatient. I said, "My investigators, Dirk's Detectives—an Internet PI company—and my company's own Web investigator, looked into the life of Wilton Johns Stuart, a school advisor and mentor to Juliet Trapp and Bunny Raddison. When I interviewed Wilton Stuart, he admitted he introduced Juliet to motorcycle riding. They wrote notes. It's all in my report."

"You telling me that Stuart and the girl, Juliet, had an affair?"

"I don't believe it was sexual, though it might have turned into that. Juliet and Bunny were friends; Wilton Stuart had a curious relationship with both girls."

"You're equivocating."

"It's what I believe to be the case."

He sat back, looking like a disbelieving satyr. Wonder where his mind was?

I told him that Wilton had kept in touch with Bunny through her missing years, and that in investigating him, we learned he owned a houseboat. I explained that Dennis Caldwell, my Web guy, found Bunny Raddison singing at a cabaret here in Atlanta before he located her on Stuart's boat.

"How does he do it, this Dennis Caldwell?"

"You can't have him. Anyway, Wilton Stuart and I went to a performance, and I talked to Bunny afterward. She obviously fears someone she believes might be involved in Juliet's murder and promised to think about a few things and talk to me the next day. When I got there, she'd skipped from her hotel, but I found a number she'd jotted down." *At least I'd thought she was the one who jotted it down until I divined the plot.* "It was the number of a kick."

"Let me guess. Your hacker traced the phone."

"Not hard. You've seen the warrant. Lake had a right to be on the boat."

"Those who might question the legality are dead. I just want to understand. There's a lot going on you're not telling me."

"I'm investigating a local murder case, which is not FBI jurisdiction."

"We're giving an assist to the GBI."

"As far as my work is concerned, Sherman Trapp died in Tennessee, probably murdered, but that's for the Chattanooga authorities to sort out. Juliet died here. Until you tell me you're in charge, I'm keeping what I find to myself and the APD."

"And Chattanooga?"

"If I find out anything that will help that department, I'll contact the chief."

He leaned back and contemplated my face like I'd auditioned for his couch. He said, "These people were all involved in something that includes murder and possible kidnapping. I intend to find out how they're connected."

"Can't stop you."

"You know what I think?"

"You're going to tell me."

"The intended victim wasn't Stuart or the Brandle girl. It

was you. They were the sacrifice for the real target. Have you considered that?"

What had Trilby said? *The fucking bitch is next. She's the one. Not the blonde. Do it.*

"That supposes I know something that I don't know I know."

He looked disbelieving and started to say something, but I was saved by the opening door.

A tall man in a dark blue suit, yellowish shirt and red striped tie entered. The Assistant U.S. Attorney from the Southern District of Florida. We stood, and he extended his hand. "Miss Dru, I'm Carter Peabody." I shook. He turned to Grady and they shook hands.

"Special Agent Locke, sorry to be late. Please have a seat." He looked at me. "I see you are acquainted with FBI Special Agent Grady Locke."

"I am."

We sat at a long table, Peabody at the head, Grady and I on either side. While Peabody opened his file and leafed through it, and, as the nervous silence lengthened, Grady continued to stare at me, his eyes, his expression, giving the impression he was sorry it had to be like this.

I looked outside. White cloud fragments paraded across the sky. What, I wondered, for the eightieth time, did the Florida authorities have in mind for me? Was my life about to spin out of my control? Should I have had my attorney with me? His secretary told me he was out of town until tomorrow. Should I have pissed a U.S. Attorney off and not shown—with an excuse, of course? In the end I had decided to take my chances, act as if I have nothing to worry about, did nothing wrong and expect no consequences. And be careful what I said.

Lake had told me not to worry. Easy for him. I recalled his upheld hand, the look of panic on his face when I glanced over my shoulder, just before I shot a young man as he raised a gun to assassinate two human beings in a cemetery. What a U.S. Attorney for the Southern District of Florida thought about that I was soon to find out.

Peabody cleared his throat. "The Criminal Division of the U.S. Attorney's Office is divided into three sections: Major Crimes, Narcotics and the Organized Crime Drug Enforcement Task Force. We are not concerned with Economic Crime or Criminal Appeals and the Victim-Witness program, so let's get on with it."

Let's do.

He turned on a recorder and identified each of us and said that this was to be a informal proceeding and that the tape was for informational purposes only. Then he looked at me, "As I understand it, as part of your private investigation into a murder case in Atlanta, you and a member of the Atlanta Police Department rode to West Palm Beach with a motorcycle club. Is that correct?"

"That is correct."

"This club is registered in our database as an outlaw motorcycle club. Did you know that?"

"Of registry I know nothing. I know of their reputation."

"Did you suspect one or more of them to be your suspect in the murder case?"

"No." I looked at Grady. "We were following a lead for any information they might provide."

Grady intervened and explained his role, clearly stating, "I sanctioned the trip, Assistant Attorney."

Peabody looked at Grady. "Why did you ride with them to south Florida?"

"To protect and further an operation we had regarding OMGs in the Southeast region."

He went on to outline our case as it connected to an outlaw motorcycle club vis-à-vis Juliet Trapp's assertion that she was riding to Florida with Wild Blood, an OMG that was a target in his investigation. He said the magic word RICO a couple of times.

Peabody nodded understanding. "Multiple jurisdictions get tricky."

I said, "The Atlanta Police Department coordinated with the West Palm Beach Police Department and the sheriff's office to grant Lieutenant Richard Lake's entry into their jurisdiction to gather information on the murder of Juliet Trapp. Also to gather information on the disappearance of Brandle Raddison, a potential witness in the case and in the death of Juliet Trapp's father in Chattanooga, Tennessee."

"I understand all that," Peabody said, shuffling paper. "Why were you at a biker's funeral?"

Careful.

"The members of Wild Blood acted appropriately in every way to Lieutenant Lake and me on the occasions that we spoke. The leaders of the Chattanooga and Raleigh clubs told us that they wanted to help us with our case—if they could." I looked at Grady. Was he going to say anything about confidential informants? He blinked. Apparently not.

"Did they?" Peabody asked.

"Yes. I believe Raleigh's leader, Joe Blade, provided information that will lead me to the man responsible for Sherman Trapp's death."

"That being?"

"We—that is I, because I can't speak for the Atlanta Police Department—believe that Sherman Trapp set out to find the murderer of his daughter. He sold his business and bought a motorcycle. Having no experience on one, he went to a riding school and started hanging out with the biker crowd. Blade came in contact with him in Atlanta. He tentatively identified Trapp's photo as that man. Another witness, Dwight Baines, head of a motorcycle school in Marietta, said a Mike Sherman plunked down hundreds in cash for lessons. I'm going there today to show him photographs."

"Admirable, Miss Dru. I admire your investigative skills and I think it's fine that you have an Atlanta police detective helping you, but you are a civilian."

"A private investigator, yes."

"You do a lot of work for the court system, don't you?" I said that was correct. He tapped his finger. "I can't see that we could make a case for involvement or disruption in an Organized Crime case by shooting a member of that gang, although . . ."

Grady said, "It's unclear that the illegal man was a motorcycle club member. More of a wannabe."

Peabody went on as if Grady hadn't interrupted. ". . . Although there are those zealots who would try to hit you with a charge." He smiled thinly to show he is not one of these zealots. "However, a case may be made for a civil rights violation." My eyes popped. He continued, "Cases typically involve situations when a person in a position of authority in state, local, or federal government uses the office to deprive another individual of civil rights, including hate crimes and racial profiling."

I opened my mouth to protest strongly, but Grady spoke up first. "As you've stated, sir, she's a civilian."

My defender.

Gathering his papers, Peabody said, "While the Fourteenth Amendment pertains to the State, courts have ruled that no citizen or person in authority can deprive life, liberty or property to another citizen no matter his race, color or nationality, or to an immigrant who has entered the country, and has become subject in all respects to its jurisdiction, and is a part of its population, although alleged to be illegally here. Have you ever called an immigrant an alien?"

I held my breath. *Had I committed a hate crime? Been guilty of profiling?* I had interfered in a murder at worst, serious injury to those going about a legal activity at best. Members of Wild Blood had committed the murder of the illegal. Yes, I had said alien. But it was Wild Blood who deprived the illegal immigrant of his right to life, but this is where I shut my mouth and wait for my attorney.

After a lengthy wait and a steady stare from me, Peabody rose. "It is only fair that you should know we are looking into the legal issues and will reach a conclusion one way or another. Good afternoon." He walked out with me holding my breath.

Feeling raw, like I'd been filleted, I turned hot eyes on Grady's face. Words rushed from him. "Please don't . . . It's pro forma . . . A matter of clearing up . . ."

That's all I heard as I slammed the door on my way out.

It was early for a cocktail, but Lake had been on duty for twelve straight hours and met me at High Time for much-needed alcohol.

Lake listened to the tape I'd surreptitiously made of the interview with Peabody and Grady. "Alien," he said. "You could get twenty-five to life, no early release, for calling an illegal alien an illegal alien?"

I let a sort-of laugh escape my throat.

But then Lake's guarded eye contact told me that he had feared from the moment I'd raised my gun that my precipitous action would cause me considerable pain. He clutched my wrist. "I think this officious U.S. prude is rattling a saber. They'll look into the entire case and how it ties in with our murder investigation and clear you. I think that's what he was telling you. When the Feds have someone in the crosshairs, they don't have a polite sitdown and spout the Constitution. Now let's talk about dinner."

Lake's phone rang. He listened, then said, "Haskell wants us. I told him about your meeting with the U.S. Assistant Attorney."

The summons gave me another *uh-oh* feeling. "Can I get drunk first?"

Haskell looked stern as he listened to the tape.

"You got a flesh-eater on your tail, Dru. You did fine. Now let your mouthpiece do the talking."

Haskell always had a way with words that somehow managed to comfort.

"Ahem," Haskell said. Not many people actually say that. After inserting a clean cassette into his recorder, he pressed play and introduced himself, Lake and me and stated the date and time. He got to the heart of the matter. "Lieutenant, Grady Locke of the Federal Bureau of Investigation, Memphis Bureau, questioned your jurisdiction at Tinny's Marina in the killings of four people. He stated that it was a matter of form in case Wilton Johns Stuart's family made a claim in that regard. His killing could, according to Grady, cause us lawsuit problems and he wanted to give us a heads-up."

Today was a heads-up kind of day.

"He a lawyer or something?" Lake asked.

"They all are; lawyers or accountants."

Lake made a noise I interpreted to mean *No wonder I don't like the son-of-a-bitch.*

Haskell said, "I acquainted him with our jurisdictional agreement." He eyed both of us as if we had better pay attention. "That being said, the Atlanta Police Department's jurisdiction extender agreement with metro counties is valid in this case. We have implemented this mechanism to better serve and support communities and counties that affect the metropolitan scope. The warrant was legal, your identity and qualifications correct as you have authority to serve warrants in extended counties within the jurisdiction when it pertains to a felony in the primary jurisdiction, which is the APD, in the Trapp murder case. That you stopped the commission of several felonies in the process of serving the search warrant supports the jurisdictional extender."

He turned off the recorder.

Lake nodded. I smiled. Small comfort.

Haskell said another, "Ahem," paused and continued, "That taken care of, I'll give you an update on the investigation the state is conducting into the matter of Eugene Fetterman and Dawn Marie Sullivan. Sullivan has confessed to taking a trip to West Palm Beach with Fetterman in the summer on a church field trip. She had her parents' permission. There was a second trip, as you know. She rode to Miami with him during the Christmas break. She says he knew that Brandle Raddison was performing at those clubs and she went with him to see her. She denies any romantic or sexual involvement with him during those trips. Her mother isn't so sure. She said the Miami trip bothered her because they didn't go with anyone like they were supposed to have. She was debating calling Pastor Fetterman. In the meantime, we've interviewed Mrs. Fetterman. She isn't cooperating and said her attorney will be in touch. We've asked for a court order to test Dr. Fetterman's DNA. He is also uncooperative and asked for an attorney. If it's not his semen, we're back to square one. If it is, he's cooked. But I'm worried about the court in this case. The district attorney's office thinks the probable cause is not very strong."

"The appearance of impropriety isn't impropriety," Lake said. "We should have raided his garbage can."

Haskell laughed. "CSI Miami has a lot to answer for." His landline rang. He picked up and said, "Yes, Chief." Lake rose and signaled me. Haskell held up a hand against our leaving. After a series of "I see's," and "Yeah, okay's," he hung up the phone. "Road trip."

"Chattanooga," Lake said.

"That was Smarr from Chattanooga PD. In the north country they found a man's body in the woods. Been dead a while. He was in the process of emptying a bag of cremains when he was shot, perhaps by a hunter. Someone called anonymously after finding him. No name or ID on the cremains bag."

I spoke up. "The funeral director told me that they provide a dog-tag ID to accompany the cremains."

Lake explained that there is no DNA in cremated ashes, that the heat is too high to allow such material to survive, so that it made it imperative to find the tag.

God, to get out of this city for a while. I stood up and looked down at Lake. "You coming to Chattanooga with me?"

"Bet your boots."

"Make sure you take them with you," Haskell advised. "Smarr says the state of Tennessee is covered in snow."

We left Haskell's office and Lake asked, "You need to go home first?"

I couldn't hit the road fast enough. "I'll buy what I need at a big-box store—toothpaste, undies and bullets."

CHAPTER TWENTY-ONE

Alfred Denton, the doctor who administered care to the comatose Sherman Trapp, stood across the autopsy table from Lake and I. The medical examiner pulled the pall from the dead man's face. "Oh my," Dr. Denton exclaimed. "I really couldn't say."

Who could? Despite being January, it had been warm enough—when whoever shot the man calling himself Robert Thomas Trapp left him face down in the woods—to attract the hardier insects and worms residing in the soil beneath decayed leaves and pine straw.

The funeral director looked austerely puzzled and shook his head. These were the only two men who had seen the man calling himself Robert Thomas Trapp.

The medical examiner removed the entire cover from the man's body. He wore a television pitchman's cheap brown suit, a tan shirt and ugly green and tan tie. His shoes were brown. The body and its clothing had suffered the effects of the recent snow.

Chief Smarr asked both men, "Is there anything about the man that looks familiar?"

The funeral director said, "Those could be the clothes he wore when he came to get the cremains of the man who he said was his brother. Of course, they fit differently on a living person, you understand."

Dr. Denton's eyes scanned the entire body, then he said, "I

don't recall his clothes, but the ring. That ring. I noticed it."

The ring was caked with mud. Like the clothing the ME had left on the body for forensic examination before the autopsy, the ME had left the ring on the man's finger for study. The ring was embedded in the man's right-hand third finger. It was a school ring, the centerpiece a big blue stone.

Smarr said, "It's from Clark Keeper Buchanan High School here in Hamilton County. We're going through the student roster for that year."

Blood sparked through my veins at something positive in this dismal room. We would soon learn who Robert Thomas Trapp had been.

Smarr said, "His body was found within fifteen miles of the high school. If the man attended that school, he was most likely familiar with those woods."

"So was someone else, and that someone else followed him and executed him," Lake said. "The small-caliber bullet was fired close range. Five feet."

Lake knows bullet wounds, having specialized in forensics at the FBI National Academy. My major study was behavioral sciences.

"Ex-ray shows the bullet in his skull," the ME said. "Deceased several days. Don't know how specific I can get yet."

We left with Smarr, who said, "A hunter, probably without a kill tag, stumbled on the body. Footprints were deer and small animals. We found the cardboard box the plastic bag was in."

"Did you find a canvas tote with a coffin on it and lettering that said 'Think outside the box'?"

Smarr shook his head. Not a glint of amusement in his eyes. "I'll get an officer to take you up there if you want."

"I'd like that," Lake said. "Not that I think I'll all of a sudden see the key piece of evidence."

The chief grinned, showing some nice dimples. "Don't

begrudge if you do." He looked at me. "Maybe he'll find that tote for you."

I smiled. *Maybe he had been amused.* I asked, "Did Jean Ann Scott ever turn up?"

"No," he said, "and we talked to the roommate day after you left here. Mean woman, had all of Jean Ann's things in plastic garbage bags ready to throw away once the first of the month came, and she didn't pay up. I got the bags in the evidence room. We're treating her as a missing person. Wherever she went, she took her identification; she left none in her room. Barstow at The Tire Store said she never came back to work. The good news, no female bodies have turned up."

I told Smarr that Dave Barstow was a Wild Blood, road name Michelin. He nodded that he knew and said that Dave never caused trouble.

"Can I have a look at Jean Ann's things?" I asked.

"With the lieutenant along, you can. Our rules state a law enforcement officer must check out evidence."

"Everyone's," Lake said. "But not every department is so co-operative with other departments."

"Like I told you, I'm not a glory boy, I just want the crimes solved. If you can do it, that's just dandy with me."

I guess he hadn't heard about my run-in with the U.S. Attorney's Office.

The hotel was moderately priced and so was its menu. I had reservations about the meatloaf, but then nothing appealed. I felt like the day had tugged off my protective covering. I was trying to pull it back on with the help of a gin martini.

"Better eat something and keep up your strength," Lake said, forking in rice and mushroom gray. "Booze keeps the nerves jangling."

He was right, and when we got to his room, mine being down

the hall, I said, "Sorry, darling, I'm buzzing to a rumba beat."

"Nerves. I'll sing you a lullaby."

Melody and Lake do not a lullaby make. "While I sweat and punish pillows?"

"I'll keep watch."

"Lake . . ."

"Humor me." He wouldn't say that he was worried, but I'd seen his neck swizzle and eyes narrow each time someone walked into the room. Same when we walked across a parking lot or when he drove. Lake was the best at spotting a tail and losing same.

Inside my small suite, Lake checked under the bed and the bathroom, even behind the sofa bed. "Really, darling," I said, laying my cheek next to his.

His arms went around me. "I can feel your heart race," he said. "Don't go having an attack on me."

Our goodnight kiss was loving but not inviting, and I loved Lake the more for his response. I loved the way he wanted to champion and reassure me, and keep me safe. He turned to leave. I had a rush of indecision, a moment in time to change my mind before the door closed, but no, that would only confuse him. It would buoy him, but then he would wonder if I'd lost my nerve. He could never doubt me. He must always trust that I was his equal in mental strength and resolve. He appreciated that I was not the kind of woman who depended on a man under stress or in a fight. It made me a good detective and protector—although maybe not the best lover when tough times arose, nor a confidence-builder in an insecure man. I got lucky when I met Lake. He possessed all the confidence he (and I) needed. More than anything, we valued our individual strengths and denied we had any weaknesses, separately or together.

CHAPTER TWENTY-TWO

At ten the next morning we were riding on the old railroad road that was still used by the timber industry, the sheriff's deputy told us. He sat in the back of the squad car and acted as tour guide along the fifteen miles of asphalt that separated two valleys. Not much traffic had passed and parts of the road were slick with ice. The temperature, our car said, was thirty-three degrees. The deputy said, "A week ago, it was dry and cold, no problem."

We passed the entrance to a trailhead for Jensen Falls and the deputy rhapsodized on the beauty of the falls in spring and fall. "The red maples give the air a red glow with the leaves and all," he said. "Mighty pretty. We get lots of tourists in those seasons. We get lots of problems with the bears, too. Tourists don't know to avoid the big guys. The bear looks friendly, they get too close, the bear takes a swipe and it's a trip to the hospital, sometimes worse." He pointed out a road to our left. "Shortcut to the Little Smoky Mountain School. One of the earliest in the area. It's still got the original little desks and blackboards. Kids take field trips and marvel at how their ancestors learned in that primitive setting. Ask me, they got a better education then than now."

I agreed, minus the woodshed visits.

"We're coming to the Sinkhole," he said. "It's a treacherous part of the Cascasia River. You don't want to wash over the bridge here because you're likely never to be found in the swirling hydraulics." A little later, he said, "Slow now, we're coming to our turn-off. It's not marked but it's called Garrity's Junction. Old Garrity owned all this land hereabouts. Died ten years ago, before he could get the road paved, so it's still gravel. Old Garrity wasn't a popular man. A right tyrant. Here we go. Make a right. We'll come to the old logging camp. Old Garrity was a logger, tried to rip every tree off the mountain, but the environmentalists stopped him. Only good I ever heard they did."

At the camp, a wide place in the gravel, he told Lake to stop the car. "Walk from here," he said.

"Is this public land?" Lake asked.

"Nope. It's still tied up in probate court. Probably always will be. Old Garrity had no children himself, but his brothers gave him ten nephews and nieces. The brothers are dead and the nephews and nieces are still fighting over about two thousand acres. The rest is National Forest. Down the road about a mile, they're fashioning a park. Going to be a fine park with teaching areas for kids' camps and school trips." He starting walking east and gestured ahead. "The body was found about half a mile into the trees from here."

The hiking shoes I bought at the big-box store served me well, and I trusted that Lake's did, too. The ice-crusted leaves and pine needles beneath my feet crunched as I walked a road wide enough for logging trucks. The deputy told us that the temperature usually rose to forty-five degrees in the daytime and patches in the sun melted, only to freeze again when the sun set and the temperature lowered to twenty-five. Lake and I walked side-by-side with the deputy leading us up the dirt road. We pretty much kept our eyes on the ground in front of us and roaming to the shoulders for whatever might become promising.

"We scoured along here pretty good," the deputy said. "Saw

a lot of junk, old tennis racket, rusty bike fenders, lots of tires. People'll dump things anywhere."

"Archeologists love our junk," I said.

I heard him grunt, "Huh?"

"Ten thousand years from now, they'll use it to figure out how we lived."

"Can't for the life of me understand digging up old crap, but that's just me."

I'd thought about becoming an archeologist. "Is this road still used?" I asked.

"When it's cleared for the trucks when they take the timber. It's been a while, as you can tell."

I looked over to see Lake step off the road and study an area bounded by a ravine or ditch. "Somebody's gone off here," he said.

I couldn't see what Lake meant at first, neither could the deputy when he paced back to where we stood. He said, "Where?" He looked around, then said, "Lot of hunters come up this way. Maybe the same hunter who saw the body and called anonymously, but I swear I checked this trail closely. Must have been made after we pulled out."

To me, it could have been anything that made the indentation in the soil. The sun had come through the branches and melted the snow on the area. Lake looked at me, expecting me to comment. I shrugged.

"Don't see it?" he asked.

"A scuffle? Somebody dragging a body?"

"No, look close. I want you to see what you see."

I could feel the deputy's confusion. *Are these people nuts or what?*

I said to Lake, "Had I your eyes and brain . . ."

"Look at it like you're going the other way on the trail, back down, instead of up."

I walked around to do just that. It did appear different from that vantage, a long narrow rut that cut deeper at the front. I was with the sheriff on it being a hunter. Someone slipping. Although . . .

Lake asked the deputy, "Once the body was discovered, did you bring vehicles up this road?"

"Not at first. We had to move downed tree limbs. That's likely what that is." He pointed at the disturbed earth. "The medical examiner didn't want us to carry the body on a stretcher half a mile, so we had to move fallen trees off the path so we could get the wagon in to take the body."

Lake said, "I saw where they used a chain saw to cut up trees and debris, but that's not what I'm looking at."

Then I saw it. The skid. "A motorcycle."

"Yep," Lake said. "He locked the front brake with the bike at an angle and went down on the high side. You can't control the front if it's locked into a skid." He stepped off the path into the shallow ravine, bent and gingerly picked through the ice and flora trash. He stood and asked the deputy if he had protective gloves on him. The deputy didn't, so Lake reached into the pocket of his suit and took out a baggie and latex gloves, things that are part of his outfit wherever he goes. He knelt and picked up a shiny object that lay beneath the crackling waste. He rose and asked the deputy, "Do you know motorcycles?" He held out the curved piece of chrome.

"Don't know what you're holding there," he said. "I don't ride."

"It's a bat lash for a bat wing."

Now the deputy was certain Lake had lost his mind.

I laughed. "It's not part of the Caped Crusader's outfit. A bat wing fairing is a type of windscreen for a motorcycle. It has curves on each side to resemble a batwing and the trim, called the bat lash, fits into the curves. There's a nose piece on the bat wing called a bat brow."

He was certain I was nuts, too.

Crime-scene tape was staked into the ground at the spot where the body had lain. "Found the cardboard box over there," he motioned toward a bramble of blackberries, "stuck in there. The vic took the plastic bag out of the cardboard. That's how Ol' Miller gives the living folks their dead folks' remains."

Men of a certain age were ol' to the deputy: Ol' Garrity, Ol' Miller.

All of a sudden Lake straightened and stood quite still. He was hearing something no one else could hear. He gestured his chin further up the trail, a slender path through bramble. "I heard a motor. Where's the path go?"

"Follow me," the deputy said.

We single-filed through the bramble for at least a quarter of a mile, not saying anything, though I watched warily for snakes. I have a deadly fear of the creatures. Don't like lizards or spiders either, and the bramble and trees were thick with webs. "Jeez, where's the birds that eat spiders?" I called to the deputy.

"Those are not spider webs, they're web worms. They come out in the fall and build their webs at the ends of tree branches and shrubs. Harmless. Don't confuse them with tent caterpillars."

I said I surely would never do that. Ever.

We huffed up an incline and came to a plateau. A sensation of danger flitted across my shoulders and I paused. Lake looked back and frowned. We came to a wide clearing. Ahead was a small wooden structure, a log cabin with the chinking largely gone from the walls. The roofline sagged at one corner. The deputy stopped and faced us. "This here is where Ol' Abe Garrity built his first home place more'n a hundred years ago. He raised five kids in two rooms. Let's walk careful to the edge of the cliff. One boy went over when we had a little earth shake over Cleveland way." He paused as if to give reverent thought to the boy. "The cliff's got a cleft in it. Over the years rock slips off the side when Ol' Man Mountain settles after a shake. There's underground springs that flow out of the rock during the wet season."

Maybe the cliff held the danger I'd felt. Add heights to snakes and spiders on my terror list. These are atavistic fears, but I thought some change in air pressure or current caused my physical reaction.

A hundred yards ahead I recognized where the cliff edge and the sky sharply defined each other. At twenty-five yards I saw the vista of snow-covered trees. That was as far as I was going. Lake edged closer and said, "How do you get to those houses clinging to hills down there?"

The deputy explained, "Jensen Falls Road curves into that valley. See that wide patch along the river there?"

I edged closer. Lake said, "Yeah."

"That's another Garrity home place that the cousins are fighting about."

"Anybody live there?"

"Ho no, not while probate's going on. Those cousins are divided into camps and are fierce with each other."

I wandered over to look at the homestead cabin. Although ancient, it had been built to last as long as the hills did. The timbers were thick oak logs laid horizontally and interlocked on the ends with notches. The corners were set on large stone slabs. There were probably stone supports to the cabin floor inside as well. Cabins set on stone kept the damp out, and stone was not hard to come by. Granite outcroppings rose from the earth's thin shell all around me.

I tested the first of three steps to see if it would support my weight. I applied pressure a little at a time and the hewn boards held. I moved up to the shallow porch. The timbers, thinner

275

here, creaked. The door cracked open. Suddenly, I heard the deputy yell, "Don't go in there."

I turned.

He came at a trot. "That place should of been condemned."

Lake had followed. "Why didn't the county tear it down?"

The deputy let out a smirky guffaw. "It's on the historic site list."

"I'd like a peek inside," I said.

"You take your chances," the deputy said. "I gave fair warning."

Spiders had spun threads across the door and its opening. Fortunately, the actual crawlies were not in web residence.

The cabin's parlor stretched across the entire front and was maybe thirty feet wide and twenty feet deep. An occasional table had been pushed into a corner. A sturdy wooden chair was placed next to a camp stove. *Someone was here recently.* There were boot scuffs in the dust. Candy wrappers and Coke cans lay scattered about. The chair was not dusty and the stove looked fairly new.

"How 'bout that," the deputy said. "That stove's been put here since we took the body away."

Lake walked into the second room. "Whoever it was left a sleeping bag. It's spread out on an old iron bedstead spring."

I stuck my head into the back room. The sleeping bag looked new.

The deputy called the chief, who said he'd send the crime people and told the deputy he should bring us on back into the city.

Heading back down the trail, I thought I saw something or someone move in the trees. I told the deputy, and he replied, "Spooked about the bears?"

"They're in hibernation, aren't they?"

"Let me tell you about the bears hereabouts. They den in

hollow tree stumps, some way up high. Black bears here don't actually hibernate. Especially panhandler bears."

"Panhandler bears?"

"You city folks ain't the only ones with panhandler problems. Bears just don't say they'll work for food. Get it?"

Lake grinned, and I said I got it.

The deputy talked as we walked. "It can get warm here in winter and they come out for a spell. They'd all be sleeping now with the snow, but if you got some good-smelling food on you, they'd be on you like vultures on a dead coyote."

Despite his odiferous warning, I didn't believe the shadow and movement was a bear.

Lake dislikes bat lashes and bat brows, but doesn't go as far as calling them *gay add-ons* like Dave "Michelin" Barstow did. "Nobody in the club pastes those things on their batwings."

It was the middle of the afternoon when Lake drove us to The Tire Store, ostensibly to ask if Jean Ann had come back to the store. She hadn't, as we knew.

Dave had shuffled things around on the counter as idle talk led to a question or two about his jail-bound pals and the Feds, and then onto the subject of bikes and eventually their accessories.

Lake said he likes his bikes as they come from the factory, as Harley-Davidson intended them. I chimed in to say that I saw a Road King with bat lashes and a bat brow on it and thought it might look good on Michelin's bike. He looked at me like I was crazy and made his politically incorrect statement. "We're kind of a classic-look club," he said. "I'm not into choppers, but lot of the guys are. Don't much like ape hangers, either. We all different, but we're all the same, see what I mean?"

"You protect each other from outsiders, don't you?" I asked.

Fret wrinkles surrounded his eyes. His lips moved without words.

Lake said, "She asks the damndest things." Sneering, he leaned his head toward me. "No different with cops. It's something we learned growing up. You get a buddy you can trust, you form a bond. It's no secret why boys build clubhouses that say no girls allowed. Girls don't build clubhouses."

I grumbled, "I was a cop. I don't think all cops are the same."

Michelin said, "I didn't say we're all the same. We're all different but the same, meaning we think alike about the big picture, but for the details, we make separate choices."

"I get it," I said. "It's been a real treat to travel with your friends and raise a glass. I'd never have thought that the leaders of famous motorcycle clubs, like Rassler and Switch, would be so friendly to outsiders."

I think he was looking for a hidden meaning in my words or tone. "Every group's got to have easy-gabbers to smooth things out. Like any corporation. Everybody works for the good of the group because it's for the good of himself. See?"

"I do," I said. "Where'd you go to high school?"

Lake took out his cell phone. "Pardon me, folks. I got to call the house. Check in." He walked away.

Michelin must have thought about Lake saying I ask the damndest things, because he shook his head, and a little smile came to his lips. "Home-schooled."

Did that mean dropout? Yet he had this job. "Are you a city boy?"

His eyes shifted. "Country."

"When did you start riding motorcycles?"

Some people are intuitive enough to know it's better to answer than evade. "Ten or so. Me and my buddies started on scooters up and down these hills."

"How did Jean Ann Scott come to work here?"

"She was hanging around the bar I go to. She asked me to give her a try. I got a lot of thanks for that."

Lake jangled his keys. "C'mon Dru. We got to get back."

At the door, I heard Michelin's voice and paused.

"My turn to ask," he said. "Why did you really come here?"

"Looking for Jean Ann," I said. "A few questions have come up she might be able to answer."

"About your Atlanta murder?"

"Yeah, and the murder of Sherman Hanover Trapp."

"Like I said, she never came back here. I had two girls since. They don't stay."

He didn't concern himself with the murders, it would appear.

After we left, I called Webdog. "Check out David Melvin Barstow, manager of The Tire Store."

I pulled on forensic gloves. The evidence officer, Chief Smarr and Lake stood around the table, too. Two large black trash bags holding Jean Ann's things had been opened and the contents arrayed on the Formica top.

Chief Smarr said, "We haven't put them through forensics, so keep the touching to a minimum. We got a few partials for testing. The five Jean Ann Scotts in the city's phone and cross-reference books are accounted for."

"I doubt that's her real name," I said, studying the garments, the cosmetics, the materials of a female's life. I said, "Look at her clothes. The leather jacket and boots, underwear, bras. They're pretty new as if she bought a whole new wardrobe to live with Trapp."

"Huns are particular," Smarr said.

"Or somebody bought them for her. According to Jean Ann, Trapp kept his money in his wallet." I wondered what had happened to that *wallet*, supposed to have been filled with hundreds of thousands of dollars?

Skepticism showed in Smarr's face. "You think Jean Ann had a connection to someone else in your case?"

"Possibly, or yours."

"A biker?"

I pointed to the motorcycle helmet. "That isn't new. It's a half-helmet, the kind favored by motorcycle clubs of the outlaw kind. Bikers and their chicks are particular about their helmets."

"You being a chick, I heard," he said and grinned.

"On occasion," I said.

"Grady told me he'd saved your butt down there in West Palm."

"I was thinking it the other way around," I said.

"I can believe it. Okay, so what I'm hearing is that you think maybe Jean Ann is some biker's chick with a fake name, keeping company with Trapp to find out what he's up to."

Lake said, "Makes sense. In looking for his daughter, Trapp went where club members hung out and asked questions no one wanted to answer."

I said, "Jean Ann said Trapp packed his duffel when he told her he was splitting. You find a duffel with Trapp's things?"

He shook his head. "If he packed it, then killed hisself— which is what we thought, and it hasn't been proved otherwise—it would have been left in her possession when we took him away. You can see it's not with her stuff now. His possessions were few." He pointed to men's size-ten shoes, boxer shorts still in the bag, white tee-shirts still packaged, new heavy socks, the kind worn with motorcycle boots. I was about to ask Lake if bikers wore boxers, but then Smarr continued, "Jean Ann said he had a lot of money. We didn't find but a few dollars. No identification, either. We learned his name by his fingerprints. He didn't have a record, but he'd been in the service."

Lake said, "Before coming to see you, we stopped by Tire

Store Dave's. He's not telling all he knows."

"No one does," Smarr said. "Especially bikers around police. He works. Not all club members are bad boys."

CHAPTER TWENTY-THREE

After our conversation with Chief Smarr, Lake and I were called back to Atlanta from Chattanooga. Commander Haskell told Lake that Bunny was ready to leave the hospital and would only talk to me, not the police. I persuaded Haskell to let her talk in Judge Portia Devon's presence. After I explained what had become obvious, he agreed. Lake would be stationed in the jury lounge, listening from a sound amplification device, although no recording would be made to avoid legal ramifications.

When I fetched her from the hospital, Bunny was pale and trembling, something to be expected from a young woman that had witnessed a gunfight where three people, one of whom was a mentor and friend, were killed.

I introduced Bunny to Portia and excused myself to let them chat. The idea was for Bunny to get comfortable in Portia's presence. I believed Portia's austerity and authority would comfort Bunny. Initially, I was right.

In the next room, I sat at a desk across from Lake and listened to Portia's and Bunny's exchange. Portia's voice was mellow as a marshmallow. Bunny sighed often, and Portia allowed the young woman to ramble, a human trait Portia abhorred.

Portia talked about her days as a thespian, something that was true. She was good in drama and comedy, the wry kind. Portia never resorted to lies when it was necessary to get at the truth, like I sometimes did. Maybe it had something to do with being a judge. Anyway, I listened to Bunny talk about her schooling in England, her longing for the English countryside, riding to hounds, and then returning to America, a place she'd been homesick for. It was all lovely, before Portia brought her back to the present.

"What are your plans now?" Portia asked.

"Find myself." Said with a sigh.

"You must have plans."

"Why?"

"Pull your hands away from your hair, sit up straight and tell me what you plan to do." No more marshmallows and riding to hounds.

Bunny apparently did as told because Portia said, "Now, tell me what you're going to do."

Bunny spoke in brisk syllables, "I plan to tour, get with a troupe and build a career. Movies, TV, stage are all on the table."

"Have you kept in touch with your parents?"

"Some."

"They can help you with your career in New York."

"They don't want me anywhere near New York."

Portia had talked to Bunny's mother earlier in the day and understood why. "When you leave here, where will you go?"

"I'll stay in a hotel, get a gig in this city. Plenty of them and I'm used to hotels." Laughter sprung into her voice. "I don't have to make my own bed."

"Do you work with an agent?"

"Through my daddy. He gets me good gigs."

"How long was the last one?"

"It was four nights. The last night was when Wilt came with Miss Dru. I'll use my own name now, even if Mama doesn't like it."

"Speaking of Miss Dru, here she is."

I had eased the door open further. When she saw me Bunny's tears bathed her face. She jumped from the chair and ran to me. She threw her arms around my neck and clung. "I'm so sorry," she sobbed. "So sorry." She smelled fresh as spring rain.

"It's all right, Bunny," I said, stroking the back of her head, feeling the silk of her hair.

She pushed back, tears still raining. "*I'm* not—yet."

I looked at Portia. Her piercing black eyes said the ball was now in my court. She said, "Sit, please."

Bunny's mouth turned up, her eyes sincere and sorry. "I got Wilt killed."

How could I dispute that?

After she settled herself in the chair, I said, "He warned Juliet against what she was doing, didn't he?"

She nodded. "He said when it came out, it was going to look bad."

Wilton always understood Bunny, I realized that now. "Were you going to stay on his boat?"

"He said I could for a while. Then those men came into the salon with him." She put her hands in her face and sobbed.

Porsh and I looked at each other while the tears ran their course, and she wiped them away with a wad of tissues I handed to her.

"Shall we look at some pictures," I said, reaching into my backpack for two yearbooks.

She waved them away. "I don't know anyone that goes to that school anymore. I have to confess, I made it all up."

"Why?"

Her faint frown told me she was trying to guess what I was thinking. "I got tired of hiding. I needed to have a career with my own name. I kept in touch with Wilt. He was my greatest friend. He meant the *world* to me. You know?"

"So you went to your old riding instructor, Hoyt Fagan, and then to your advisor Samuel Chapin?"

"I needed advice, what to do. I didn't want him following me everywhere."

"How long did Juliet Trapp carry on with him?"

Bunny sniveled, a child getting over a tantrum. "I don't really know. She didn't tell me about him because she knew I would tell her it was wrong and she should stop. But I saw them in the library, on the fourth floor, where they keep the microfilms and stuff. Later Juliet said it was nothing, but I knew better."

"Were you jealous?"

"No, absolutely not. It was *just wrong.*"

Portia leaned forward. "Was this the man you called a motorcycle creep?"

"She and Wilt rode all the time. I hated calling him a creep. He's a love, really. But it was wrong then."

"Let me get this straight," no-nonsense Portia said. "Juliet and Wilton were carrying on an affair and you caught them."

"I really don't . . . don't want to say it right out, like. It's all so awful. He's gone now and I don't want to ruin his reputation."

I didn't think Wilton would care one wit about his reputation, but he did have a thing for the truth. "Bunny," I began the probe. "Why do you think *he* looked you up twice in south Florida and showed himself to you?"

Her mind hadn't yet made the leap. "I . . . It must have been coincidence. He wouldn't want me seeing him, would he?"

"But what if *he* did want you to see him? *He* sat in the forward rows. *He* didn't hide himself in the back rows. What would *he* be saying to you, do you think?"

She shook her head, the quality of her eyes changed from clear to opaque and her hands shifted uneasily. "I can't imagine . . ."

"Why did you run after Juliet's death?"

"I wanted to be away from where she—I couldn't stand she was dead. I wrote that note to Wilt, but he was . . ."

285

"He was what?"

She looked at Portia for relief from unrelenting questions she knew weren't going to stop.

Portia said, "There's a saying, Brandle. Once is coincidence, twice is on purpose. You get my meaning?"

Bunny swallowed the creeping realization of what was being said, and nodded.

"*He* wanted you to see him, didn't he?"

Her eyes shifted. "What are you talking about?"

"*He* wanted you to see him with another girl, didn't he?"

My emphasis caused her to blink, but she was good at recovering. "No," she said, tears lacing her lashes, then flowing down her cheeks.

"You got too old."

"Please." Even distressed, she was beautiful, a cool Kim Novak. If Bunny hadn't ruined her own life, she would have been a fabled actress. But the act was over.

"You fell in love with *him* and you thought he meant it when he said he would love you forever and that as soon as he could get away from his wife you would be together. You believed him, didn't you?"

Comprehension flickered in her eyes and she looked suddenly venomous. "You're crazy."

"No, Bunny," I said. "I know how it was and what really happened."

"Nobody knows."

"There are people now tracing his steps in south Florida. Ticket people, credit card people. Hotel people. You and he kept in touch through the want ads, or some signal so he knew where you'd be. You used disposable phones, maybe. We'll unravel the truth, get the evidence, and, learn that before he threw you over for a younger girl, he visited you as often as he could. The police talked to the Sullivan girl. Yes we've identified

286

the girl who took your place because you got too old for him. The girl told the detectives that he wanted you to see that it was over, and that he had another *woman.*"

She shot up. "*I* was his woman." She stepped to Portia as if it were Portia that accused her. "I did things for him."

Portia sat steely-eyed, hands folded on her desk. "Including murder."

"It was an accident."

"Juliet Trapp was not strangled by accident."

"I just wanted to shut her fucking mouth." She'd startled herself; maybe she hadn't meant to be profane in front of a judge.

"You did exactly that."

Portia can be so unemotional.

Bunny whirled to me. "It was an accident."

"You called Fetterman and told him what you'd done. It was Juliet who found *you* and Fetterman in the microfilm stacks. It was Juliet who told *you* to stop the affair or she was going to report Fetterman."

Her breath caught in her throat like she couldn't believe we knew the identity of the man. "Silly slut." She threw herself into the chair. Meryl Streep. *Postcards from the Edge.* "It was my business and his."

A hour ago, Portia had talked by phone to Babe Brandle. It was a sixty-second conversation wherein Babe said that her daughter was a compulsive liar. *She is artful and compelling because she believes her lies the moment they hatch in her brain and come out of her mouth. To her, lies become truth. Some day she'll be a great actress, but I could never trust her.*

I looked at Bunny. Her eyes were closed as if she were savoring the urgency of his touch.

I said, "He's a pedophile, always was."

Jerking upright, her skittish eyes bulged. "I was not a child. I

287

was a woman, same as I am now. I could have a baby. I fell in love. I am a woman. His woman. Sex was great with us."

"Until you got too old."

She burst from the chair and took a swipe at me. I caught her arm. She twisted to get away. It had to hurt like hell. "Stop or it will break," I said.

She relaxed the arm. "Bitch."

"Juliet was raped."

Standing over me, she deliberately cocked her hip and raised her chin. "There goes your theory. I couldn't rape her." A husky-throated Marlene Dietrich. She was going to have a hell of a time in prison skits.

"Fetterman did," I said.

She tossed her blonde hair. "He didn't. He left her there by the motorcycle club's house. She was alive. Someone in the neighborhood raped her body. Gene said that happens all the time with bodies." You could see a touch of cleverness coming to the fore. "I only warned her. It was that damned scarf. It got caught when she slipped and fell." To her it was the pinnacle of truth and logic.

"That didn't happen," I said.

The phone on Portia's desk rang.

She listened. "Yes, Lieutenant. I see. Fine." She hung up. With her hands folded, her eyes fixed into Brandle Raddison, she said, "I am sorry to have to say this, but Fetterman hung himself in his back yard."

"Bastard," Bunny said. "Fucking bastard." Glenn Close. *Fatal Attraction.*

Then Lake walked in. "Brandle Raddison, please stand. You are under arrest for the murder of Juliet Trapp."

Her howl came from hell. Drew Barrymore. *Scream.*

CHAPTER TWENTY-FOUR

"Classic narcissist," Portia said. "The mother, too. I had to threaten her agent with extradition if she didn't call me back in an hour. Without telling her our hypothesis, Babe Raddison wasn't surprised that her daughter had a role in Juliet's death. She'd said, 'I wouldn't be surprised if she didn't harm that girl in some way, she was always manipulative. I know she egged those two into a steeplechase. Louise was the only one who could control her. She shoved me on the steps one day, pushed me from behind.' " Portia shook her head and rose. "Like mother, like daughter. Narcissists. Fetterman was vile, but the girl is dangerously malevolent."

I said, "I think Fetterman was going to kill Bunny, his partner in Juliet's death, to protect himself once he started with the Sullivan girl. I think Bunny feared him."

"Too much thinking going on," Portia said.

That ended that line of postmortem.

Portia's clerk stuck her head through a crack in the door. "Miss Dru, you need to call Webdog. Developments in the north country, he said."

As I fetched the cell phone from my backpack, Portia said, "Get this case over with, Moriah. You look like a wild sea is battering your tenacity."

Not true. Right now it's my best friend and favorite judge.

★　★　★　★　★

Web said that David Barstow was home-schooled after his fresh-man year at Clark Keeper Buchanan High School because his parents opposed sex-ed classes and began an online home school program. He was granted a general equivalency diploma by the Garrity Community College Action Project. There were ten graduates in the class. One was Jeanine Kaplow, who had taken the same online course as Barstow and lived five miles from his parents' home. Jeanine Kaplow belonged to the Garrity clan, after whom the community college was named. Her mother's last name was Scott. The mother was widowed and now deceased.

"The warring Garritys," I said.

"I'll be sending out the photo," Web said.

"Thanks and, as always, good work."

When Lake finally called me back, I related Web's information. He asked, "Another road trip?"

"Chattanooga."

"You got it. I'll contact Chief Smarr."

"How was Bunny at the jail house?"

"Smug. Sexy." he said.

Basic Instinct. Sharon Stone.

The snowstorm dove south from the Ohio River Valley, across mountains, only to meet its end on Atlanta city streets, which are hot with traffic twenty-four hours a day, seven days a week. They call it a heat island.

Wearing blue jeans and leather jackets, we got into the unmarked and Lake turned on the windshield wipers and the heater. I like fine dining as well as anyone with a refined palate, but I also like eating hot hamburgers and fries in the car, head-ing out on a case. Between bites we discussed the case and its possibilities. Our conjectures differed only in the small details.

Having finished eating, I got on the phone to Webdog. He told me that Grady Locke had called to congratulate us on solving the Juliet Trapp murder. He wanted me to call him. That wasn't going to happen. Then Web said that in purging the fishnet, he'd found an interesting fish in it, meaning a number and corresponding location for the call. He said, "You know these fake towers are tracking devices. They don't record text messages, emails or listen in on the calls. They can operate legally under the rule that you purge all the calls that don't pertain to your investigation, which is what Dirk was doing when he came upon three calls that wouldn't purge, nor deactivate the tracking device on the cell phone like we could with Wilton's."

I knew that the fishnet spoof tower software netted all calls taking place in the target area at the time the device was in use. The controversial device had proponents and opponents. Proponents say since no confidential information is gathered by speech or text, there was no invasion of privacy. Opponents contend that tracking someone's movements by electronic devices was per se an invasion of privacy. The device was a boon to law enforcement and PIs in pursuit of suspects or persons of interest who use a kick phone for alleged illegal purposes. To me it's no different than hoofing it behind a target, so long as such tracking is not considered stalking. Oh, these fine lines.

Web continued, "You know what that means?"

"Yep, is Dirk's handling it?"

"He's doing the purging, I'm trying to find out who the fish is."

That meant a different kind of spoofing that if successful would result in voice and text identification.

"Get me in touch with Rassler, if you can run him down."

Rassler had given me a number and I rattled it off to Web. "Ask him to meet us at his favorite dive."

We took the Ringgold exit off I-75 to gas up. Ringgold, the Wedding Capitol of the South.

We were back on the road, having left the little city famous for quickie marriages from blood test to I-do's in two hours, when Lake said, "If one has to get married, the no-fuss way is the way to go."

"If one *wants* to get married . . ." I said.

We seldom spoke of marriage in our years together. Although I can't read Lake's innermost thoughts on the subject, we both rather liked being lovers and our living arrangements—what with our careers, etc. The idea scares me more than snakes or cliff edges. People start out in love and end up in divorce court. It had happened to Lake. I lost my fiancé in a drive-by; I had to get used to him being gone. I don't think I could take a divorce.

Lake said, "If a couple wants to get married, seems to me they have to get married."

Where was this going and what was I supposed to say? Lake can be more romantic with words than me, so he should know I'm not saying a thing.

He said, "Don't you agree?"

"Hmm. Sounds logical."

"I am nothing if not logical," he said. "Having gone through the machinations of a formal church wedding, only to see my marriage end, I was just thinking the no-fuss way would lessen the loss."

"Of what?" I said. "The money spent, the waste of time?"

"The high expectations, the loss of friendship and love."

"You are waxing philosophic."

"I'm waxing up to something."

"Lake . . ."

"It would be nice though."

"There are always expectations."

"As we have of each other now."

"Like your not sleeping with anyone else as long as you're sleeping with me?"

"That's elementary. It's being there for each other. It's compromise. When the man likes bare windows and the woman likes window treatments, the woman wins. When the man wants lean red meat and the woman wants seafood, the man wins, every time."

"And here I thought you were getting all serious on me."

"I was."

I had to keep my mind from scattering in fifteen different directions at once and said, "Grady Locke was quick to point out that our case was solved."

"I heard." He gave me a hard glance. "You did not disabuse your admirer."

That quashed the marriage talk.

CHAPTER TWENTY-FIVE

Web gave us the address of the chopper dive, and forty minutes later we arrived at the concrete block square building, painted gray with day-glo multicolored lettering on the side that said this was "Frank's Place." A smattering of old to middlin-old cars were parked on the cracked asphalt. Two Harleys were parked at the side of the lot.

"Pabst Blue Ribbon, two bucks a pop," Lake said, turning off the key.

A stream of cold snow smacked me in the face when I got out of the car. The bartender wore a cap turned backward. A woman sat at the bar with teased platinum hair and cleavage riding up the top of her Harley tank. The two men playing pool in the corner were the bikers with plenty of ink running down their arms. I didn't recognize them. Tina, of the cobra neck, came through a door that led into the bar from the back. Ladies' room, I thought. She saw me and rushed across the room and exited a side door. Thirty seconds later a man came out, smoothing his shirt and adjusting his belt. I leaned over and reminded Lake that I'd met her at Tire Store Dave's.

The barkeep sidled down, wiping the bar with a gray rag. "What you doin' here?"

He was rather young to have so few brown teeth. When he reached over for a coffee can and spit a stream of tobacco in it, I saw why.

Lake said, "Gimme a Coors."

"One sissy's piss comin' up," he said.

First time I've known Lake to order a mild beer. I said, "I'll take a Bass Ale." First time I've ordered an ale.

The barkeep stuck up his thumb.

I heard at least a pair of Harleys bark into the lot outside.

Rassler came in first, flanked each side by twin red fireplugs. The men must have run the artist out of red ink. Lake hoisted his bottle of Coors and Rassler separated from his bodyguards and strolled over. He hit his upper left chest. Lake reciprocated. The bartender's mouth opened enough for a swarm of flies to enter.

"My man," Rassler said. "Grab your lady and let's watch the play." To the bartender, he said, "Bring my brew, Bud."

After we'd slid into a ratty booth with a good view of the pool players, but far enough away not to be heard, Rassler said, "What's the deal?"

Lake said, "We found our girl, but we're looking for Dave Barstow's."

"Why's that?"

I said, "When I met her she was calling herself Jean Ann Scott, but her name is Jeanine Kaplow."

"Jeanine? Why are you looking for her?"

The bartender came with Rassler's bottle of beer and a frosty mug. *Interesting.*

When he'd left, Lake said, "She lived for a time with a man calling himself Hanover."

"I heard a man by that name hung around. Lots of wannabes do." He sat back holding his frosted beer. "Let me tell you something. Being a leader in a club isn't much different than running a business. You got responsibilities, meetings to attend. I'm away from here half the time, going to corporation meetings."

I gave a quick thought to these meetings: *how to more ef-*

ficiently manufacture and move crank around the Southeast.

Lake reminded Rassler that Hanover's full name was Sherman Hanover Trapp and that he was the father of Juliet Trapp, the murdered girl in Atlanta.

Rassler leaned forward and put his beer mug on the table. He seemed more interested in the pool break than talking to us. Then he said, "You putting Michelin in the middle of that?"

Lake said, "Trapp came to Chattanooga looking for the biker who murdered his daughter."

"We've gone over this," Rassler said with an air of displeasure. "Our club members are accounted for, and that includes Michelin."

"Remember Joe Blade telling us about this rich urban biker with the V-Rod?" I asked.

"Sure. Switch was hanging in Atlanta at that time. I told your man that Switch's pretty sure he's the RUB. He was growing a beard, trying hard to be a biker."

"Sherman Trapp bought the bike after Juliet was murdered to go after the killer. He enrolled in bike school, learned to ride and started hanging out with bikers to pick their brains."

"Yeah and stuck out like a boil on Switch's backside. I'm going to tell Switch about this Trapp. You got to admire a man that does that. I'd do that. I'd go after the shit-bird that killed my kid, that's damn sure. So what's this to do with Michelin?"

"Two clues brought Trapp to Chattanooga. One, his daughter told her mother she was going to ride to Bike Week with Wild Blood."

Rassler shook his head like that wasn't going to happen.

Lake continued, "And, two, she wrote a note to her father asking for money for a field trip to Chattanooga just before she was killed. There was no school field trip. He put Chattanooga and Wild Blood together and came here."

"I see it, sure. But Michelin had to work. He wasn't going to

Bike Week. I can account for all club members during that time. I did my own investigation. The Atlanta club came out clean; their blood didn't match." He stopped and appeared to consider something. "Why did you say you're looking for Jeanine?"

Lake said, "We believe Trapp got to know Barstow through a bar. Barstow didn't trust him and asked his girlfriend to keep an eye on the man he knew as Hanover, a lone biker wannabe. Eventually she moved in with Trapp."

"Uh, naw." He shook his shaggy salt-and-pepper hair. "Not Michelin's girl. They been together since kids."

I was beginning to think Rassler spent too much time away from his own club. I asked, "Wouldn't a biker woman do that for her man?"

I had skirted close to calling biker women whores.

Rassler said without rancor, "I couldn't guess at the whys of that."

"Did Barstow hang with anyone in particular?"

"Used to hang with a lone wolf that was a customer of his. I never got a look at him; members said he wore a do-rag with the stars and stripes and aviators. Inked up his face and arms, but it was fake. Michelin called him a squid, gave him Squid for a road name."

"His V-Rod got stolen."

"Yeah, Michelin said. Nobody's ever found it, I know of. I'd like to talk to this Trapp. Give his hand a shake."

Lake said, "He's dead; most of his ashes are in police custody. Chattanooga police believed he died as a result of a suicide attempt. I believe he was murdered."

Rassler gave a quick shake of his head. "I don't know how Michelin got mixed up in this, but I know he's no killer. You need to talk to him."

"We will," I said. "Jeanine was working for Dave."

"Yeah," Rassler affirmed.

"I think she's in danger."

"From Michelin?" He scoffed.

"Of whoever killed Trapp."

"I know my members. It wasn't Dave, but he should know where his girl is."

I thought so, too.

The morning chill was bone-aching. I thought about summer and the hot sun. Didn't help to warm me up. After a country breakfast, we set off for the Chattanooga Police Department.

Walking off the elevator, we passed a kid who argued with a uniformed officer. "Aw man, half a ounce. Gimme a break." The officer looked like he was tired enough to wish he hadn't looked in the kid's glove box.

Speaking of tired, Chief Smarr sighed like a man who had too much to think about. In answer to Lake's questions, he said, "I know Butch Garrity; he used to be a deputy before the old man died and the cousins squared off against each other. Now his full-time job is thinking up ways to piss off his cousins. Jeanine is on his side, so I gave him a call. He was cagey as a bear after a honey pot with bees swarming, but he swears he hasn't seen Jeanine and he goes around to all the properties to see that the enemy cousins aren't squatting on the places. He did say she could be in any one of them. He'll probably be on the lookout now."

I didn't know if that would be a good thing or not.

Lake asked, "What's Dave Barstow's relationship with the Garritys?"

Smarr grunted. "He's been Jeanine's boyfriend on and off for years, and he's never gotten close to any of them. The Barstows are pretty new to the area—from West Virginia. They're fundamentalists. Churchy." He said it like someone who wasn't churchy. "The Garritys go to church but they don't wear you out with it."

"But are they killers?" I asked.

He bared his teeth in a kind of smile. "They're mountain folks."

That was all we got, except for a reminder that we should be mindful of whose territory we were searching through.

So we left the office, and I asked "What's a squid?"

Lake laughed. "An acronym for a rider who is Stupid Quick Undressed Imminently Dead."

"If it's Trapp we're talking about, sounds like he didn't master the motorcycle."

"Trapp's not the squid. He learned who did not kill Juliet from the squid."

"He thought it was Dave Barstow."

"Can you tell me why?"

"Someone told him that Barstow was the biker with Juliet on the night before her murder?"

"Who?"

"The squid."

Lake said, "On learning that Dave Barstow wasn't his target, Trapp packed his bags. Where was he off to?"

"Beside the crematorium?"

These questions could go on and on, and often helped delineate the case. I said, "We've got a packet of photos to show Jeanine, if we could only find her."

"Before her killer does."

Dave's face looked like we'd thrown a handful of flour on it. He was finishing with a customer and began stammering so much the customer looked perplexed. The customer paid, then headed through a door into the garage for his car.

"Miss Dru, Lieutenant," Dave said, trying to keep his voice under control.

Usually it's the third official visit that breaks them.

"Where's Jeanine?" I asked.

He tried to swallow dry spit. "I can't tell you."

"Yeah, you can," Lake said, opening the leather jacket to show his badge and gun.

"This ain't Atlanta."

Lake gesture toward the phone on the counter. "Call Chief Smarr."

Barstow stared, not daring to blink.

"We know Jeanine is your girlfriend. Once your do-rag *customer* told you that Hanover was the father of the murdered Atlanta girl, you got scared. You knew you didn't kill her, but you didn't know what else he could tell you. He suggested strongly that you make Jeanine get close to Hanover and find out what he was up to."

"Like, up to what?" he squeaked.

"What had you told your *customer*? The one you called a squid, but who is, in fact, an accomplished biker?"

"Why would I tell him anything?"

"You tell me."

"I can't tell you something I don't know."

"Trapp thought you killed his daughter and was after proof, maybe from someone in your club."

"That's a lie. He would of never found proof of me, because I did *not* kill his daughter."

"Why did Trapp suddenly chuck Jeanine out and pack a duffel?"

"Who said he did?"

"Jeanine told me the first time I saw her. I have her words on tape."

"I don't know nothing about that."

"I'm sure the Chattanooga Police Department has a contract with a lie detector service."

"I never killed anyone."

"Did Jeanine lie to you? Did you kill her, too?"

"I never. I wouldn't."

"Then why did you have a friend of yours masquerade as Trapp's brother and have the body cremated?"

"I never. That's another damn lie."

"You know who did. Squid, who had you by the balls because he knew you had been in Atlanta several times to see Juliet, and that you promised to take her to Bike Week."

"It's not—true."

"Dave, we've all but figured it out. You got caught up in a sting. Squid killed Trapp."

"Hanover shot himself. Jeanine called me," Dave said, voice in a panic. "I went to that house. He was still alive. He didn't die."

"Not when his killer shot him, but later in the hospital."

"I got to get back to work. I can't stand here . . ."

"Hang tight," Lake said. "We have some photographs you need to look at."

I slipped outside, called Webdog and told him what photographs to email to me and to the Atlanta PD and the Chattanooga PD. He told me he'd identified the fish in the net and that the fish had set up the hit on the boat after I was lured there. I thanked him again and didn't bother to ask how he'd spoofed out that information.

Back inside the tire store, I set my laptop on the counter.

Meantime, Barstow had gone into the back area, and Lake was outside, in the squad car, talking to Chief Smarr.

Lake came into the store and signaled for me to join him at the door. He said that the body of the imposter, Robert Thomas Trapp, had no ties to Clark Keeper Buchanan High School, despite the class ring he wore. His fingerprints were not in the national or state databases.

I said, "Somebody wants us to think he's a local."

"The unraveling continues," Lake whispered. "That's what happens when killers try to be too clever."

At the counter I booted my computer.

Barstow came from the back area, and Lake asked, "You know anybody that lost his Clark Keeper Buchanan High School ring?"

Perplexed, Barstow said, "No."

"Did you have one of those rings?"

"I didn't graduate there."

"Did you tell anyone you did?"

His eyes shifted. Caught, he said, "Sometimes, but I never had a ring."

After downloading the photographs, I turned the computer to face Barstow. "Let's take the first photograph." It was the dead face of the imposter, Robert Thomas Trapp.

"Oh God," Barstow said, looking away

"Do you know him?"

Barstow glanced back at the screen. He looked ready to up-chuck. "I seen him. He came in here. He had a beard, though."

"Was he with Squid?"

"Yeah."

"How about this photo?" I said, scrolling to Hoyt Fagan astride his motorcycle.

"Never saw that dude." Fagan looked like a dude.

He'd never seen Wilton Stuart, either. When he saw the photo of Sherman Trapp, he wanted to lie, but said, "That's Hanover."

"When did you find out he was the father of Juliet?"

"I can't . . ." He clamped his mouth, maybe thinking of his Fifth Amendment rights.

"So you asked Jeanine to get close and keep an eye on him."

"Yeah, but that's all I did. He used her to keep house. He

was very particular."

"You told her to tell anyone who asked that she was his girlfriend."

"That was her idea, then he shot himself."

"You know he did not shoot himself."

I had scrolled to the photograph of Eugene Fetterman.

Barstow squinted. "Maybe. Don't recall where I seen him though."

A photograph of Grady rolled up. "Know him?"

"He's in the news. Some of our members have problems with the Feds."

I brought up the photograph of Geoff Howard.

Barstow said, "Don't know that dude."

"He saw Juliet Trapp with a biker the night before her murder on December twenty-eight. Were you at the White Dot Reboot on December twenty-seventh?"

Before I stopped speaking, he picked up the telephone. "I need to call a lawyer."

"And the police," Lake said.

Chief Smarr said he would send a car to bring Barstow in for questioning in the Atlanta case and the Sherman Trapp case—cautioning Lake that the Chattanooga case was closed, it being ruled a death resulting from a suicide attempt, which he still believed was the correct finding. He would be, he said, calling Special Agent Grady Locke because the cases could relate to his investigation into OMGs.

He also said that Jeanine's Garrity cousin called to say that Jeanine claimed the rights to a property on Jensen Falls Lane and that he'd seen Dave Barstow ride his motorcycle from the lane onto the state road.

Lake explained that we wanted to talk to Jeanine and show some photographs, which was all right with him.

Lake accompanied me to my hotel room and checked the place out, admonished me to double lock the doors, then left for the Chattanooga police station. He said he wouldn't be gone long because David Barstow would have an attorney, and it would be a matter of negotiation because the Atlanta Police Department wanted to question Barstow to wrap their Juliet Trapp murder case. Bunny Raddison, of course, had recanted in a tear-filled scene before her parents sent a famous attorney to silence her.

"There's also a possibility we'll lose the cases to the FBI, in the person of Special Agent Grady Locke," Lake said. "He might link the cases to his ongoing outlaw motorcycle gang investigation. Murder by an OMG member could come under the RICO statute if a conspiracy could be shown. Dave didn't kill Juliet, but he could have conspired to murder Sherman Trapp."

Don't think so.

While he was gone, I did the whiteboard thing on my laptop, setting out the facts as we knew them, leaving aside speculation. I started with the steeplechase accident between Juliet Trapp, Bunny Raddison and Lawrie Taylor—a blamable accident that was never reported—and ended with Fetterman hanging himself and Geoff Howard positively identifying the photograph shown to him by Pearly Sue. It was a cell photo taken by Lake on a visit to the tire store. Howard also identified the man in another photograph as the "policeman" who'd followed him after he'd regained his memory and talked to a reporter. Howard is, I think, lucky to be alive.

Okay, the last sentence I typed was speculation, not fact. Portia had said, *Too much thinking going on*, but I disagree. Thinking leads to proving. Sometimes.

★ ★ ★ ★ ★

Lake came back from the cop shop with unsurprising news. Barstow was questioned with his lawyer present, but not charged. The investigation would roll forward. Barstow and his legal representative promised to show up in Atlanta on Sunday for a friendly chat with homicide detectives. The Tire Store is closed on Sunday, and good employee that he is, Barstow didn't want to jeopardize his job.

"Sweet," I said. "And Grady?"

"Didn't show. No interest. They're state cases."

"He didn't have to take my word for it," I said.

CHAPTER TWENTY-SIX

The global positioning satellite is a marvel.

Four o'clock in the mountains, the winter sky is a gray smear blending into shadows of naked bark and green pine needles. Lake drove the squad car over the hills where the landscape was white and sooty and vertical. Parts of the road had been bulldozed. Snow and ice clung to ridges and fields and floated in creek beds.

It occurred to me that the abundant quarries and rock caves were good places to dump dead bodies, which made me wonder why the imposter, Robert Thomas Trapp, wasn't deposited therein. Me thinks there must have been murder interruptus—a hunter, a hungry bear, a Garrity checking out his future property.

We began the descent into a small valley that was a wind tunnel for the flurries sweeping across the winding road, driving against the car. According to GPS, we would be turning onto Jensen Falls Lane in two-and-a-half miles.

Once Lake skidded onto that road, he asked, "How many cabins on this stretch of road?"

I had opened Google Earth—another marvel—on my computer. I typed in the road name and hit the link for street view. The screen showed the level view of a small house by the river, an unattached shed and a gazebo near the river bank. Moving the pointer farther along, I spotted a larger house and a barn. The river didn't show in the panorama. "Three houses," I said. "Our destination is at the end of the road, a large single-story log house with a wide front porch. Looks like out buildings hulking beyond it. That's Google's last panoramic still of the road, heading east."

"What's the landscape like?"

"House faces the river to the south." I used the mouse to do a virtual walk to the south and north. "Woods within two hundred yards of the house on the north. Open spaces overgrown with weeds and shrubs. Snow doesn't show on the still. It was shot in the summer, the sun high in the sky. Trees in full leaf and flower. On the road, to the west, are two older cars. With tires. That's not always the case in the country. Several dog houses and animal pens scattered behind the house. A children's play set looks lonely and forlorn. Near the river is a boat on a trailer. Heavy equipment parked at the dead end of the road. Beyond that, woods that travel up a mountain. There is overgrown shrubbery on the east and west sides of the house. Trees in back. No cover in front."

Lake parked between two old John Deere tractors. Passing the house, I looked for the boat and trailer ensemble. It was gone. Lake opened the trunk and extracted Kevlar vests and ammo belts. We hadn't talked about going in like a SWAT team, but I guess Lake had absorbed my anxiety, and I his tension. Closing in on our mission, the unspoken language of menace surrounded us. I could touch it, cut it. Jeanine may be here, but she might not be alone. Who was this Garrity to lead us here, and why? Was this yet another trap? Where had Dave Barstow gone when he left the cop shop? The Tire Store had been closed when we drove by.

I attached the vest with velcro straps and buckled the ammo belt. Lake brought out the guns, an automatic rifle for him, the tactical shotgun for me and magazine carriers for our total arsenal. As we moved out, the sound of barking hounds echoed from the hills, but none came from where I'd seen dog houses and other animal pens scattered around.

We kept to the east side of the house, winding through rusty hay rakes and bailers until we reached a window. It was covered with black cloth or paper. Coming upon another window, it, too, was blacked out. Whoever was inside, and Lake signaled his belief that someone was, they wouldn't see us if we couldn't see them. At the front porch, Lake led the way up the granite steps to the creaking floorboards of the porch. He rapped on the door. "Open up."

No response.

"Open up, Jeanine," I called. "It's me, Moriah Dru from Atlanta. We've come to talk. Is Dave with you?"

Lake cupped his ear. "Footsteps," he said.

I couldn't hear them.

Lake looked down the road, the way from which we'd come. "Bike."

A black curtain was pulled aside and a white face appeared like a ghost in a fun house. She saw me and drew back. She moved something away from the door and I heard the clinking of a chain and the knob yanked.

By this time, I'd heard the familiar Harley sound.

"Dave's coming," Jeanine said, stepping onto the porch. "The hounds tell me. They bark at his bike."

"Dave shouldn't come here," I said. "It'll blow his cover and get you both killed."

"Dave's no chicken."

She hadn't denied that Dave was a confidential informant.

Lake of the keen ears said, "Movement from the river."

I heard nothing.

"Inside, quick."

We scrambled into the dim room. Lake tore a piece of black construction paper from the window and lifted the combination day-and-night vision binoculars. I peered out the rip and saw only a mountain of snow rising from the sliver of river.

River. Oh God.

That was my last thought when the biker abruptly stopped fifty feet from the granite steps and the rattle of an automatic rifle blew him off the bike.

"Dave!" Jeanine ran for the door, but Lake caught her and dragged her back and right. The AR rattle strafed the front door and blew it off its hinges—just as another burst of fire came from the back of the house, ripping wood and plaster. Lake returned fire from the window with his automatic. I ran straight through the front room into a hall, paused, leaned into the shotgun and pulled the trigger. The echo bounced along the walls. I had fourteen more shells in two tubes.

Jeanine moved up behind me. "He's come for me. Dave was right. I didn't do nothing to nobody. Dave didn't do nothing to nobody. He made us. I figured out who he was even though he disguised hisself."

Stop whining or die.

I said, "Take cover."

Jeanine shot away, bound for the door, prepared to race out into the dusk after her man. Lake caught her as a single rifle shot zinged off a metal hinge.

"Get to the other rooms," Lake shouted.

An AR burst slammed into the front of the house. Lake shot back. I fired a round into the kitchen and looked back. Jeanine was down. Blood spilled from her shoulder. Damn woman. "Crawl away!" Lake yelled. "Out a window, side of the house."

She moved in a belly-crawl to the threshold of a side room and collapsed. We were all in peril in here. Eventually to run out of ammunition.

"Cover me, I'm out the west side," Lake yelled, jumping over Jeanine into the room. I covered the front with a blast from the shotgun, then turned to shoot through the hall into the kitchen.

After the echoes rumbled into silence, I took in the lull. The shooters outside had to know we'd try to escape. They'd stopped firing. They had a plan and were likely rethinking it. I prayed Lake got out the side window before they got to him. *Please Lake, be nimble. Like always.*

There would be no sirens coming to the rescue. The homesteads along the road had been empty. It was up to us. Live or die. I wasn't ready to die. When faced with danger, my thinking clears, my adrenaline doesn't suddenly jump and dissipate quickly. Rather, it comes in a steady flow like an IV drip into my veins—there to stay, there to assist me.

"How many doorways into the rooms?" I asked.

"Most have two." Jeanine huffed out. "From the hall, parlor and kitchen."

I picked up the binoculars and scanned the shadows in the crusty countryside—studying the surreal landscape that always reminds me of dream sequences. Dave's bike was on its side. Dave beneath it. I hoped there was some life left. Two shooters moved up the bank from the river, assault rifles in hands.

I swung the binocs right. An eight-year-old Volvo moved slowly up the road. "Who drives a brown Volvo?" I called to Jeanine, still crouching in the doorway. "Jeanine, who drives a . . . ?"

"Squid. He made us watch Hanover." She broke into tears again.

Shots echoed from the back of the house. Handguns. Seven, eight barks. I turned the shotgun toward the kitchen in time to see a shadow sweep across the stove. Hiding the shotgun under the blown front door, I grabbed the Glock from its paddle holster at my back and looked into the room where Jeanine lay slouched in one of its doorways. Another door into that room led from the kitchen. I doubt the shadow figure knew he'd been seen. I motioned to Jeanine and hoped that she understood I was telling her we had an intruder in the kitchen.

I asked loudly so the hidden assassin would hear. "Did you know Dave was an informant?"

"I never asked Dave questions. He didn't like people snooping."

"Didn't you ask why he wanted to hide you here?"

"He said it was for my safety after somebody shot Hanover and you came."

Time ticked slowly to the rhythmic beating of my pulse. I heard a click. The killer was on the move. I signaled for Jeanine to press back. Footsteps came from the kitchen just as Jeanine scooted her butt past me into the front room.

All of a sudden, outside, an exchange of fire from automatics pierced the air like hell rose up and was thundering through the valley.

Just as suddenly quiet descended. In that aftermath, I heard a door hinge squeak. It came from the kitchen door that led into the room Jeanine had vacated. I rushed across the threshold and shot the man in black as he turned to me, his Luger a second from firing.

Outside gunfire came from the other side of the house. I helped Jeanine over the man's body. "Out the window. Hide in the shrubs. Get to the woods if you can."

She shook her head. Her face was pale with pain, but the shoulder wasn't bleeding much now.

"Fire," I said. "They'll pin us in and burn the place."

Two shots roared from the kitchen.

"Dru," Lake shouted. "Not the windows. Too late."

I pulled Jeanine into the front room as Lake backed in, shooting into the hall. The rattle of an AR erupted from the front.

"They're at the east side now," Lake shouted.

"How many?"

"Too many."

"One's dead in the west bedroom."

"I got one I know of."

"Dave?" Jeanine asked. "How's . . . ?"

Lake went to the east room door. "Cover me," he said and reached for the door knob, but suddenly stepped aside, back against the wall. I did the same.

Five nine-millimeter bullets cracked through the door, but not the walls. These log houses were sure good for stopping nine mils.

"Ready?" Lake asked.

"Yep," I answered.

We waited for another fire burst and reload time. If they were good, we had only seconds.

Lake kicked in the door and I shot the man on my right as Lake shot the man on the left.

Lake looked at me. "I got to take the rest out," he said. "How's the ammo holding up?"

"Holding. But hurry."

Automatic rifle fire came from outside, through the blown front and back doors. Lake pushed Jeanine through the east window, then climbed out. I'd picked up the shotgun, changed magazine tubes and returned fire, front and back. I wouldn't win this game. I would run out of ammo, but if I stopped firing they'd be waiting for one or all of us to escape. *Three dead in the house and one outside. How many had he sent?*

The bullet barrage from the back halted. But the front gunner kept rattling his AR, probably to keep us fastened on him, while other thugs sneaked into the house. From the front room I ran into the kitchen, ready to fire out the door frame, and saw a man down in the weeds. *Save your shells.* He was all in black. Lake's kill. I heard a handgun shootout at the front. I ran, keeping out of the line of fire through the blown door. I spotted the

AR shooter and fired a shotgun round. And missed. Then all went silent. *Please Lake. Not you.*

Time to escape. In the kitchen, I put the shotgun in a cupboard, and, pulling the Glock's trigger every five seconds, I moved to the back door and looked out. The man still lay in the weeds. Taking a shooter's stance, I swung the Glock left, then right, fast, twice in sequence. No one. I dashed to a doghouse and crouched.

I was wrong. The AR shooter had seen me. He'd come around the house from the west when I made my dash. There was no cover but the doghouse. He walked slowly. I could see the evil smile pulling across his white teeth. He thought he had me.

A frontal attack could get me killed, but . . . Jumping up, arms outstretched, Glock in both hands, I ran at him. His eyes widened with surprise and the rifle in his hands jerked skyward, rattling off three rounds. I shot him in the thigh. He collapsed to his knees and the rifle fell into the weeds. He tried to rise, tried to cry out to whoever still lived, but with one trigger pull to his head, he lay dead.

I grabbed the AR. The time had come to show the son-of-a-bitch what I thought of a man who would send killers after a woman—even one that was more than a match for him. Was I riding on hubris or skill? We'd both had the same training, after all.

An exchange of shots came from the front. I fired the Glock to see if Lake would answer. He knows my 17s. No answer. I tried to fire again. Click, the magazine was empty.

Where was Jeanine? Where was Lake? I reached for the butt of the Glock at my ankle, freed it from its holster and, holding my breath, remained stock still. The man who wanted me dead would come, thinking we were all dead, to check that no one faked it.

Lake. Lake. Where are you?

I entered the house through the back. I thought of taking off my boots, but had no time. I heard his creeping black shoes crossing the front room floorboards. Lake would have been proud of my hearing now. Raising to the balls of my feet to quiet my boot steps, I slid my fanny along the kitchen wall into the hall and then toward the west bedroom. I reached for the knob—holding the Glock firmly, finger on the trigger. I heard him in the hall now. He was circling carefully.

Inhaling deeply, I turned the knob and opened the door. Its hinge still creaked. I swung the Glock around the room and stepped over the dead man. Picking up his Luger, I went to the threshold where Jeanine had lain and fastened my sight on the blown front door, waiting for someone to rush inside. I heard footsteps along the squeaky floorboards, but didn't know where they were headed.

A rasp came from behind. I froze. *You're in the open. Move.* Three strides took me to where I could lay my back flat against the wall leading into the hall. No sounds from there. I looked around cautiously and slipped quietly down the hall and into the kitchen. I swung the Glock from window to window. No one rushed through the destroyed door, but movement sounded from the bedroom where we'd shot two assassins. Gun in both hands, I walked down the hall and stood outside the door. Through a crack I could see him checking for neck pulses. I believe I heard him grunt softly.

Disappointed, you bastard? That I'm not one of the bodies.

I heard the rasp behind me and froze again. If it wasn't Lake, I was dead. Crazily, I thought about the caul that was supposed to keep me safe and let me live a long life. Maybe my actions had something to do with safety and a long life.

I heard, "Shhhhh. Me. Rassler."

He pushed me aside and crashed through the door just as

Grady straightened from the bodies of his men. Rassler flew at him and punched him twice in the solar plexus. Grady made a choking sound as he went down. I sensed something, someone behind me and turned.

Sneaking up was a dark-bearded man with a Luger tucked into his belt. Then I saw the knife as he thrust it. I knew that action. The attacker from my house. A true dumb ass. Once you've lost a knife fight, don't do it again, not to the same opponent. He charged, ready to slice into my heart. I spun left and kicked him on the right side of his neck. He anticipated and stayed on his feet, but off-balance. I caught sight of Lake behind him, looking for a way into the fray, a way to save me. I slipped sideways, giving him room. Dark-beard had good instincts; he turned. Lake shouldered into him, ramming his back into the wall. His hands spread, then he brought them together, fists tight like a prizefighter. Lake landed a blow to his gut. He bent forward and apparently remembered the Luger. He reached for it, freed it from his belt when a shot drilled his forehead. I turned. Rassler—with a big revolver. Colt, I think.

I looked into the bedroom. Grady lay on the floor. He wasn't dead but looked soon to be. Blood poured from his mouth, a knife stuck to the hilt in his chest. I went over and looked down at him. "Your third mistake was coming here, Squid. You always sent paid killers to do the jobs. Your second mistake was sending someone to cut me. Your first was being born with too much ambition and no morality."

His face registered understanding mere seconds before the light went out of his eyes.

Rassler came in. "Good work, Wonder Woman."

Lake was beside him. "My Hippolyta."

Aw-shucks moments are for the movies. I left the room, eyes rolling.

Catching up, Rassler said, "Michelin didn't kill your girl, Dru."

"I know," I said, feeling my pulse slow. "But you knew that he was the biker Juliet planned to ride to Bike Week with."

"Wasn't going to happen. I told him so."

We walked outside to join Lake at Dave Barstow's body. Jeanine lay with her head on his still chest.

Looking for a moment at the dead man and Jeanine, Rassler turned away and said quietly, "He rode to Atlanta occasionally and met the girl there. He showed me a video, a real beauty, but looking young and innocent, if you get my meaning." I nodded. "That made me wonder. Michelin's no good-looker. I could tell the girl was high on fun, the kind of thing we're used to. Bad boy cool, you know? Michelin had to admit she was sixteen. No one in my club rides with sixteen-year-old girls, not even their daughters. I told him no; he said he told her no. End of story."

"You should have encouraged Michelin to tell the police he was the biker. He could prove he wasn't the rapist. The case might have been solved three years ago."

"Yeah, and her daddy would still be alive. Life is not fair, is it?"

"Fairer for some than others."

"Not for Jeanine," he said, glancing back at her sobs. "When did you get onto the Fed? I never heard anything against him."

I thought about my barely formed suspicion when Grady asked me where I learned martial arts. How did he know, except that he'd sent a killer to get me, and the killer failed? Then there was the warning about the school. I said to Rassler, "Webdog spoofed a fishing expedition and found that Grady was the fish in the fishnet. Or maybe I should say the squid."

Rassler looked perplexed, and I grinned at him.

I said, "Grady told me he had a confidential informant in

one of the clubs that could help me with the Trapp murder. That was all bull. He wanted to watch me, manage my investigation. Then his informant began to crack. You know that Barstow was his CI, don't you?"

"I do now. Surprises the hell out of me. Michelin's a local kid, no dummy about ratting."

"What would have happened to him if you found out before he was killed?"

He grunt-laughed. "He would best be leaving Chattanooga. There's some that would be after his tail with a carving knife."

"Once Trapp—calling himself Hanover—fell in with Dave Barstow, Grady learned who Hanover really was. At some point in their relationship, Barstow must have confided to Grady that he was the biker with Juliet. When Geoff Howard got his memory back, and the Atlanta police turned up the heat on the cold case, Grady sent an assassin to murder Trapp. It was botched. Maybe interrupted, who knows?"

Lake said, "It seems Grady had a stable of assassins on call, some not so adept."

Like the oafs that killed poor Wilton.

Lake said, "We started looking at him when he told us to concentrate on the school in Juliet Trapp's murder. The reason was obvious. He wanted us out of Chattanooga and his case here. I had to ask myself, what did he know about Winters Farm Academy, and how did he find out? We can only speculate, but I'd guess during the times that Juliet hung out with Barstow, she likely talked a lot about the school and what went on. Barstow, in turn, told Grady. Juliet knew Bunny and Fetterman had a thing going. That's why she was killed."

"So in the end Grady did help you."

"With unintended consequences. You can't kill everybody who knows something. A lot of times the pieces don't fit together."

"We supposed to be the bad guys. Goes to show, the world is a crazy place. Locke couldn't understand us, but man, I sure can't understand why he did what he did."

"The Juliet Trapp murder case threatened his operation. Once Wild Blood came into the homicide equation, he followed every detail to make sure his OMG—you don't mind being called an outlaw motorcycle gang, do you?"

"I take great offense."

I laughed. "To make sure his investigation into motorcycle clubs wasn't compromised. He was what I call a glory seeker on the 'Highway to Hell.' "

Rassler contemplated Barstow's body until the medical examiner arrived. He urged Jeanine up and let her lean on him. "It's over now." He hugged her. "Don't you worry, girl. We'll take good care of you until you're well again."

The day they buried Federal Bureau of Investigation Special Agent Grady Locke, the Assistant U.S. Attorney from the Southern District of Florida called to tell me that the investigation into the death of the illegal immigrant had been ended as far as I was concerned. He added, "Special Agent Locke instigated the civil rights allegations. We had no choice but to look into the matter."

A Fed ratting out a Fed. Beats all.

ABOUT THE AUTHOR

Gerrie Ferris Finger is a retired journalist and author of several novels, five published in the Moriah Dru/Richard Lake series: *The End Game, The Last Temptation, The Devil Laughed* and *Murmurs of Insanity. Running with Wild Blood* is the fourth in the series published by Five Star. Ms. Finger lives on the coast of Georgia with her husband, Alan, and their standard poodle, Bogey.